GOING TO CALIFORNIA

GOING TO CALIFORNIA

DAVID LITTLEJOHN

Coward, McCann & Geoghegan
New York

The author is grateful for the permission to quote from the following materials:

"I've Been Everywhere" by Geoff Mack. Copyright © 1962 by Hill & Range Songs, Inc. Copyright Assigned to Unichappell Music, Inc. International Copyright Secured. ALL RIGHTS RESERVED. Used by permission.

"The Golden Rocket" by Hank Snow. Copyright © 1950 by Hill and Range Songs, Inc. Copyright Renewed, Assigned to Unichappell Music, Inc. (Rightsong Music, Publisher). International Copyright Secured. ALL RIGHTS RESERVED. Used by permission.

"La Vie en Rose" by Mack David and Edith Piaf. © 1947 Editions Arpege. © 1950 Warner Bros. Inc. Copyright renewed. Warner Bros. Inc. controls all rights for the Western Hemisphere. ALL RIGHTS RESERVED.

"The Song From Moulin Rouge" by William Engvick and Georges Auric. Copyright © 1953. Screen Gems–EMI Music Inc. Used by permission. ALL RIGHTS RESERVED.

The fictional diary of Ellen McCue in the pages that follow owes a great deal to the many actual diaries and memoirs written by overland travelers to California in 1849 (and other years), which the author consulted in the Bancroft Library at Berkeley.

Library of Congress Cataloging in Publication Data

Littlejohn, David, 1937–
  Going to California.

  I. Title.
PZ4.L78115Go 1981   [PS3562.I785]   813'.54   80-16698
ISBN 0-698-11042-0

PRINTED IN THE UNITED STATES OF AMERICA

Love is patient, love is kind, and envies no one; it is never boastful, nor conceited, nor rude; never selfish, nor quick to take offense. Love keeps no score of wrongs. There is nothing love cannot face.

I Corinthians, 13

For Sheila

1

The black of night is never really black. If a honey-colored moon lights it up, and such a moon did, it becomes instead the deepest of deep blue. Then pitch darkness is not pitch, but luminous, darkness made visible, like the incandescent ocean deep. It is as if, even at night, far above a thousand intervening veils, there is still somewhere a shining blue sky.

If you watch the skies at night alone for a long, long time (as Timmy had done), you begin to feel how full of light and even color the darkest sky can be. If the night is unclouded, stars begin to leap out at you, penetrate the membrane of your mind, assume their places in the patterns men have been fitting them into for thousands of years.

This particular night was only random-scattered with cloud. Torn fringes of paleness floated with terrific slowness across the moonface, then disappeared again into night. They interfered with the light of only a very few stars. By refracting the moon's luster, in fact, they enhanced the sky's luminous deep blue.

No, the dark, as any amateur astronomer could tell you, is never truly black. But as star patterns wheel imperceptibly about their orbits, inches every hour, and the amber host of moon begins to pale, a true blue comes visibly to dominate the inky blue-black of middle night. From about four-thirty A.M., Timmy could distinctly notice (rather than dimly sense) the luminescence of night. Now only the brighter stars were left, rearranged since midnight. The fading moon shone upon him from lower in the sky.

First hints, then, of new morning: disappearing stars, fading moon, lightening sky. With them came a hazy visibility that sketched the shapes of sleeping trees, sleeping buildings, an all-but-sleeping road. Along the wide, west-running road, widest of all the roads in this part of the state, one red car had been driving through the night.

All you ever see from a freeway is the freeway, the driver thought to himself.

They cut out too wide a piece of country, to begin with. Then they close in your view with empty verges and hundred-yard dividers, extra lanes, signs, light poles, huge hedges like institutional walls.

But then driving 65, I suppose you wouldn't see very much anyway. Even after the sun comes up (it was now beginning to come up), all you do is watch the white lines, steer your car between them. Do it long enough, it drives you nuts.

He remembered the end of one long day's drive out west, years ago, when his head left his body and soared aloft. His brain and eyes moved up on a high, retractable stalk. The road surface was yards and yards below, and suddenly he was driving as if from the cab of an otherwordly truck. Road boredom and freeway fatigue had disoriented his sense of space. Lights, going and coming lights, red and yellow lights, became much smaller than they should have been, bent and twisted their angle of approach.

Each time he shook his head hard, the road and the other cars came back to his level. But the hallucination kept returning. Consciousness kept soaring, like a lost balloon.

Sometimes he looked at other cars (and trucks and vans and buses and campers) and tried to think about the people inside them. Where they'd come from, where they were going. But this early in the morning, in this corner of the state, there weren't any other cars. It was his own private freeway.

Funny feeling, driving so early in the morning, sunlight only starting to touch things. It's as if I shouldn't be here. (As if *we* shouldn't be here. Have to start thinking *we*.) We should be home. Home in bed.

But where is home? No home, now, either of us. This car is home.

He rolled down the window. Cool air, funny-cool, coldish. Not fresh so much as smoky-smelling, but still newborn from last night, the night just ended; night all mine. Tomorrow now, tomorrow Saturday, July . . . 13.

Each new day, such a wonder. Clean, wide open, not cluttered up by other people. I like early morning. I like the middle of the night better. But I like early morning.

Fields asleep, stores not open. Houses just waking up. Good time to be around.

My time of day.

He looked over. The woman in the corner was talking softly to herself.

She's waking up. Still dreaming, maybe. What, I wonder.

"Hi, honey," he said softly. "It's morning." She yawned, lost in her halfway world.

"What were you dreaming?"

She writhed, smiled, curled back into her corner, into her dream.

Doesn't want me in.

He gripped the wheel hard, pushed his right foot all the way down. O.K. with me. Eighty-five, going for ninety. Heading west.

With just over 5,000 miles on its clock, the car rolled as fast as he could push it down the New York State Thruway, at ten after six in the morning. Five months ago, this car—a flame-red Mercury Cougar—had been a carefree bachelor's fortieth birthday present to himself. Timmy, the carefree bachelor, then met Audrey, the girl on the seat alongside him who was trying not to wake up. He had just spent the third night of their marriage driving across the width of two American states.

This is the story of their honeymoon trip.

Timmy McCue had been an electronics technician at Aerojet General Nucleonics, on Highway 128 in Framingham, Massachusetts. Audrey, born Audrey Hunter (she was twenty-two), was a secretary there. They had met the way people usually meet in such places. One day she was asked to type some of his test evaluation sheets. She made a lot of mistakes. (She always did. She was a terrible typist.) He came upstairs to go over the corrections with her.

Timmy was old, by her standards, tall and rawboned and thick-muscled, not at all like the soft suit-and-tie men she was used to seeing in Sales. He wore faded jeans and a short-sleeved shirt. She looked at the curls of hair on his forearms. They made a few nervous jokes about her typing, then got on to first names. Where are you from? How long have you been here?

The next day, he came upstairs and asked her to have lunch with him in the company cafeteria. A week later, they were having lunches out alone.

Things moved rapidly after a party one Friday at the department manager's house, where each saw the other in the company of someone else, and hence as more desirable than before. Rides home followed, rides to work, evening drinks, early breakfasts at highway cafés.

He was not her type, nor she his. But they were in love before they had even got so far as a proper date. He asked her to marry him, and she said yes, and they were married in her parish church at Dedham, to the dismay of her older relations, six weeks after they had learned each other's names.

"At least he's a Catholic," Auntie Momie had said.

"That's as it may be," snapped her mother. "Doesn't act like any Catholic I ever knew."

"County Tyrone people. From the north."

"Never knew a McCue I could trust," said her grandmother.

"And his mother's people . . . Eyetalian." Eileen.

"And the age of him!" Aunt Kath, speaking for them all.

"I don't see why she couldn't have taken up with one of those boys from Holy Cross, like the Deane girl did."

"Someone from around here. Someone whose people we know."

"Who's to look after this house, now? After me? That's what I'd like to know."

"Now, now, Teresa. We all will."

"Hmph."

"Teresa's right. Audrey had no business marrying at all."

"I don't like the look of him, neither. No woman can tame a bull like that."

"Not our Audrey, surely."

The teapot was offered, chipped cups were refilled. They all sighed around the oilcloth and thought of our Audrey's last romantic episode, although of course no one mentioned that. If she could have brought herself to talk civilly to such a buffoon, her mother might even have told Timmy the whole story, in the hope of frightening him away.

"It may be all for the best," said Cousin Elsie, at the last; Cousin Elsie, who had never married, who had prayed for a man like Timmy for twenty long years.

"God's will be done," said her grandmother, who made a sign of the cross, and sipped her tepid tea.

Its gray air filled with that keening chorus, Dedham was no place to start again. Framingham, where they worked, was little better. Timmy's Boston apartment was out of the question. New England, as far as he was concerned, was out of the question, the whole worn-out East.

So he quit his job, and asked his boss for a letter of recommendation to the Aerojet headquarters in California, on his side of the country, which is where they were heading now.

Audrey's family, fisherfolk from Ballyconneely in County Galway, had never left Dedham since first they came to America in 1913. The family was dominated now by widows and old maids—her grandmother; her mother; the three aunts and their families; her two older sisters, Catherine and Barb—Sister Mary Mechtilde and Sister Mary Sylvester as they were now, of the Sisters of Mercy. They taught in parochial schools of the Boston archdiocese, and lived in brick convents that looked like prisons, sisters more in misery than mercy.

Timmy's home, and his parents', and grandparents', and great-grandparents', and *their* parents', had been in California ever since the Gold Rush. Five of his eight great-great-grandparents had come to California in 1849 or 1850 in order to escape poverty and parents in Ireland, Italy, or the eastern United States, to find gold and get rich.

None of them found enough gold to live on, except those who gave up looking for themselves and went to work in huge company mines, where they earned two dollars a day for twelve hours' work underground. But some of them did become at least moderately rich.

His mother's great-grandfather, for example. Emilio Portale had sailed for California at seventeen from a village in Calabria. Failing in the mines, he opened a restaurant in a tent in what is now Grass Valley, where he sold cheap meals for high prices to miners. His establishment, many times rebuilt and enlarged, is still there, "Italian Family-Style Meals, Portale's Since 1853," run by Timmy's next-oldest brother Mark and his wife. His mother and dad had retired sixteen years ago to the family ranch up near Downie-ville, although they still dropped in the restaurant now and then to inter-fere.

"You want breakfast yet?" he asked, presuming she'd say no. Audrey had uncurled again, and was making I'm-awake-and-want-to-be-fussed-after noises.

"Oh, no, darling, I couldn't. But could we stop for a cup of coffee? I like a cup of coffee first thing in the morning. Don't you?"

Coffee? What a dumb thing to stop for.

"Do you really want to?"

"Not if you don't," she smiled over at him, uncertain. Much as she loved him, she couldn't pretend to know him very well yet, so she didn't insist.

Stiff and cramped from sleeping all night in the car, she pushed her feet hard against the floor, arched her back against the seat, and stretched her arms as far as she could over her head. With her eyes shut tight, she yawned deeply and held herself taut in the hope of easing the cramp in her mus-cles.

Timmy looked over, and liked what he saw: a perfect little body, curved like a dolphin caught in mid-leap. He felt it with the fingers of his mind.

She collapsed back in the seat, yawned again, took a mirror out of her bag. What a mess I look. She found a brush, and started tugging hard at her hair. I suppose I could learn to do without morning coffee.

Outside the window, trees in late-summer green rushed past along the parkway verge, muted by the early morning mist. She wondered if anyone ever walked through them. (Maybe you're not allowed to.) I'd love to stop and walk under those trees, hug their trunks, touch their branches and leaves.

She rolled down her window. The smoky morning smell reminded her of coffee. Her stomach surged up, craving, a demanding hungry cat. She rolled up the window again.

"Leave it down. I like that."

"Happy to. Sweetheart."

She moved over close to him, kissed him good morning on the cheek. Still feeling her fine body in his mind, he replied with a smile, a wide smile of uneven white teeth. The tanned skin wrinkled at the edges of his eyes. With such a smile he had won her, back on Route 128. With his right arm, he pulled her up against him, a gesture of compensation for their lost last night. She tucked one hand inside his thigh.

Oh, Audrey, Audrey (she said to herself, leaning her head against his shoulder). What a long way you've come. Aunt Kath, Sister Mary Assumpta, the girls at St. Rose's: creatures of another world, now, of a dream that was gone. She thought of all she had learned in the last three days.

BATAVIA SERVICE AREA
FOOD. GAS. LODGING.
12 MILES.

11

"Compromise. We stop at this next place, you have your coffee, I get breakfast." Gas near E anyway. Nice to have her hand there.

"Lovely." She kissed him again, then slipped out her hand to light her first cigarette of the day. "Whatever you want."

The fog was just beginning to lift as they drove into the Howard Johnson's parking lot. Inside were silent travelers and truckers. "Sit anywhere you like," a blonde-wigged crone at the door told them. A waitress was pouring their coffee before they even sat down, but Timmy stopped her in time.

"No coffee for me, thanks," he said, turning his cup upside down. He didn't need or like coffee, and he disapproved of people who did.

Audrey gulped hers like a life saving potion. He watched as she did it, uncomprehending.

"Four eggs," was his order, "sunnyside. Hash browns. Double side of sausage. Toast and marmalade. Large orange juice. No coffee." She couldn't believe it. It wasn't even seven o'clock.

"I still don't understand why you wanted to drive all through the night. You're going to be *dead* the rest of today."

With a third cup of coffee, she was gradually coming to life, trying not to watch him mop up strings of still-liquid egg white with half-eaten bits of marmalade toast. No doubt about it, he was harder to love when he was eating.

"I like staying up all night. I got in the habit overseas. I still do it sometimes. Go down to the plant and work till morning, or go for long drives. The roads are empty. You get to see the sun rise. The whole world is asleep."

"But I thought . . . "

"It doesn't do you any harm. Anybody healthy can stay up all night, if you don't overdo it. Your body catches up."

"No, but I mean now."

"Now?"

"Now that you're married. Now that *we're* married." She forgot to say it sometimes, too.

"Oh. Well." Hmm. "Yeah."

"It's just that I thought that we . . . that we would always sleep . . . together." She twirled an empty saltshaker.

"We will." He took her hand across the table, sticky with other people's jam. "I promise."

She squeezed his hand tight with both of hers. Soft little white hands, big knuckly hairy hand. Two brand-new gold rings.

"Oh, I *do* love you, Timmy."

"I love you, too."

"Forever and ever?"

"Right."

* * *

12

Hungry for conversation, the check-out woman asked the same thing of every white customer.

"Whaddya think of them niggers?"

Behind her, a portable radio was rattling out bulletins from a troubled midwestern city.

"Animals. Just like animals. They oughta be in cages."

She had placed a towering ash-blonde wig, teased into extravagant curls, atop a sapless face. Her Howard Johnson's pinafore costume, bright orange and brighter blue, went better with the wig than the wizened face.

"Up here, we put 'em in cages. My husband, he keeps two shotguns, one for the front door, one for the back. Wants me to keep a gun here, too." She suddenly glommed onto the difference in their ages, and looked narrowly at them through a pair of butterfly glasses, held around her neck by a drooping chain.

"Where you folks from?"

"Massachusetts."

"You got nigger problems back there?"

"Well, hard to say. Not like some places, I guess."

"Headin' west?"

"Yep."

She found the right keys on her register, and punched them. Timmy watched his change tumble down the little chute. He scooped it out.

"Behave like that they oughta be in cages. That's what I say. Just let 'em try and come up here."

Audrey smiled politely. She hoped Timmy wouldn't say something liberal and offensive.

"You folks have a nice trip now." She peered at them again through her violet glasses.

"Thanks," said Timmy. "We will."

He pushed open the glass door to let Audrey through. The woman stared at his broad shoulders, his thick brown arms. Old enough to be her father.

On the road again, fresh and full of breakfast, Timmy pushed down the accelerator, and let the woods of western New York state fly on by. He felt free, now, free like flying. So little effort, so much power. He loved driving fast, loved the satiny friction of tires against road. Sitting erect, knees widespread, hands gripping the wheel, he felt independent, in control. There were few things he found more beautiful than a wide-rolling highway running through a landscape of dark green trees. Three, four hundred miles he could make today.

"Oh, Timmy, look!" Audrey pointed to a large green sign coming up.

AMHERST. TONAWANDA. NIAGARA FALLS.
EXIT 50. KEEP RIGHT. 3 MILES.

"Uh huh."

"Couldn't we just turn off and have a look? Like for half an hour? I've never *been* to Niagara Falls."

You've never been west of Worcester. "It's a drag. Look, it's just ten miles of cheap honeymoon motels and souvenir shacks, then a lot of water. You'd hate it." He didn't really mind Niagara Falls. He just wanted to keep on driving.

"No, I wouldn't, Timmy, I'd love it. Oh come on, honey. You're *supposed* to go to Niagara Falls on your honeymoon. Everybody does."

"As far as I'm concerned, that's one great reason not to go. What do we care what everybody else does?" Man Mountain McCue. "Listen. There'll be a million fat mamapapa tourists and their kids. It'd be at least four hours before we got back on the turnpike. And you'd hate it. I've been there, I tell you it's nothing. We got all kinds of great things to see, baby, once we get west. Let's just stay on the turnpikes till Chicago. After that we can take our time and start acting like tourists."

He turned to her, pressuring, male, smiling with his lips, not his eyes. "Okay?"

"Okay," she said, sulking. "I guess." Bully. "You're the boss."

She felt mildly crushed. He was still punishing her for Provincetown, she was sure of it. That was why he had driven all night.

Things were going to have to start working out better than this soon, she told herself.

It really wasn't fair. The weight of his years, the size of his body, the timbre of his voice could make her feel tinier and more helpless than she was.

"I don't care. I mean, if *you* don't want to."

It annoyed her that she couldn't think of anything more grown-up to say than that.

"Hey honey, that's not the reason. I told you, you wouldn't like it, I know you wouldn't. It's just another tourist trap. Like the fake Indian museums in Dakota. The snake farms in Tennessee."

Timmy had been through this battle-of-wills bit many times, and had become a pretty good player (for a man). But to Audrey, the game was still new, and in that sense she was right. It wasn't entirely fair. She felt imprisoned in his will, *his* car, *his* route, *his* part of the country we're going to, on his terms, at his times. *He* doesn't like Niagara Falls. *He* doesn't want to stop for coffee. Sometimes he seemed to hold all the cards.

She paused, thought about it, looked at his right profile. For all his age and strength and power of will, he *had* fallen in love with her. For some reason, he needed her. She had that, at least, and she must learn to use it well.

When they reached the Niagara turnoff, neither said a word; Timmy moved the steering wheel left, and now they were heading southwest along the pike, towards Erie. Somewhere out of her window, the map said (unless she was reading it backwards), there should be a lake. She stared into the trees, and tried to see a lake, but all she saw was leaves. She thought about green leaves, and lost summers, and boys she had liked, and their first two unhappy nights.

I must make an effort.

14

She snuggled over on the car seat. In her cutest voice, she asked: "When did you first decide you loved me?"

Jesus Christ, he thought. This woman is hard to believe.

Since turning south, Timmy had been trying to ride on one of his fantasy trips, a high foamy wave from the night before, full of German women, ripe-breasted frauleins pressing close.

Reality was Little Audrey. Twenty-two, barely out of high school, interrupting his daydream to ask when he first decided he loved her. A little sparrow with everything to learn.

"Hard to say, sweetheart. First you were just there, like everybody else. Then I got to looking at you, then thinking about you. A lot. Then you had me trapped."

"Come on, Timmy: *exactly*. I want to know. Exactly when did you first fall in love with me?" She loved saying the words, *fall in love*.

"Oh, I don't know. At Emery's party, I suppose."

"You must be kidding. You were with that fat nurse all the time. You never even looked at me."

"Sharon wasn't fat. She just had a great build." Whoops: quick reverse. "Anyway, I had to take somebody. I hardly even knew you yet, except as a secretary, I mean. I mean, I thought you were cute, and fun to talk to, but that was the first time I saw you, well . . . as *you*.

"And what do you mean I never looked at you? I couldn't take my eyes off you. You had on that purple-colored sweater and skirt outfit . . ."

"Lavender. My Spagnoli." (Go on, go on.)

" . . . yeah, and a scarf around your neck, and those hoop earrings, and high heels. You never dressed that way at work, that's for sure. You were dancing with Wayne Lockhart. I couldn't take my eyes off your butt."

"Timmy!" That wasn't what she wanted to hear.

"I mean it. Sharon chewed me out for it all the way home. You were one hot little number."

"But I mean what made you *love* me? That's not love, staring at someone's butt."

"Yeah, it is. I wanted your bod."

"Stop it. Be serious."

Two nights before, on the Cape, he had tried talking dirty to her in bed, in the hope of exciting her into compliance. It was one of his standard routines, and sometimes it worked. She fussed and protested, of course. But in the end, he thought, she had begun to stop fussing.

"I am serious. I wanted to see all your smooth white skin, I wanted to hold your bare round ass right in my two hands, and kiss your sweet little tits, and get my fingers way up into your . . . "

"STOP IT! Please stop it. You know I don't like that."

"Sorry." He drove on, his face flushed. A forty-year-old kid. "I thought you did."

"You know I don't." She moved back to her side of the car.

"Well. Maybe sometimes. But not now." She was piqued, peeved. This was supposed to be a romantic conversation. "And I still say that isn't love. Love is when you need someone and care about them and want them with you day *and* night. Isn't *that* what you felt?"

"Sure. Of course. You know that." Three thousand more miles of this, he thought. Three thousand more *years* of this. "I guess I just can't talk about it very well, baby. I love you, I want you all the time, I worry about you being happy or not. You're the only woman I want. Ever." (Liar.) "But I'm just going to have to *show* it to you, not talk about it. I don't like talking about it."

"I do."

"I know."

He smiled at her with closed lips—one of his third-best smiles—and switched on the car radio. This was his way of ending conversations he didn't want to continue, as she had learned on the trip back from Cape Cod. She learned it then by asking how many babies he thought they should have. Click: end of conversation.

So they drove on into the fetid outskirts of Erie, Pennsylvania, to the rabid racket of Radio WBS, the Big Sound of northwestern PA., and the silent, separate rhythms of their thoughts.

Audrey knew what being in love meant, well enough. They were in love now, weren't they? She knew that, anyway. The way he looked at her, the way she felt, all those red roses. They wouldn't be here, for heaven's sake, if they weren't really in love.

She had thought she was in love before, a couple of times, back in high school. But she wasn't. This was the first.

High school was St. Rose's Academy in Dedham, where you wore navy-blue pleated skirts and white blouses and said a Hail Mary before each class. The nuns let them have dances once a term. Sometimes you got asked to the boys' dances, too, at Sacred Heart, on the other side of the park. There were well-chaperoned teen club parties at the church and, between school years, long humid summers full of promise.

Audrey was short—five foot one, maybe two—and small breasted. She worried a lot about both these deficiencies, these failures to meet the norm. Actually, she had a perfect and very desirable body, but she could never quite bring herself to believe that. She didn't get asked out a lot, or make out, much. Two sisters in the convent, all those manless females at home: it wasn't exactly an inspiration. She had never been one of "The Clique," as the tall bosomy girls at St. Rose's who had boyfriends four years straight called themselves. The only times she had thought she was in love were during muggy summer days, when she and her girlfriends rolled up their towels and took a 17 bus out to the shore.

The boys could be horrible. The ones at their end of Adams Beach, from Sacred Heart, were no better than the ones from Dedham High. They were always shoving and fighting and dunking one another, swearing, smoking, opening more cans of beer. The girls in Audrey's gang (a minor circle at St. Rose's) stayed together on their beach towels with their radios and Cokes and chips and movie magazines and *talked* about the boys, who showed off for

16

their benefit down by the water—until it was time to go home. Then, if they'd had enough beer, the guys who weren't going steady might come looking for a girl to go home with. Sometimes she was asked. Sometimes she said yes.

In her senior year, two guys had *told* her they loved her. The first, John Hannigan, was a creep who just wanted the usual thing, but Andy Brady she liked. She made out with both of them, up to the venial sin/mortal sin boundary, in order to learn how, and to be able to compare notes with the girls in her gang.

Andy, they all agreed, was neat, and kind of a stud. He played J.V. basketball and varsity hockey. His face was corrugated with acne, but he had tattoos on his arms, and hair (as well as pimples) on his chest, and detectible erections they all discussed. One night, under some pressure, she told him she loved him *too*, but if he really respected her, he wouldn't ask her to do that again.

He didn't ask her to do that again. But he also stopped asking her out. That annoyed her so much she half-wished she had let him do it, half-wondered if she should become a nun like her sisters. This whole business with boys was so confusing. Sister Mary Assumpta, the principal, had almost convinced her freshman year that she had a vocation, too, like Cathy and Barb, that the whole Hunter family had been specially marked out by the favor of the Blessed Virgin Mary.

The *real* truth, though, was that "love" (before Timmy, of course) was only something she watched in movies or on TV, read of in books and magazines, heard about on records or from other girls.

Oh, and Mark Robinson.

Mark Robinson, Robby to his friends, was out of her reach. He was student body president at S.H. *and* captain of the football team. He pumped gas at Daley's Esso, except during football season. He was great-looking and super-popular but nice, too, not stuckup, not a showoff. Like Audrey, Mark was shy, though of course he didn't know she existed. He stuttered terribly when he had to give speeches and hardly danced at all at their dances, student body president or no, because he didn't know how.

Still, someone like Mark Robinson could hardly be expected to notice a girl five foot one and a half with hardly any breasts.

Audrey thought she loved him. She used to watch him obsessively: pumping gas, serving mass, playing football, lying on the beach. He had one steady date, Margie Dempsey, whom he married the summer after graduation. But all the girls talked about him, and wrote it down in their diaries whenever he noticed them. If he didn't notice them, they pretended he did, and wrote down what they imagined.

There was one event involving Mark Robinson which Audrey could recall with such vividness that every layer of time since became utterly transparent. All she had to do was think of it, and there it was, there *he* was.

They were all at Adams Beach, as usual, this particular afternoon. Late August, a sunburning sun, air heavy, no breeze to cool the skin. Robby and six

17

of his friends were fooling around, wrestling listlessly, tossing one another down in the sand. Suddenly, Robby was fighting seriously with Billy O'Brien. Then he broke off and swam out in the bay. The boys ran after him, splashing and swimming out in the water. There they ganged up on him, held him under in the deep water, and pulled off his swimming trunks. They left him alone in the bay and ran back up onto the sand. There Billy climbed up on someone's shoulders and stuck Robby's trunks up on top of a Beach Regulations signpost where no one could reach them to get them down.

All the people at the northern end of Adams stopped what they were doing. They looked at Robby's head, arms, and shoulders, as he swam around in circles far out in the deep water of the bay. They looked at the red trunks, hanging like a damp flag at the top of the pole. They listened to his beer-thick friends, who kept laughing and calling out dirty remarks. But nobody, not even the lifeguard, did anything to help him. So after half an hour or so, Robby just swam in and walked out of the water, stark naked in front of hundreds of people, boys and girls, grown-ups and children, and shinnied up the signpost like that all by himself. He lifted off his trunks, slid down the pole, and put them back on.

Audrey had no brothers, and as her father had been killed when she was five, it was the first time (except on statues) she had ever seen those parts of a man.

People laughed, or stared nervously, but Robby just went loping back to his friends, smiling his big goony smile, as if nothing had happened at all. The gang at school talked about it for a week. Audrey knew for sure she was in love now. She was disheartened by the thought that Mark Robinson would never be hers.

Last night, scrunched up in Timmy's red Cougar, she had dreamed about Robby. It was a dream she had been having on and off now, with variations, for almost five years. He was coming up out of the water, very slowly, almost motionless, heading straight for her. Only in her dream version, *she* didn't have anyting on, either.

No. She checked herself. That's not a good thing to be thinking about now. She snuck a private look at her own big man, lost in his thoughts, head bobbing to the radio music, smiling secretly about something. (Maybe me.) He sat back very straight, and held the steering wheel hard-gripped in both hands, like a wagon driver holding the reins of his team. I wonder what it's like, she thought: being a man. Being forty.

Timmy was very, very tall—taller than almost anyone she knew. He looked frighteningly strong, like someone who would break things more naturally than he would make them. He had told her about skiing, and climbing, and fishing in the mountains. She had never done any of these things, of course, and she was sure that she couldn't learn now, and wouldn't want to, which would only mean that he would go on doing them without her, once they got to . . . "California."

He had semilong, curly, reddish-gold hair, except on top, where he had none. She loved the little bald spot as much as the curls. She loved that, and the freckles, and his drooping gunfighter mustache, and the side-wrinkles next to his eyes. She loved all of those, and the hair on his arms, and the look of his back, and the shape of his bottom.

The nicest thing about men's bottoms, she thought to herself, was that you could stare at them as long as you wanted without the person you were staring at knowing you were doing it. She was fascinated by the way Timmy's curved inside his trousers, especially when he ran or bent over. There was something vulnerable and yet appealing about it, little-boyish and yet very sexy. She liked it for being the softest and whitest part of his body. She liked the fact that she could see it and he couldn't.

To a man, she supposed, it was just something you sat on, or went the bathroom from. If he thought about it at all, it was probably as a kind of comical necessity.

To women it was different. All those centuries of mothers wiping and powdering their boy babies, changing them, spanking them—in its funny way, a man's bottom *did* seem one of the few visible signs of male weakness and female power.

She didn't object to the harder parts of his body. His penis alternately frightened and obsessed her, depending on its state, and his intentions. But the soles of his feet; the back of his neck; his stomach; his inner thighs; his bottom—these were less under his control. Less aggressive, less alien. More like parts of her own body. These she could more easily love. By means of these, she might one day gain some control over him, as he so easily did over her.

On their wedding night, he had finally given up trying to get her to *relax*, goddamn it, and gone off to sleep. After half an hour's twitching, he rolled over on his stomach. Awake in the predawn light, she found herself fascinated by the curve of his hindquarters under the sheet, as she had been earlier by the soft rise and fall of his stomach. Now that he was still, unthreatening, sleeping like a baby, she felt completely relaxed, and warm love came surging back.

The second night at Provincetown was (from Timmy's point of view) no more satisfying than the first. Like a creature in a fairy tale, Audrey waited again until he was asleep. This time she lifted down the sheet, ran her fingers very gently up the hills and down the dales, touched them with her lips.

Doting on it now, she suddenly caught herself up sharp. "That's not love!" she had told him, offended and insulted, just a few minutes before—"staring at someone's butt."

Well, maybe. Maybe partly it is.

Very different things were going on inside old Timmy's head, during their long silence on the edge of Lake Erie. What went on inside his head when he was driving often made little sense. Strange pictures ran past according to a logic of their own, intercut by images from the other side of the windshield.

So as Audrey was daydreaming of the white middle of Mark Robinson where his trunks ought to have been, and then shifting, by satisfying stages, up to Timmy's own curves, he began by remembering the feel of hot stones

19

and cold water under his toes, and rain pelting down on a tent; of mud puddles, and the taste of female flesh, and blood that pooled around a little boy's head.

What went on in his head most of the time didn't make sense. In many ways, getting married hadn't made sense. As he drove along towards Erie, he tried to pull that idea free from a stew of disordered associations.

During the weeks before he met her, he had got to the point of spending hours alone in his Boston apartment, doing absolutely nothing. First he abandoned his exercise routine, the firm spine of discipline in his flaccid days. Then he started cutting work, and spent whole days in which he just sat around: never went out, never got dressed, never ate except Cheez-Its and cold crud out of cans. He let his rooms decay into a moldy heap of unwashed socks and shirts and underwear, unopened mail, unread newspapers, unfinished cans of food.

He watched hours of television without seeing it, sat in baths till the water grew cold and turned his skin clammy. He read the Yellow Pages, phoned the Time Lady, drank beer from the can and whiskey from the bottle. He took all his belongings out of closets and drawers, and piled them on the floor.

The only reason he could think of for this brainless degeneration was that he had turned forty, and had lived alone for too long. If he pulled himself together, there were half a dozen girls he could get to move in, or even marry him. But he had sworn never to risk marriage again.

In the better times since he had moved east, he had often had two, three, four women to pick from at a time. Carla, JoAn, Jerrilyn, Pat, *two* Pats, Dierdre, Sue, who else?—Sharon, *and* her roommate. The Dutch girl. Brenda. Lots. More than he could remember now. He did his job at Aerojet better than anyone could do it; no one could fault him there. Until three months ago, he could work like a son of a bitch all day at the plant, AND get a good-looking woman to his place (or himself into hers) damn near five nights a week. He played basketball and tennis, swam two miles every day after work, and took off on weekends to wherever the action was. He put in plenty of bar time, caught Russell at the Garden and Yastrzemski at Fenway, and collected chicks like a fucking machine.

He was good, goddamn it, he *knew* he was good. Good skier, good defensive forward, good sackman, good development technician. He kept in shape. He earned decent money. He had been promoted three times in four years. He had six technicians working under him. He had a drawer full of medals, a shelf full of trophies, and a box full of letters from ladies.

So why was he suddenly yelling at the men at work, goofing off, screwing things up? He got into nasty, meaningless fights. He broke a guy's nose in a bar. He fell asleep in his Gran Torino on the way to Marblehead, damn near totaled it—and then tried to punch the kid he ran into! The not eating, not getting dressed, not going to work: all that garbage at the apartment. It was like the worst years with Dee, all over again.

See a shrink? No. Shrinks were out of the question. He didn't believe in shrinks. He had seen too many of them in California, rich fakers who leeched off sickies for years without doing them the least bit of good.

After he blew it completely with a couple of pneumatic stewardesses he picked up at the Sixes (*nothing*; absolutely nothing), he even gave up sex. He was on a downhill run to hell, and saw no way to stop or get off.

Until Little Audrey.

There was no way to explain it, really. It *didn't* make any sense. She had just turned up, that was all, this very, very young chick. He went upstairs to Sales one day to give some girl hell over screwed up test reports, and whammo: that was it.

Was it "love"? Hell, he didn't know. Given the downhill slide he was on, all pits and no poles, you could call it anything you like. She was his lifeline, his ladder to escape. She had to be right, because there was no other way.

Somehow this chirpy little bird (a type he usually detested) had put it all back together. She knew *nothing*—he found that out in half an hour. But it didn't matter. At twenty-two, her talk was still high school trivia: gossip, giggle, and slush. She believed whatever she heard on Johnny Carson. She took the whole Holy Water scene as seriously as Grandma Portale. He had spent the first two nights of their marriage, at a romantic old inn on the Cape, trying to convince her that the things he wanted to do weren't mortal sins.

Which was the main reason he had decided to drive through night number three. Watching her frug with Wayne Lockhart in that purple knit number, tight as a sock, had convinced him that this was one lady who knew how to use her ass. But damn if she didn't play Virgin Saving It All, whose idea of hot times was still a prize little snake-tongued French kiss some seventeen-year-old stud had taught her in high school. When she finally let him take off her blouse and her bra, you would think she was Joan of Arc, closing her eyes and giving herself up to the flames.

Oh, shit. She was all right. Better than Sharon. Better than all those Boston whores, round-heeled nurses and stewardesses and sluts from Assembly. For her, he had cleaned up his apartment. For *her*, he had cleaned up his act at the plant. He bought new shirts he hoped she would like—he bought a *suit* (well, a leisure suit), and tried to find decent restaurants for lunch. He *listened* when she talked all that chirrupy chatter, and tried to care about what she said. He bought a six-dollar bottle of Brut, rolled Roll-On under his arms, brushed his teeth before they went out. He even shaved twice some days, because he thought she liked it. He worried about his age. He started buying a one-dollar red rose, on his way to work each morning, and leaving it on her desk before she arrived.

She ate it up. After all his women, women who knew everything, women who would do anything, this pure little Boston Irish doll-baby was perfect. He would do anything in the world to make her smile, make her happy, make her his.

* * *

21

The odds against it, even between newlyweds, must be pretty high. But coming from totally different mental galaxies, with no outside prompting but the wind, Timmy and Audrey McCue hit on exactly the same thought at exactly the same time, heading west on Interstate 90 out of Ashtabula, Ohio.

"I love you, baby."

"Oh, Timmy. I was just thinking the same thing. I love you so much."

She slid over to his side and threw her arms around his neck. In return, he risked both their charmed lives by closing his eyes for several seconds to kiss her deep and warm on the mouth. His right foot, the soft sole of which she loved to fondle, kept pushing them on. The red Cougar sped forward, 75 on the dial, momentarily undirected.

2

There had been more to their two days at Cape Cod than sexual fears on her part, and frustration on his. After driving down from Dedham, they had walked up and down narrow Main Street until dark, looking in all the tourist shop windows. They ate fresh lobster at a friendly seaside shack.

Timmy was unhappy, but not angry, about the white wedding night. Things went like that, sometimes. He could wait. In her shy smiles that morning, her pliant yieldings, the way she hugged his arm when they went out he read a silent promise that she would try harder next time.

As they walked along the beach in the sunshine, he realized how much more there was to love. All along, ever since he met her, the days had been good. She lightened them, brightened the very air with her freshness.

He watched her now as she ran along, kicking up surf with her toes, laughing for no reason. He could easily have overtaken her, but he preferred to stay behind, where he could contemplate the tiny, perfect roundness of this delectable pink prize he had won. After a while, she would stop and look back, like a puppy playing games with its master on the sand, the tiniest bit afraid it was being teased or abandoned. Then he'd open his arms wide, and she would run back and leap into them, holding him tight.

Barefoot, carrying their shoes, they ran in and out of the lapping film and runnels of foam. They looked for pretty shells and polished stones, and lashed each other gently with wet seaweed whips. They stopped to admire children's sand castles, and giggled at fat bodies reddening in the sun. Audrey got into a comical tug of war with someone's black cocker spaniel, the two of them running in circles at either end of a long, bulbous snake of seaweed. Timmy, desultorily skipping stones into the sea, watched their game from a distance. He remembered an old ballad Joan Baez used to sing, a song about a king's son who had been forced into marriage with a grown woman while he was still a boy. In the song, his bride sits at her chamber window weeping and untouched, looking down at her boy-husband playing with a ball in the courtyard below.

At the far end of the beach, they came upon a traveling carnival set up inside a white picket fence. Inside the enclosure were a miniature merry-go-round, a circuit of kiddie cars, a baby Ferris wheel, a Tilt-a-Whirl, and, for daring teenagers, a pair of rocket ships that circled high and then rocked upside down at the ends of long metal arms. Timmy bought a long string of tickets, and they took rides on everything, as if to prove they were really on vacation and starting life anew. They ate hot dogs and ice cream cones and popcorn, threw baseballs at lead milk bottles, shot corks at moving ducks, tossed Ping Pong balls into (or rather at) the narrow openings of goldfish bowls. Audrey lost two dollars in dimes on a wheel of fortune, but managed to toss a hoop around a brightly colored statue of a hula dancer, which she gave to Timmy as a present. In return, he won her a stuffed purple snake with long eyelashes by placing six basketballs in a row through the highest hoop of all.

He, they felt suffused with joy, joy that came not from the rides and games, but from Audrey herself, her merry impulses of delight—her giddy fear of the rides, the thrill she felt at each ten-cent gamble, her sloppy bliss at breaking her own rules and stuffing herself with popcorn. When he purposely rocked their yellow cage (stopped on a Ferris wheel all of thirty feet up in the air), she squealed with the hysteria of a seven-year-old, and he realized that part of what he loved in her was just this: how close she still stood to the fountains of youth.

They were catching their breath, leaning against a rail and watching others—almost all of them children—riding on the Tilt-a-Whirl. He was rubbing the back of her neck.

"Oh, Timmy, I love this. I love it, love it, love it."

"Why do you love it?"

She looked up at him, for a second puzzled—didn't *he?*—then broke out all smiles.

"Because I'm a grown-up married lady and I can still do whatever I want."

"Of course you can."

The canvas sides of the Tilt-a-Whirl dropped down. Everyone riding it screamed as the striped caterpillar suddenly reversed course, plunging them backwards in the dark. He kissed the sweet nape of her neck.

On the kiddie cars—a circle of bright, minute police cars and fire engines and speedboats fixed to a moving floor, where all you could do was spin a play steering wheel and toot a horn—Audrey made friends with two little girls by showing them where the horn was, and pretending to race them around. Enraptured by the fantasy, the two girls, sisters about three years old and five, laughed and laughed, as Audrey waved at them and tooted; they kept

24

waving and tooting back. Timmy leaned against a pole and watched her, utterly lost in her game. On about the tenth revolution she remembered him and waved, and he realized he'd never seen her so happy. Twice more she asked him for tickets, and rode around the track with her new friends.

Audrey had always loved the gaudy, safe adventures of amusement parks. One of the few memories she could still identify with her father was going out on the streetcars with him to the rides and games at Revere Beach. To have found one now, free of Dedham and yet firmly fixed in love, left her happy as a balloon on a string, almost but not quite breaking loose.

The little girls started tagging along after the pretty lady who spoke their own language. When Audrey asked where their Mommy and Daddy were, it turned out they didn't know. They had been left with a long ribbon of ride tickets and ordered not to go outside the white gate. At the revived thought of her missing Mommy, the three-year-old began to cry.

"What do you think?" she asked Timmy.

"About what?"

"About the girls. Don't you think it's criminal to leave children this young all on their own in a place like this?"

"What can happen to them here?"

"Why, anything can happen! They could fall off something and get hurt, or wander off, or get kidnapped, or lose their tickets. Anything. I think we better stay with them till their parents get back."

She talked the three-year-old out of her tears, and they went on another round of the gentler rides and easier games; first the four of them, then, as Timmy grew tired of cramped seats and preschool chatter, just the three girls. He waited on the sidelines, in charge of the tickets and the change, and watched his girls at play.

Having found a more than adequate substitute, the girls grew oblivious to the absence of their parents. But after another half hour, Timmy and Audrey began to get worried. They asked around the various concessionaires and ride attendants, but they knew nothing of the parents. Consulting with the merry-go-round man, as the two girls waved at them once each circuit from two stable peacocks (they didn't like animals that went up and down), they decided to wait another thirty minutes, and then call the police.

Audrey asked Timmy for another dollar, and bought three great puffs of pink candy floss. She sat the two little girls down on a patch of grass, gave one puff to each, and showed them how to eat them. They were entranced at the rosy miracle of food that disappeared at the touch of a tongue, and yet stayed so lovely and sweet. Timmy bent his long legs akimbo and joined them on the grass. Without any candy floss of his own (he couldn't stand it), lost in the rituals of nursery school conversation, he felt a little left out. Even so, he was impressed by Audrey's magic in comforting two abandoned little girls, by the closed and silvery world she had created to protect them from the panic of being lost.

A number of other holiday-makers were aware by now of what Audrey was doing. They looked over at the little party on the grass, or hovered nearby, smiling approval. Audrey was so absorbed in her conversation that she didn't notice the smiles and nods.

She didn't even notice the lost parents running up. Father was at first defensive and suspicious, mother torn between panic and relief. Audrey was wiping sticky pinkness off her charges' chins with a licked hanky when the two arrived, tripping over excuses and explanations.

"Mommy, Mommy!" The younger girl saw her first.

"Oh, my poor, poor babies!"

"I'm so, so sorry. Our car . . . you see the traffic . . . we had no idea."

"Oh, no problem, it was no problem at all. They were *such* good girls. Weren't you good girls?"

"Yes. We were."

"Mommy, where *were* you?"

"Well, angel, Daddy and I got to shopping, and completely lost track . . . look, we bought you both presents!"

Timmy held an arm tight around his wife, as they stood by the merry-go-round and waved to the girls, running off now with their parents. He felt proud of Audrey's power to turn tears into laughter and chaos into order. But· he also felt uncertain: alien, older, male, able to admire but unable to enter the clear sphere of childhood in which she was still so obviously at home.

At the last minute, as the reunited family was disappearing out the gate, Audrey ran after them and gave the girls her stuffed purple snake with the false eyelashes. As Timmy stood watching them, clutching his own chalk hula dancer doll like an Oscar, the merry-go-round man came up to him and said, "That's a great little girl you've got there."

Timmy smiled in thanks and agreement. Both men looked on, as Audrey traded a final set of hugs. "Yessiree, a great little girl. She'll make some man a wonderful wife."

Timmy felt slapped by the man's mistake. Now as he looked at her, running back to him laughing, her hair bouncing in the sun, he felt his heart falling through space.

3

Mile into hour, hour into mile: Ohio, on the pike. As three P.M. crawled into four, they were running out of talk. Timmy had been in the saddle for nearly twenty hours, with time out only for the Howard Johnson's breakfast and a similar lunch. He had a sore ass and stiff leg muscles, stiff muscles all over. He longed for a shower, a swim, sleep on a firm mattress. His all-night high had long since worn through. Now his brain and body were feeling the fuzz of fatigue, and crying for their lost sleep. His nerves had been frayed by a roadblock outside Cleveland, where convoys of National Guard buses and trucks had forced his car and thousands of others into two hours of stop-and-go, bumper-to-bumper traffic.

The industrial suburbs of Toledo promised little. But he could go no more today. He told Audrey they were turning off at the very next chance to escape. Soon after, for the first time in 800 miles, they quit the Interstate.

The drive had begun at their honeymoon hotel, on the tender, slender tip of Cape Cod. What with one thing and another, they hadn't got away until three o'clock on Friday, and then spent another three hours retracing their route to the Mass Pike. It was after dinner that evening in Framingham that Timmy told Audrey of his decision to drive through the night.

Twenty hours and 800 miles later, he was still glad he had done it. For one thing, he regarded total, earned physical fatigue as a positive good. For another, he had had the whole blue night to himself. This had given him a chance to think by himself, about Audrey and their future.

Marrying Audrey may have been irrational, and may not yet have provided much in the way of sexual kicks. But it still seemed the right thing to have done.

She picked at her food, he had discovered. She knife-and-forked everything into teensy little bits. She ate peas, even, one at a time, cut out every last sliver

27

of gristle and fat, daintily removed peels and seeds and minute discolorations.

Timmy had planned to camp out during part of the trip. He had imagined the two of them cooking fresh-caught fish over a campfire and eating them with pocket knives and fingers; then snuggling down together under the stars in his well-used double-mummy bag. But he was beginning to wonder how well that was going to work, with a girl who couldn't eat fat, and didn't like one food to be touching another.

She drank coffee (with cream, which made it look even worse) and smoked, both addictively. She washed more than she needed to, brushed her hair obsessively, and giggled when nothing funny had been said—sometimes when *nothing* had been said, which made her seem a loon. She had a nervous dislike for long silences, which were as essential to him as water or air. She despised country-western music, which had been his nourishment almost from the womb. She liked going barefoot, which he approved of; he liked going barefoot, too. He even took off his shoes to drive. She had the broad-voweled, slightly nasal accent of Greater Boston.

But she was thoughtful, and compliant, and she tried, at least, to do what he wanted. She seemed, a) to know about cooking, b) to care about housekeeping, and c) to have no desire whatever for a career of her own: three marks over his first wife (whose existence she knew nothing about). When she was truly, freely happy—as she had been at the little carnival—she opened up a whole world of joyful possibility.

One of her jolly ways of breaking silence in the car was to insist on playing games in between real conversations. She would announce that they were going to count up out-of-state licenses, or play "I Spy," or "Twenty Questions." He had guessed Paul Newman in twelve, and their two wedding rings, and—on the last question—a single red rose. She had guessed their car in ten, and Niagara Falls; but couldn't even get close to "U.S. Interstate 90" (which is, perhaps, unfairly abstract). After six rounds Timmy declared a halt, by switching on the radio. Spinning the dial, he happened across a whiny old Roy Acuff song about the Bible, and started singing lustily along. That was when he learned that Audrey Ann Hunter McCue thought that, quote, Hillbilly Music Was Just Gross, unquote.

Tough shit, little lady, he said to himself. But he stopped singing, and eventually changed the station to Top 40 crap, which she loved: she knew all forty by heart.

Reminded by the radio news bulletins of what was going on all around them, they got onto the subject of blacks and whites. Audrey was afraid of Negroes, who had begun moving into her neighborhood in Dedham a few years before. When her grandmother was knocked down and robbed by two black teenagers, the Hunter family's raw Irish-American racism flared into the open.

Timmy, on the other hand, believed himself sympathetic to people of all sorts. (He wasn't. He just believed himself to be.) One of his best friends was an Indian in Wyoming. He had played basketball with black soldiers when he

28

was overseas. If he were black, he told Audrey, and had to live in Cleveland, he'd probably be throwing bricks through store windows, too.

Beyond these sociological discussions, and Audrey's car games, conversation that Saturday consisted mainly of efforts to learn more about one another's past.

Timmy's dealings with her family in Dedham had been so charged with hostility that he had taken away very little sense of the world in which Audrey had grown up. These narrow-faced, narrow-minded females, and their shadowy men, had been for him like nuns and priests out of uniform.

During the day's journey, she told him more about them—which one drank, which had traveled, which she liked best—adding form and color to her past.

Timmy listened with varying degrees of attention. At the very least, he liked the sound of her family-recollecting voice. For all its tonal flats and emotional shallows, there was a lyrical up-and-down lilt to her babbling which filled the car agreeably when he had had enough silence. She may have been only conjuring up aproned aunts and gossiping cousins, but Audrey's chirruping was proof that a sweet living female was now sharing his world. And that was good.

Timmy gave up glimpses of his past more cautiously. He had told her almost nothing of his life outside the plant in the weeks before they married. If she knew that he swam and played basketball at the Y, and had tennis and handball matches with friends, it was only because they had to fit their meetings around these irrevocable events.

He hinted at more exotic feats. He had climbed mountains, apparently, and skied in white places all over the world. He had glided on wings, played basketball in Germany. He had balanced on a board through ocean waves, and swum far under the sea.

She tried to imagine it all—the white mountains, the basketball games, riding the ocean surf—but she couldn't. It struck her as very odd that a forty-year-old man who could do all these things had chosen her.

In every sense but one his life seemed richer than hers. (The one lack, for which she pitied him, was religious faith.) He had the advantage of age, of course, all those extra years of freedom; and freedom of a man's kind, a free-wanderer out of the West. But his life also seemed richer because his people were so different from hers.

From the beginning of their friendship, whenever intimate conversations began to founder, she headed for the safe waters of his family. They were fun to hear about, these hearty westerners of his. They sounded like good people. The more she learned of them, the more shape she could give to her unknown and slightly frightening future. And since Timmy didn't mind talking about them, it helped to pass the time.

Of his parents, he had so far said virtually nothing. He never told Audrey if they knew about the wedding (and she never asked). None of his family came, in any case.

But she liked the idea of the restaurant in Grass Valley, and the feasts he

29

described at which thirty or forty relatives gathered to cook and eat and drink, and then nap and clean up and trade stories all day long while the children played out of doors—all this at a big family farmhouse in the Gold Country hills. She prayed that these robust men and women (she imagined them all as tall and strong as Timmy) would be willing to move over and make a small place for her.

He told her about going on a fishing trip in the mountains with his father and his brothers, where he had broken a leg falling off a high rock into the water. She could have wept with envy at the thought of a father who took his children to such wonderful places, and then carried them on his own back when they broke their legs in mountain streams.

Timmy knew about five generations of his family in minute detail. To a girl whose own living grandmother had been born in Ireland, but whose relatives never said a word about anything beyond eight square blocks of Dedham, or anything older than their own petty grievances, it was like being adopted into a legend.

He told her of two of his ancestors who had crossed the country in a covered wagon in 1849. The wife, his great-great-grandmother Ellen McCue, had kept a diary of the trip in a cloth-bound school notebook. Timmy's dad still had the notebook, which he kept locked in a metal box at the farm. He used to read the whole account aloud to his sons every year, censoring it with a few silent omissions.

4

The farm-country road they had turned onto was accumulating the sleaze that signified the approach of a lesser American city. Used tire dealers squeezed between Dairy Queens and little stucco bars blinking their names.

But no motels. For six miles, so far, no motels. Hoping for better luck, they turned onto an Ohio state highway signposted "Toledo."

NO VACANCY. NO VACANCY. SORRY, NO VACANCY.

It was growing late on a midwestern muggy afternoon. With each mile, Audrey could feel her new husband growing more impatient, fouler of temper.

"There's one!"

"FLAMINGO ROYALE" was spelled out in giant neon script. But in tiny letters beneath it, "NO VACANCY."

"Oh, dear. I am sorry.

"Look, there: across the street. A TraveLodge . . . oh. No."

Another, and another, and another: all full. No Vacancy. No room at the inns.

"Why would anybody want to stay *here*?" Timmy demanded aloud: "It's not even Toledo yet!"

He snarled a vile word Audrey had never heard him use. She whispered a pious ejaculation. The nuns at St. Rose's had taught their girls that this was the way to ease the pain smutty talk caused the suffering Jesus, hanging on the cross. As he stepped on the gas to make a sudden left turn, a siren whined behind them. A red searchlight pierced the rear window.

"Oh, screw! I didn't see a signal there, did you? Must be a fucking speed

31

trap. What a shitty asshole place!" He pulled over and braked with a jolt. She uttered four more silent ejaculations.

"Timmy," Audrey whispered. "Please don't argue."

He said nothing. A policeman came up to the window, dripping sweat.

"Don't believe in red lights, do ya buster?" He leaned his arms on the car door, stuck his head inside the window. In that hot, enclosed place, his large shaven head had the effect of a noxious presence, like a giant fart. "License."

"I didn't see any light." Timmy kept looking straight ahead. Audrey glanced anxiously from one man to the other.

"Wanna come back with me and look?"

"It was green when I was there."

"Look, buster. I got witnesses in the car. I been here all day. It's hot; you broke the law. I got other things to do. If you wanna argue, you can follow me to the station."

"Sure. Sure, that's just what I want to do." He ached with desire to break the fat red nose with the knuckles of his open hand. Instead, he pulled a sweat-damp wallet out of his back pocket, and handed over his license.

"California license, Massachusetts plates. What's the deal?"

"No deal. I lived in California when I got the license. I lived in Massachusetts when I bought the car." *Ass*hole.

"Where you live now?"

Timmy finally turned and looked him in the face. "We're going back to California."

"Not through red lights, you're not." The policeman glared back at him, eyeball to eyeball. He looked over at Audrey, who was praying to the Virgin Mary that nothing would happen.

"I think you better follow me."

Timmy sighed furiously and reached into his wallet again. Audrey couldn't make out what he was doing. In a sordid tableau, the two men seemed to be shaking hands. Then the policeman smiled at him (his smile was more sinister than his frown), dripping fat drops of sweat.

"That help any?"

"Maybe."

"Now can we go?"

"I said maybe. Maybe not. This isn't California, buster."

"You're telling me." Timmy tried to stare him down, but the pink pig eyes had shifted to Audrey. They drank in her bare arms and shoulders, her small buds of bosoms. Finally the policeman backed his head out of the car, stood up, stuffed his hands in the tight pockets that were squeezed beneath his gun belt and rolling belly.

"Okay, buster. Get the hell out of here, before I start asking where you picked up the kid."

Timmy peeled rubber, as he slammed back into the traffic. He was blood-red with anger, silent as a rock. Audrey waited three blocks before asking.

"What was all that about?"

"I slipped him a ten. Fucking bastard."

"That's why he let us go?"

"Corrupt as hell, cops around here. Worse than Chicago."

It was so vulgar she wanted to cry. This wasn't what her honeymoon was supposed to be like! She wondered where they would be now if they had turned off at Niagara Falls. Maybe they would have stayed the night.

Night. As afternoon edged into dark, she began to be apprehensive about night number four. Street lamps were lit. Bar signs flashed. The sky pressed down, reddened by the neon, enervating, close, wearing tempers to threads. Perhaps he'll be too tired.

Martin Road. Pemberville. Woodville Road. Curtice. Jerusalem. Each intersection looked just like the one before. Every cross street duplicated whatever road they were on, as if giant mirrors had been set up at the corners. Beautiful Ohio, in dreams I hear you call . . .

Another three miles of gluey traffic, adhesive heat, the poisonous smells of hamburger stands blending with engine exhaust, discount furniture warehouses, Thriftee gas stations, lines of little used car lot flags limp in the breezeless air, red lights, green lights, yellow lights, cut-rate drugs, Pizza Huts. Overweight ugly people in short-sleeved shirts walked slowly through the stinking heat.

A big Holiday Inn: "NO VACANCY." Three forlorn palm trees marked the Monte Carlo Trailways Palm Resort Lodge. "SORRY," said an insincere sign.

"Should we ask at a gas station?"

"No."

Leave him alone.

After another half-hour, Timmy turned at a huge church surrounded by empty asphalt. Traffic was thinner here. The neighborhood began to grow more tawdry—vacant stores, boarded-up windows, painted graffiti in Spanish on blind walls. Down the road, they spied at the same time the outline of a heart in green neon: "HEART OF AMERICA MOTEL. HEATED POOL. REASONABLE RATES. COLOR TV." There was a red "NO" before the green word "VACANCY," but it was still unlit.

It was shabby, the Heart of America, more an old-fashioned tourist court than a proper motel. Two rows of pink-painted stucco units (with car spaces in between) flanked a patch of browning crabgrass. Behind it was a swimming pool, enclosed by a steel fence. Gauze curtains lay unmoving in the open windows of the manager's bungalow.

Timmy wiped the sweat off his forehead with the back of his hand. "I'm sorry, honey, but I'm afraid it'll have to do. Do you think you can bear it?"

"Sure I can, sweetheart. Please let's stop."

"I'll try to find somewhere nice to eat as soon as we get a room."

He parked alongside the office, leaving the keys. As he went in, Audrey looked at the faded pink cabins, twelve on each side. To her mind's eye, they were beds, nothing else, big soft beds separated by thin walls. Motels like these were places where homeless, evil men made love to the evil women they picked up in bars; flesh-colored cubicles full of sin. John Hannigan had stopped at a place exactly like this one after the Sacred Heart High Junior Prom, and tried to persuade her, dressed in her aqua tulle strapless ballerina-length formal, to go into a room with him. She could see slippery bodies, writhing, encoupled; half-empty whiskey bottles; cigarettes. Sheets on the floor. Sin.

No: not sin. Not any more. Relax, I must try to relax. Try to feel married. I mustn't make him angry with me anymore. Sitting in a car in front of a cheap motel office, she said a prayer: "Please don't let him hurt me," she prayed.

He was back. She wiped her cheeks, and smiled the best she could.

"Number eleven. Down at the end." He turned on the engine, drove the bug-spattered Cougar down the row of huts, and pulled into a space alongside the second-to-last cube.

"Those other motels weren't really full up. They just don't want any more business tonight."

"Why not?"

"Some kind of emergency alert. They may be declaring a curfew. Apparently there was a riot in Toledo earlier this afternoon, and the police are afraid it'll start moving in this direction. The lady at the Flamingo Royale knows someone in the riot control center. She had just phoned the guy here to tell him when we drove up.

"Look: he's put his 'No Vacancy' sign on. We just made it!"

"Timmy, I don't like this."

"I don't like it much either, honey. But I'd rather be in here than out on the road. Instead of looking for a restaurant, though, I think I'll just go out and get us something we can eat in the room. If that's okay with you."

"I'm not hungry."

"Well, I am. And you will be. Come on, let's move in."

He gave her the key, chained to a big plastic heart with the motel address engraved on it, and went to get their suitcases out of the trunk. She unlocked the door to number 11, and turned on the light.

One lumpy double bed seemed to fill up the room. It was covered with a white chenille bedspread, just like her mother's. Squeezed in alongside it were a purple armchair and a dressing table. Over the table, a metal bell lamp hung on a chain. The walls were covered with some kind of ridged, wheat-colored vinyl spattered with gold flecks. The plaster on the ceiling sparkled, too. Timmy came up alongside her.

"Not bad for fourteen bucks."

"No." She bit her lip. "No, it'll be fine."

"I tell you what. Let me grab a quick shower, then jump in the pool and cool off. You take a nice long soak in the tub. Wouldn't you like that? Then we can both have a little nap on the bed, before I go out for eats. I think we'll feel better after that. It's been a long day." He gave her a hug and a kiss.

A little nap on the bed. "That's a good idea," she managed to say.

He was already taking off his sweaty-wet clothes, letting them fall where he stood, without even closing the drapes. Audrey pulled them closed, then sat on the edge of the bed with her back to him, brushing her hair. Now he was behind the glass door of the shower-bath, singing. She brushed harder, harder. Remember, O most gracious Virgin Mary, that never was it known that anyone who fled to thy protection, implored thy help, or sought thy intercession, was left unaided. I must stop this weeping, make myself attractive. Oh, this *room*! She tugged at the snarls in her hair until it hurt, and cried a little more.

He was back, singing softly, toweling off his back. He sat down alongside her on the bed. She forced herself not to cringe away. He kissed her on the ear with a warm gentle breath, and pulled down the zipper of her dress. Must relax.

Kindly, he moved aside her hair, and touched his mouth to the back of her neck. She turned and smiled bravely, and he saw the tears on her face. He touched them with his fingers, licked them away with his tongue, kissed her closed eyelids. Grateful, she found the courage to reach out one hand over his wet thigh, close her fingers softly over his penis. Still as night, they sat for several seconds, his lips to her eyelid, her hand between his legs.

"I'll try, Timmy. I promise."

"I know you will, baby." He kissed her cheeks, then her lips. "Don't worry about it. I love you, you know?"

She threw herself onto his chest, into his arms, sobbing great gulps.

"Hey, easy there. Easy, baby." He rubbed her back, inside her dress; unhooked her bra. "Come on, now, into the bath. Here, you lie down. Let Daddy help."

She lay back and let him undress her, like a baby, like a helpless child.

"Don't go away." He kissed her face, then her nipples and her belly, gently touched her little bush. "I'll be right back."

He went into the bathroom to run her bath. She could see him in the mirror bending over the tub: shoulders, back, bottom, legs. She felt a surge of longing to love him the way he wanted. When the tub was full of hot water frosted with bubbles, he turned off the tap, and strode back into the room with that apelike lope of his, naked and grinning. He picked her up in his arms, carried her into the bathroom, and gently set her down into water that warmed and soothed, hot water topped with a layer of white foam that smelt of her own perfume.

"You just relax, baby doll. Daddy's going for a swim. I'll be right back."

"I love you, Timmy."

"I love you, baby."

Erect on the board, ready to dive: the sky cracked with a long drum roll, and broke into rain. Instantly the water was pockmarked by a hundred thousand drops.

He raised his arms, made a single jump, and dove to the bottom. Pushing the water aside, he swam two quick underwater laps, then rose to the surface and turned his head to the sky. Hot, heavy rain pelleted on his face. The thunder drums pounded, lightning still flashed. With a vigorous kick, he pushed himself off and began swimming hard.

Whenever he began to swim steady like this, lap after lap, he could feel the machinery of his brain start to wind down. For a while, back in Palo Alto, he had tried running instead of swimming, because so many of his friends were doing it. But then he would find himself thinking, thinking of the landscape, of other runners, of the strain in his calves. He found he could even run and *worry* at the same time, which was no good at all.

A game of handball fixed his attention more closely. In a good game, he could reduce his mind to a kind of electronic beam that focused on the ball and nothing else. Then the rest of his system would respond instinctively to the place where this semiconscious sensor told it the ball would be, to its speed and its spin. In a good, fast game he could short-circuit his reason altogether, which was why he played.

But after the first few hundred yards in water, he could feel his brain dissolving altogether. Here there were no other people to think about. There was no goal. There was no strategy. Arms reached and pulled, then reached and pulled again; legs kicked like an independent machine. Head rose and turned, mouth breathed in; head dipped under water, nose breathed out. It was all as involuntary and natural as breathing in your sleep.

He pushed on, hurling himself back and forth. Near the end of each lap, his radar sensed the coming-up of the wall; body spun down and over for the turn, legs thrust back for the kick. Then he was off again like a batted ball, in less time than it takes to think. Arms, legs, head flashed on like a fish, like part of the water.

Any way of losing yourself was good. But swimming was one of the best. It had none of the exhilaration of skiing or sex, none of the danger-highs of surfing, the emotional rhythms and ecstatic peaks of more dramatic sports. It wasn't a "sport," in fact, the way he used it. It was an escape from the antigravitational strain of pretending to be an upright human being. It was total self-transformation. Every muscle in his body was vigorously engaged, his whole physical self supported by a jellylike fluid through which it made its fishy way, a fluid that slipped so suavely along all of his skin that self became water, water became self. He didn't count strokes, or keep track of laps; he tried to think nothing but water, let his body swim of its own accord, smoother, faster: lap, and turn; lap, and then turn. . . .

In earlier years, he had fretted over strokes, listened to coaches, exercised ashore, timed himself, driven his limbs and his lungs past exhaustion. In the mid-1940s, he had been a finalist in the All-Northern California high school championships two years running—the nearest to a state championship Nevada Union High had ever come. Now he swam only to pull his body free of his mind. When that process was complete, he stopped, instinctively, and surfaced. He stopped now.

It had poured rain the whole time he was underwater, but the atmosphere was no less close, the air no less hot. He pulled himself up, sat on the edge of

36

the pool, and breathed with conscious slowness. He let the rain pour down his hair, down his shoulders and back, drip off his mustache and his nose.

Fifty feet in front of him, a group of fat travelers had got out of their Winnebago and were standing in the rain, arguing with the motel manager. From behind the screen door at his bungalow, he kept repeating that there were no vacancies. The travelers, in wet pin-curlers, baseball caps, ham-thighed Bermuda shorts and soaking T-shirts that stuck to their bellies, kept insisting that half his units were unfilled.

Timmy walked to the Cyclone fence and stood there watching the scene, his hands resting high in the lozenges of iron.

Out in the street, cars squealed and skidded. Distant sirens wailed, rising and falling.

The manager shouted a last word, slammed and locked his door. The family went on arguing, with the door, with one another. An elephantine young woman, in huge curlers and red plaid shorts, saw Timmy behind his fence. She waddled over, nearer the fence. One by one, the others turned around too. There were six of them, round, squat, soft, all in tropical Bermudas with their Madras plaids bleeding, the hair plastered wet to their faces. They all stopped their quarreling and gathered by the iron fence to stare at the lone man in a swimsuit. Rain kept pouring, thunder rolling, lightning cracking. No one spoke.

Feeling outnumbered by this family of voyeurs, an ape in a cage, Timmy grabbed his soggy towel and hurried out the gate towards number 11. As he knocked on the door, he looked back over his shoulder. All six were still standing there, staring after him like some animal escaped from the zoo.

She smelled of lilac bubbles and love, soft and fresh and beautiful from her bath. She had put on a new lemon-yellow nightie over nothing but clean, powdered skin. She unchained and opened the door. There, looming above her under the amber porch light, were dark shoulders, dripping curls, fine body hair pressed wet into curving allover patterns against the contours of chest and arms: green eyes that looked into hers.

What Timmy saw through the steam and the wet, and the fire of new energies drawn from the water, was a sweet, dark-eyed, very young girl, her face full of willing affection. Beneath the soft folds of lemon transparency, he saw a flawless sequence of soft curves waiting to be touched, kneaded, grasped: one sinuous song of silken skin. Shoulders and breasts were half-bared above the ruffled neck of her gown. The lines of waist, hips, and thighs were silhouette-clear from the light of the lamp that hung behind her.

He kicked the door closed with his heel, tossed his towel into the room, and, wet as he was, pulled her body up against his, clutched her buttocks in his hands through the fine nylon. They stood by the door locked together and kissed like a husband and a wife.

That evening, they made love as he wished, and though she suffered, she was pleased. During his solitary night drive, he had decided to defer his plans for wringing maximum pleasure out of this exquisite little body: time would

37

come for all that. If he could rein in his urges for a while, he sensed years of docile apprenticeship stretching ahead. So he tried to go easy.

She could not yet take much delight (though she tried to, and pretended to) in all this unfamiliar handling of her most private person. The greatest pleasure she took came from the belief that she was giving *him* pleasure, in the way he wanted it.

She was amazed at how much vigor he still possessed, after twenty straight hours of driving. At times, she feared that his ardent holds were going to cause her permanent damage, as well as temporary pain. But she dared not beg off. Whatever she was feeling, she tried to make satisfied purrs, while he puffed like a breathless sheep dog, and mixed tender phrases with obscenities in one general guttural grunt.

The secret, she told herself, was simply to *yield*, and not to think of the strangeness or the pain: to let him, as they said in her novels, have his will of her.

Unfortunately, his will seemed to demand more than passive yielding, from the way he kept pulling her arms and legs around. But she didn't know the right moves, didn't understand what he was after. She concentrated all her energies on self-abnegation, and ended up achieving it the only way she knew how: by prayer.

Having penetrated her standard fashion, Timmy had flopped her over onto her stomach, hoisted up her bottom, and spread her cheeks wide, in order to thrust in again. (How many times she wondered, could a man his age do it?)

As he bit into the back of her neck, muttering indiscriminately of love and fuck and fuck and love, as the fingers of his spare hand squeezed painfully hard at her nipple, she was praying herself out of the ignominy and pain, offering it up, *thanking* the Blessed Virgin for giving her this animal on her back, defiling her, filling her; for teaching her how to be a good and patient wife.

> Brethren: let wives be subject to their husbands as to the Lord; because a husband is head of the wife, just as Christ is head of the Church, being himself savior of the body. But just as the Church is subject to Christ, so also let wives be subject to their husband in all things. Husbands, love your wives, just as Christ also loved the Church, and delivered himself up for her, that he might sanctify her, cleansing her in the bath of water by means of the word; in order that he might present to himself the Church in all her glory, not having spot or wrinkle or any such thing, but that she might be holy and without blemish. Even thus ought husbands also to love their wives as their own bodies. He who loves his own wife, loves himself. For no one ever hated his own flesh. . . . For this reason a man shall leave his father and mother, and shall cleave to his wife; and the two shall become one flesh.

Father Doyle had looked very keenly at her during the marriage ceremony. Even behind her veil, she could not face his hard glance, or comprehend his hard meaning. Timmy was certainly trying his best, at this moment, to cleave to his wife, and make the two of them one flesh. Holding on for dear life to the iron headbars of the bed, her bottom up in the air, her hundred pounds hammered by his two hundred plus, she tried to focus on her white wedding in Dedham just three days ago.

5

Drained and (temporarily) satisfied, Timmy lay on the bare mattress, arms and legs spread in the shape of an X. The sheet, pulled free by his exertions, lay wadded up between them. The blankets were on the floor. The hair of his head and body was matted and wet. The mattress and bedclothes were covered with hundreds of tiny hairs. He stank, the sheets stank, even she, sweet she, stank of sex, sweat, and fatigue.

She sat up, leaned over, and picked up the wet towel he had tossed alongside the bed. Slowly, carefully, she rubbed him cool with it, first his forehead and face, then the rest of his body.

The thing lay like a dead eel over his thigh. For all the damage it had done, she could look at it now with curiosity instead of fear or disgust.

Smiling with his eyes, he reached one arm beneath her neck. She curled up against him, head nestled on his chest, both knees bent on top of his leg, one arm across his rising and falling stomach.

When they awoke in the same embrace, it was dark. Timmy's right arm had gone all pins-and-needles from the weight of her head. With his free hand, he picked up his wristwatch from the dresser alongside, and made out the luminous hands: ten o'clock. He said it aloud: "Ten o'clock." Audrey, waking, was pleased to learn the time—her dreams had been distressing—but unhappy to remember where she was. Both felt rested, and ravenously hungry.

"There's bound to be a market that stays open late somewhere around here." He was squatting beside the suitcase, fishing for clothes. "I'll find us something."

"No, Timmy, don't. Remember about the police. About the curfew. You

yourself said it wasn't safe. Please, sweetheart. We can wait until breakfast."

She was devouring the shape of his back. How I do love him.

"Maybe you can, but I can't." He had pulled up and buttoned his Levi's
cut-offs, tugged a dirty soccer shirt over his head. He shoved his wallet and
car keys in the pockets. "Don't worry. I'll be back in no time. Get ready for a
feast." He kissed her, and was out the door. The rain had stopped.

Audrey waited for the sound of the car driving off. She told herself she
would get out of bed, put something on, try to tidy the little room. Instead, she
sank back and fell into another deep sleep.

Once more her dreams were bad. Timmy was surrounded by other women.
She was unable to get to him. Other men seized her, took her away. Her
mother locked her in a room, from which she could only escape by a high
window. Now she was walking down a church aisle, endlessly long, with Mark
Robinson. Both of them were naked. Father Leonard was waiting at the end.
Her feet were so heavy they dragged in the sand.

She struggled to get out, and was finally pulled free by a long rising
scream, demanding and ugly, right there in her room.

It wasn't a dream. Her waking mind took over, with a jarring electric jolt.
The scream was real.

Shivering, naked, she hurried to the window. She pulled aside one corner of
the drapes, and saw two police cars outside. The scream had been their sirens.
They were parked near her door, red lights flashing around, casting an awful
glow through the drapes.

Four policemen were talking to the motel manager, who was standing in his
bathrobe and slippers near the pool fence. Lights went on in cabins across the
way.

They were talking about Timmy, she could tell. Other Heart of America
guests looked out their windows, or opened their doors. A few went outside.
Audrey stayed where she was, waiting for the manager to point to her door,
for a policeman to come up and knock.

But no one did.

After a few minutes, the police got back in their cars and drove off. The
sirens rose, the lights flashed around.

She put on her robe and slippers, switched on the light, sat down at the
dressing table. She lit a cigarette and started brushing her hair. Her eye in the
mirror fell on the reflection of Timmy's wristwatch, where he had left it when
he went out. Almost midnight. She picked it up, shook it, listened to it,
studied the face again. It was ticking, both hands were near the twelve.
Twelve o'clock midnight? But then where *is* he?

He's been kidnapped. No, shot. Run over. Arrested. He's hurt somewhere,
knocked out, his head crushed and bleeding, I know it.

Why didn't they come in and tell me?

No, he's gone off and left me, changed his mind about being married. I
wasn't what he wanted. He decided it tonight in bed when he learned I wasn't
pure. That was my last chance. It was a mistake, he decided. Now he isn't

41

coming back ever. He's left me alone in this room, with no car, no money, no one, nothing.

No, that can't be. All his things are here. (I'm one of his things.) She went over and switched on the television, clicked around until she found a news program.

A camera tilted and fell, trying to catch a running crowd. An official sat at his desk. There were sirens, breaking glass, looted store windows, smoke. A bombed police station. An overturned car burst into orange flame. Through it all, reporters kept reading out names in a flat Ohio drone. She got up and fixed the chain on the door. On the TV screen a platoon of policemen were clubbing down one black man and dragging him away by the feet. "After this message . . . " She clicked it off.

Think. (I'm trying.) *Think*! There must be another explanation. No store open for miles, his heart set on getting this meal, just for us. . . .

Then why didn't he phone? She looked around. No phone. He could have called the manager. Maybe the manager wouldn't answer.

Ran out of gas, maybe? When did he last put in gas? On the Interstate. After Erie.

Maybe he read the time wrong before, maybe it was eleven, eleven-thirty even. Not ten. He was looking at his watch in the dark then. Now he doesn't have it. I have it. He doesn't *realize* how long I've been waiting.

Twelve-forty. He'll be back any minute. I must hold on. Mustn't go to pieces. (What would a wife do? I mean a *good* wife?)

She turned the television back on, found a talk show, tried to get lost in that the way she usually did when she couldn't sleep. She fixed her hair back with a ribbon, started painting her fingernails, but her fingers shook so badly she missed the nails and painted the skin. Then she dropped the brush. She lit one cigarette, then another, put them both out before they were finished. She went to the toilet, couldn't go, washed her hands and face. Back in the bedroom, she paged through a pamphlet she found in the dresser drawer, "This Month's Fun in Toledo." She lay down, got up again, changed the channel.

"It's one o'clock," the announcer declared.

He *is* gone.

What will mother say? "I was right," is what she'll say. In her bag, she found two candy bars, and almost swallowed them whole. She turned up the TV, took a Gideon Bible out of the drawer and started reading it at random. Nothing made any sense. She put on earrings, brushed her hair violently, lit another cigarette, stared at herself and an old Topper movie in the dressing table mirror.

He's not just gone, he's dead, a corpse lying somewhere in the street. In an alley. They took his money and keys. He didn't even have shoes on. Nobody would know who he was. They would think he was just some vagrant. He got caught by one of those mobs. They rocked his car and turned it over and then poured gasoline on it and set fire to it with him in it, that car I saw on TV. "Burned so badly as to be unrecognizable." If I went down to the morgue,

42

they would pull down a sheet and show me this long, blackened hulk on a table.

Was it my sin that killed him? Letting him do that to me, like dogs, pretending that I liked it, lying? Was it my mortal sins that killed him? Yielding to him like a whore: was that why God let him die? His head cracked and bleeding now. Or because I lied to him before, let him think I was a virgin? Because of my past, my unforgivable sin? She could see the light of a street lamp shining in a sticky puddle of almost black blood.

I'll say a rosary. That's what I'll do. No more crying. Listen to Johnny Carson in my nice new robe and furry slippers and say a rosary at the same time, to calm my nerves. By the time I'm finished, the Blessed Mother will have brought him back.

She was feeling around in a straw bag for her pearl rosary, the rosary she had had ever since her First Communion, when she heard a knock, a tap really. She waited: another, louder knock.

"Audrey? Are you awake?"

Through the narrow opening over the door chain she saw him—whole, unwounded, unbleeding, looking the same as he had when he left her, except that now he held two big bags. She unlocked the chain and threw herself upon him, but he escaped her grasp to put the bags down.

He tried to explain. He had spent all this time trying to find a grocery store open. Everything was closed, see, for blocks and blocks around. After he found the groceries, he decided he wanted them to have champagne as well, so that meant he had to find a liquor store, too, understand, and all the liquor stores in Toledo were shut down, with iron grilles or sheets of plywood over their windows.

She was sitting on the bed; he was standing by the dressing table. He began to take out the things he had bought and show them to her, one by one. But she wasn't ready to pay attention. She kept sobbing, and between sobs asking the same questions, over and over and over. She told him about her nightmare, and the police siren, and the burning car on TV. Not once did he offer sympathy. And all he did was keep telling the same story, in fewer and fewer words, glib, uncomforting, more defensive than sympathetic. He was looking past her now, around her, less and less interested in her complaints. He kept trying to reach inside her robe. She kept pushing his hand away. He was back, but he brought no relief.

Timmy had set out his store-bought feast on the top of the dresser. Hard rolls, a loaf of pumpernickel, a cube of butter, salami, a jar of herrings in sour cream, a tin of anchovies, potato salad, marinated mushrooms, fresh green onions, tiny pickles, a chunk of cheddar cheese, Wheat Thins, macaroon cookies, a Swiss roll. A bottle of cheap champagne perspired on the glass dresser top. It was more than enough for two, even if they were the two hungriest lovers in the world, even if one of them had not just sat out a miserable vigil; even if the other were not lying through his teeth.

For of course Audrey was right. Timmy had *not* spent three and a half hours looking for food.

He had left, full of hunger, and love, and the best intentions, to bring home a feast for his tender mate. But once he was driving alone in his car, he tasted the salt air of freedom, and set off again into the night.

Wiping Audrey and marriage out of his mind, he headed out Jerusalem for the dead center of Toledo, to look at what was left of the fires, the barricades, the milling nighttime crowds.

He ended up in a bar full of neckless flat-tops who talked a good lynch mob, but didn't have the guts to get off their stools. He listened to them and argued with them, and bought drinks for a scaggy tart who rubbed his crotch and whispered wet offers in his ear.

About midnight, the bartender grew tired of hearing his maudlin, guilty tales, and virtually ordered him to go home. He told him where he could find an all-night liquor store and delicatessen on the way back.

Timmy left, found the store, did his shopping, and went back to comfort little Audrey.

But little Audrey would not be comforted. Through the lies and the whiskey, both of which she could smell, comfort was not in his gift to offer. They picked at their indigestible feast with the help of his pocket-knife, and drank champagne out of plastic tumblers from the bathroom. The television buzzed blankly to itself. He tried for more sex, groping and thick-tongued, but this time she simply said No—no excuses, no misgivings: No.

While he was in the bathroom, she scraped the mess on the dresser into a wastebasket, piled the leftovers into a bag, turned off the television and the room lights, put on clean underwear and a flannel nightgown, and got back into her side of the bed. She curled tightly under the covers, facing away from the side he would lie on. She heard him flush the toilet, and stumble out of the bathroom. In the dark, he tripped over something and swore. He shed his clothes and collapsed on top of the bedspread. No kiss, no good night: within seconds, he was snoring.

Audrey stiffened with rage, then closed up wounded in a shell, emitting powerful rays of disaffection. For twenty minutes, she ran around and around the circuit of her grievances, to the noise of his drunken snore.

Only then did she switch on her bedside light and look at his carcass, sprawling, unconscious, and she hated it. It looked so animal and gross. She could not believe that she had allowed this thing to have mauled and man-handled her just a few hours before.

She got out of bed, tugged the bedcovers out from under his dead weight. Then, to hide the loutish spectacle from sight, she threw them back over him.

One arm and half a leg hung heavily off the side of the bed. She tried to shove them back on. A bleary eye opened.

"Hi, babe. Whatcha doin'?"

"Nothing. Just go back to sleep."

"Night, swee'heart." He reached up a hand, but it dropped of its own weight.

"Good night." She tucked the blankets over his chest, switched off her light, then went over and sat by the dark mirror to smoke a cigarette and feel miserable.

What had she locked herself into?

She woke first, as the morning sun penetrated the curtains, and slipped out from under his arm She had washed, dressed, cleaned up, and very nearly finished packing before Timmy opened his eyes.

Both up, they said little, and avoided direct glances. He had suffered a husband's deficit of guilt; she had earned a wife's credit of wounded self-righteousness. No mention was made of his three and a half hours in Toledo, his whiskey breath, his transparent lies; of his behavior after he returned. She had packed away the remnants of their unfestive feast, to serve as lunch the next day on their way to Chicago. Timmy hurried through his shaving, showering, and dressing, careful to keep covered up in her presence, to keep his voice low, to pick up his clothes. He offered, silently and superfluously, to help with anything that needed doing.

He was not precisely contrite; he did not exactly crawl. He had lost a round, and he knew it. Now was a time to be quiet, and let the little lady make a few decisions. Which is why he didn't question, let alone protest, her announcement that she wanted to go to church.

6

"In nomine Patris, et Filii, et Spiritus Sancti, Amen. Introibo ad altare Dei."

"Ad Deum qui laetificat juventutum meam."

Timmy and Audrey were standing in a pew at the back of the church. Taking their cue from the altar boys, they knelt down with everyone else.

In the name of the Father, and of the Son, and of the Holy Ghost, Amen. I will go to the altar of God.

To God, the joy of my youth.

On the off chance that what they had done so far *was* a mortal sin, Audrey had asked a priest she saw in the vestibule before mass to hear her confession. Timmy waited for her outside.

("And I committed . . . unnatural . . . sexual acts."

"With whom?"

"With my husband."

"Go on.")

Now he was kneeling alongside her, in a clean white shirt and a blue Air Force tie. She couldn't have ordered him to come with her, of course. But after last night, she wasn't surprised when he came. Knowing how he felt about such things, Audrey had been afraid she'd never get him to church again after the wedding. It pleased her that they were together now.

She glanced up to see Timmy staring at the priest, who had just finished (*"Mea culpa, mea culpa, mea maxima culpa,"*) hurrying through his Confiteor. Now the two kneeling altar boys bowed their heads to the floor and began repeating the confession of sins. To her astonishment, Audrey saw Timmy's lips moving along with their prayer.

She closed her hand tight over his, on the back of the pew ahead. The priest ascended the steps, kissed the altar, and went over to the right side to read from a huge missal on its stand, red ribbons dangling from between its decorated pages.

"*Kyrie eleison,*" intoned the priest. "*Kyrie eleison,*" answered the boys. "*Gloria in excelsis Deo . . .*"

During the gospel and the sermon, Audrey let her eyes wander into blue-painted vaults, past stained-glass saints, up to the stone pinnacles and plaster statues and groves of candles of the alter. All things eventually drew her eyes to the plain pine doors of the tabernacle (the old bronze ones had been prised off by vandals). The doors, now closed, were set between red-veined marble colonnettes, and surmounted by a golden crown the thieves had been unable to unbolt. High over the altar hung a larger-than-life-sized crucifix. The familiar figure of Jesus, with its crown of thorns and drooping diaper, was nailed to a gigantic cross of polished walnut. Painted blood dripped from the nails in its hands and feet, the mangled forehead, the carven slit in its side. The cross hung in space on bronze chains, which were screwed at one end into the high vault of the choir and attached at the other into hooks in its arms.

As the mass droned on, Audrey thought about the night before. "Those who marry," Saint Paul had warned her, "will have pain and grief in their bodily life." But "better be married," even he conceded, "than burn with vain desire."

She looked up at the gaunt figure in his green and gold robes, muttering his pre-communion prayers. Priests never married. She recoiled from the thought of one young priest she had known, and suddenly felt burned, deep inside.

They had convinced her two sisters; they had almost convinced her: all her life, she had been warned by drab, holy people against the sins of the flesh.

Now she had given herself entirely to the flesh—to his flesh. How could she feel sufficiently undefiled, after yesterday, to receive into her mouth the body and blood of her Lord?

But she did.

The priest had finished offering up the pure Victim, the holy Victim, the all-perfect Victim. The bell rang three more times. Professing his unworthiness, the priest swallowed his wafer, drank his cup of sweet wine.

At the bells, Audrey rose and walked up to kneel at the altar rail. Up and down the rail the priest moved, plucking wafers one by one from his golden cup. One of the altar boys held a gold saucer beneath each chin, just in case a wafer should drop.

"*Corpus Domini nostri Jesu Christi custodiat animam tuam in vitam aeternam, Amen,*" he mumbled, as he slid a pale host onto her tongue.

Audrey forced it down her throat, walked back to their pew, slipped in beside Timmy. She tried to feel full of every grace and heavenly blessing, but immortal longings kept slipping away. Immoral ones kept pushing into their place: sweating shoulders, curling red hair.

47

She was overcome by the futility of it all. When she looked beseechingly up at the cross, the Son of God looked like just another naked man.

"*Benedicat vos omnipotens Deus,*

"*Pater,*

"*et Filius,*

"*et Spiritus Sanctus.*" The priest lifted his right arm over them, high, low, right, left. It was all over so quickly.

Audrey held tight to Timmy's arm on the way back to the car, trying to keep her pious daydreams from melting under the morning sun. She hoped other people would look at them. "What a good-looking couple!" she hoped they would think. Timmy looked so nice in a white shirt and tie.

But "Damn!" he said, as soon as they got back to the car. "I can't wait to get out of these things."

"Oh, please, darling! Please leave them on, just for today? For Sunday? You look so nice, all dressed up."

"Don't be dumb. It'd be crazy to keep these clothes on all day, just to sit in a car."

"But you'll look so nice, in restaurants and places. I want people to see you."

"What people? What restaurants and places? You know the sort of restaurants they got along the Indiana Toll Road?" He unknotted his tie and roughly yanked it off: this penance had lasted long enough. "Nobody dresses up to go to lunch on a freeway."

"Well," she sighed. "Okay." Minor victory, minor defeat.

"But maybe we could go somewhere nice for dinner, for a change? And put on some decent clothes *then*?"

"Maybe. Depends where we are."

He drove to a gas station, and pulled in. While an attendant was filling the tank, they went into their respective restrooms, gleaming in soft Sunday pastels. Minutes later, they emerged in their touring costumes: for her, a striped sun-top, tan wrap-around skirt, and huaraches; for Timmy, the same old YMCA T-shirt, Levi's cut-offs, and dirty tennies he had worn for the last two days.

7

The Indiana Toll Road, Main Street of the Midwest, is a world in itself.

Once you drive through the first toll plaza, you need never leave this ingeniously outfitted corridor. You could live on it for years, if you liked, though most travelers cross it in half a day.

It is six lanes wide, split by a grass median divider, with broad safety verges and rights-of-way on either side. For 156.9 unexciting miles, from the Eastpoint Terminal near Angola, Indiana, to the Westpoint Terminal just inside the Illinois line, it hugs the northern boundary of its unexciting state. The Toll Road, in fact, is all of Indiana that most Americans ever see.

It was approved during the far-sighted administration of Governor Henry F. Schricker. It was built, seven hundred and eighty-six days start to finish, during the efficient administration of Governor George N. Craig. It cost two hundred twenty million dollars to build, and seventy million more to finance. If all goes well, the 3½% bonds issued for its construction will be completely retired by 1994.

So far, all is going well. The summer Timmy and Audrey used it, the driver of an ordinary passenger car was charged three dollars and fifty cents to drive the whole length from east to west or west to east. A truck with five axles paid nine dollars. Although this was no more or less per mile than one paid on the Massachusetts Turnpike or the New York State Thruway, the fee often came as a surprise to first-time travelers from the West, accustomed as they were to authentically free freeways, roads at least as noble as the Indiana Toll Road, which cost nothing at all to traverse.

But few travelers were deterred by the tolls. About ten million cars, and five million trucks and buses, use the Indiana Toll Road every year. There is no other practical way to get from northern Ohio to northern Illinois, or vice versa, unless you need to visit the Indianapolis Speedway, or New Harmony, or the banks of the Wabash, or Tippecanoe, or hate toll roads. Every year, on their journeys across, more than twenty thousand vehicles break down, freeze up, suffer flat tires or dead batteries, run out of gas, oil, or water, wear through their fan belts, or skid off the road.

The Indiana Toll Road bulges out in eight carefully spaced nodes for the intricate minicivilizations of its service areas: *sixteen* service areas, in fact, since each node includes one center on the north, for westbound vehicles, and another on the south, for eastbound vehicles. Pedestrian bridges spanning the wide roadway connect each pair of service areas, should an eastbound traveler ever wish to compare his restaurant, cafeteria, gas station (Standard of Indiana or Union 76), truck center, gift shop, picnic area, playground, or rest rooms with the rival facilities across the road.

When the Toll Road was first being planned, in the early 1950s, the state highway commissioners in Indianapolis had the patriotic idea of dedicating each service area to a distinguished son or daughter of Indiana. There were cynics in those days who doubted the state's ability to come up with sixteen Hoosiers whose names would mean anything at all to travelers from the rest of the country, but they were wrong. Today, the names are emblazoned on mammoth Interstate exit signs, and honored by bronze plaques outside service area gift shop doors. Eastbound, from Illinois to Ohio, you drive past (or better yet, visit) the George Ade, T.A. Hendricks, Knute Rockne, Benjamin Harrison, George N. Craig, Thomas R. Marshall, Gene Stratton Porter, and James Whitcomb Riley service areas. Westbound, from Ohio to Illinois—the route our newlyweds were traveling—you encounter first the Booth Tarkington; then the Ernie Pyle; then the William Henry Harrison; then the Henry F. Schricker; then the Schuyler Colfax; then the Wilbur Shaw; then the C.W. Fairbanks; then the John T. McCutcheon.

Timmy and Audrey McCue made a point that Sunday of trying to spot the eastbound cars' honorees as well as their own. They did this by looking out the rear window, or through the rear-view mirror, as they zipped past the signs whose backs were to them, intended for drivers on the other half of the highway. Timmy, who had driven across the country six times (not always through Indiana), remembered some of the names from before. Both of them knew who the two Harrisons were, and who Ernie Pyle was, and (vaguely) Booth Tarkington. Timmy knew about Wilbur Shaw, and of course Knute Rockne. Audrey had not only heard of James Whitcomb Riley, she could (and did) recite "Jest 'Fore Christmas" and "Out to Old Aunt Mary's," two of his poems she had memorized, out of a book called *101 Famous Poems*, for a fifth-grade Christmas assembly. They argued over Gene Stratton Porter. Timmy was sure he played baseball for Cincinnati. Audrey thought she had read a book by a *woman* with that name, an old-fashioned book about a pioneer girl in the woods. Timmy wanted to bet on it, but Audrey didn't like gambling.

Neither had heard of any of the rest.

Picnicking that afternoon at Governor Schricker's service area, she bought a *Guide to the Indiana Toll Road*, which included capsule biographies of all

50

sixteen. She was unusually pleased to find that she had been right about Gene Stratton Porter. "What a dumb name for a woman," Timmy said.

She also bought a pile of postcards at the gift shop to send to relatives in Massachusetts, including—for her mother—a fold-out affair that dropped down twelve separate, almost identical views of the Indiana Toll Road. She had promised her mother to write every day until they got to California. (She had even telephoned, secretly, from Cape Cod.) Despite a certain sameness in the postcard views (which reflected a certain sameness in the toll road), Audrey remained impressed by the experience of these broad, flat, endless highways, and she knew that her mother would be, too.

The day's drive, on the whole, went better than they had expected. The sky, for one thing, was pure blue, and looked wider than usual in this totally flat land. The air was warm, the breezes fresh. The traffic flowed like brookwater. They passed occasional mounds of trees and mountains of clouds, but very little else.

Sunday mass had left Audrey feeling oddly uplifted. Through his fault, through his fault, through his most grievous fault, Timmy had confessed his Saturday night sins—whatever they may have been—before her and the Blessed Sacrament, and thereby anaesthetized the sharp ache of her vigil. She positively glowed with fresh happiness, as she looked up at the wide, bright Indiana sky, interrupted by nothing more than an occasional overpass or sign gantry flying over their heads.

Cruising well over the legal speed limit (but then so was everybody else) down the Main Street of the Midwest, Timmy felt pleased with himself, too.

He was pleased not because he had been to church, or confessed any sins. Church had been a drag; the words Audrey had spied him mouthing were nothing but an unconscious recollection of altar boy days at St. Patrick's, in Grass Valley.

No, Timmy was pleased because he had got off so easily. He had known women who would have punished him for such an escapade with five *days* of silence and moral superiority—during all of which time he would have been expected, wordlessly and without thanks, to take on extra tasks, to anticipate trivial requests—or to sit quietly in disgrace in some unobtrusive corner, unwanted as a person but available as help: and in general to grovel and cringe until the female in question felt disposed to forgive.

At the very best, he would have got one full twenty-four-hour day of insult, argument, and bitter recrimination. So many of his past women seemed to relish raking over their griefs, whining or yelling the same phrases hour after hour. First they would vent their wounded sense of self, noisily complaining; then immure themselves in untouchable silence; then, for no reason, break out with exactly the same abuse they had been hurling about a few hours before.

Eventually this treatment would grow intolerable. However wicked his

51

original lapse—and Timmy had not been a model mate—he could only stand so much. Once his limit was exceeded, he would begin defending his sin, belittling his guilt, returning insult for insult. Next he would dredge up real or imagined faults on the other side, to shore up his own eroded self-esteem. He might go on to attack one of the lady's more unpleasant but incorrigible traits, in malevolent, perfectly chosen words she would never forget.

Worst of all—if he were pushed hard enough—he might go on to commit the cardinal sin in any love affair, and say what he was actually thinking. Sometimes, unfortunately, he was pushed beyond that. Then he would begin hitting. How many days, weeks, months of his life had been eaten away by these mutually destructive sexual wars!

But no more. In choosing Audrey he had chosen well. One hour, last night, of tearful complaining; no sex (but he had anticipated that); one morning's silence; one hour in church.

And now they were sailing away under the Republican blue Indiana sky as if nothing had happened. Audrey was pressed up against him hip-to-hip, with one hand on his leg. With the other, she fiddled with the radio dial. Bumping into that noise she so disliked, that unmistakable nasal whine, she fixed the dial, turned up the volume, and smiled over for approval. God love her sweet ass!

From old Montana down to Alabam'
I've been before and I'll travel again,
You triflin' women just can't keep a good man down . . .

Part of the pleasure they were taking in each other that day was self-deceiving. But another part was genuine. They were enjoying one another's legs.

Audrey was fascinated by Timmy's bony knees, by the fur on his long-muscled thighs. She let her fingers tickle over the top of it, then run up under the sawn-off edge of his jeans.

He could not be quite so free with his hands, since he needed them to drive. But he could look at, from time to time, and think about, as often as he wanted, her smooth, unveined limbs, stretched out tanned and bare beside his. When the thought became too warm, he would steer for a while left-handed, grasp her knee firmly, then squeeze his way up the inside of a plump thigh with his fingers, moving span by span under her skirt to her crotch. At that point she would halt his progress, take his wayward hand in hers, and move it back to Square One. Then they would smile at each other, like children caught in some bit of nursery naughtiness, and start the game all over again.

They stopped for breakfast at the Booth Tarkington service area, eleven miles over the Ohio-Indiana line. This time Audrey ate as much as he did. Going to communion always left her ravenous. It was as if the presence of God within her, like a fetus in the womb, demanded extra nourishment. She managed to get down, very delicately, two waffles with melted butter and lingonberry syrup, two glasses of milk, bacon, toast, juice, and coffee. Lots of

52

coffee. Timmy had a hamburger steak and French fries *plus* fried eggs and sausage, and a strawberry shake.

They continued down the uneventful Toll Road. Around one-thirty, remembering the leftover fragments of last night's feast, they decided to make use of the picnic tables of the Henry F. Schricker service area. Timmy went inside to buy drinks—a root beer float for her, a beer for himself. Audrey picked out a table back under the trees, and set out what was left of the Toledo delicatessen treats. Less than four hours had passed since her hearty breakfast, but already she felt prepared to finish the lot, little French pickles and all.

They ate greedily and happily into the afternoon. Sitting on opposite sides of a picnic table, they took to popping bits of cheese and salami into one another's mouths, allowing their fingers to be licked, sucked, and savored along with the food.

After they had eaten their fill of food and fingers, Audrey sat on the grass with her back against a tree, and invited Timmy to lie down with his head in her lap. It was something girls like Janet Leigh and the St. Rose's cheerleaders were always doing with their boyfriends, in the movies or at Adams Beach. It looked, and (she now discovered) felt wonderfully possessive. *She* was the one awake, erect, in control; he, the male animal, was supine, flat out, his hair and cheeks caressed by her fingers, his own folded harmlessly over his belly.

Audrey enjoyed the weight of his head between her thighs, the look of his long body stretched out to rest. It was warm and sensual and yet . . . safe. She touched his bald spot, fingered his mustache. As he closed his eyes in infantile contentment, she plucked out a hair from his chest.

"Ouch!" He opened his eyes, flushed and flared. "Don't do that."

"Does it hurt?"

"Of course it hurts."

"Baby!"

"What are you, some kind of sadist?"

She plucked out another.

"Goddamn it, stop it." He lifted his head, started to raise himself on his elbows. But she bent over and kissed him, deep, tonguing past his teeth, at the same time she touched his chest gently. Then she bit his lip hard, and pulled out another hair. He collapsed in her lap, twitching in the unison of pleasure and pain. He lifted his hands to hold her face, but she pushed them away.

"There. That wasn't so bad, was it?"

"Goddamn. You do learn fast."

"Learn what?"

"You know what I mean."

"No, I don't."

"How to turn someone on."

"Was that what I was doing?"

"Don't give me that. You knew damn well what you were doing."

"I *didn't* realize it, honestly. Maybe it's something women just do natural-ly."

53

"It's possible." He settled back down. "My brother Micky had this theory that all girl babies are stolen out of their cribs when they're about six months old, and taught how to seduce men by female spirits in the woods."

Audrey was touching her tongue to his strange, useless nipples, running the edge of her front teeth gently around them. He grinned at her upside down, tried to break his hands free, but she kept him pinned down.

"What *is* with you females?"

"I don't know." She set him free, and thought about it, one hand on his cheek, one hand on his shoulder. They talked for a while, half-seriously, about female instincts, about how women learned about men, about women without men, about her family.

"Most of the men in my family let the women run things," she said. "That's the way it's always been. And everyone defers to my grandmother. She has to approve of boyfriends, jobs, where you live. Everything."

"She didn't approve of me, I bet."

"No. No, she didn't. The family was very upset about you." She tickled his chin with a blade of grass.

"What did they dislike about me most?"

"That's not a fair question."

"Tell me."

"You know."

"My age?"

"Yes."

" 'He's too old for you,' they said. 'He's old enough to be your father,' they said. Right? Isn't that what they said?"

"Yes."

"What do you think?"

"Oh, Timmy, you know what I think. I think you're perfect."

"I'm getting fat. And wrinkled. And bald."

"You'll never be fat. I like your wrinkles. I adore your bald spot." She bent over and lifted his head so she could kiss it.

"I'll be sixty when you're forty."

"Forty-two. John Wayne is sixty."

"You think of me like John Wayne?"

"Cary Grant is sixty. Jimmy Stewart is sixty. All really sexy men are forty at least: Paul Newman. Anthony Quinn, Rock Hudson, Harry Belafonte."

"What about women?"

"With women it's different. When a woman's forty, she's over the hill. I don't ever want to be forty."

"It's not all that bad."

She bent over and kissed him again. Her left hand was playing gently over the skin of his chest, down across his stomach. The sun cast longer shadows around their tree.

"What else didn't your family like about me?"

"They didn't think you were a good enough Catholic."

"I'm not."

54

"I know."

"Do you mind?"

"No," she lied.

"What else?"

"They didn't know enough about you. About your family, your past. You seemed like something off the moon to them, coming from so far away. My grandmother called you an ox, a bull, a cowboy. They thought you were wicked and rough, and they hated the idea of your taking me away from Dedham. Away from them."

"Funny now, to think how much they hated me."

"You hated them, too."

"But I *tried* to like them, didn't I? I was polite, I asked questions. I brought your mother presents. They didn't even try. They hated the sight of me from the start."

"That's not true. Not Cousin Elsie, anyway. She adored you. When you walked into that front parlor it was like something out of the movies. Don't let this go to your head, Timmy McCue, but you were probably the most gorgeous man any of them had ever seen. I honestly believe they all envied me. They couldn't admit it, of course, any of them. But they'd never seen anything like you. Not even in the films."

He reached up his hands again to pull her face down to his, and this time she let him. Audrey felt a little guilty about playing the game the way she knew he wanted it played. But then, you could never flatter a man too much. That much, at least, the fairies had taught her.

They kissed, stood up, and began preparing to leave. Timmy got his road map out of the car, and spread it out on the table to show her where they were going next.

With a felt-tip pen he lined out the route they had traveled so far, on the pale patchwork quilt of the American states.

To Audrey, the land they had still to cover looked distinctly uninviting. There was so much of it, for one thing. After driving for three days, they were less than a third of the way across the map. Her part of the country was all so tidy and small, busily laced with highways, speckled with towns. The splash of the Great Lakes was refreshing to look at, a happy counterweight to the dour pointing prow of New England. Even here in the boot of Indiana (where the "highest point in the state," she noticed on the map, was only 1,257 feet), it was agreeable to think of all that water.

But as Timmy began inking out the route for the rest of their trip, the state oblongs began to get larger. City cells and road veins occurred at wider-spaced intervals. There were fewer and fewer blue splashes.

Illinois was the next state they had to cross. It was pale green on the map. It looked reasonably narrow and densely settled. An appealing blue river-line ran down its left edge.

They would have to go through Iowa after that (it was pale orange), all the way on the Interstate. She didn't care for the look of Iowa much. It was a big square with uneven sides divided into smaller squares, by means of a sparse network of roads that ran either straight up and down or straight right and left. But it was edged by a wide river, too, which was nice. She liked the idea of rivers.

Nebraska—a sort of grayish-purple—came next. It was even wider. It would take them forever to get across—and there seemed to be almost nothing in it. Here, Timmy told her, they would cut off from the Interstate, in order to follow a river that looped down and then up again, almost the whole width of the gray-purple state. That sounded sensible.

After that, the United States of America got very unattractive. Between Nebraska and California, *all* the states seemed to be vast, waterless, and empty of dots. She found it hard to share Timmy's enthusiasm for this part, which was obviously the "West" he was always going on about. It reminded her of those huge sand-dotted spaces on world globes at school: Mongolia, the Sahara.

Drawing the red line up into the Grand Tetons, he grew excited, even eloquent, going on about geysers and canyons and Indian reservations. "You'll love the Tetons," he told her. "They're fantastic. Steeper than the Alps."

Oh, great, she thought. Lovely.

After the Grand Tetons, where he wanted to camp out, they would turn south to Salt Lake City. Timmy loved the brown mountains east of the Mormon city, and the great white desert to the west, but his descriptions of them turned her off completely. She asked about the lake itself, the one inviting blue patch in the gray-colored emptiness of Utah, but to her horror she learned that it was thicker with salt than the sea itself, thick enough to hold one afloat; impossible to drink, unpleasant to be in. He had unfolded for her a map of the dark side of the moon.

Nevada she didn't even want to hear about. As Timmy raved on, she reached under the table for his bare knee. For ending a conversation, she thought, this might work as well for her as turning on the radio did for him.

He stopped halfway into his description of Wendover—the first sign of life, apparently, after the Great Salt Desert—and broke into a grin. He blushed, and stared into eyes she had purposely made as loving as she knew how to do.

Audrey was beginning to enjoy testing her new powers. She could warm his blood, it turned out, speed his pulse, change the very shape of his body, just by letting him know, with her hand or her eyes, that she was willing. If not yet his equal in the field, at least she was becoming an interesting opponent, now that she had discovered this secret cache of weapons. Daring beyond thought, she was consciously trying to arouse him.

She succeeded. They got up off the bench, and ran, almost fell down a grassy slope behind the picnic area, to where a little jump-across creek trickled past.

On the other side of the creek, they found a stand of tall bushes bursting into yellow, trumpet-like blooms. In the center was a sheltered alcove. There,

56

on the sixth Sunday after Pentecost, Timmy McCue lay down with his wife, and made sweet and equal love.

He could be gentle, even considerate, when he wasn't feeling rushed. It wasn't his favorite way of making love, but a wise German girl had taught him this approach (along with several others), and there were times when it worked best.

"Tell me when it's good," he whispered. "Tell me when to stop."

"Not now. No. Now. Easier. There."

They lay still. Then he began probing again. "What should I do?" she asked. "Move back," he answered. "Move when I move."

He rolled them onto their sides, to ease the weight, and she began enjoying more and more her share of the game. After what seemed to her an eternity of searching, he hit the spot precisely, and she shivered with a new kind of delight: selfish, not loving. Such an unexpected treat, to have a thrill all her own.

"More," she ordered. "Again." He complied. "Right there." By digging her nails tightly first into his shoulders, then his back, finally into the cleft of his buttocks, she could pull him as close and as deep as she wanted. He kissed her ferociously, biting her lip till they both tasted blood. Now he was hurting her again, thrusting as hard as he had yesterday; but now she didn't mind. Today he was alongside her, not crushing her from above; today she could move with the thrusts, place them and space them so that the pleasure was at least equal to the pain. Today they were lying on God's earth and under his sky, not in a little room in a shabby motel. When he shuddered, epileptically, she clamped him tight as a vise with her arms and legs. At the same time, she tried to relax her own insides and enjoy all there was to enjoy.

They raced one another back to the picnic table, then on to the car. Timmy won both races, but Audrey didn't mind. She was happy enough staring at his backside as he ran.

Driving west into the sun, to the end of the Toll Road, to the Illinois line, they felt somewhat more married than they had before.

57

8

Civilization, of a sort, came back a short distance into Illinois. Grubby suburbs, traffic lights, factories: they had entered the Inland Empire of Chicago. Illinois Light and Power chimneys poured black smoke into the hot afternoon sky. Billboards flaunted chromo-seductions. Traffic slowed.

"What do you say we quit soon?"

"Fine with me. What time is it?"

He looked at his watch. "Only about four-fifteen. But this country is getting to me. I feel like calling it a day."

"I'm all for it." She looked out the window. "Where were you thinking of stopping?"

"There's a good-sized town coming up, Joliet. It's nothing special, but it's big. We ought to be able to find a decent place, especially if we stop this early. Better than" (don't say it) "last night." He said it.

"Somewhere with a bar, maybe, lawns, a nice pool. You feel like a swim?"

"Love it. Then could we go out and eat at a nice restaurant, after? Like you said?"

"Sure. Best place in town. Steak, lobster, you name it."

They reached Joliet a few minutes later. Every motel they passed, and there were plenty, still showed its "Vacancy" sign; but today they could play at being fussy. Nothing but the best.

They cruised for about half an hour, until they found what they were looking for—a little chunk of Las Vegas fallen into eastern Illinois. It was called the Joliet Marquise. They turned off under a cantilevered porte cochère big enough to shelter a Boeing 747.

"Oh, yes, sir," said the desk clerk, sliding him the registration form. "No problem, sir. MasterCharge will be fine."

Dapper in company blazer and tie, he seemed not to notice Timmy's scruffy attire. More like Vegas all the time. Timmy remembered overhearing a girl croupier once, near the entrance to the Desert Inn's supper club, talking to a group of tourists who thought they needed jackets and ties. "You pay the freight, baby, you can walk in here bare-ass."

The motel lobby, air conditioned down to the Arctic level that passes for luxury in the Midwest, was semipalatial itself—considering that no one ever used the room except to check in and check out. Its wood-paneled walls were hung with original oil paintings in white and gold frames. On a furry white carpet stood four gigantic lamps with tasseled shades. There was a glass coffee table big enough to play Ping Pong on, if you were very short. Atop it one copy each of *Town and Country*, *GQ*, *Fortune*, *Vogue*, and *The New Yorker* had been artfully fanned out, like cards in a losing poker hand, between two symmetrically set ashtrays the size of bricks. Audrey had to touch one of a six-foot-high fountain of flowers to be certain they weren't real: they certainly *looked* real. Ice tinkled in from the Monseigneur Piano Bar off the lobby. She peeked, but it was too dark to see inside.

"Did you have any special preference in rooms?" the clerk asked. Wherever did they dig him up in Joliet? Timmy wondered. Must be a fag.

"Like what?"

"We have standard doubles at thirty; our deluxes at thirty-five; and suites from forty-five up."

"Got a honeymoon suite?" Timmy asked.

Audrey shook her head, shaped the words silently with her lips: "Timmy, no!"

"Oh, yes, sir, yes" (he deciphered the signature upside down) "Mr. McCue. Mrs. McCue. In fact, we have two. The Madame du Barry Suite and the Madame du Pompadour. They're quite, quite splendid. And as it turns out they're both vacant, at the moment. Oh, I'm so glad you asked! I do think you'll be pleased. Would you like to look at them first, and then decide?"

"Either one'll do. You decide. What'ya say, Aud? Nothing but the best?"

"Oh, Timmy. I don't know. Do you think we should?"

" 'Course we should. We're who they're for."

"May I ask, sir, if you are indeed on your . . . ah . . . "

"You better believe it." He gave Audrey a proprietary squeeze. "Five days today. Boston to California." Sultan displaying prize harem addition to chief eunuch. Whatever a smirk was, he was smirking one.

"In that case, sir, madam," smiling, smiling, "a chilled bottle of champagne will be delivered to your suite, courtesy of the Joliet Marquise and our parent firm, Luxury-America, Incorporated. And if you do indeed have no preference yourselves, *I'd* suggest the Pompadour. It's my favorite. Très, très chic. It has a sunken marble tub and private garden in the bathroom, which the Du Barry doesn't. Otherwise they're identical, though of course in different decorative motifs. One is white and *moderne*, the other pale blue antique. There's a round waterbed, stocked wet bar, remote control color TV and stereo, dressing room, actual working fireplace, Arabian ceiling effect, et cetera, et cetera. Both are seventy-five dollars for the night, plus whatever you use from the bar."

"We'll take it." said the sultan. New harem girl gasped. "You want my MasterCharge now?"

"Only to copy and verify the account number, Mr. McCue. When you check out, we can add in anything you've used from your room bar, plus any other charges you might wish to make in our restaurant or lounge. All you need do is tell the waiter your room number."

"Sounds great. Now how do we find it?"

He handed Timmy a pair of keys. "You drive through the entry here, sir, to the end of the front parking lot. Then turn left, through the arches, and park your car in the space numbered two. There's a passageway adjacent. It leads to the pool terrace. On the gate between the terrace and your private patio, you'll see a large two."

"Fantastic."

"I'll send the waiter with your champagne straightaway." He was all in a flutter: he adored honeymoons. "And may I offer you both my warmest congratulations?"

"Thank you," said Audrey, who was beginning to feel deliciously married.

Timmy seized the clerk's slender, manicured fingers, pumped them up and down.

The Madame du Pompadour was everything the fag clerk said it was: the deluxest deluxe either one of them had ever stood inside. Through their own little garden off the poolside terrace, they walked into a mind-blowing Thirties Hollywood musical set.

Everything was white. In the sunken living room just ahead, two low, cushy white sofas were set on more of that furry carpet, in front of a genuine fireplace stacked with real logs.

They dropped their bags at the door. Like Hansel and Gretel when they first hit the gingerbread house, they ran around nibbling at everything. They flicked every switch, felt every surface, opened every door.

"They're real *logs*. I mean of *wood*."

"Hey, look here: Chivas Regal, Beefeater's, Canadian Club. The works."

"When you push this button here, the curtains open, Timmy. Oh, they close, too. Automatically."

"What's the other button for? The one next to it."

She pushed it. The muted music of a thousand strings wafted out of somewhere.

"Far fucking *out*!"

They ran to see the other rooms.

"Oh my God, you won't believe this bathtub!"

"Bathtub, hell! Come and try out this fucking *bed*."

She came into the octagonal bedroom (white furry floor, striped red and white walls) and lay down alongside him on a circular bed covered in fake ermine.

60

"Oh dear. Oh my God. It's rolling."

"No it's not. It just gives. It moves *with* you. You never slept on a waterbed before?"

"Which end is the top?"

"Any end you like. That's the fun of it."

She lay back and tried to yield to it, but it left her insecure and queasy. The absence of a proper head to the bed was even more disorienting than the squishy give of the mattress. You just put your pillow (there were five) wherever you wanted. Suddenly she saw someone staring at them from a skylight, and she screamed.

"Look! Up there!"

"That's us. Mirror on the ceiling."

"What on earth for?" The ceiling was draped with red and white striped cloth, like a sheikh's desert tent in some old movie. In the center a round mirror was hung exactly over the bed.

"You'll find out."

Inevitably, they made love: the room virtually ordered it. Midway in round two, a young black waiter let himself in with the courtesy champagne. Audrey freaked, but Timmy held her arm so she couldn't run off. He was taking an exhibitionist's delight in playing the nonchalant nude.

"Just bring it in here, fella." He leaned up on his elbows, flushed and on display, and looked up with his new proprietary smirk at the teenaged waiter, who was carrying a silver ice bucket on a tray. Audrey cowered under one corner of the fake-fur throw, and buried her face in several pillows.

"Shall I open it now? Sir?" The boy kept his eyes vacant of expression, and stared at the wall. Naked white assholes showing off in their seventy-five-buck room: big fucking deal.

"Yeah. Yeah, why not. Then you can take a buck out of my wallet. It's in those pants on the floor."

With that Timmy tossed off poor Audrey's cover and went back to work, pretending to be oblivious as the boy behind him uncorked, popped, and poured. What the hell. Give the kid his kicks.

They drank their champagne together in the sunken tub, which had an underwater Jacuzzi, as Melachrino strings purred in through a speaker over their heads. The tub—a small pool actually—was surrounded by a mini-jungle of indoor plants, so whatever water they splashed in their play ran into the white gravel underneath the plants.

Me Tarzan, you Jane, two bodies in a jungle pool, tropical plants, light streaming in the steam from a skylight overhead. Tarzan, Jane, and a bottle of non-vintage Taylor State.

As they drained the tub, and the champagne, Timmy persuaded Audrey to run with him out to the motel pool. Without stopping to dry off, they found their swimsuits, slipped them on, and raced outside. Timmy dove straight in; true to form, Audrey fussed. First she toe-dipped, and squealed, then timidly let herself down the ladder inch by chilly inch. Cavorting about like a randy porpoise, Timmy jeered at her from the water.

Once in and fully wet, she let herself go, too, and for half an hour they had the pool all to themselves.

Other guests, fat old cats sunning themselves on chaises longues, watched them like a stage show, as they chased one another, hugged and pinched under water, then curved up like the stars of an Esther Williams movie for a wet kiss in the middle of the pool. At one point Timmy got her bikini bottom down to her knees, but she pulled it back before anyone noticed.

They took dive after dive off the board. Audrey was clumsy, but gorgeous, Timmy the country club showoff, slipping, twisting, knifing into the water like a choreographed seal. When one paused for breath along the edge, the other would swim over and press limb to limb, lips to lips.

Exhausted and high, they ran back in and collapsed onto the bed, victims on a fur-covered altar. They got their breath back, dried off, and lay there making jokes about the clerk, the waiter, the senior citizens around the pool. They felt sorry for anyone who wasn't as beautiful and as much in love as they were.

Audrey lit a cigarette, but had to put it out almost at once when Timmy started tickling her. He made her laugh till she cried. Then he eased down her wet bikini again, in order to demonstrate what the ceiling mirror was for.

"Hey! It's nearly seven o'clock. We better eat if we're going to."

Audrey lay euphoric, drunk on more than champagne.

"Oh, yes, let's." She rolled over on her back. "I'm ravenous."

"Somewhere fantastic."

"What about the motel restaurant? We can put it on one bill, the man said."

"Oh, no. Better than that. Much better. This is too good to quit now." He bounded off the bed and started flipping through the phone book on the dresser.

"Hey. What do you say we drive up to Chicago? It's only about twenty miles. Get all dressed up and go to some ritzy place there? Floor show, dance band, the works?"

She was staring at herself in the ceiling mirror. She lifted her legs slowly, then moved them apart; cupped her two breasts in her hands and tried to make them seem larger. "I love it. I love it."

Timmy was tearing through the Yellow Pages. "Fuck, there's hundreds of restaurants in Chicago. How do I know what's the best?"

"Why not ring up that desk clerk and ask him?"

"Right. He oughta know." He dialed zero.

"McCue, number two. Hey, we want to eat at the best restaurant in Chicago. Dance floor, entertainment, the works. Price no object. What you recommend?

"Uh huh. . . . Wait till I get a pencil. How do you spell that?
  . . .

"Got it. Now, how do we get there?"

He copied the directions on a pad.

"You will? Great. Table for two, eight o'clock, best seats in the house. Name McCue, M-c-C-U-E. Oh, right. You know that. Hey. Do *they* take MasterCharge?"

. . .

"Great. Thanks a lot." He hung up, and turned around grinning like a cow eating cactus.

She was reclining on all five scrunched-up pillows, glowing with self-satisfaction, still holding her breasts in her hands. Timmy drank her all in, his own private page out of *Playboy*, ruddy-rosy and soft against the fake fur and almost-silk sheets.

"The Cafay Ducell. It's French. It's on top of the tallest building in Chicago, he says, and it goes around and around. He's gonna call up and reserve a table.

"Oh baby, baby, baby," he made a leap for her. "This is gonna be our night!"

They emptied everything out of their suitcases on top of the bed, in order to decide what to wear. Shyly, Timmy offered Audrey a present he had stashed away for later on. When she opened it, it turned out to be a full kit of Frederick's of Hollywood peekaboo underwear in nylon and lace, the like of which she had never in her wildest dreams imagined. Despite all he had taught her so far in his cram course, she was shocked that people could manufacture or buy such lewd things.

But she put them on, and Timmy kissed her through each of the unexpected holes. Over that, she put on her new going-away suit of watered silk, as white as the room around her, with a rose-colored blouse. Out of her precious jewelry box, full of family treasures, she took an amethyst pin, and her great-grandmother's gold locket and chain.

Timmy put on red bikini underpants, a mauve silk shirt with green stripes, and a lime green leisure suit—his one and only suit, in fact—with matching white shoes. Her Miss Dior. His Brut. Presents to each from the other. His wallet and keys; her purse.

They were beautiful, and they were ready, Cinderella and Prince Charming. Their eyes danced with extravagant expectations. Timmy swooped his little lady up in his arms, and carried her out to the car.

9

The Café du Ciel wasn't really a very good restaurant. Even the Mobil Guide, which was usually more impressed by expensive 102nd-floor restaurants that offered large tasseled menus printed in French on white parchment, gave it only two stars, and misspelled its name.

However, the usual run of clients didn't know it wasn't very good, and wouldn't have believed you if you told them. It offered, on clear nights, an unbroken view of over 50 miles in every direction. As the whole restaurant slowly revolved (one revolution per hour) on top of the 1,200-foot Richard J. Daley Tower, diners could examine at their leisure not only the bright lights of Chicago, but also the lesser lights of large portions of northern Illinois and Indiana, the southern end of Lake Michigan, and—so the waiters were instructed to tell them—an edge of southern Wisconsin as well.

The outer, up-against-the-glass ring of tables was assigned to Chicago business people and flacks who booked regularly there for out-of-town visitors, or to diners who overtipped the headwaiter when they arrived. Timmy and Audrey, who were not known to the headwaiter, and who had given him nothing, were shown to a table in the inner ring. These tables shared the flat, fabled view, however, since they were elevated on a round terrace up three carpeted steps, and the Café du Ciel's windows were huge.

The outer ring tables had imitation antique gold chairs. A long-stemmed yellow rose slipped into a Steuben tube bloomed in the center of each white linen cloth. The high windows were draped with brocaded French hangings and valences, also in gold. The draperies seemed to stay still as the windows revolved (in fact, it was the other way around), so that the bronze-anodized strips between the double panes were almost never properly centered. Planter tubs filled with real live orange trees divided one waiter's section from another's.

From the upper, inner ring, one could watch these waiters hurrying about, with or against the direction of rotation: lighting cigarettes, filleting sole, offering sample sips of wine in balloon glasses, maneuvering vegetables (lately frozen, now overcooked) with a large silver fork and spoon lightly held in one hand, tossing salads, grinding pepper out of gigantic wooden mills, flaming desserts, sliding out chairs, bowing, always bowing.

Timmy and Audrey's ring, rotating at the same speed about the same axis, had been done in an entirely different decor. It was as if the Daley Tower were an upended ocean liner, with its Tourist Class Dining Room inserted concentrically into its First Class. Audrey was seated on a black leatherette banquette, one of several by which the whole inner section was divided. Timmy was placed opposite her, on an ill-balanced tubular steel chair. Their tablecloth, napkins, and rose were all blood-red instead of white or yellow-gold. Their carpet was a hard-finish red and black, not deep-pile gold Louis XVI style. Outer ring waiters wore midnight-blue dinner jackets; inner ring, dried blood. Over Timmy's and Audrey's heads hung a lighting arrangement of sharp chromium icicles and black cubes, which continued all the way around, and moved as they did. Over the Versailles drapes, the outer ring tables were dimly lit by cream and crystal chandeliers (which didn't move).

The period style was obviously intended to connote greater taste, or cash, or prestige than the moderne, although all diners paid the same price for their meals. The psychology behind it was perfect. The favored patrons could look out at Chicago, Lake Michigan, Illinois, Indiana, and (perhaps) part of southern Wisconsin, and enjoy feeling superior because they had been seated next to the windows. The less-favored could also see Illinois, Indiana, et cetera, although not the immediately adjacent streets of Chicago, which weren't all that attractive anyway; and at the same time enjoy looking down on their more fortunate fellows at feed.

In the very hub of it all was a small circular dance floor, which revolved much more slowly than the rim. (In theory, there was a point in its geometrical center which didn't revolve at all.) A steel-railed shelf had been cut out of one side of the inner ring for a small dance band, avec chanteuse. The band was now on break, so discreet music was piped in to fill the gap, and allay the diners' dread of total silence. Over the dance floor disc hung, or bloomed, or exploded an intricate metal sculpture, half-Louis XVI, half-moderne, which reflected colored lights off mirrored baroque facets and thin shivering stalactites of steel.

Audrey was drinking her second Manhattan (she liked the cherries), Timmy his second double Scotch on the rocks. At first they just sat there, and held drink-free hand in drink-free hand across the red cloth. They stared, alternately, at the twinkling perspective of the Midwest—such a different Midwest from the afternoon's—and into each other's eyes.

In this light, in this place, in this gauzy, alcoholic glow, Audrey had matured into a woman worldly and infinitely desirable. Her short auburn hair was brushed gleaming and chic. Her eyes were outlined in black, and blue-shaded. Her gold locket and chain, and the rose-pink of her blouse, set off skin as soft and fine as a TV soap commercial model's. It was the kind of skin a forty-year-old woman would do anything to have again, and it enchanted this particular forty-year-old man.

The leathery skin and hard bone angles of his face, meanwhile, were smoothed by the light into a Hollywood gloss. Above silk collar points of mauve that fell loosely over lime green lapels, he looked (to his wife) movie-star sophisticated, a magazine cover. The dark red cave they were in, the gold and silver below, the 8,000 square miles of gradually disappearing lights out beyond the wheeling windows all seemed an emanation of their own champagne-and-roses high. They felt perched on a thin peak of perfect felicity; unstable, perhaps, impermanent, but all the more magic for that. At a florist's counter in the elevator concourse, Timmy had bought a gardenia corsage, and pinned it to the white silk of her jacket. Its heavy scent drugged them even deeper into bliss.

The dance band returned, and started playing: mirrored piano, sad saxophone, bass, muted horn, drums ever so suavely dusted by a brush. A middle-aged imitation Hildegarde stood by the mirrored piano, dressed all in green. Mermaid's green sheath, green gloves to her elbows, a yard of lime chiffon hanky, fake emeralds. She lowered her false lashes and began to purr:

When you press me to your heart
I'm in a world apart
A world where roses bloom . . .

Timmy invited his Lady of the Gardenias to dance. They downed the last of their second drinks and stepped out on the little circle of polished wood. There they pressed close together—her chin came about to his navel—smelling one another's scents, in love with the idea of being in love. Swaying romantically, they shuffled their toes back and forth about an inch at a time, as the room made its slow way around. Just as close, as warm as sex, Audrey thought: but so much nicer.

After "La Vie en Rose" came "The River Seine," first in English, then in French. "Darling, Je Vous Aime Beaucoup." "The Last Time I Saw Paris." "I Love Paris." "The Song from Moulin Rouge." This one brought tears to Audrey's eyes.

Whenever we kiss, I worry and wonder—
You're close to me, dear,
Oh but where is your heart?

Her Medley Parisienne done, the Café du Ciel's mock-Hildegarde bowed, fluttered, blew kisses, and waved chiffon to 360 degrees of polite applause, her green-sequined hips rippling under the lights. The little band continued quietly on its own, and Timmy led Audrey back to their table.

They were now facing Chicago's huge round sewage treatment pools on the

66

shores of Lake Michigan, instead of the highway from Joliet. A fresh Manhattan cocktail, a full Scotch on the rocks were waiting. Timmy liked having his wishes anticipated. There were also, now, a silver bowl of almonds, a basket of French bread, and two enormous menus, with silver satin covers and white tassels.

For the next twenty minutes they ate salted nuts and buttered French bread, sipped their third round of drinks, recalled moments of their day, and puzzled over the French of the menus. They looked, at first admiringly, then enviously, at last hungrily at the outer ring diners, who were handed dish after steaming silver dish by an endless parade of waiters. Up above, they had been left unattended with their nuts and bread. One sleek, seal-like party of six who had come in (they would swear to it) just *after* them was already pointing to gooey things on a regal trolley of desserts.

The glamour began to fade under the double strain of hunger and envy. Audrey had finished the nuts, Timmy the last of the buttered bread. He had cracked the last ice cube in his glass between his back teeth, chewed it up and swallowed it—a habit Audrey disliked almost as much as he disliked her habit of snuffing out cigarette after unfinished cigarette in an already full ashtray. They were no longer holding hands. Conversation was dead. He waved at several waiters. As each looked straight through him, he pretended, haha, to be holding his arm up in the air for some other obscure reason, so other people wouldn't know he was being ignored.

Finally losing his rosy glow, then his cool, he got up, walked down the stairs, and stopped a blue-jacketed waiter by grabbing hold of his arm.

"Excuse me."

"M'sieu? Ah, the gentlemen's lounge is now"—he checked the horizon for landmarks—"down those steps and to your right, in the elevator foyer."

"I don't want the john. I want a waiter. We been here since eight, it's after nine, and we're ready to start chewing on the flowers."

"Ah, *pardon*. And you are seated where, M'sieu?"

"Up there. See the lady in white?"

"I am so sorry, those are the tables of the waiters of the red jacket. If you will be so good as to ask one of them, I am sure he will fetch your waiter directly."

He smiled, slid away, bowing towards a table of large people with full plates.

By the time Timmy had returned to Tourist Class, their waiter was (of course) standing behind his chair, pad in hand.

"You are ready to order now, M'sieu-dame?"

He smiled his professional grimace. "I had come two times before. You were dancing." He had a way of dealing with people who complained to First Class.

"Oh. Sorry." Timmy felt like a fourth-grader bawled out for being tardy. "Yeah, we're ready. At least, I think we're ready." Their first survey of the menu had left them perplexed.

"You enjoy dancing, Madame?"

"Oh, yes, I love it. She sings so beautifully."

"I took the liberty of refreshing your drinks. Perhaps you would care for another?"

"Not if it's gonna take us another hour to eat. Let's get some food."

"Très bien, M'sieu. Something to start, then?"

"Like what? Soup?"

"Soup, yes, if you like. Or perhaps an hors d'oeuvre." He leaned forward and pointed to a long list of hors d'oeuvres. Timmy looked at the prices. He had eaten two-hour meals that cost less.

"Could you explain what these are?" cooed Audrey sweetly. "I'm afraid we're not terribly up on our French."

"But of course." He moved alongside her and ran his pencil down her menu, translating as he went. "We have fresh Belon oysters, oysters Rockefeller, snails cooked with garlic, caviar from Persia, poached egg on spinach, stuffed crêpes—ah, pancakes, you would say—, avocado and shrimp, grapefruit, smoked salmon, whole artichoke with hollandaise, duck and pheasant paté, salade Niçoise; and this one, this last, is raw steak, raw ground steak with egg and onion."

"You don't want any of that stuff, do you, hon?"

"Well. Yes. Yes, I would." If he could say yes to a seventy-five-dollar room, surely she could find out what caviar tasted like. "I'll have the caviar."

His eyes popped as he checked the price. O.K., little lady. Two can play that game.

"What's in this salad? The three-fifty one?"

"That is a classic Mediterranean dish, M'sieu. It is composed of tuna fish, black olives, French beans, green peppers, salami, onions, anchovies, sliced tomatoes, and hard-boiled eggs, all on a bed of lettuce with vinaigrette sauce."

"Okay. I'll have that."

"And then perhaps a soup?"

"What's good in soups?"

"They are all good, M'sieu. It depends on what you like. Perhaps something light, if you are planning several other dishes. The consommé Madrilene, for example . . ."

"I'll have that," said Audrey.

"A buck-fifty for one cup of consommé? You can get a can of Campbell's for two bits."

"This does not come from a can, M'sieu. A proper consommé takes many hours to prepare. The beef and vegetable stock is simmered and strained many times, egg shells and whisked egg whites are added to clarify the stock, the best sherry, fresh tomatoes and tomato purée, noodles, freshly chopped herbs . . ."

The Café du Ciel's consommé, in fact, *did* come from cans. It was delivered by truck in gallon tins. But this guy had worked better places. He knew how to keep the green leisure suit crowd in its place.

"Okay, okay, I don't want the recipe. You got a good potato soup? My mom used to make a great potato soup," he confided to Audrey.

68

"Would you care to try the Vichyssoise?"

"Is that soup?"

"Yes, M'sieu: a classic leek and potato soup."

"All right, I'll take that. What's next?"

Never in his life had he had to order so many things to get one meal.

"Well, if you wanted to follow the traditional pattern, a fish course would come next. Before the entrée." With the tip of his pencil he touched the word *Poissons*, written in red script on Timmy's menu.

"Ha. We thought that meant 'poisons'!"

Audrey kicked his ankle under the table.

"Ow. Not for me. I don't like fish. Whaddya say, Aud? Shall we skip it?" A busboy had brought more bread. Timmy started tearing again, buttering and stuffing.

"I don't know, sweetheart. I was thinking of maybe having a fish for my main course. They're all so . . . so reasonable." Sole was the only main course she could find under six dollars, and she was having guilty second thoughts about her caviar. It was also one of the few words on the menu she understood. The only trouble was there were six different kinds.

"Don't be silly. You can't celebrate with fish. Save it for Lent."

"Well, then, how about lobster?" Pop go good intentions. "Or is that just for Lent, too?" True child of New England, Audrey adored fleshy morsels of lobster dipped in melted butter. She held a happy memory of their lobster feed at Provincetown just four nights ago.

"Sure. Have a lobster."

The waiter indicated with his pencil. "Homard, Madame, is lobster. We have Americaine, Newburg, or Thermidor."

"I want the plain kind. The fresh boiled kind with melted butter. Like in New England."

"Ah, that, I am afraid, we do not have. In all three of these, the lobster meat is removed" (in fact, the chain that ran the Café bought frozen lobster meat in bulk) "and prepared with other ingredients. Tomatoes, wine, brandy, and onions for the Americaine. Butter, cream, egg, and sherry for the Newburg. Mustard, wine, shallots, herbs, and cheese for the Thermidor. In the Thermidor, the mixture is browned and served inside its own split lobster shell."

"I'll try that, then. The Thermidor."

Timmy had just found it on his menu: twelve dollars.

"And you, M'sieu?"

"What I'd really like is a steak. One big, juicy steak with a baked potato. What's that in Frog?"

"These are all steaks of different sorts, M'sieu." He pointed to each in turn, rattling them off in rapid French to intimidate this redheaded giant in his J.C. Penney suit.

Timmy—who was ready to stalk out and kill for meat by now—saw only one thing in his mind's eye: a thick, marbled slab of perfectly cooked, rare-red sirloin. "Which one is the best?"

"Mmmm. Probably the Rossini." It was also, after the châteaubriand, the most expensive.

"Okay, gimme that. With a baked potato."

"No baked potato, M'sieu. Lyonnaise, Parisienne, au gratin . . ."

"What do you *mean*, no baked potato? Christ, we got them at Howard Johnson's. How about mashed, then?"

"Pommes de terre duchesse."

"Whatever."

"And vegetables?"

"Sure. Whatcha got?"

Never had it taken him so long to order one blessed meal!

"Broccoli, endive, asparagus, cauliflower, eggplant, spinach . . ."

"Come *on*, bud, *American* vegetables. You got any peas?"

"Oui, M'sieu. Petits pois Parisienne. And Madame?"

"Peas will be fine with me, too. No potatoes. Maybe this instead." She had spied what looked like rice in veal sauce on the menu, but she didn't want to make a fool of herself by pronouncing it wrong. She underlined it for the waiter with her fingernail.

"Ris de veau, Madame? As *well* as the lobster?" Eyebrows doubting, daunting.

"Yes. Yes, that's what I want." She was *not* going to let this know-it-all Frenchman (Belgian, actually) sneer her out of having rice with her lobster. What's wrong with having rice with lobster, anyway? She gulped what was left of Manhattan III.

The waiter took a breath. "Salade?"

"I already ordered one, remember? The antipasto? You did get that down, didn't you?"

"Oui, M'sieu." Patience standing on a monument. "Would you like to order dessert now, or wait until after?"

"What for? To see if we're stuffed by then? Or broke?" Timmy laughed. The waiter waited till he was finished.

"No, M'sieu. But there are some *specialités* which must be ordered in advance. They are only cooked to order, and take a long time to prepare properly. The *soufflé, par exemple*."

"Oh, I want that!"

"They can only be ordered for two, Madame."

"Can we, sweetheart? Please?" She squeezed his hand. "I've always wanted to order a soufflé."

"Sure. Too sooflays."

"*One* soufflé, for two. We have *chocolat, orange, framboise, et Grand Marnier*."

"Chocolate, I think. Is that all right?"

"Fine with me."

"And to drink, M'sieu-dame: I shall send the sommelier with the wine list as soon as he is free."

"We've waited an hour and a half already. With our luck, the guy won't be free till next week. You pick. Okay?"

"Very good, M'sieu. Since Madame will be having the lobster, and Monsieur the tournédos, I would recommend one bottle of white wine and one bottle of red. You can share them as you choose during the first two courses."

"Great."

"Perhaps a nice white burgundy with the lobster; shall we say Corton Charlemagne sixty-two? And with the tournédos a fine red. We have several excellent Chambertins."

"You're the boss. Just get us *something*. And quick, hey."

Exhausted by the ordeal of ordering a six-course pseudo-French meal, Timmy collapsed back into his modular chair. He thrust both long legs out before him, and banged his head against the chromium frame. Reaching out for succor, he came up with an empty glass.

"Hey! Hey, fella!"

The waiter, just disappearing behind a curved and mirrored screen, reappeared. There was no escaping such people.

"Two more of these."

"Oh, no more for me, Timmy!"

"Listen. I drink, you drink. We're gonna need it to get through this meal."

It was important for Timmy to feel on top of things. Able to cope. In control. In control of the surf at San Clemente, of KT–22, of the hairiest new prototype reservisor some M.I.T. whiz kid could toss at him. But at the moment he was not one hundred percent sure he could handle a dinner for two at Chicago's Café du Ciel.

New glasses arrived, old glasses departed. He was just clear-headed enough at this point to know that he was asking for trouble, drinking like this. But he thought of it as an investment: fortitude on the cheap—well, not so cheap— for the ordeal ahead, paralyzing into a warm fuzz his mounting insecurity.

He was also beginning to wish Chicago would stop moving around: it was like drinking on a giant merry-go-round stuck in low gear.

The voices around him grew louder. Silver started crashing against china. He had to talk louder to himself in order to hear what he was saying.

"Shhh."

"Shush, yourself," he snapped. The man at the table next to theirs looked up startled from his sole Veronique. Were you talking to me? his face silently asked. He looked back, eyebrow arched, at his companion, shrugged his shoulders, and slid another forkful of sole into his mouth.

"Timmy," Audrey whispered. "You *are* talking a little loud."

"So's everybody else! I can hardly hear what I'm saying."

"I can hear you fine." She stubbed out another half-smoked filtertip into the saucer of melted ice and melting butter.

"Why don't we dance again while we're waiting?" Audrey was feeling a little woozy herself, but she wanted to do something to calm Timmy down, and stop him drinking. In her Irish-American girlhood, she had seen more than once how a man who drank too much could ruin a lovely party.

"Sure." Timmy pushed himself up from the chair, which tipped over backwards and hit a passing busboy, who then lost *his* balance and fell flat, dropping a tray of dirty dishes. An explosive clatter resounded through the restaurant. Hit in the back of the neck by the unexpected noise, Timmy fell forward onto their table, and tipped Audrey's cocktail onto her lap.

"Oh motherfucking, cocksucking *shit!*"

His words rang out with the clearness of a chime in the hush that had followed the crash.

"I'm sorry, baby. It's these fucking chairs. Here, let me help."

He dipped his napkin in the water jug. As waiters and busboys scurried to scrape up the debris—the whole restaurant seemed to be watching—he leaned over the table and tried to shove a dripping wet red napkin into Audrey's lap.

"No! No, don't!" She slid off the banquette, squeezed out between the tables. Their neighbors were staring fish-eyed, sole forks suspended in air.

"Please. I can fix it, dear, really. It's no trouble. Let me just get to the ladies' room. I don't want this skirt to stain."

"Gee, honey. Gee, I'm sorry."

"No, no, it doesn't matter."

"Christ, I'm sorry. Your best dress."

After she ran off, he pulled up his righted chair and collapsed into it again. This time he just sat there, numb, dumb, nursing his Scotch, determinedly chewing the rocks. Waiters fussed around him like busy ants, changing the tablecloth, mopping the seat, replacing glasses, picking up shards, scraping off crud.

I'm definitely out of control, he acknowledged. With another deep swig, he dismissed the sober, vigilant half of his brain altogether, and let the outlaws in. What the hell.

Their corner was tidy again when Audrey returned; but her small stain was now huge.

"It's all right," she said softly, sliding back to her seat. "I took off the skirt and rinsed the front in cold water. It'll all dry out evenly now. A lady in the powder room helped me."

He drained his Scotch, she sipped her fresh cocktail. Timmy flashed a crooked smile. It was still all right, then, she thought. Hoped. Wished.

"Caviar for Madame, salade Niçoise for Monsieur."

"Aha! The lost hunter. We thought you'd never get here."

The waiter poured a half-inch of the Corton Charlemagne into a glass with a very long stem. Timmy drank it, and started wolfing down tasty bits out of his salad. The waiter poured a half-inch of Chambertin into another glass, shaped like a goldfish bowl on a stand. He gulped that down, his nose poking into the glass, and went on eating.

"Fill 'em up, mate. What are we waiting for?"

"Both the red and the white now, M'sieu?"

"Yeah, live it up. The lady too, don't forget."

The waiter half-filled each of the four glasses, and left. They drank indiscriminately first from one, then the other, and gorged away on their respective treats. They didn't give you as much antipasto here as they did at Portale's in Grass Valley, but Timmy was devouring his with gusto. His wife was discovering for the first time the pricey pleasure of those tiny black pellets, bursting with salty fishness. She spread them on dry circles of toast, sprinkled with chopped egg and dotted with lemon drips. Bravely, she bit. She chewed. She swallowed. Waited. Thought.

"Oh, Timmy, I *adore* it! Here, you try one." She spread one knife's tip of caviar on a round. He closed his eyes, leaned forward, and held out his tongue. She slipped the laden wafer into his mouth.

" 'Sgreat," he mumbled, chewing. "Far out. You have some of mine."

"Let me just pick a little from this side." Trying to dislodge a chunk of tuna, she set off a miniature landslide. Miscellaneous savories rolled onto the fresh cloth. They both giggled. Timmy topped up all four glasses; this time to the rim.

"Here's to us."

"To us." Spilling just a bit, they clinked, drank, then kissed the gold-ringed knuckles on each other's left hands.

"Happy anniversary, sweetheart."

"Happy anniversary."

"Five days already."

"And four nights."

They bowed till their foreheads bumped, and broke into giggles again. The waiter's quiet cough announced soup.

By the end of that course, Audrey was beginning to be apprehensive. Timmy didn't like his cold soup, and was drinking too much wine. For safety's sake, she vowed not to touch any more of hers, lovely as it was. The chill golden yellow in the tall glass was one of the most beautiful things she had ever tasted; the smell of the dark red was like the deepest perfume. From now on, though, she would just sniff and pretend to be drinking. She had once seen her fat Uncle Arthur being hauled out from a funeral parlor like a corpse by four other men, when he got too drunk to walk at Aunt Maudie's wake.

"What's this?"

"The ris de veau, Madame. I presumed you wanted it before the Thermidor." This time *he* refilled Timmy's glass, finishing the red, now, as well as the white.

She stared at the gluey, gray mess that he had just laid in front of her. Whatever it was, it wasn't rice.

She felt trapped in silent combat. The waiter knew she didn't know what it was. She knew he knew she didn't know. But if she could just face it down, ladylike, and pretend, damn his eyes, that she *always* had this junk before her lobster, she might still end up winning this round.

"Of course. Thank you very much."

He bowed and departed, smiling more genuinely than usual.

"What's *that* stuff?"

"Shhh. I don't know. I thought I was ordering rice."

"Well hell's bells, let's call him back and tell him. That's no rice. Looks like the Air Force's Friday night shit stew."

"Please keep your voice down. I *know* it's not rice. But it's my fault. I didn't ask what it was when I ordered it. Now I don't want him to know I don't know. It's called Rida Vo or something, but it was spelled 'r-i-s.' I could have sworn that meant rice, and I thought Da Vo meant veal sauce. There's some rice at the bottom, it looks like. Maybe these things on top are veal." A pause: moral combat in progress. "I've got to try it anyway."

Very gingerly, this fussiest of female eaters scraped off the sauce from one Thing and detached a cubic centimeter of it with her knife and fork, like a pathologist dissecting one diseased slice of surgically removed organ for microscopic examination. She pronged it on a tine of her fork, looked at it, smelled it, finally dared to touch it to her tongue. Timmy stared, transfixed: her lips pursed over it, her jaws began moving.

"Well?" he asked. "Well?"

"I don't know." She kept chewing, slowly. "I still don't know what it is. It's like nothing I ever tasted."

"Want me to try some?"

"Please." She cut a sort of Red Sea path midway down her plate, and shoved slightly more than half of the gray mess towards Timmy.

"Smells weird."

"I know. It does, doesn't it? Do you suppose it's bad?"

"How could *we* tell? Tastes weird, too."

"Well, help me to finish some of it, anyway, so the waiter won't think I'm a total idiot. If we both eat a little, I can sort of push what's left into a corner, to make it look half-gone."

They dutifully set to, scraping off the stinking sauce and cutting the pale gray slabs into tiny bits, which they then tried to swallow straight down, without thinking of or feeling the slimy, lumpy texture. It was like slices of rubbery cooked cauliflower, somehow made gelatinous and soft. Like congealed gobs of phlegm. Like nothing else on earth.

Finally, she put down her fork and took a large swallow out of the goldfish bowl of red. She had to break her vow to get rid of that taste, of the memory of that experience. Her stomach was on the brink of a turn. "I give up."

"Me too." He gulped at his red wine too, drained it, stared at Audrey and the restaurant behind her all deformed into a blur through the bottom of his goblet. It had been a sobering experience.

"Finished, Madame?"

"Oh, yes. Thank you."

He looked critically at the uneaten mess. "It was . . . not satisfactory?"

"Um. Well. I, uh, I don't think it was done the way I'm used to having it. Do you cook your Rida Vo in some special way?"

"No. No, I don't think so. Perhaps you are more familiar with the Milanese, in brown sauce. But this is, I believe, the classique. The sauce is your basic cream with herbs and white wine added to the reduced liquid, which is left after braising the pressed and sliced meat in a vegetable-wine base. Of course, we first blanch and peel the membrane from the sweetbreads, and remove the gristle."

"From the what?"

"The sweetbreads."

"*Sweet* bread?" Timmy asked, disbelieving. He must be pulling their legs. "Sweet *bread*?"

"Oui, M'sieu." The waiter was relishing his big scene. "Ris de veau. The two large lumps of the thymus gland extracted from the throat of a young calf." He touched his neck. "A great delicacy, as of course Madame is aware."

"Excuse me." The room's persistent revolution had displaced the exit to the toilets. Audrey had to run the gamut of waiters and tables twice before she found it.

Nothing as simple as calf's glands could affect the numbed state of Timmy's stomach, but he suffered in sympathy with Audrey, who was throwing up in the ladies'. He poured a drink; nothing came out. Other bottle. Same thing. He lifted the two empties high in the air and kept clinking them together until the waiter came running back.

"One more of each."

Both new bottles were half-empty by the time Audrey returned. Timmy was sloshing away at a bowlful of purple burgundy, so dark it was almost black. Since the staff seemed to have deserted them again, he proposed another turn on the dance floor; weak as she was, she agreed.

Careful not to tip over his chair this time, he hauled himself onto the disc with the help of the steel rail. It was spinning much faster than before, like that platter at the Fun House where you had to sit dead in the center to avoid being spun off altogether.

This time, Hildegarde offered her other medley, made up of old Cole Porter show tunes. Timmy tried to twist and stomp instead of slow-dance, dead against the beat, which only led him to bump into everyone else on the floor.

Audrey kept her ground, gently moving with the music, maintaining as best she could the fiction of a happy bride in a silvery celebration. On the fringes of the circle, she could see clinging couples swaying and embracing. Beyond, at dimly lit tables, men and women looked into one another's eyes, tasting delicate foods off silver forks, sipping gold and ruby wines. Further beyond, the fairy lights, America.

Before her, this ludicrous ape. His shirt half-unbuttoned and untucked, his hair disheveled, wet with sweat, he was assing about and having the time of his drunken life. Her husband. "Mr. and Mrs. McCue." He smiled at her. She smiled at him; inside him, through him, beyond him.

Starlight, she thought miserably, back at the table: roses, gardenias, caviar and champagne. A supper club high in the sky, a French chanteuse in green sequins cooing "La Vie en Rose" just for her. Beautiful rich women in real jewels, silver-haired men who wore cuff links. She let flow a few tears; he was bellowing along with the singer, and too blind now to notice.

Maybe the steak would sober him up. She wasn't sure her stomach could even look at a lobster.

But there it was, crumbled over with gold and brown, steaming in its scarlet shell. It *did* look beautiful. Unfortunately, the oaf sitting opposite chose this moment to blow his cork again.

"A *steak*, I said, goddamn it. What's *this* dinky thing? And what's all this crap on top of it?"

This time, the waiter said nothing. Instead, he turned ever so slightly to the side. First a second waiter, then the headwaiter came over and stood beside him. Audrey prayed he would behave. They looked like security police, like guards ready to take him away. She toyed with her beautiful lobster, sipped tiny sips of her wine, trying magically to will Timmy into silence. She leaned over, touched his cheek, buttoned the buttons of his shirt.

"It's all right, sweetheart. It's like a filet, I think. Sometimes the best pieces are the smallest."

"But what's this shit on top of it? I didn't order any of that glop." She glanced up in fear at the ice-faced attendants.

"Never mind, darling. I'll take it off." With her knife, she scraped off what looked like liverwurst and bits of black olive, lifted the meat off a piece of gray-green stuff, and unwrapped from around it a ribbon of fat. All these she dumped in her saucer.

"There, dearest. Do you think you can eat it now? I'm sure it's lovely. I'll cut it up if you like."

He shook his head, sullen. He hated this Mommy-do treatment.

"And see the nice mashed potatoes? And peas? Just like you asked."

The pacifying cream only maddened him more. The patronizing edge in her voice was about to puncture his calm. But he didn't know what to do. If he let go now, he was going to break something, hurt someone. It had happened before.

To the waiter, she asked, "Do you have some Calso water or something? Something fizzy? I think we've had enough wine."

Who's had enough wine? He glowered at her, grabbed onto his bottle. Who do you think you are, my fucking *mother*?

One waiter signaled the other, who signaled a third. A bottle of mineral water appeared. A glass was poured.

"Here, Timmy. Try some of this."

He drank it, made a face, grabbed for his wine glass instead.

"What the fuck was *that*?" he shouted.

The headwaiter moved forward, slim and erect, foreboding.

"I am very much afraid, Sir, that you are disturbing our other guests. There have been complaints. If you cannot be more quiet and orderly, I regret I shall have to ask you to leave."

"*Leave*? Because you guys can't bring me what I ask for, you're telling *me* to leave? Who the fuck are *you* to tell me to leave?" He was half out of his chair.

Audrey had been waiting in fear for this moment for almost an hour. She could hardly bear to watch. There were five waiters, now, blocking the view of their table from the rest of the Café.

"Paul, the gentleman's check."

It appeared, on a silver tray. Timmy pushed it off the table. Crash.

"I haven't finished my steak, goddamn it! If that's what you call this horsemeat. And the lady hasn't finished her lobster."

"Timmy. Timmy, I'd rather not. Please. Please let's go. Now." She wiped her eyes on her napkin, pushed the platter aside. "Let's pay them and go." Audrey reached over for his hand, but he pulled it back.

"What about our dessert?"

"No. No *please*. Let's go now."

Glassy-eyed, a disaster, he tried to look at her, but she was out of focus. Then he turned and looked over his shoulder: the Café du Ciel goon squad was still there. Audrey was terrified he was going to try to fight. Under equal impulses of terror and disgust, she reached under the table and began to rub his leg.

"Please, my darling. Let's go back. Back to the motel. To our lovely suite."

The glaze over his eyes clarified just a bit, the twisted frown began to ease. Thanks be to God. She squeezed harder on his knee, moved her hand up his thigh. He reached for the check, which a waiter had replaced. He turned it over, and read it.

"You gotta be kidding."

"M'sieu?"

"This is insane."

"Is there something unclear?"

"This isn't a robbery, it's a joke."

Audrey had been trying to add up in her mind the cost of what they had ordered, but she kept losing count. She had no idea how much the drinks were, for one thing, or the wine; or even, now, how much they had drunk. The precious lobster, growing cold in its shining shell, had been twelve dollars all by itself. Timmy's tournédos had been ten. That's twenty-two. Maybe two, three times that . . . ?

"Look, baby." He handed her the bill. "Look at that and tell me what's a rip-off."

Crossed sevens. Capped ones that looked like sevens. A long line of French scrawl, impossible to read. She scanned to the bottom: $147.40.

"Does that include the soufflé?" she asked, in a thin voice she tried to keep firm. "We never had it, you know."

"Oui, Madame. It is nearly finished cooking, it must be served at the precise moment. It could not be sold to anyone else."

"That doesn't seem fair to me."

Le shrug Gaulois.

"And these, I suppose." She nodded at their pièces de résistance, desolate, uneaten.

"Oui, Madame."

She took a deep breath and tried to go over the addition, but it was no use. She couldn't even decipher the numbers, let alone keep juggling in air which ones to carry from one column to the next.

"What's this for?"

"Le couvert, Madame. The cover charge."

Timmy had given up entirely. He let her take charge, and slumped down again in his chair. His chin was now near the level of the tablecloth. The skin of his face had drooped and turned yellow. He looked older than she had ever seen him before.

"I think it's right, darling." She pushed the tray back. "Things are always more expensive than you expect in a place like this."

He reached inside the pocket of his jacket, which hung over the back of his chair, and took out a wallet. On top of the unbelievable bill, he laid a plastic card.

No one touched it. He looked up at the waiter.

"I'm very sorry, M'sieu. We do not accept MasterCharge."

Audrey froze.

"What do you *mean*, you don't accept MasterCharge?" He sat up straight, flared bright red. "How am I supposed to pay for all this, then?" Everyone around was attending closely.

The waiter shrugged again, and signaled for the maître d'.

"We do accept Diners' Club, Sir. And American Express."

"I don't *have* Diners' Club or American Express!"

Staff consultation.

"Do you have a Chicago bank?" asked the Number One Man.

"Of course I don't have a Chicago bank. Why would I have a Chicago bank?"

Audrey felt undressed in public, stared at by the whole restaurant. He had been revealed as a deadbeat, a vulgar interloper. What did they *do* to people who couldn't pay, at places like this? Arrest them? Seize their cars?

"Listen" said Timmy, who was sweating now himself. "This guy in Joliet called here and reserved for us, and I specifically asked him if you took MasterCharge. He said you said yes."

"A man in Joliet?"

"Yeah. At the motel."

"At the motel."

"Right." He fished in his pockets for the key. "The Joliet Marquise."

"Ah, the Marquise. The Café du Ciel is under the same management as the Joliet Marquise, Luxury-America, Incorporated. Perhaps if you would come into the office with me, Sir, I could telephone the Marquise to verify that you are indeed a guest. Then an arrangement might be made to add the cost of this meal to your room bill there. Your luggage is still at the Marquise, I presume?"

It was like air in the lungs, after being trapped under water. Timmy's knees gave when he first tried to stand, but he managed to stiffen them out. He tucked in his shirt, put on his jacket, and stumbled away behind the maître d', holding tight to their waiter's arm. All three disappeared around the curved and mirrored screen.

Left alone, Audrey opened her little white wedding purse and tried to repair her face. Then she stared out the windows at the lights. There must be millions. Well, thousands.

Half an hour later, down in the exit level of the Daley's underground garage, she was doing her best to maintain the tattered fiction of their elegant evening out. Perhaps by just standing there, placid and ladylike, she could hold together all the evening's broken pieces and keep them from falling into a heap.

This meant, for one thing, ignoring the spreading stain in her lap, which would never come out. It meant, which was harder, pretending that Timmy was now making a quite reasonable protest to the parking attendant over his delay in retrieving their car, and not shouting like an obnoxious noisy boor; that he was dipping and slipping and leaning onto greasy poles out of exuberant high spirits, and not because he was out-of-his-mind drunk.

She fingered her already browning gardenia corsage. How sweet he had looked when he bought it for her and pinned it on her jacket, just a few hours before. Without knowing what she was doing, she pulled off the petals, one at a time.

10

"Timmy!"

He swerved over the white line, then oversteered back, scraping a City of Chicago street-washing machine.

"I wish you'd be more careful."

"Listen. I been driving cars since before you were born."

"I'm sorry, I don't mean to nag. But nothing here looks familiar. Are you sure this is the way we came?"

Now he was lost as well as drunk, she decided. And beginning to get belligerent.

"Don't you worry your pretty little head. I'll get us home." He smiled an idiot grin, swerving right as he turned his head.

Just a few blocks out of the Loop, they descended into rock-bottom slumland. Now they were driving through blackened brick shells, in which people apparently still lived.

It was late, and wet, and the streets were dimly lit. But an unhealthy number of black people lingered on the streets.

After leaving the Daley Tower garage, Timmy had continued in a straight line down Michigan Avenue. It was the easiest thing to do. But in almost no time the grand hotel and office facades across from the park thinned into cheap urban motels, car rental agencies, parking lots, night cafés. Now, into No Man's Land. It was as if they had crossed over some invisible frontier.

The hulks rose on either side; 14th Street, 22nd, 30th. Audrey felt herself being sucked deeper and deeper into the blackness. Night-walking Negroes were beginning to stare.

"Timmy, *please*: I'm sure this isn't the way to the expressway."

"This is south, goddamn it. I'm driving south. Joliet is south of Chicago."

She took a map out of the glove compartment, unfolded it, switched on the

80

overhead light, and tried to find Chicago. But it made no sense at all. Hadn't they doubled *back* from Joliet to get here? And wouldn't that mean it was west they should be going, rather than south?

Unfortunately, reading maps in a moving car made her sick. When Timmy first learned that, on their way down to the Cape, he had cursed at her weakness. Since then he had taken to reading maps himself, propping them against the steering wheel, navigating as he drove. She cringed at her own incompetence. There was nothing she could say.

36th. 40th. Try once more, very gently.

"Timmy, I'm sure you're right. I'm sure if we keep going down this street, we'll eventually get back to the motel. But this place scares me. Can't we *please* go back and try to find the way we came?"

Her voice rose to an involuntary shriek, and she started sobbing, then tried to stop sobbing and choked, distracted more by frustration than by fear. She covered her face with her hands, and turned against the seat.

He braked to a halt, exasperated by her noises and (worse) by a nagging fear beneath his alchoholic fog that she might be right. He was beginning to suspect he had driven *over* their expressway about two miles back up the road. But he certainly couldn't admit it. And he wasn't going to move until she stopped that awful noise. If he kept on going, he'd eventually hit the Dan Ryan, in any case. Then he could get back to Joliet via 80. Unfortunately, his directional sense was awash in booze.

From the dark of a half-demolished building, shadowy youths began to emerge. Others, who had been sitting on the steps of a building next door, stood up at the same time. A third group, leaning against a store front, pushed themselves erect, as they began to take notice of the red car parked in the middle of the intersection, a celebrated battleground just a few months ago. Lean, skull-like black faces were converging on them from three sides.

The car's jarring leap forward threw Audrey off the seat and onto the floor. A missile hit her side door with a thump. Tires in pain, Timmy turned the car in a giant arc that spread across all lanes, rammed on ahead, then squealed again back up State, torn rubber crying into the jungle of night.

Audrey lifted herself up from the floor and tried to light a shaking cigarette. State Street, here, was as ugly as Michigan. Even if they never made it back to Joliet, she would feel better in the safe haven of downtown.

In a few minutes, they were out of the horrors, driving through something closer to civilization.

"We drove past a big Sears store downtown," she offered. "It was on the same street we came into town on from the expressway. We drove around a giant interchange, I remember, then through a big building and over a bridge, and came to this big Sears store on the corner, all lit up. Right afterwards we came to that park by the water, where we turned left. So if we come to a big Sears store *this* time, we should turn left to get back, shouldn't we?

"Shouldn't we?"

"Timmy?"

He was not receiving advice.

"There!" Half a block away, she saw the green and white neon letters. "Timmy, *here*. Here's the road!"

They reached it, passed it. In a brightly lit window, two white manikins in red swimsuits tossed a beach ball that never moved.

He ignored her cries. Steadily he continued up State, past the parkway intersection, past Sears, Goldblatt's, Lytton's, Ward's, the Palmer House; past Carson, Wieboldt's, Marshall Field.

"Will you please just shut the fuck up? Will you please? I got us here, and I'll get us back. The more you keep throwing me off, the longer it's gonna take."

She had seen it, their one road of escape; now it was gone. She stared at the pointillist outlines of one mammoth old movie palace, then another, the baroque curves of their marquees carved in red neon and marked out with hundreds of light bulbs. "The Green Berets" was at the Chicago. "The Odd Couple" was at the State-Lake.

"Shit." Timmy braked to another jolting halt. "We're back at the river." Their road was turning into a bridge.

"This can't be right. The river's over there!" He turned sharply left, onto the lower deck of a highway full of honking taxis cutting across lanes and great farting one A.M. trucks.

What *he* dimly remembered was a mammoth city parking garage, just as she had remembered a Sears. (The two buildings were in fact on opposite sides of the same intersection. The Sears store had been out her window, the parking garage out his.) He kept looking for his parking garage, unconsciously swerving the car right or left each time he thought he saw one.

There. No. *There.* No, not yet.

That's it! That's the one. Washington Street.

"It was Washington. I remember. I'm sure it was Washington."

She said nothing. He had told her to shut up. She would not say one word more.

One way the wrong way. You drive *in* on Washington, out on the one before. At the next intersection, he cut right, crossed the river, and started heading west.

Past a train station, he drove into a neighborhood of brick warehouses. Amazing how suddenly this city kept flattening out into nowhere. Street corner followed street corner, with no sign of an expressway approach. The warehouses moldered into more rows of three-story slums, cages for the blacks of Chicago. Again the menacing night-wanderers, leaning up against the hulks.

What *was* it with Chicago? Timmy wondered. It looked like war-damaged German cities he had seen twenty years ago. Boy, do they keep a lot hidden from the tourists.

Madison was giving him the creeps. He turned right, then left again down Warren. Maybe it was on Warren.

Dead-straight the street ran, between the teeming hives. He felt a million rats staring at him in the night. His nerves and muscles began to tighten. He pushed on in sullen frustration.

The city was so walled in by these ghettoes that escaping became a monstrous game. If you chose the unmarked exit, the one and only way out, you were home free. Choose any one of a thousand others, and you drive on forever.

Gasoline sprays down the valve holes, wheels spin faster down the desolate street. A black Buick noses into the intersection. The red machine curves to avoid it, but not far enough. Silver nose rams into rear door, hits, wounds, buckles it. Sheets of heavy steel collide in sudden pain.

In the echoing lamplight of a hot Chicago night, two cars lock in violent copulation. Inside them are a young black man, unhurt but mad as hell; a young white woman, bruised, lucid, frightened for her life; and a white middle-aged man, slumped unconscious over his steering wheel, where he collapsed back from a shattered windshield. His face is a mess of blood.

11

The garage was a greasy shed made of concrete blocks, lit by a few hanging bulbs under metal reflectors. As soon as the mechanic unlocked the door and let her in, Audrey saw their red Cougar hanging helpless in the air. Pieces of its insides and all of its face still lay scattered about the floor.

"Had to send Dennis to Cicero for some parts," he said. "Be another couple hours. I done the new windshield and brakes. Problem's mostly your radiator, now. It's shot to hell. Fan, too, hoses, headlight, some other stuff."

"Will it run?"

"Oh sure, it'll run. Long as you don't mind driving a noisy car with a mashed-in grille. And keep your eye on the oil and water."

"Is that dangerous?"

"There may still be some leaks. I'm not too sure about the head. All I'm doing is a patch-up, ma'am. But it'll get you back on the road."

"Tonight?"

"Tonight's most over. Morning. I ends my shift at eight."

"Can we wait here?"

"Sure." He went over to a dismantled car seat that lay propped against the wall, and started clearing off engine parts. "You and your old man can sit here. There's a radio if you want music." Stuffing poked out of splits in the upholstery, which was stained black from engine grease. He got some newspapers and lay them on top of the seat.

For two and a half hours, Audrey fidgeted, exploring every inch of the garage. Prickly nerves were pushing her down the far side of fatigue. She smoked a pack of cigarettes. Each time she asked the mechanic a question, he grunted and went on with his incomprehensible work.

Timmy, meanwhile, was sleeping off his booze and his shots, oblivious to his pains. He lay sideways on the dismantled car seat, with his knees bent and his feet on the floor. When the mechanic saw that he was taking up all the room, he dug a three-legged wooden chair out of his office, and propped it on a carton of oil cans for Audrey to sit on. But she couldn't sit. Staticky rhythm and blues rasped out of the radio, which the mechanic had turned on for her. She dared not turn it off.

At five-thirty A.M., Dennis, a tall skinny boy who looked about fifteen, come back from Cicero with a new radiator core and some hoses, plus a headlight, a fan, and other bits.

Dawn brought light through a dirty back window. It also brought stiffness, sadness, the taste of death in the mouth. Audrey was freezing, but strangely untired.

The coming of light burned through the last of Timmy's fog. He opened his eyes, tried to sit up, cried out in unexpected pain.

"Where the hell are we? My *God*, I hurt!"

"We're in a garage. We were in an accident, remember? They're fixing the car now. You were knocked unconscious in the crash. Do you remember the hospital?"

"Yeah. Some damn nigger kid in a black sedan."

"Howard. He's the one you hit."

"*I* hit? He hit me, the little prick."

"Dearest, he's the one who got our car here. He talked his friend into working on it tonight. He drove you to the hospital, then brought us back here. He was really very nice. I don't know what we would have done without him. Does it hurt terribly?"

"My face feels pulled apart. And it itches like crazy. My arm; hey, what . . . ?"

"You've got some stitches in your face. And you sprained your wrist. They had to tape up your wrist and your ribs."

"Jesus, how can I drive? I can't drive like this!" He looked at his fingers, splinted and taped together. "How could I shift?"

"I . . . I think I can drive. I just have to get us back to the motel. That's not very far. About thirty miles, the man said. Then we can go to bed. It's been a terrible night."

"I'm sorry, Audrey."

"I know."

She kissed his cheek between the bandages.

Howard's friend opened the sliding front door. The morning light lifted some of the gloom. In daylight, everything looked cleaner. Audrey was pleased to think that the Negroes in Chicago's West Side got a chance to see daylight sometimes, to move out from under cars. They could even wash, and take off their dirty overalls. Young Dennis was doing that now, as the older man lowered their car down from its long stay on top of a pole.

"That's it," he said.

Timmy rose, stiff with his pains, sick with his hangover, and went over to talk to the man about the car. Audrey stood back, trying to recall what she had once known about clutches and gears and changing lanes, and arm signals, and cars coming up behind you. She stared at the disfigured face of the Cougar in the cold light of day, and knew she wouldn't be able to do it.

While Timmy was settling up the bill, she walked over to the wash basin. Young Dennis was scooping gritted soap out of a tin and rubbing it on his hands. He stopped and looked at her as she approached.

"I wonder if I could ask you a favor."

"What was all that about?" Timmy came over from talking with the mechanic.

She knew this was going to make him mad. But there was nothing else she could do.

"This is a nasty thing to bring up, Timmy, after everything that's happened these past eight hours. But this whole mess started because you couldn't find the way back to the expressway. I was just asking Dennis . . . "

"I wasn't *looking* for the goddamn expressway. I told you that last night! I was driving down South Michigan Avenue, which would eventually have got us to Joliet. The only reason I turned back was that you started bawling. Ouch!"

"Now, that's not true." Stay calm. "Howard showed me on a map. We *did* miss the turnoff that would have got us back home. It was right where I said it was, at that Sears store; the Congress Avenue Parkway. If we'd stayed on South Michigan like you were doing, we'd have ended up back in Indiana."

"Goddamn it, woman, I'm not as much of an idiot as you seem to think. We *could* have gone back on the Stevenson, right. But if we'd stayed on South Michigan a few more miles, we'd have been able to join up with the west leg of the Dan Ryan, which hits Interstate 80 about fifteen miles east of Joliet. Do you think I drive across the country blindfolded? I checked out both routes before we ever left the motel. I *had* to. I sure as hell couldn't depend on you to read a map."

Even when he was wrong, he could act so obnoxiously right. He had got evil-drunk; ruined their dinner; wasted an hour and a half driving through the worst parts of Chicago; crashed up their car—his car; and *still* he could manage things so that she was at fault; so that she should be apologizing to him! How could anyone stand up to such an arrogant bully? He *must* know he's wrong this time.

"Timmy, I don't want to argue. Just listen to me, for one second. I don't want to drive, but I have to. I know that. That's okay. But I haven't driven a car for over three years. I haven't driven one with a manual shift since I passed my first driving test. And I've never driven on a turnpike in my life.

"So I'm scared. You must understand that, and try to help me, not criticize me. *You* may not mind driving down the whole length of Michigan Avenue, but I do. I just want to get out of Chicago and back to our motel the quickest and safest way possible. It's going to take all the brain power I've got left to remember how to shift and steer, and I can't be worrying about how to find my way as well or I'll just . . . I'll just . . . "

She sniffed, tossed her hair back, and took a deep breath. Don't cry.

" . . . I don't know what. So I asked Dennis if he would drive in front of us to the nearest expressway approach in the direction of Joliet, and let me follow behind. I'm sure you could direct me to it just as well. But if I can just follow his truck I won't have to think about anything else except how to keep the car running, stay on the road, and not get hit. And I'll need you to help me do that."

In her very weakness she felt strong: strong enough to confess the weakness direct, to insist upon the truth. They looked at one another on a straight, simple plane. Timmy felt a new balance of powers quietly shifting into place.

"All right, baby." He reached for her hand with his good left arm. Let's go."

Dennis waited in his pickup at the curb while Audrey practiced on the gear shift and pedals, Timmy quietly coaching at her side. She still jumped when she started and jerked when she stopped, and mixed up second and third. She made one hiccuping test-drive up and down the block, during which she kept taking her right foot off the gas pedal when she pushed the clutch with her left, which caused the car to shudder and stall; or else left the clutch down for too long, which resulted in awful grinding noises. She checked everything she could find to check twice. Seat adjust, lights, seat belts, wipers, window spray, mirrors, blinkers, handbrake, radio, heater, fan, horn, cigarette lighter, glove compartment. She even released the hood latch, which meant that Timmy had to get out and close the hood. She made him put on his seat belt, lock up all the doors, and let her know when there were no cars visible in either direction for at least two blocks.

"Now," he said, and patted her knee to reassure her.

"Don't do that!" she screamed.

With a wave, and a sigh, Timmy signaled the pickup to start off.

At 10:15 on a muggy morning, the battered Cougar turned under the porte cochère of the Joliet Marquise. Audrey down-shifted smoothly, and drove under the arch to the space they had left so ecstatically sixteen hours before. She stopped the car, turned off the key, pulled back the brake: then collapsed into her passenger's arms.

They gave themselves one more day and night in Madame du Pompadour, making use of all her amenities. Then they moved to a cheaper room, a decent poolside double for only thirty dollars a day. No ceiling mirror, no sunken tub; but it would do: a clean, comfortable place hidden from the world, in which they could lick their wounds.

For four more days they stayed at the Joliet Marquise, letting injuries heal, eating and drinking in their room or at the pool, doing laundry, writing

87

postcards, and getting to know one another better. On the fifth day, Audrey drove her husband to a Joliet doctor, who took out the stitches, undid his tapes, and gave him a prescription for his headaches.

They spent their last afternoon lying side by side next to the pool, talking quietly about their childhoods. That night, by playing on her sympathy for his pains—it was so much easier on his ribs that way, he explained, just a temporary expedient—Timmy persuaded Audrey into sexual acts and positions she had never heard of before. Afterwards, they slept innocently in each other's arms, like Hansel and Gretel in the woods.

Next morning, they bathed and dressed, then packed all their things and stowed them in the car. They ate breakfast in the motel restaurant, then charged the whole imperial tab—including $147 (plus tip) for the Café du Ciel—to the gods of MasterCharge.

12

St. Joseph, Missouri
April 10, 1849

It seems we shall be obliged to stop here a while longer, whether we fancy it or not. (I do not. St. Joseph is mean, crowded, and dirty.) So I purchased this exercise book at Mr. Tyler's store in town, in order to record some of my impressions of this journey.

We are now at the limits of civilization. The United States are all behind us. Across the river lies Indian territory. After all the time and effort we have spent getting to this point, I wish we could be on our way. "Camping out" here, to no apparent purpose, begins to grow tedious. And one hears fearful tales of what befalls emigrants who set out too late.

But I confess myself also not a little frightened of what lies in store across the river. Two thousand miles of wilderness is a mighty undertaking even for a man as hardy as James, with only one wagon, three yoke of oxen, a cow, and whatever poor assistance I can provide. Crowded as it is, I will be loathe to see the last line of chimney-smoke rising from the rooftops of this little town. There is one fort 250 miles west of here. Another 500 miles after that. But that is all we shall find in the way of "civilization."

St. Joseph
April 12, 1849

It is now five weeks since we left Vermont. We spent 27 days traveling, by railroad, lake and river boat, and have now been at "St. Jo" for more than a week. We have been told that we must wait here at least until the first of May, and the spring rains. Sooner than that, there will be insufficient new grass on the plains to forage our stock.

Others are already leaving. Each day the line of wagons at the ferry grows longer and longer, though the two boats now ply back and forth from dawn until midnight. The line is two wagons wide, and it reaches far back from the bank. Even if we chose to leave now, we should have to take our place in line, and wait two or three more days for our turn.

James spends the time bargaining for more provisions, seeking a good trail horse, and, I fear, gambling and drinking. There is little for me to do.

Doubtless it is this lack of occupation that magnifies my apprehension. Except for the time I spend preparing our meals, my days are void of needful work. Having tidied the wagon for the hundredth time, I knit till I can no longer make out the rows, then walk about the camping place exchanging greetings with the few females here. There are far more emigrants in our city of wagons and tents than there are permanent residents in the city we surround, and appear to invade.

Has the world ever witnessed such an extraordinary sight? It is like a gigantic fair, or encampment of gypsies. Thousands of chattering, anxious Americans, from almost every one of the thirty states, wander to and from all day among the canvas-covered wagons and tents. By night, they gather around blazing fires that light up the dark as far as the eye can see. (We make our fires here of prairie grass, cottonwood stumps, chokeberry wood, sage-brush, and greasewood.) The men sing and dance in the evening to music from banjos, fiddles, and accordians, or drink and play cards by lantern light on improvised tables. Many of the wagon tops bear designs and humorous inscriptions, announcing the sanguine expectations of the argonauts.

The town I do not like to visit, for its filth and profanity, and the jostling mobs of ill-bred men. It troubles me to go to the river and stare at the long line of white wagons and patient animals, waiting day and night, day after day, for the two poor scows that must ferry them across.

So I come back to the wagon, where I am writing this now, and remain alone with my thoughts. On our first night here, after the wagon had been unloaded from the steamboat, I felt quite wretched and fearful. There is a bleak dreariness in feeling the darkness descend over you without the shelter of proper walls or a roof. And this is to be our situation for many weeks, even months. In my heart, I begged for escape. But I said nothing to James, who fell asleep, easily and quickly, just as he does at home. Despite the comfortable straw and blankets on the wagon floor, the sense of homelessness kept my eyes open for a long time that first night.

But I did, of course, sleep, and woke in the morning quite ashamed of my faint-hearted longing for home. Such discontent is a mark of female weakness and wicked insubmission.

Our wagon is one of hundreds assembled in a kind of temporary city which surrounds the town. Our encampment is located in a fine grove of oaks on a rise to the south. There are a few hotels and lodging houses in St. Jo, but space in them is very dear, and the beds are long since taken up. Despite its discomforts, I would rather stay in the wagon. Our one meal at a hotel—greasy and indigestible fare, served at a common table to us and forty ill-mannered men—disposed me to prefer the healthiness of the open fields.

Camping in this way also seems to be a sensible preparation for the rigors ahead, which are sure to be greater than these.

Despite the huddled crowding, which deprives one of any sense of privacy, there is some comfort in the very size of this extraordinary assembly. For all my secret fears, for all the dire rumors, for all the competition for precedence at the ferry (over which two drivers shot each other to death with pistols last week), there has been much co-operation and Christian sharing. Men aid one another in breaking mules and repairing wagons. They band together to search for provisions, and compare what they learn concerning the prices asked for stock.

Oxen hereabouts are selling for more than fifty dollars a yoke, but there are very few to be had. Good American mules cost seventy dollars and more. James is mightily pleased with himself to have purchased ours at St. Louis. Downriver at Independence, he is told, things are no better.

We few women trade female wisdom, in our makeshift rolling homes. I have been assisting a Mrs. Cluett from Buffalo, New York, in caring for her three ailing youngsters. Yielding to the enforced delay, she has fitted up an outdoor sitting room and kitchen by moving some furniture out of their wagon, and hanging carpets and canvas out front. They brought along far more than we did: a fine brocaded chair and footstool, a spinning wheel, a loom, a brass bedstead and a lamp. It makes a most delightful place to visit, even though it recalls so painfully the world of four-square homes, and clocks, and quilts, and dear, dear friends we have left behind.

One problem of all this sociable commingling, in camp as in town, is that it increases the spread of rumors. Those who are for leaving early remind us of what was endured by the Reed and Donner group just three seasons ago—as if one needed reminding! Those who vote for waiting longer threaten us with starving cattle on the still-barren plains. We are told by some that there is no more grass beyond the river than will serve for two days' march, and by others that there is plenty; that only pack mules, and not ox-drawn wagons, can make the journey across the Rocky Mountains, and that the South Pass is as broad and as easy as a boulevard. Rivers are either impassible torrents, or easy to ford. There is water aplenty, one insists. No, declares another; there are barren deserts to traverse beyond the endurance of man or beast. Either Fort Kearny and Fort Laramie are well stocked with provisions for emigrant parties; or we must pack all one could possibly require for a five months' trip, at the risk of starvation. We are frightened by tales of barbaric Indian massacres, along the valleys of the Platte and the Humboldt, and the cruel usage of the Mormons toward Christians. Others carry back stories from returning travelers, who insist they could never have survived without the kind help of these same Indians and Mormons.

Night and day, the men exchange rumors. They argue heatedly (and, I daresay, ignorantly) over Indians, provisions, livestock, and routes of travel. The greater part of them are already equipped like comic-opera soldiers, each with his private arsenal of rifles, guns, knives, and powder. They bravely boast of what they will do to the first "redskin" who tries to impede their progress to the mines. James is a positive villain in this regard. Already, on the boat from St. Louis, these brave new frontiersmen began practicing their aim at any living thing, deer, dog, or hog, that had the misfortune to appear along the bank.

Most people, like us, stocked their wagons with provisions and supplies before arriving at this "jumping-off place," which is just as well considering the outlandish prices the merchants are demanding. Each day higher prices are set—and only for us emigrants, not for local citizens! The merchants appear surly and indifferent to this mob that is making their fortunes. "If they're going to find all that gold, and get all that rich, they can d---ed well pay what we ask!" I heard one saucy grocery clerk remark. I cannot abide this low, trickish, cunning disposition. It is people like him who keep me from going to town.

We now have about 250 pounds of flour (it is selling for a dollar a hundredweight here), 100 pounds of bacon, 60 of sugar, 50 of rice, 12 of coffee, as well as beans, salt, soda, dried fruit, and hard loaves of "pilot" bread. We shall depend on the cow for milk, and hope for fresh game and fish as we travel. Fruit and vegetables we must from now on do without, except for my own preserves and dried fruit—though there may be edible berries on the plains.

Some of our fellow campers have made excursions across the river in order to gather supplies discarded by earlier travelers, who took loads too heavy for their animals. They bring back not only bacon and flour, but also tools, spare wheels, axletrees, and clothes. It is hard to know the right thing to do.

All male emigrants of sufficient age let their whiskers grow, as a mark of hardiness, and wear a common "uniform" of broadcloth pantaloons tucked into boots, flannel shirts, and broad-brimmed hats. The only exceptions are the companies formed along military lines, which dress in army uniforms with brass buttons, and are made to parade and drill like schoolboys playing at soldier. The men gather around one wagon or another and argue over the merits of "Ware's" guide or "Hastings'," debate this "cut-off" against that, each waving some favored map or account torn from a newspaper back home. But I believe that not one in a hundred of them knows the first thing about the country ahead. They refuse to hire a guide, since this is regarded as a sign of pusillanimity. The trail to California, all insist, is as wide as the sea and as plain as a pikestaff. We shall soon find out.

One thing is clear: a great number of them could use someone to teach them the rudiments of the countryman's life. Watching a city-bred mechanic (who may never have seen such creatures before) trying to break a mule, or drive three yoke of oxen, is a wonderful thing. If it were not so frightening, in view of the road ahead, it would be mirthful indeed.

St. Joseph
April 15, 1849

Emma Cluett's youngest died this morning, after a fearful night of chills and fever, vomiting and diarrhoea. The poor little girl's sufferings were pitiable to behold. She grew pale as a sheet, choking and weeping with the pain of her cramped little stomach, as wet with perspiration as if she had been left out in a warm rain. A doctor from the Cincinnati party administered laudanum, and advised us to rub her cold extremities. She was too weak to cling to her mother. I stayed with them through the night, trying to comfort her brother and sister (whose afflictions seem to mend), and to keep them from noting too keenly the agonies of dear Rachel Anne. James helped Mr. Cluett to dig the tiny grave, and a minister from the large Pittsburgh party read prayers. Such suffering troubles the soul. God's will be done.

Coming up the river, we heard many tales of sailors and travelers stricken with the cholera, but this is the first death we have witnessed ourselves. Suddenly there are rumors of victims from surrounding encampments, and the doctors among us are kept busy. Some have fled further upriver to board less crowded ferries; they hope to escape the scourge by setting out at once into Indian territory. But the wagons of two sad families returned to town yesterday, having buried four members along the trail. The survivors are going back, abandoning dreams of gold. The disease, it appears, has crossed the Missouri.

James purchased the horse he has been seeking last night. He found it at a street auction in town held by a discouraged man from Illinois who had been robbed of his stake and forced to return home. He rang a large bell to announce the sale.

In the same street, earlier in the day, I witnessed a sight shocking to Christian eyes: the sale of a human being. A strong Negro boy of about 18 is now destined for a life of bondage. Surely this is a crime against nature, even for an African Negro. The bidding started at five hundred dollars, and ended at eight hundred. God will punish the state of Missouri for its decision to ally itself with the barbarians of the south.

St. Joseph
April 18, 1849

James returned to camp this evening quite crestfallen, to confess to me that he had lost most of our small fortune of four hundred dollars—the sum we were paid for the house and smithy in Burlington. He fell victim to a band of unscrupulous gamblers in town. They have, I am sure, set up shop in St. Jo precisely in order to fleece unwitting overlanders like James.

This is a serious calamity. Everyone tells us that one must have on hand several hundred dollars in ready money in order to reach California. There are ferries to cross, all charging high rates. (The rate here is five dollars per wagon.) Indians demand tribute if one is to cross their lands unmolested. And most travelers can be certain to require supplementary provisions in later stages of the journey. These must be purchased either at the forts, or from the Mormon traders, or from companies that are larger and better equipped.

I assured James that I did not blame him, and that I did not want to turn back. But inwardly I did both, and I suspect that he knew this. He is cast down and very morose. He is trying to sell either the new horse, the cow, some of his weapons, or the mining equipment he purchased in Ohio. If that fails, he will try to obtain two places in one of the large companies that are forming here, in return for his services as a smith. All he wants is the assurance that our expenses will be paid until we reach the mines.

I would be happier if we traveled as part of a company, and have made my feelings on this clear all along. We could have traveled so all the way from Burlington. I have developed the liveliest fear of red savages, who apparently respect white women even less than white men. But until now, James insisted on the greater honor and freedom of what he calls "independent" travel.

He does not get along well with other people. He works hard, and is a good husband, and in his own way a Christian. He will help a neighbor in need. But he dislikes asking for help. He believes that other folk look down on him because he is Irish. No doubt his bitter experiences with his own family (and mine) have helped to make him what he is.

He has his faults, but who has not? I have mine. One reason I am writing in this exercise book is that I cannot talk easily to James about the things that lie heaviest on my heart. Our burdens are lightened when they are shared, even if it is only with the unattending page.

And yet it seems unwifely and deceitful to keep any confidant other than one's lawful spouse. I am oftentimes tempted to toss this book into the fire, to keep no counsel but my own, and the Lord's.

Six more died this day of the cholera in our encampment. Next our wagon, one of the stricken lay under a canvas shelter. His groans continued through a day and a night. Sometimes it is difficult to sustain a proper Christian sympathy, when affronted by dire and awful noises. I must confess I hoped that if he did not recover soon, he might die even sooner. It kept me from sleep the whole night.

St. Joseph
April 26, 1849

After a week of trying to peddle his services, James has been elected a member of a 30-wagon company from Carthage, Illinois. He has had to resell his horse, and some of our supplies, and guarantee his free labor to all, in order to make up the price of two shares. So we shall have the security of companionship across the plains.

Mrs. Garner, one of the two other women in this company, was surprised that James and I had not traveled by sea, living as we did near to the great eastern ports. I told her we had been near-persuaded by the advertisements, but were eventually converted to overlanders by the greater cost, as well as the perils and unhealthiness of sea travel. I dared not admit that it was only my terror of being cooped up for weeks in a fragile, storm-tossed craft around Cape Horn that obliged James to abandon his original plan of sailing from Boston last January. Had we done so, as he often reminds me, we would be in California by now, ahead of these legions of "dirt farmers" from the western states he professes to scorn.

Four days ago, the "captain" of the Carthage Company invited a young clergyman from a neighboring party to preach our Sunday sermon. He took his text from the Book of Job, chapter 22, verse 24. "Then shalt thou lay up gold as dust, and the gold of Ophir as the stones of the brooks."

94

This is all very well. But these words are spoken by one of Job's three worldly counselors, who understood not the ways of God. Job himself later declares, "If I have made gold my hope, or said to the fine gold, Thou art my confidence, If I rejoiced because my wealth was great, and because my hand had gotten much, This was also an iniquity to be punished by the judge; for I should have denied the God who is above."

The young preacher, sunburned and bewhiskered like the rest of the men here (and dressed no better than they), lauded us as brave heroes and patriots and I don't know what else, building the greater glory of God and the States. Folks listening looked very puffed up and pleased with themselves. But everyone knows we are only heading west to find gold and get rich. Almost none that I talk to plan to settle in California—only to get gold as quick as they can, so they can go back and "show folks" at home, and then live like kings and queens ever after in Illinois or Missouri.

I do trouble me about our sin of Greed. When I scorn the vicious merchants and landlords of St. Jo, I then reconsider and ask myself, which of us is more guilty of avarice? The only difference I can see is that they are stripping and gouging fellow children of God, whereas we plan to strip and gouge only His insentient earth.

Last Friday, the body of one poor overlander from the camps was found three-quarters of a mile outside of town with his throat cut, apparently a victim of robbers. With the deserts and mountains, and the red Indian savages ahead, it is appalling to consider that we may harbor worse savages among our own kind. The dread disease of covetousness, more mortal than the cholera, shows its marks.

St. Joseph
May 5, 1849

It is now four days past the last safe day on which we were to have crossed the Missouri. Still we sit. The problem now is the rain—the very rain we had been waiting for. The sky has been pouring with it for the last five days. The camping ground is turned into a bog, the streets are thick rivers of mud. Many wagon tops, including ours, have proven less weather-worthy than their owners expected. The confusion and filth are past description.

People are rushing to join the long parade at the ferry, where they stand up to their ankles in mud. But our wise "captain," Mr. McClellan from Carthage, has determined that we must now wait for the prairie mud to dry, and the spring grass to sprout. If we wait here much longer, I fear, the animals that are now swimming the river every hour will have eaten up whatever grass is left.

One whole month we have sat here in St. Jo. Surely this is only to invite disaster at the other end of the trail.

A boat arrived yesterday from St. Louis, on which eighteen men had died of the cholera during the journey. There seems to be no escaping the disease. Poor Mrs. Cluett lost her younger son as well as her daughter, before her party left for California last week.

Lying in the wagon last night listening to the rain, I heard someone playing the notes of "Home, Sweet Home" on the key-bugle, and burst into tears. This is no home, nor shall we know a real home again for many months. James was dazzled to blindness last winter by what he had read of California, and could be persuaded out of his phantasy by no arguments of mine. Our home, my parents' house and church, our neighbors, all the things I depended on most became for him unsupportable chains and fetters once the gold fit was on. There was nothing for it but to go. Had we a child, I believe, he might have stayed. But God has not willed it so.

St. Joseph
May 10, 1849

Rather than wait any longer for grass, the Carthage Company has bought corn sufficient to feed our stock for the first three days on the plains. We leave tomorrow.

"I will both lay me down in peace, and sleep; for thou, Lord, only makest me dwell in safety."

13

On day number eleven of their marriage, Timmy and Audrey kept to U.S. 6, which from time to time became Interstate 80, all the way across Illinois and Iowa, except for one emergency detour. This highway—which is toll-free—runs a few miles north of the Illinois River up to the Peru-Depue exit. Here the river turns south to Peoria. The highway, and the McCues, kept heading west.

They crossed the Mississippi River between Rock Island in Illinois and Davenport in Iowa. The river was very wide, but crossing it was not a Meaningful Experience. The water looked like dirty milk chocolate. Even though she was disappointed, Audrey asked Timmy to stop so she could buy postcards. On the cards, she was pleased to find, the river looked more nearly blue.

That evening, from the balcony of a Holiday Inn in Council Bluffs, they could count barges tied up in the Missouri River. Across the river they watched a bloody sun set over the billboards and antennas and parking garage roofs of Omaha, Nebraska, whose listless skyline was pierced by a few skyscrapers. From one of them, the words "Northwestern Bell" flashed on and off all night in red letters.

Some human systems can absorb a great deal of stress without breaking. Creatures less resilient than Audrey and Timmy, equipped with less efficient shock absorbers, might have undergone radical deformation under the batterings of that particular Sunday night. For such creatures, an episode like Chicago might have caused visible and permanent damage.

Things had changed for the McCues—but the changes were deep inside. Nerves, in their way, have memories. The brain snaps a candid photograph of a lover—let us say—seen for the first time as a belligerent, drooling drunk.

97

That photograph is not just filed away in the brain; it becomes part of it, inalienable, ineradicable.

Consider: the feeling of terror in an alien place; the physical impact of a crash. The sense of being abandoned, lost, in real danger. Willingly or unwillingly, awake or asleep, we go on recalling such moments. We are made of our separate Chicagos.

But scar tissue forms, scabs dry over the ugliest wounds. We square our shoulders, toss our hair, and move on, pretending.

They had started the day with the feeling of fresh wind in their sails.

That feeling lasted about an hour. Then the midwesternness of the Midwest closed over them. Audrey tried to pump something out of the surrounding terrain, but nothing came.

They stopped for lunch at a Hinky Dink's along the highway, where they made fun of the other tourists. When they got back to the car, the weather had turned brain-baking hot. Forced down by the heat, the flow of consciousness ran sluggish, turned selfish. Conversation ceased.

A gas-and-toilet stop at an Iowa crossroads became a drag through the tarpits of middle America. By this time, Timmy had stripped off sweatshirt, T-shirt, tennis shoes, and socks, which bothered some folks in Iowa. He was hardening into one long forked and sunburnt root that kept a car moving, nothing else. A fragment of his brain clicked off the slow-moving miles.

Audrey, meanwhile, was getting sick. When she finally told Timmy she was getting sick, he seemed to pay no attention.

"We're almost there," is all he said.

"Where?"

"Don't ask. Somewhere."

The barns were huge, their roofs shaped like half-octagons in section. Most of the buildings were painted white; some barns were red with white trim. The houses looked like a child's drawing of a house, house ideal, House Platonic: horizontal white siding, peaked gable roofs, dormers, porches, chimneys, square-paned windows, front door set squarely in the middle. Audrey tried to imagine their rooms; she saw lace curtains, drugstore calendars, wallpaper, corners of shadow in which clocks ticked loudly. From the wide porches at ground level, to the lightning rods and television antennas that sprouted from their roofs, the farmhouses grew white and upright, two or three stories tall. Each stood back from the freeway on its green hillock of lawn, shaded by a cluster of trees.

The barns had lightning rods and metal ventilators—some as many as four—on their roofpeaks. Alongside them rose silos, their silver shafts and heads glistening in the heat.

Between the buildings lay thousands of acres of land planted with green corn. They drove past a tiny figure seated high atop a tractor. How could he possibly cover all that space?

"Have you ever lived on a farm?"

"Only my grandfather's. Where my parents live now. It's not really a farm, though. Not like these. They've just got vegetables and fruit trees. Two horses. Some chickens."

"So the place we'll be going to won't look like this?"

"Like this? Hell, no. It's not at all like this."

He looked out his side window, and felt a warm wave of homesickness. These were dull homes where dull people led dull lives. To each farmhouse, its litter of outbuildings; between each cluster, acres of grain. No shops, no steeples, not even grain elevators or water towers emblazoned with the names of passing towns.

"In the Gold Country, you never stare out at space the way you do here. To me, this is like a desert. What farms we have are just family farms, small. You could walk the whole spread in an afternoon."

"Tell me about California," she said, like a child asking for a favorite fairy tale.

"Well," he said, thinking. "The town where I grew up has about five, six thousand people now. It's in the foothills, out of Sacramento on your way to the mountains. Live oak trees, evergreens, manzanita and scrub brush, hills covered with dry grass in the summer and fall. It gets hot in the summer, but it's dry heat, not humid. Not like Boston.

"I used to like summer there. Crickets, woodland smells. You could hike down trails in the dust and throw rocks at the lizards and snakes, or wade in the creeks to catch crawfish. Everyone sat out at night on the porch or under the trees. Some nights it got too hot to sleep. Then we sat out till real late.

"The winters get cold, but never too cold. Some snow. They plow the main roads. Rains a lot around Christmas. Then the creeks fill up. Sometimes flood over. Once, when I was about ten, the whole town flooded."

How can I describe it? "Farms, ranches, little country towns in between. A few tourists on weekends, up to pan for gold, or to look at old buildings. There are a lot of Gold Rush buildings left. Main Street stores, bars. Cafés. Gas stations. The family restaurant."

He kept trying to place it, define it. Home. Where they were going.

"It's more small-scaled than this, human-sized. Easier to live in. Trees, rolling hills. I don't know." He looked out the window for a long time.

"Places like this really bother me."

"They bother me, too. I thought I'd like it more."

"WELCOME TO THE LAND OF LINCOLN," said a billboard: "S. SHAPIRO, GOVERNOR."

"I'd go nuts, living in flatlands like this. There's no mountains, no coast you can escape to. It's like you can't breathe, like you're abandoned in the middle of a huge open space. This continent doesn't get interesting till you're three-fourths of the way across Nebraska."

Audrey remembered the vacancy of Utah and Nevada. "How long will it take us to get there?"

"Two more days, probably. We've got all of Illinois, all of Iowa, and the farm part of Nebraska to get through first."

She stared at the green corn, which reached to the horizon in a haze of late afternoon. The tiny tractor inched its way along. "Will it look like this for two days?"

"Like this or worse." They sighed in unison, laughed without joy. Illinois, Land of Lincoln. She tried to imagine rolling hills, pine and fir woods, oak trees, a cozy country town. But she couldn't picture a California without palm trees.

"That man on the tractor," she finally said. "It can't be much fun, doing that."

"It isn't," Timmy turned and looked at him, a doll on a Tonka Toy. He was scarcely moving.

"I suppose farmers like feeling close to the earth, or something like that. Being a part of nature, planting, harvesting, adapting to the weather, just like . . ."

"Just like animals. Just like peasants. You'd have to be pretty dense to enjoy working in a place like this. No one with half a mind could sit up there all day, day after day, driving that thing back and forth."

After the tiny man disappeared, Audrey kept asking questions, to keep from sinking into flatness and haze. What were those wire mesh storage bins for? How do they get things in and out of silos? Do cows sleep in barns? She watched a hay baler chewing up grass and excreting grass cubes. "How does that work?" she asked, a city schoolgirl on her first field trip to a farm. "What do you suppose the winters are like here? I mean, what do they do for fun, do you think?"

"Watch television. Read *American Farmer* and *The Soybean Digest*. Go to church. Bitch about price supports. Eat." His hand started up her leg. "Screw."

A tractor appeared ahead of them in Timmy's lane. He zapped around it, honking.

"Do you think they mind having the freeway here?"

"They got a million each for their piece of the right of way. Gets them to their Grange meetings faster." He slipped into midwestern nasal-hicky. "Gives th' ol' lady sumpin' t'look at out t'winder."

"I wonder what they think of us."

"They wet-dream about going to California. They'd give anything to trade places." His hand had reached her crotch. Absent-minded and bored, she let it stay.

The morning had started overcast and close, but by ten o'clock it turned clear again, with a scattering of eggshell clouds. Within another hour, it had broken into a splendor of pure blue.

Eventually, Audrey ran out of things to ask about farms. She let the country-and-western music on the radio take over. She was growing numb from the sensory deprivation of the middle western plains. Very plain, the plains.

Hinky Dink's, where they stopped for lunch, was one of a midwestern chain with identical walls of pink plaster and glass under roofs of a violent blue.

Their conversation was running dry, and the fire of affection burning dim. So they diverted themselves over hamburgers and French fries by taking note of their fellow travelers. Audrey even tried to sketch some of the more interesting types on her paper place mat. But her drawings kept turning out either poor or comically unfair, so she scribbled them out.

Fat fathers and mothers kept yelling at and slapping their overweight children. There was one couple with eight children, all obviously theirs. Men with large bottoms and white legs wore overlong plaid Bermuda shorts, with black socks and leather shoes. Beer bellies, squeezed into knit polo shirts, rolled over their waistbands as they slid into booths. Those who weren't bald wore their hair cut very short.

Sons were miniature copies of their fathers: long shorts, blond crew cuts, mashed-potato faces. Their cow-sized moms, in teased hair or pageboys, wore sleeveless nylon blouses, sunglasses, and Bermuda shorts like their husbands', which encased bellies, thighs, and bottoms even more fleshy than the men's. Audrey shrank from this image of American family life.

The other childless couples in the place looked like retired people on vacation. The old men wore a uniform of duck-billed caps, short-sleeved shirts, and roomy cotton pants colored tan or silver-gray. The old women dressed in the standard female costume of bright blouses and shorts, or sometimes slacks. One whole wall of the restaurant was taken up by a Greyhound tour group from Maryland, homey old ladies in permanent silver waves and rayon print dresses. It was their faces mostly Audrey was trying to sketch.

As they were eating dessert, the waitress pulled their table in half and seated next to them another couple, perhaps midway between her age and Timmy's. Man and woman both had the blond hair and bright eyes of college sweethearts; he wore a short-sleeved orange sweatshirt which bore the name and seal of Northwestern Illinois State. But their fresh young features were now fitted incongruously into puffy necks, attached to gargantuan rears and wobbly pads of flesh. Averting her eyes from the sight of them eating, Audrey searched for someone more interesting to draw.

"Who's that?" Timmy asked after a few minutes, reaching for her place mat.

"Oh. No one." She quickly scribbled it out.

At a table directly in front of her, but behind Timmy's back, two boys had been seated, midwestern college kids in the regional uniform of crew cuts, shorts, and T-shirts. But unlike the rest of the crowd, they were trim and tanned and athletic—and to Audrey's eyes, beautifully young. The handsomer of the two was sitting looking right at her, staring at her unselfconsciously, with his legs spread apart. She was trying to catch the contour of his head, but her eyes kept dropping down to his crotch. She wrinkled up the place mat, put her pencil back in her purse.

"Let's go, hey."

Timmy pushed back his chair.

As they got up, Timmy's glance fell on a gang of people near the entrance.

101

"Look," he said.

"Look at what?"

"Those people. That family that just came in."

"The fat ones?"

"Yeah. I *know* them."

"You must be kidding."

"I don't mean personally. But I've seem them before. At that motel. In Toledo. In the rain, remember? I went for a swim? This huge Winnebago drove up, and those pigs got out, the very same ones. They started arguing with the manager about a room. He wouldn't let them have one, and they got pissed. He slammed his door in their faces, and they all came over by the pool fence and stood there staring at me."

"Are you sure it's the same ones? They look like half the people here."

"I'm sure it's them. They out-gross the whole crowd." He looked sideways at her, "Maybe they decided to spend a week in Joliet, too." She didn't think it was funny. "I wonder if they'll recognize me."

"Not with your clothes on."

Cheeky bitch. He gave her bottom a pinch, then rubbed the place he pinched. Nice little ass, he thought, as they made their way through the stockyard of corn-fed flesh.

When they pushed out the glass door, the heat hit them a flat-handed smack. Shimmering waves rose from the blacktop. Door handles, seat covers, steering wheel burned to the touch.

"Jesus, it's hot!"

"Could we open the air vent?"

"That would only let in hot air."

"What about the air conditioning?"

"I don't have air conditioning. Try closing your window most of the way, and leaving the little side window open. If we both do that we may be able to get some kind of breeze flowing through."

They tried, but it didn't help. They drove on, and just stayed hot.

The Interstate looped south of Quad Cities, where they crossed the brown river. Timmy pulled up at a discount drug and liquor store in Davenport so Audrey could buy her postcards. He got the ice chest out of the trunk, filled it with two bags of ice and two six-packs of beer.

By now the car was an oven. He popped open two beers. Beer made Audrey sick to her stomach, but she hadn't the will to refuse. At least it was cold. She sipped the bitter foam, and tried to write a postcard on her lap. She leaned over and scooped a handful of ice chips out of the chest, rubbed them over her face, her neck, her shoulders and arms, the throbbing places behind her ears.

It was on the hundred-mile stretch between Iowa City and Des Moines that she began to feel sick. At first, it was only an indefinable malaise, a kind of heartsickness at the absence of any tangible surroundings. Moline and Iowa City may have been dispiritingly hicky, but at least they offered the tangible security of a lot of people and buildings close together.

The rube cities of Illinois-Iowa were built around bus depots and twenty-four-hour cafés. With that as a center, they spread out to boarded-up department stores, vacant movie houses, a couple of tired office buildings, a bankrupt hotel. There was less life downtown than in the gaudy entrance and exit parades of gas stations and Kentucky Fried Chickens, the motels and used car lots with their shouting signs and flapping flags.

Speed limits fell: 70, 55, 45, 30. The car lots gave over to houses with screened porches, set back from the road under trees; houses yielded to little stores, little stores to bigger stores. Finally you entered the weary blocks of downtown, trying hard: "ATHENS, ILLINOIS: ALL-AMERICAN CITY."

Going out, the same in reverse: smaller shops, gas stations, car lots, motels, McDonald's, flashy signs, nothing. 45, 55, 70, and out. End of city.

Audrey had known open country before, but never emptiness like this.

Her city soul craved brick walls, sidewalks, traffic lights, the hard surfaces and multi-colored things which prove that people have come together for mutual support.

She sipped her bitter beer, and listened to the radio's staticky whine. New stations rose out of nowhere, calling hog prices, peddling living room suites at thirty percent off, pouring out the same nasal truckers' laments and dirges to Mama. Then they died out again in the static. Timmy would twirl around the fading fiddles until KRAM-Prairie City, or whatever, came in loud and clear enough to take over for KOOK-Oskaloosa. If he hit it real lucky, he could ring a country-and-western jackpot, like Johnny Cash growling out "Folsom Prison Blues" twice in a row. Audrey kept hearing tantalizing snatches of a powerful pop station from Des Moines—Engelbert Humperdinck! The Monkees! Simon and Garfunkel!—but Timmy kept twirling past it in search of his hillbilly trash.

He was feeling the heat, too. It left him numb, rather than sick. He felt heavy and drugged, and in no frame of mind to sympathize with anyone else. He knew how much worse heat could get (how much worse it was *likely* to get, in fact). There was nothing to do but drive on, and wait for the sun to set.

Eastern Iowa offered indetectible variations on western Illinois. The roads ran so straight, across terrain so nearly level, that he could sometimes make out a slight rise or curve of the road, a building or a clump of trees, 10, 20 miles ahead. He tried to guess distances to these landmarks, to help eat up slow-moving miles. Audrey played the game with him for a while; but that still left all the times in between, when the only sounds in the car were the cries of the engine, and some doleful steel guitar rag from Oskaloosa. To keep from becoming road-hypnotized and drifting over white lines, Timmy sang along with the radio. But even that effort grew too great.

Not so many cars, here. No wonder. Nearly all midwestern plates; a few Californias. He passed one of those foreign travelers' "D" stickers, on a Volkswagen Beetle. Diesel behemoths strained and strained to pass him. Invariably, once they got in front, they would relax and drive slower than he had been going. This forced him to go either 72, in order to get past them, or

68, to stay behind them; when what he wanted to do was drive a neat, unthinking 70, forever.

Occasionally, some fool would pass on the right; some oaf in a family-filled wagon would glue himself alongside at exactly his speed, never overtaking, never falling back. How easy it was to hate other drivers. Cross-country Greyhounds sailed by, double-decked, silver quartered red-white-and-blue. Jalopies smoked and sputtered along, unlikely to make it to the next county. Bumper stickers, patriotic, Christian, silly, raunchy, advertising tourist traps or local radio stations. Toy dogs nodded their heads like idiots in rear windows. A pair of feet sticking out a window. A Mustang. An Impala. A Bel Air. A Capri.

He glanced at his dashboard dials. Oil pressure right of center, engine temp up, gas at half, speed stuck at 70, tach 55. He looked in his rear view mirror: nothing there. The less attention it took to drive, the more he felt trapped, a blank mind in a steel thing on a long conveyor belt, speeding through a time warp tunnel all the way across. If only she'd go to sleep and stop fidgeting. She lit another cigarette. He reached down and popped open another beer, steering with his elbow. Ahead, the road pushed towards him in ever-narrowing, never-changing perspective. At his side, rows of green corn spun on like a Cinemascope film.

He made an effort to arrest his motion by fixing on a single weed in the blur. Hiking in the mountains, he used to stop and study things one at a time: peer into flowers' most personal cups, trace the veins in a rock, break open rotting logs to watch the termites scurrying about as if the end of the world had come. Now billions of things were passing every minute, and he was missing them all.

A tree, far in the distance: gone. A farmhouse; gone. Landmarks spun past him as if they were set at various places on a giant turntable of which he was the center. He played the meditative game of watching a faraway piece of the dotted white line until it raced past the car at 70 miles an hour. It was like following drops of water in a fountain, motes in a sunbeam, waves as they broke on a beach.

In mid-afternoon, they drove in and out of the state capital. Audrey wanted to stop—by now, Audrey very much wanted to stop—but Timmy was in no mood for a town like Des Moines. So he drove on through, and didn't stop till they reached a roadside turnout 20 miles west of town.

Set down in the middle of what looked like a million acres of nothing was a little parking area with picnic tables under shade trees, running water, and flush toilets.

"KEEP IOWA CLEAN AND BEAUTIFUL," admonished the garbage cans. Well, he thought: clean maybe.

His gas pedal leg was cramped, his ass was sore. The buttons of his jeans pressed tight against his middle. He got out, unfolded, stood up in the shade, and stretched his arms high over his head. God, it felt good. Then he headed for the Men's, Audrey for the Women's.

In the toilet, he enjoyed the feel of a river-running flow of ex-beer running warm through his spigot. He changed from jeans back into his old cutoffs, then took off his shirt at the sink and splashed face, arms, hair, everything above the waist with cold water. Back at the car, he got out two beers, and sat down at a shaded table to wait. Audrey was taking her time, probably washing and changing, too. He opened a can, glugged a deep glug, sipped, took off shoes and socks, stretched his legs, ran his bare feet through the grass, flexed and unflexed long bony toes. A hundred more miles to Council Bluffs: an hour and a half, two hours at most. No sweat. He finished his beer and started on hers.

Audrey finally came out of the toilet. She had changed into a halter top and short shorts, which should have done wonders. But she didn't look too good.

"Have another beer?" He held it up, half-finished.

"No, thanks." She seemed to be looking purposely wan, so that he would have to ask her what was the matter.

"What's the matter?" he finally asked. "Heat getting to you?"

"I'm afraid so."

"You should wash yourself down. Like a horse. Turn on the cold tap and just pour it all over you. Hey, babe, you look great in that top."

"Timmy. I'm afraid I'm sick."

"Sick? Sick how?"

"I've got diarrhea." It embarrassed her to admit it. "I feel terrible."

"Yuck. Well, we're almost there."

"Where?"

"Somewhere. Don't ask. You just tell me when you need to stop."

The last 90 miles of the day were painful for both of them, but for Audrey they were torture. As the heat grew more and more intense, she curled into a ball of sick, shivering with both fever and the fear that her stomach was going to explode before she could get to a toilet.

Timmy was feeling his burdens, too: the burdens of her annoying female weakness, 102-degree heat, the car's frightening groans, his growing white-line fever. Zombied out with driving, he stared at the odometer. The miles passed more slowly than ever. His eyelids weakened, dropped, fell: he kept catching the car as it drifted over the line. Audrey sucked and cracked LifeSavers, and prayed that her stomach would stay still. Timmy kept drinking beer.

They made one last stop, when Audrey's gut pressures grew urgent. She moaned like a woman in labor; he turned off the road as soon as he could. Three miles down, they came to Shelton, Iowa, "A FRIENDLY AND FORWARD VILLAGE": one paved block, one grocery-post office, one gas station. An old man, shirtless in overalls, watched as they pulled into the station. Audrey got out and ran to the john. As a long-necked teenager with a huge Adam's apple filled his tank, Timmy got out to look under the hood. The radiator holes were stuffed with bugs, large moths, one mashed little bird.

The old degenerate got up from his pile of tires and come over to chat. "How'dja smash it up, then?"

Rheumy eyes were taking the measure of Timmy, gaping at his hairy torso.

"Chicago. Guy plowed into me."

105

"Head on?"

"Not exactly."

"Nigger, was it?"

Timmy looked at him.

"Matter of fact, yes."

"I knew it. I been to Chicago, oncet. Right after the war. The first war. Place was fulla niggers. I heard on the teevee they're burning the place down."

"That what you hear, huh?"

"Best thing could happen to it."

The long-necked kid came up as Timmy was looking at his dipstick.

"How's your oil?"

"Down. Gimme a quart. Quaker State. Ten-forty."

"We ain't got Quaker State."

"Anything, then."

Audrey was tottering back, white in the heat. She looked terrible. The brief halter and short shorts belonged on a healthier woman.

"Feel any better?"

She smiled a weak, false-heroic smile.

"How about a Coke?"

"I had some water." She paused, thought, belched. "I hope it was all right. The toilet was filthy."

"Lady sick, huh?" Now the whiskery geezer was taking her in: all that pale, bare flesh.

Mind your own business, you old fart. Several lumpy local types had gathered near the Coke machine to stare. The boy was filling out Timmy's credit slip for the gas and oil.

"California, hey?" he read off the credit card. "I had a buddy went to San Diego with the Marines. Ever been there?"

"Yep."

"You got a lot of nuts out in California, my buddy says."

You got a few nuts here in Iowa, kid, he thought, looking at the loonies by the Coke machine.

One of them walked over—a bald, red-faced man in suspenders with a great wen on his neck, who had been standing with two women. "Where these folks from, Hector?"

"California."

"Massachusetts, actually," Timmy corrected. "Near Boston."

"Folks dress like that in Boston?"

"Dress like what?"

"Like you two." Audrey was still leaning against the car door, taking deep breaths. "Round here, we'd call that indecent."

"Round here you folks don't much mind your own business, do you?" He signed the slip, took back his card, and got into the car.

The man came up to the car window. "This may not mean nothin' to you, but we're Christians here in Shelton." The two women were now standing behind him, staring hard at them both. "We don't take kindly to immorality.

106

Folks like you best do to keep your scanty clothes and sinnin' ways outa here. We know the Lord's will." The two women nodded.

"I see. The Lord came right down to Shelton Iowa and informed you of that now, did he?" Timmy turned on his engine.

He squealed out past the Lord's delegation, backing up and then curving his wheels so they came within inches of the bald man's toes when he drove forward. "The fuck he did!" As he U-turned into the main and only street, he lifted a middle finger for them all.

Two hours later, at the Council Bluffs motel, Timmy and Audrey collapsed on separate beds, solipsistic as two eggs, aware of nothing but their separate, selfish griefs. The climb up the Inn's two outdoor landings had been almost more than Audrey could manage. She had already had another long siege in the toilet. Timmy had opened the sliding glass door onto the balcony, but still the place stank. Amazing how offensive someone else's smell can be. He was lying with his hands behind his head, staring at the ceiling. I never notice my own.

It was just as well they had two beds this time. Sex was the farthest thing from either one's plans. Audrey's mind was disgusted with Audrey's body, which felt like one limp, befouled rag. If she could get up the energy to take a hot bath, at least she might feel reasonably clean. Then she could slip under a sheet and try to sleep. Alone.

Timmy knew she wasn't well. The poisoned air proved it. And she had told him enough times. But he was too exhausted himself at the moment to spare any genuine sympathy. (Fake sympathy, maybe; genuine sympathy, no.) His leg muscles felt like rusted steel springs. His butt was saddle sore. His eyelids burned, his head ached: the day's road kept unrolling in his head. Four hundred seventy miles of the Midwest, drinking Rock Island Select in the sun.

"Do you feel any better?" he finally worked up the manners to ask. Have to say something.

"Not really." Christ, I thought you'd never ask.

She sighed a great suffering sigh, the sort that usually melted her mother. "My whole insides are churning. I feel just wiped out."

Me, too. "What do you think it was? Just the heat?" How the hell are you going to cope with Nevada? he wondered. Or life, for that matter?

"The heat, yes. And all that driving without stopping. I *asked* you to stop. Worrying about all those noises in the car. And that beer. I never usually drink beer. It's not good for me." She burped menacingly.

I see. It's all my fault.

"And I'm wondering now about that hamburger I had for lunch. It did taste funny. Remember I said so?"

"I had one, and it didn't bother me."

You had two. Raw horsemeat wouldn't bother you. "I don't suppose they have room service in a place like this."

"Sorry. This isn't the Joliet Marquise. You don't want something to *eat*, do you? After all that?"

107

"Oh, no. No, don't talk about food. But I'd like something like a soda water. And some Pepto Bismol."

"Sure."

Marriage, he thought, sulking. I haul ass all day. Little sweetheart doesn't like to drive, so I get the wheel every fucking mile. With a sprained wrist and stitches in my face, *I* keep the car going, *I* find us rooms, *I* carry all the luggage. I pay for the whole thing. Doctor says go easy because of my stitches, I feel my head splitting in the sun. And as soon as I lie down for one minute, I'm supposed to run out in the heat again and go shopping, because Ladybird's got the trots.

"Sure." He sat up on the edge of his bed, and started pulling on his shoes. "There's a shopping plaza across the street. Anything else you want?" He looked at the limp body, wet hair, wasted little face. Hell, she *is* sick. He felt suddenly ashamed.

"No," she whispered. "Just something for my stomach, and something fizzy to drink. Maybe some aspirin."

He sat down on the edge of her bed and started to straighten her hair.

"Don't. Please don't touch me."

"O.K. Sorry." Sorry, sorry, sorry sorry.

He stood up and walked to the glass door, drew the curtains closed.

"I might pick up a McDonald's or something. Think you'll want something to eat later on?"

"*Please*, please don't talk about food. I asked you not to. But do get whatever you want. And don't worry about me."

Sure. His hand was on the door.

"You will hurry back, though? This time?"

Low blow. "Of course I will. You try to sleep."

He slid open the door, ducked under the curtain, pushed it closed.

She was in the bath when he returned.

"I'm back, honey "

"Oh, good. I was beginning to wonder. Could you pour me a glass of soda water and bring it in here?"

The Holiday Inn bathroom was almost tranquilizing in its antiseptic, daisy-yellow way. Audrey was curled up in the low shower-bath behind half-shut frosted glass. The floor was already wadded with her towels. Timmy took a plastic tumbler out of its sanitized wrap and filled it with Calso. He had brought back a paper bucket full of ice from a machine at the end of the balcony. From it he picked out two hollowed lumps, and dropped them in.

"Here." He pushed open the frosted door. "You want your Pepto Bismol, too?"

"Oh, no, thanks. Just leave it by the sink." She smiled almost coyly out of her soapsuds. "I'm feeling better."

"Great." I'm not. It's fucking hot out there. Street's coming up in tar bubbles.

"Did you get something to eat?"

"Yeah. I'll keep it out on the balcony, though, if the smell bothers you."

"No, don't do that. As a matter of fact, I'm feeling a little appetite coming back. Funny, isn't it?"

Funny as a crutch. Oh no, don't buy me anything, I couldn't possibly think of eating.

"I think there's enough for both of us. I'm not all that hungry anyway." He had brought up what was left of the Rock Island Select. I can always live on beer.

"Thank you, sweetheart." She blew him a kiss from the tub.

He took off his shoes and socks, dropped his cut-off jeans and underpants, and lay back down on his bed with a can of beer. He propped his head up on a pillow folded in two. He drank several mouthfuls, then set down the can. He ran a hand up and down his chest and stomach, fingered his sore balls. He could feel his dried sweat, his own grit.

"Where's the food?"

Audrey had come back in, a tiny thing wrapped in one towel, her hair wrapped up in another.

"Here. You can eat me." He waved it at her.

"Don't be disgusting. And put something on. You left the curtains open."

"Then I'll close the curtains. You're not supposed to mind." He got up and pulled the cord.

Audrey sat on her bed and started brushing out her wet hair. Looking at his back, rawboned and furry, she remembered the blond boy who had sat opposite her at lunch; Dennis in Chicago, scarcely fifteen. Mark Robinson. There were lines of loose skin on Timmy's elbows and buttocks she hadn't noticed before. His long arms looked red and dry in the afternoon sun. He *was* getting old.

"Here." He handed her a paper bag with grease spots. "Four Big Macs and four bags of chips. Take whatever you want."

"You planned to eat all that yourself?" She started sniffing into the bag. "I wish you had bought something decent to eat. For heaven's sake, Timmy, you know what I've been through." She began to peer daintily inside each wrapped bun.

"Listen. You *said* don't get you anything. You *said* you couldn't stand the idea of food. You specifically told me . . ."

"Well, you must have known I'd need something to eat eventually. And please put on some clothes. Did you get me something to drink?"

"Yeah. That Calso." He pulled back on his underpants.

"I mean like a shake or something."

He looked at her hard, underlining his unspoken meaning. She looked right back.

"I suppose this will do." She unwrapped a Big Mac, pulled out the pickle, scraped off the relish with a plastic knife. It was gone in about a minute. "Do you mind if I have two?"

"No. Take whatever you want."

How can he buy such junk? She started on one greasy bag of fries, pale yellow things like wet cigarettes.

"I'm sorry about my stomach earlier. It must not be very nice for you."

"Worse for you. Sorry I couldn't be more help."

"I never usually get carsick or anything."

"Today was rough."

She lit a cigarette, and switched on the television. A soppy soap opera: just what she needed. "Aren't you going for a swim?"

"Nah. Dinky little pool. Water looks putrid."

"It'll make you feel better."

"I'm okay."

Actually, she wanted the place to herself for a while, and hoped she could persuade him to leave. Now that she felt clean, healthy, and at least moderately cool, he depressed her by looking so filthy and hot, filling up the space with his acrid maleness. She was beginning to feel a little of her pampered, pre-married self, soft and pink and girlish, ready for mindless television and clean sheets and a mother's cool hand on her forehead. There *he* lay, boorish and uncommunicative, like a selfish old log. For all her faults, Mother knew how to take care of people who weren't well.

"What's that you're watching?"

"Oh, nothing. I just wanted to get my mind on something besides the heat."

He sat up and looked at the screen.

"You've got to be kidding! You don't mean to tell me you can watch that junk? That'd make anyone sick to their stomach."

"If you don't like it, don't watch."

"Kind of hard in the same room."

"Then take a shower or something. You must be filthy. I can smell you from here."

They finished the Big Macs and fries, then watched a little television neither really enjoyed, nursing private wounds while pretending they weren't. At eleven o'clock, Audrey fell asleep, and started snoring in a high-pitched, uneven female snore. She was curled up like a baby, naked under a sheet.

It was Timmy, healthy-as-a-horse Timmy, who was unable to get to sleep. He blamed everything he could think of: Audrey's snoring, his twitching leg muscles, the neighbors' television, bug noises, traffic noises, Northwestern Bell, and the roads that kept running in his head.

Three A.M. He sat up and looked at her body in the near-dark. Any desire he felt was more mental than real. His muscles were still too tired for him to want even imaginary sex. But he had to admit she looked cute, flashing on and off under the red neon. The temptation to peel down the sheet and do something was strong.

It was hard to sort out feelings sometimes. He felt some love, a little lust; aches and pains, fatigue, dislike of the Midwest, bitterness at his lot, envy of her sleep. Beneath these were deeper-lying worries about his head, his car, his age; about how things were going to work out in California.

Hell, maybe I'll just slip in with her now.

110

Nah, she'd just fuss and play sick. Tell me to go away.

Shit. What's the point of being married?

He got up and went out on the balcony. It had rained a bit, but now it had stopped. The glass was stippled with glistening symbols, water drips stopped in their tracks. Raindrops sparkled on the plastic-cord chairs lined up along the balcony. Under each door light hovered a cloud of tiny gnats. He looked at the line of wet car roofs below. The oval pool was empty, the water dark except for one underwater light.

He pulled the door almost shut, walked quickly in his bare feet down the balcony to the outside stairs, then down the stairs to the pool. He glanced around, slid off his shorts, and slipped silently into the water.

The pool was too small for serious lap swimming, so he just coiled around underwater like an eel, easing himself into the element, curving round in ovals and S's. Up for air, he stretched his arms along the coping and looked up at the long balconies, the curtained glass, a few doors still lighted from inside. Nude, wet, alone in the dark water, he felt better. Down again he plunged, his legs a coiled spring that kicked him far. His arms pulled back hard. Four strokes brought him to the other end.

The size of his space was frustrating; he felt a trout thrashing around in a goldfish bowl. But the near-invisibility of it all appealed. He had always liked skinny-dipping under the stars. The day had been full of light, full of heat. It was good to look into deep nothing, to plunge and curve free through dark water. The water relaxed and invigorated, cooled and enlivened, softened and pleased.

He had been foolish not to go for a swim earlier, when Audrey had proposed it. He had been trying to play martyr, then, trying to make *her* feel more uncomfortable by staying uncomfortable himself. It was so dumb.

It was dumb for you to have been so mean, too, closed up in yourself. You're supposed to be the stronger one, aren't you? You may have felt stiff, and tired, but she was really sick. All she wanted was a little sympathy. A little tender loving care. And you wouldn't give it. Fuck it, McCue. What a bastard you can be.

He got out and mounted the board. He poised, strode forward, stopped, raised his arms; took one thudding bounce, then rose and cut the water in a perfect, splashless dive. When he surfaced, he reached for the edge and looked up at the third-floor balcony. Sixth door down; the one open just a crack. As he looked, the crack widened. The curtain parted. Dressed in nothing at all, his bride came out and stood at the rail. He swam to the pool ladder, climbed out, and stood up facing her in the moonlight. She saw him and waved; he waved back. He felt thrilled, shot with shivers, glowing fit to burst. God, I do love her, he thought: I really do.

A room light went on, down near the pool; then another, next to it. A bright spotlight from above lighted up the pool, the pool ladder, him. Timmy dove back in. Audrey disappeared.

14

We have now been three days traveling on the plains. By Captain McClellan's reckoning, we have covered only 28 miles. We shall have to travel much faster than this if we are to reach California before the snows. According to James's interpretation of the guide books, we have over two thousand miles to go—and through heaven knows what sort of terrain. May that same heaven guard and protect us every mile of the way.

Our beginning could not have been more ill-omened. On mounting the steep western bank of the Missouri, the axletree of our lead wagon broke. We all had to stop until it was repaired, in full view of hundreds of other travelers. A quarter of a mile further, we encountered a bluff so steep it appeared to be nearly perpendicular, perhaps 200 feet in height. There was nothing to do but unload the wagons, unhitch, and double team. The drivers shouted and cracked their whips at the poor beasts, while other men blocked and pushed at the wheels to keep them from rolling back.

In the process, another broken axle. It is dispiriting to be halted thus before one is fairly underway. Of course everyone walks at such times. The city-bred among us quickly learned what so much walking means—sore feet and tired legs.

From the top of this bluff we had a fine view of St. Joseph, with the new courthouse crowning the town and the busy river at its feet. To the west, we looked for the first time at the limitless green prairie which is to be our home for many days. If it enlarges the heart with its vastness and verdure, it also causes the soul to recoil in terror of its uncharted freedom, stretching (it would appear) to the ends of the earth. It rolls in green waves like the open sea, enameled with countless wildflowers—pink verbena, wild indigo, larkspur, blue lupine, a kind of sweet william. There are almost no trees. One

112

longs for something solid and upright, to which the eye and the spirit could hold fast.

Having traveled a very few miles, we made camp that first day along with other wagon trains which had undergone difficulties comparable to ours. In so crowded a place, there was no grass left for the stock. For miles opposite the ferrying places, the terrain has been grazed to bare earth by our forerunners. Fortunately, we have corn enough for a few days, and hope to encounter better forage soon.

We are now out of civilization entirely, cut loose from the rest of the world to care for ourselves. Despite the security I feel in James's protection (and the presence of our new friends from Illinois), I must confess to a feeling of loneliness and apprehension at the thought of our prospects. Henceforth, we shall have no settled society, no sympathy in our troubles, none of the comforts to which we have been accustomed. We must work across these vast wastes in our own strength, and in His who takes care of us all. I try to keep my fears to myself; but I have asked James to pray with me at night—a thing that I rarely do, knowing his reluctance.

The second day our misfortunes continued, and indeed increased. Like a warning message from Heaven, a storm broke before we had even left camp. It continued through a day and a night, and made progress difficult. Thunder and lightning terrified the cattle, and not a little myself.

A storm on the plains cannot be compared, I believe, with a similar phenomenon anywhere else. The water pours down in cascades, accompanied by ceaseless peals of thunder and flashes of lightning from a wide and ink-colored sky. Winds sweep all this water with terrific force across the flat land, tearing up tents, pulling wagon covers loose, and soaking everything within. Two wagons were overturned, tumbling their contents. There is nothing for it but to travel on drenched to the skin, trying to keep one's wagon on the trail through mud up to the axles, aware that all one's possessions may be as wet as if they had lain under water.

The second night we lay wide awake in wet garments beneath wet blankets, listening to the constant downpouring and the angry eruptions of the sky, praying that our tent stakes would hold. (We moved into a tent when our wagon cover proved permeable to the rain.)

For all the terror and discomfort, the tempest was sublime, a convincing demonstration of Divine Magnificence. One is put in mind of the deluge in the Bible: the sky so dark, the wind and rain so mighty, thunder shaking the earth. "All the foundations of the great deep were broken up, and the floodgates of heaven were opened." One could not help but be struck by the littleness of man against the mightiness of nature. Our thin line of white tents and wagon tops appeared fragile toys, at the mercy of a giant hand. When at last the sky cleared to admit the sun, the rainbow it created arched over many miles, like God's sign to Noah.

The third day we tried to dry out our wet things on the ground, but had little time to linger. We traveled again mired to the hubs, trying to straddle the deep ruts made by those before us. The trail is impossible to lose at this point, being three to four wagons' breadths across. The soil of the Territory is light black loam, which may be fine for future cultivation; but it turns almost immediately into thick mud after rain. Men's boots are coated with huge balls of the stuff. What the books describe as creeks "narrow and easy to ford" have become so rapid and full that we have had to unload and double-team time and again. One thread of a stream took us four hours to traverse. Trees had to be cut and bushes spread on the muddy bottom before the wagons could be let down by ropes. Even then, many stalled and stuck. We double-teamed up the far bank. Such are the obstacles and discomforts of one's first days on a journey across the plains.

If some of our troubles are the products of the heavens and the earth, others are the result of our own ignorance. A great many amongst us are patently unfit for such an undertaking. Green teamsters deal with ill-yoked oxen. Two mornings we have had to delay while parties went in search of strayed livestock. Some of the bacon we bought cheaply in St. Joseph has had to be scraped and smoked free of insects! Goods are clumsily packed in overloaded and oversized wagons. In three days we have passed 20 or 30 outfits already broken down. The grander and better-provisioned the wagon, it would seem, the less able it is to deal with the mud and ruts, the steep banks and bluffs. Proud equipages lie like dying elephants. Many parties are dumping piles of surplus, iron cookstoves, brass kettles, furniture, mining tools, even food. Doubtless they will wish a few weeks or months hence they had kept it all. The waste is sinful: but what is there to do? We commiserate, and drive on, making scant yards through the mud every hour. California seems so far away.

Yesterday, our first Sunday on the trail, was by grudging consent allowed a day of rest. A few of us gathered early for divine service. All put the day to good use by washing, mending, and overhauling gear. But many of the men seemed to chafe under the necessity of losing place to the teams that rolled past us, as if the Lord's Day were not to be honored according to His command in the open country as well as in a church. I cannot but think we will get better service out of our oxen by allowing them, too, this weekly respite. It is both good sense and good religion. But I know not how long this practice will prevail.

At the Namaha River
May 17, 1849

Although another sudden storm, with heavy hailstones, continued to impede us, we have begun to make consistent and regular progress: 15 to 20 miles a day. We are now overtaking perhaps 50 wagons each day—but twice that number overtake us, which causes some anxiety. The fear is less that the gold will be gone before we get to California, as that the grass along the way will be, which is a concern much more pressing than yellow metal.

At our noon and evening stops, there is much visiting among the men of companies camped near to one another, to compare distances traveled and difficulties endured. The great decision, James informs me, is whether to hurry on one's animals in order to escape the crowding, reach good grass, and avoid the early snows; or to drive tham at a gentler pace, in order to avoid overtiring them and running them to death. One cannot easily adjudge the relative merits of having one's team dead from starvation, or dead from exhaustion, in the midst of the American desert.

Those who favor mules argue hotly with the partisans of oxen. The more expensive mules, it is obvious, travel faster. But I believe our plodding, patient beasts, like the tortoise in the fable, will prove in the end the more dependable.

We are not lonely for company. To the eye of heaven, we must seem an extraordinary procession, hundreds of white-tops stretching for miles across a flat and barren land, accompanied by a veritable exodus of teamsters, outriders, cattle, horses, and pedestrians like myself. (I find it more satisfying, most days, to walk than to ride. Mrs. Garner thought it unseemly, but no objection was made by the men.) "An army on the march," the captain calls us—an Army of Gold.

In the midst of daily exertions and chores, I feel quite sharply the ludicrousness of my own position. Torn from home and town, from my family and friends, I am one of a great swarm of people walking alongside wagons across an immense and barren continent. And why are we doing this? Because we have been led by the newspapers to believe that there is gold to be discovered on the far distant shore. Surely this is a fairy tale adventure from some other time.

After six days on the march, we have come near enough to a routine that it may be described. The camp is wakened by a bugle call before dawn, and the stock are let out to graze. One person in each wagon-group, or "mess," of six is designated as cook. In our group, naturally, this duty falls to me. I prepare breakfast, in the heavy morning dews, over a fire made in the shelter of two wagons. Like almost every meal in camp, it consists of fried bacon, fried bread, and coffee, although I am able to vary the evening meal somewhat from my store of dried fruit and wild plum and crabapple preserves. Game, on which we had depended, has so far eluded us, except for a couple of marsh hens and one boiled raccoon roasted on a stick, a dish I cannot in Christian candor recommend. We are promised abundant quantities of buffalo meat once we reach the Platte. This terrain yields scrawny pea-vines, chokecherries, and a bitter "prairie onion" about the size of a hickory nut, which I am pickling against the scurvy later on.

By six A.M., the call to "Catch up" is sounded, and the daily struggle to persuade the oxen back into harness begins, to the incessant crack of whips, the "Gee ups!" and "Whoa haws!" of the men. The driver and his assistant have the duty of yoking the cattle. Another man's task may be to pack the wagon, set up tents, gather wood, and so on. Others may share night guard. But the duties vary.

By seven o'clock, we are ready to move on. The captain shouts "Roll out!" The cry is echoed through the camp. One by one the wagons leave the circle to fall into their assigned place in the order of march. Our slow, mile-long parade rejoins the great march.

At noon, we pause to rest ourselves and our stock from the worst heat of the day, and eat whatever fare we have prepared in the morning. We stop near

115

trees, if any are to be found, in or under the wagons if not. At two o'clock, we move on again, and usually make camp about five or six o'clock, depending on our proximity to grass, wood, and water. At times, we must drive somewhat longer. Captain McClellan and one of his two "lieutenants" ride ahead each day in search of likely places for nooning, and for evening camp. The other lieutenant—the jobs vary by turns—leads a party of men each day in search of game. Last night, our hunting party lost its way, spent a dreary night in the open without food or shelter, and only found us as we were leaving camp this morning. There is grass now for the cattle, thanks in part to the rains. But sufficient wood for fires is becoming hard to find. So far, thank the Lord, we have always been able to stop near good water.

The camp is formed, by prairie custom, of a "corral," which makes in this wild country a novel and splendid sight. To form this affair all thirty wagons are pulled up, wheel against wheel in the form of a circle, with the tongues pointing out. The oxen are then loosed inside the circle, to prevent their straying or being stolen by night. Tents are set up and horses staked outside. A search is made for fuel, and dinner prepared. Members of the company visit back and forth in our rustic, white-roofed village, and among others nearby. There may be music and singing. But as we must rise early, and as the days are so wearying, we tend to retire soon after supper.

We hear many reports of Indians, but have so far seen none. It is said that the Pawnees, through whose hunting grounds we are passing, are reduced to a starving lot of horse thieves, harrassed by stronger tribes from the east, and wasted by white men's diseases. The main thing they are said to beg for (in addition to food) is whisky. James thinks it is a national crime that such prime agricultural land should be wasted on ignorant and nomadic barbarians. I, on the other hand, feel that we are the intruders, and wonder how long we shall be allowed to travel their country and kill their game unmolested.

Rumors abound of the predatory tribes farther west. One band of disgruntled emigrants, returning with four wagons to the States, affirmed that they had been attacked by a war party of five hundred wild Cheyennes, who robbed them not only of their food but also of their cattle and horses. James thinks they are lying, blaming imaginary Indians for their own weak spirits and poor preparations. Whether or not he is right, many of the men have set to cleaning and loading their rifles in preparation for an attack. I look forward with some dread to our first encounter with these children of nature.

Somewhere in Indian Territory
May 19, 1849

Since first we crossed the Missouri, we have passed hundreds of rude graves. These are the last resting places of fellow gold-seekers, who have succumbed to the pestilence which reaches its fell hand out from the settlements to seize the weak and unwary. Until today, our company had passed unscathed, and we regarded ourselves as blessed.

Late yesterday afternoon, Abner Frizzel, a handsome young man of our own mess, began to complain of pain and sickness. He was obliged to lie down in the wagon, behind my leather seat. Soon he was convulsed by spasms. I ministered to him as best I could, recalling my sad experience with Emma Cluett's children at St. Jo. The captain was called. He examined young Abner, and ordered the train to a halt. Medicine was administered from the company stock, and a man rode ahead for a doctor we knew to be traveling with a company that had passed us earlier in the day. He returned within the hour, and confirmed our worst fears: it was the Asiatic cholera. Everything that could be done was done, but nothing availed, and in two or three hours the poor boy expired. He died with heroic fortitude, crying out not once against the pain. He made a plea for Christian burial. He held my hand at the end, and made me promise to write his last words of love to his mother in Illinois.

While young Abner's body was laid out on a rude bier alongside, the company fell to work disinfecting our wagon and all that it contained, in fear that the contagion would spread to us, and from us to others. We were offered the use of a spare tent while the process of disinfection went on. That night, the sheet that was stretched over the body flapped in the wind, with a sound like that of some ghostly creature trying to burst its earthly bonds. The white fluttering of the cloth, dimly seen between two fires, confirmed this horrible phantasy. His death-dirge was howled through the night by savage wolves and one mournful owl.

This morning, the body was dressed in clean clothes and sewn in its blanket, for lack of wood to construct a coffin, and buried thus in the fresh-dug sod. The whole company marched in procession behind the body, borne aloft by four men. Then they stood at the graveside as the captain read prayers and delivered a short address. Next came the work of cleansing our wagon, washing bedclothes, and thoroughly sunning and airing all our things. Fortunately, the sun shone early today.

A deep gloom has settled over our company. Everyone is fearful of another attack. Many who had been stricken with diarrhoea—the result of our tedious and limited diet, or the poor water along the trail—now interpret it as a first sign of the approaching disease. Our own wagon party is regarded as tainted. People, heretofore friendly, keep their distance.

Cholera or no, this journey is certainly no undertaking for the unfit. We have passed whole days in the open under torrents of rain. Other days we are baked by the sun. And *each* day one must be prepared to walk on foot 15 or 20 miles, over whatever terrain the trail affords. Men stand knee-deep, even waist-deep in rushing water for hours, shouting at the swimming cattle, trying to keep wagons upright. Then they must hurry along, shivering with the ague, without a moment's pause. Crossing the Little Vermillion, we saw one man (not of our company) swept to his death in the current.

Some weaken and grow sick. Some turn back. We are meeting more and more wagons accompanied by folks who have given it all up as a sorry job, and are returning to the States. They talk with bitterness of the trials that lie before us, and insist that theirs is the choice of wisdom.

Many die, and leave their remains to wolves and other scavengers. For all, the perpetual vexations and hardships are well-calculated to maintain the nerves in a state of great irritability. An attitude of Christian charity is becoming difficult to maintain.

But others tested by the trail seem to harden and grow. Already I feel stronger and more fit from my daily march and chores, and from living in such intimacy with nature. The inspiration for this emigration may have been nothing more than greed. But I believe that the ordeal will end in making better men and women out of those who survive it, men and women for whom comfort and convenience, let alone luxury, will have diminished in importance before values more enduring. The Lord turns all things to His proper ends.

On the banks of the Big Blue
May 23, 1849

We are now approaching one of the major crossroads of the trail, where the wagon road from Independence joins up with ours. It is impossible to put into words the image of bustle and activity that surrounds us, the whoops and hollers of the drivers, as hundreds of wagons gather together in advance of the river crossing. At our fording place, the river is very rapid and steeply banked, perhaps 50 yards across, gravel bedded, no more than a yard deep. Morning and evening mosquitoes have become a veritable plague out of Egypt.

I do not know that our company is meeting the test of this journey as well as I had hoped. Last night was held a second "democratic" gathering of all male participants. It went on, increasing in noise and acrimony, until very late in the night. It is remarkable the degree to which a petty will to self-rule can demonstrate itself under adverse circumstances, and frustrate the most salutary interests of the group. Some men complain about night guard duty, protesting that since we have seen no Indians the practice should be abandoned. James—who spent two extra nights on duty when others shirked—is outraged at this nonsense. Others want only to cast insults and spread blame, attributing to everyone but themselves the faults of our lost stock, or poor hunting, or lack of sufficient progress. This our slow pace, and the fear of contagious disease, prompt others to propose that the group split into smaller units. There are bitter disputes over the ownership of wagons and stock.

But the rebels seem to rankle most at the very necessity of order and discipline, unused as these "free Americans" are to accepting such a yoke. There is talk among them of trying to vote out Captain McClellan and put one of their own number in charge. James would gladly oppose them, but he feels too keenly his position as an outsider, an indigent, a late-comer, and a foreigner to take sides actively.

A major dispute arose, as I anticipated, over the question of Lord's Day rests. The impious and impetuous have carried the day. From now on we are to hurry through the week like any heathens, in total disdain of the Third Commandment, and may keep the day holy only in our hearts.

I cannot believe that intelligent men would act with such mean-spirited factionalism at home. We have crossed beyond the frontiers of civilized society, and the rule now seems to be, Every man for himself.

The land alone is test enough of one's spirit. The sense of grandeur and sublimity I once felt at the illimitable prairie has long since declined into wearisome fatigue. One would pay dearly for the sight of a tree, even a shrub, even a *rock* on some days; for any object that would break the sterile monotony of this landscape. We must perforce make our fires now of an oily, stinking stuff called rosin weed, which fortunately burns quite easily. The very flatness of the land seems to weigh upon the soul. Earth and sky blend into one seamless expanse, which creates an appalling loneliness within. What mild undulations occur only heighten the sense that one is lost on a barren sea, swayed to a kind of seasickness with the rocking wagons. An old trader we encountered swears that no part of the road ahead is as tedious as this journey to the Platte.

Except when there is a breeze, we are now subject to intolerable heat. Not a cloud appears in the vastness of sky. The drive to Turkey Creek was 22 miles without water. Along the way, men drank the contents of stagnant green puddles. Arriving at the creek, they plunged into the current to drink deep draughts, cool roasting flesh, and to purify limbs and faces of the dust accumulated during the march. Some of the oxen, mad with thirst and heat, tore down the steep bank before they could be unhitched, doing considerable damage to the wagons they dragged behind. Once in the stream, they refused to leave.

We women must be content to refresh ourselves as best we can with buckets of water fetched back to the wagons. Yesterday we rode jolting down innumerable deep gullies and over innumerable high rocks, shaking bones and biscuits to powder. According to the reports of both Frémont and Bryant, there is another dry march of 25 miles before we reach the Platte.

15

A lot of cross-country drivers hate Nebraska. They feel the same way about North Dakota, South Dakota, Oklahoma, and Texas—all those states halfway across the country that never seem to end. But they hate Nebraska most.

Part of the reason is the change that comes over America midway through the state. If you're heading east, whatever is distinctly "western" about the West seems to end around the 100th meridian. You may not be fond of mountain roads, or of long desert drives. But to most travelers they're more appealing than straight lines between flat farms.

If you're heading west, on the other hand, by the time you reach Omaha you've already had one full day of flatland driving. When you start up next morning and realize that you're in for another 400-plus miles of the same hog, hay, corn, and cattle country, the hate-Nebraska mood can settle in good.

It's not that Nebraskans don't try. They work very hard to divert the hustlers-through. There's plenty more to Nebraska, they point out, than the dreary S-curve of the Platte River road. (Perfect name, Platte.) At the roadside rests along Interstate 80, they've now got abstract metal sculptures, wheelchair-accessible toilets, and forty thousand signposts to tell you about the Emigrant Trails. In the summer months, they hire cheerful Nebraska vacation guides, who sit behind counters at the rest areas and try to entice you up to off-the-pike attractions like Boys' Town U.S.A., or Willa Cather's Birthplace, or authentic ruts made by the wheels of covered wagons. When they bulldozed out billions of cubic feet of dirt for the new freeway, they made a point of leaving the holes between Grand Island and North Platte, filling them up with water, and calling them the "Chain of Lakes."

You would think all these attractions would oblige people to pause. But Americans in cars, going from point A to point Z, can be very cruel in their

120

contempt for points B, C, D, E, F, etc., in between. Nebraska is for getting through.

But Timothy McCue was a sentimental, old-fashioned kind of westerner, who had driven across the country six times. In the process, he had developed a special affection (west-going, in any case) for the states of the 100th meridian. At Council Bluffs, on the Missouri River, he knew that he still had two full days to go before he would reach the Continental Divide. But he also knew that halfway across any one of these 100th meridian-straddling states, and Nebraska in particular, the landscape was going to start looking and feeling like what he thought of as home.

He also liked to drive.He always worked out his problems best with one foot on a gas pedal and one arm out a car window. But today, for some reason, it wasn't working.

He looked over at Audrey, profiled against the window, eyelids shut, hair blowing in the wind, lost in the easy harmonies of Creedence Clearwater Revival. (It was her turn to pick the stations.) Throat, shoulders, bare tender arms, sweet swelling tits, soft tummy, the curve of her shorts, those flawless brown legs. Nothing wrong there.

Last night, in fact, had ended very nicely. He first had to get through a nasty scene with the motel manager's wife, who had come out from the apartment with the lighted windows and stood over the edge of the pool in her bathrobe and curlers until he had to come up for air. When she discovered that he had nothing on, she called him a drunken pervert, and threatened to phone the police. After he convinced her that he was a paying guest, and not drunk, and that those were his shorts by her feet, she allowed him to put them back on under water and go back to his room; but only after delivering a tirade about the laws of the state of Iowa, and Holiday Inn's rules, and common decency, and never in all her born days, which drew a lot of folks out to their balconies to listen and watch. By now all of Iowa had decided he was some kind of degenerate. Audrey followed the whole scene silently from her window, and enjoyed every minute. Seconds later (her tummy was all better!), she welcomed him back with giggles and affection.

"Where are you going? Is something wrong?"
He had braked abruptly.
"I just figured it out." He was turning off on an exit to nowhere in particular.
"What?" she demanded. "Is it the car?"
"No. It's this road."
"What are you talking about?"
"I've been trying to figure out what was wrong. Why I wasn't enjoying driving. I usually love driving.
"It's not my hand. It's not my head. It isn't the car. What I've been fighting all this time is that goddamn Interstate. I just figured it out. It was like sitting on a fucking conveyor belt. I felt like I was going nuts."

"But what will you do instead? I mean, where will you go?"

"Same place. But on a normal road. One of the roads people *used* to drive on, before they built that monstrosity. There must be a decent old-fashioned east-west highway somewhere around here."

"But you don't know for sure? I mean, can you just drive off at the first turn and expect to find another road?"

"Last time I crossed Nebraska, I took Highway 26 down from Wyoming, then 30 all the way along the Platte. They hadn't finished much of the Interstate then. When we get to the next town, I'll try to find the quickest way back to 30."

The next town was Seward, the county seat, population 4,208. At the one arterial stop, a road sign pointed left: Grand Island, via U.S. 34.

"That's it! We can cross the river at Grand Island, and pick up Highway 30 there."

Over coffee—since Chicago, he had become more flexible about things like coffee stops, and Top 40 stations—Timmy unfolded a map of Nebraska on the table.

"I promised you we'd start looking at more things once we got west. Well, today we get west."

"Is Nebraska west?"

"It stays farmland and grass plains for a while yet. But around North Platte things start opening up. Sagebrush, sandhills, giant buttes. It's one big John Wayne movie from then on. You'll like it, babe. Now's where we start slowing down to look around."

"Look at what, like?"

"Lots of things. This blue line is the Platte River, the old emigrant road to California and Oregon. We'll stay on 34 to Grand Island, then follow 30 to North Platte and Ogallala." He outlined the route with the same red pen.

"Then what?"

"Then I'm not sure. I've got some old friends in Casper I thought we might visit. That's up this road here, a little ways into Wyoming. There's my Indian buddy in Wind River. Then I'd like you to see the Grand Tetons."

(He had actually worked it out long ago. It was his secret plan to make a city-bred girl from Dedham, Massachusetts, fall in love with the West. He didn't see how it could fail.)

"For today, I thought, we could stop and look at a few places along the way. We'll be going past Fort Kearney, here. There's a pioneer village next to it." He was looking for Point-of-Interest stars along their route. "Here's a Pony Express Station. Buffalo Bill's Ranch. Ogallala. Ash Hollow. We'll just play it as it goes, okay? Depending on the time. What do you say?"

"I don't know." He was trying to be nice, she could tell, make the trip more interesting for her sake. The least she could do was sound agreeable. "It's up to you."

"Don't you want to?"

"Sure. It can't be any worse than Iowa, can it?"

She meant it as a joke, but it came out more like criticism—as if he were personally responsible for everything west of the Berkshires. He looked disappointed.

"I'm sorry, Timmy. I guess I liked the idea of our moving more quickly from here on. I was getting excited about finding out where we'd be living, about meeting your parents and all. I didn't know you wanted to do all this touring."

"It's not all that much, honey. I mean, it's on our way anyway. You might never get another chance to see some of these places."

"I'm not all that sure I want to. Who are these people in Wyoming?"

"Gerry Gleason. He's an old Air Force buddy. We worked in California together, too. He and his wife have a bunch of kids. I haven't seen him for four years."

Why would anybody want to stop off and see an old Air Force buddy on his honeymoon trip? she wondered. Shouldn't your wife be company enough? The idea irked her.

"And this Indian?"

"Paul Denio. I met him climbing in the Wind River Mountains, about fifteen years ago. He lives on the Shoshone reservation, not far from the Gleasons. You'll like them."

"I'm sure."

He looked over at her with an uncertain smile, and risked another proposal.

"I thought tonight might be a good time for us to start camping out."

"Oh. I forgot we were going to do that."

"Once you get out here, it's really the best thing to do. It's a lot more fun than motels." He smiled and squeezed her leg. "I'll make a frontier bride out of you yet!" She moved his hand away. No more tub baths, that means; no nice mattresses. No restaurant meals. No flush toilets, probably. Bugs. Dust. Snakes, even. Air force buddies and Indians and freezing cold nights sleeping on the ground. Oh, this will be just *great*.

"It sounds wonderful." She grasped his other hand, the hand that held the pen.

It had stopped, like a Ouija board pointer, at Casper, Wyoming. "Like a real honeymoon."

"It will be. I promise."

Basically, eastern Nebraska along U.S. 34 doesn't look all that much different from western Iowa along Interstate 80. But Audrey took his point. You did see more, driving on an old-fashioned highway; you felt closer to the townsmen and farmers. Fences were built just a few feet from the narrow road-shoulders, so you could see what was going on as you passed. People even waved at you from their porches and tractors. Roads ran straight as a yardstick, still, but they kept making unexpected pairs of 90-degree turns to jog around the corner of someone's farm. This slowed you down, of course; but Audrey liked the idea that farms could tell roads where to go, instead of vice versa. There was far less traffic here. What there was went more slowly.

Birds became visible. A great wheeling flight of blackbirds rose out of a field. A single red-tail prairie hawk soared on sail-like wings, for the sheer drunken pleasure of floating in the sky. You could distinguish the different kinds of trees. Without realizing it, Audrey had begun to thirst for billboards along the toll roads and the Interstate, where they were decorously forbidden. Now they were back in force, telling them in large letters and bright colors about new cars and old whiskeys, about the mortuaries and motels of Grand Island. Small hand-painted posters promoted a Buick dealer in York, the number one feed and grain merchant in Aurora. Tourist attractions—Minden Pioneer Village, Old Ogallala—kept selling themselves on little placards, all across the state.

Every five or ten miles the small towns promised by the signposts would materialize, as the highway sort of meandered down into Main Street. Tamora, Utica, Waco, jog left, jog right, Bradshaw, zig, zag, Hampton, Aurora. Timmy had planned a picnic lunch somewhere on Grand Island, but as they were crossing the bridge, the car's engine began to misfire in a disconcerting way. So they had BLTs and shakes next door to the Lincoln-Mercury dealer's on East 2nd, while a young mechanic started probing the car's insides.

After lunch, Timmy went in to see how things were going. First he got back inside the car, and kept turning the engine on and off while the boy tightened this thing and disconnected that. Then the two of them leaned under the raised hood, fiddling and poking, contemplating the engine together. While they were eating lunch, the boy had done the better part of a tune-up, but he was still troubled by a number of things. The plugs were not simply burned or worn (which would have been O.K.), but oil-fouled, which suggested either pump problems or engine wear. Compression was a little low in two cylinders, and valve clearances were off, which might account for some of the noise and misfiring. The kid wondered whether something in the transmission or differential might be causing that awful noise. Timmy's ear placed it farther forward. The boy reset the valves, replaced a leaking hose. Timmy agreed to a new head gasket, but told him to leave the carburetor alone—carburetors took forever to put back together. He let him take out the oil pump to check it out. Christ, was this going to cost.

If transmission was ruled out, then the rumbling and grinding, as well as the oil drain, pointed to engine wear somewhere—main bearings, rod bearings, maybe even something worse. But taking the engine apart would mean another full day or two in Grand Island, and another couple of hundred dollars at least. He'd rather live with the noise, hope for the best, and keep pouring in oil till California. What the hell.

She left the boys to their game, and went for a walk by herself. Up the street she walked, past the Court House, then down to a small city park. There she stood under a tree and watched mothers and their children. The air was heavy with summer smells. The shade under the tree was very nice. She pretended it was home.

* * *

The kid mechanic came up wiping his hands on a rag and grinning at Audrey.

"How do, Miss. How'd you like Grand Island, then?"

"Oh, it was fascinating." She meant it to be ironic, but pricked by his wide country-boy smile, her irony leaked out like air.

"I mean, really. It's very nice." She quickly looked him up and down. Blue overalls hid everything but his head, his shoulders, and his arms. Grease and all, he was kind of cute.

"People here seem very nice."

"You bet your life they are. Couldn't pay me to live anywhere but Nebraska. You folks headin' right out?"

"I think so." Timmy had gone back to listen to the engine.

"That's too bad. You ought to spend a day here, at least. See the museum, picnic along the river. It's a great place, Grand Island."

"Were you born here?"

"Oh, no, Miss. My family's from Holt County. That's cattle country, up north. I came down to the city for school. Central Nebraska Tech. One of my teachers there got me this job for the summer."

"You like cars?"

"A lot. I like cows better, but I like cars. Your dad knows a lot about cars."

"My dad?"

He nodded in Timmy's direction.

"Oh. Yes. Yes, he does. Did he tell you he smashed this one up in Chicago?"

"He told me a colored boy ran into you."

Blue as a prairie sky were his eyes. He kept trying to smooth down his white-blond hair, daubing at his makeup of grease stains with the rag. It was as if he were trying to clean up for her benefit, embarrassed by her charm.

"Sounds okay," said Timmy, coming up. "Sounds better, at least."

"I think it'll hold, sir."

"I hope so."

Timmy went to the cashier's window to settle up, then to the men's room to scrub his own blackened hands. Audrey and the boy exchanged a last smile.

West 2nd in Grand Island runs straight into the old Platte River Road. Soon they were back on course, following the same route the Mormon pioneers took in 1847.

The sky to the northwest horizon was beginning to show a black edge as they drove into the Fort Kearney parking lot. Audrey tried to rise to the occasion, but it wasn't much to rise to. In the Visitors' Center, glass cases full of artifacts and a continuous slide show tried to explain the fort's romantic past.

But there was nothing left of it now, not a stone upon a stone. A forty-acre square of dry grass south of the river had been marked out by plaques and rustic signboards, to let the blank-eyed tourists know where things used to be. Audrey dutifully followed Timmy around. He read the signs for her and tried to force the past back to life, without success. Kids ran around inside the new stockade fence, playing cowboys and Indians, while their mothers and fathers rested at picnic tables. Inside a facsimile of a sod-roofed blacksmith's shop, families stared at old tools without interest or understanding. Then they went outside and took one another's pictures alongside a covered wagon built in 1952.

"So this is the West."

"There's lots more to come."

"Great."

"Better than this, I mean."

"I sure hope so."

"Oh, don't be such a piss!"

She turned on the picnic bench and looked angrily away. Sipping lukewarm Pepsi, they watched people popping in and out of the mock-historic log cabin. Quaintsville, Nebraska. The inky clouds were hovering closer, covering the declining sun. The tourists moved quickly through their rounds.

"You're not still thinking of camping?"

"Sure. Why not?"

"It's going to rain, for one thing. I don't know where you were thinking of taking us, but it's already after five."

"I know what time it is. There are four state park campgrounds between here and North Platte. I looked them up. We'll pick up some groceries in the next town, then start checking out the camps as we go along. Anyway, those clouds are moving away."

"They're not clouds anymore, Timmy. They're the whole sky. When that line moves on, everything turns black. I tell you, it's going to rain."

"Even if it does, we've got a tent. It's fun sleeping in a tent in the rain. Come on, Audrey. You'll never camp out if you're going to worry about every cloud."

"I don't ever want to camp out."

"Well, I do."

Oh, I see. No discussion, no debate. Man the dictator, woman the stifled subject. The Niagara Falls turnoff all over again.

As they walked back to the car, she detached her hand from his. When they got to the next grungy little town, she let him do the shopping. "You go ahead. You know better than I do what you want to cook. I'll wait in the car." That way she could sulk to her heart's content, play *her* radio station, and say what she was thinking out loud.

By the time they reached the first state park on his list, it was already dark. Large drops were bursting on the glass. Timmy refused to turn on the wipers: that way he could pretend the drops weren't really there. He drove up a twisting gravel road into the park, staring fixedly through the rivulets of water.

* * *

126

"Sorry, buddy. All full up."

"You're kidding. In this weather?"

"Bible School outing from Cozad. They book the whole place every year."

"How far to the next campground?"

"You could try Gallagher Canyon, about thirty miles on. Back the road you came, right on 23, right on 21. But the Bible people usually fill up that one, too."

"Fuck 'em. How about after that?"

"Next one's quite a ways. That'd be Lake Maloney, just south of North Platte. Nice fishin' lake there. No showers or shelters, though. We got nice showers here. Nice cabins, too. But we're full up."

"I don't suppose you could squeeze two more in—for a slight extra fee?"

The ranger stared at him as if he had made an indecent proposal.

"If you're tryin' for Maloney, quickest way now'd be to head on up to the Interstate to North Platte." The sky cracked a bass roll. " 'Specially with this storm comin'."

"How far's that?"

"Oh, 'bout sixty-five, seventy miles. 'Nother hour's drive, little more. Take you least two hours back country."

So back they were on I-80, steering into the wake of cars ahead, windshield wipers going bravely. For a full hour, as rain poured and thunder cracked, they argued about setting up camp.

"What the hell's a little rain?" he asked, raising his voice above the downpour. He tried to make out tail-lights and lane markers through the waterfall before his eyes, the oily spray sent up by the rear tires of other trucks and cars. After one close crack of thunder, a sheet of white lightning lit up the rolling plain.

"Please, Timmy. I don't like this, I really mean it."

He was growing slightly less enthusiastic himself. His left wiper got caught in a blast and blew up off the glass. Now he couldn't see out his half of the windshield.

On he drove, guessing at the road. The engine sped up and slowed down, ignoring his attempts to control it by gearshift or pedal. It was as if it were choking on the rain. He tried to steer by the red halos that formed around other cars' tail-lights in the mists of water before him. It was like driving under water. The most he could do was 30 miles an hour. 25. 20.

"Shouldn't you stop and fix it? I can't see a thing out your side."

"Neither can I. You want to get out and do it?"

"No. But I will if you won't."

He started to pull over onto where the shoulder should have been, when a diesel truck blasted its air horn and ploughed through a pond on his left. Veering back on hydroplaning tires, he oversteered and nearly hit another honking blur.

127

"I'm *not* going to stop. I can see well enough, goddamn it. We must be almost somewhere." He flicked the wiper switch on and off in frustration. At last the left blade dropped down and began working again, scraping clear its arc of glass, losing it to the rain, scraping it clear, losing it, over and over, one thin rubber blade doing battle against a sea. Through a momentarily cleared wedge, white letters appeared out of the dark.

NORTH PLATTE.
EXIT. 2 MILES.

"See? See? I was right. We'll go off here."
"And . . . ?"
"And find somewhere with a roof."
Relieved, she touched his knee, rubbed it gently, reached her hand inside his thigh. "Thank you, Timmy. I'm sorry I was such a baby."
"Nah, you were right. It'd be dumb trying to set up camp in this mess, this late in the day. I'm sorry I get so pig-headed."
I'm sorry.
No, *I'm* sorry.
The secret passwords of marriage.
"Maybe tomorrow, though."
"You bet."

16

I have begun keeping a record of the graves that we pass. I cannot explain
the morbid impulse that leads me to do this. These poor men, women, and
children are beyond any help I can offer. I am unlikely ever to be able to
inform their families of the places where their remains have been laid.

But there is so little other occupation or diversion to animate the days. The
men escape by going off hunting. Each day they ride farther and farther from
the trail, in larger and larger bands. Often they are gone from sunrise to
sunset. They are not so much anxious for game, I believe, or the sport of the
chase, as they are impatient with the slow pace of our wagons, and the
maddening sameness of our days.

But I have not their opportunity. So I count the grave markers, and copy in
my book the penciled or carven inscriptions, most of which are already
wearing away.

No tended graveyard with its chiseled stones could impress one with the
fact of mortality as do these sad little crosses and boards. A few days or weeks
ago, the bearers of these names were fresh and eager travelers like ourselves.
Now the flesh decays upon their bones, laid where buzzards or wolves may
claw them up and devour it. Of course, the souls of the just rest in the bosom
of Jesus. But the presence of these fresh-dug mounds, all along our trail,
forces my thoughts more upon death than resurrection.

How can I keep telling myself that God will protect us, when He has not
protected these? Surely they were no more wicked, more weak of faith, more
undeserving than we are.

129

We are only an army of the greedy led on by the Prince of Darkness, marching blindly at his beck into the Valley of the Shadow of Death.

The bottom of the Big Blue, which we are following, is sterile and parched. Its water is marshy and unfit to drink. Trees are still very scarce.

Our brave hunters left today in a great gallop and halloo after a herd of antelope grazing near our camp. This is a peculiarly pretty little animal, stub-horned and shaped rather like a goat, with small and sinewy limbs, and a coarse coat of light chestnut stippled with white. Beneath the tail they sport a small oval-shaped patch of white hair. As soon as they discerned the band of hunters, they fled like the wind, first pulling all four legs together, then thrusting them fore and aft in order to leap with great bounds, as if in flight. Never have I seen an animal that could run with such ease, speed, and grace. They skim over the ground with bounding and buoyant strides. Would that we could do likewise.

Needless to say, our nimrods caught nary a one, but seemed to enjoy the chase nevertheless. They did return to camp at evening with two fat deer, however, and several wild turkey, so our supper was at least varied from salt pork.

It is extraordinary what black savages the men of our party begin to appear. Their hair and whiskers grow wild, their faces and arms are sunburnt and covered with the dirt of the trail. They seem to vie with one another in the carelessness of their attire. Ragged shirts are left unchanged and unwashed. Hats assume grotesque shapes. All, even professional men and merchants, seem determined to cast off their respectable selves, every aspect of their civilized nature, and descend to a common type scarce to be distinguished from the wild mountain men and traders we encounter. Among these latter are men who have lived far from the States for years. Some have taken on Indian wives and ways.

We continue to hear rumors of Indians, but see none. We were assured by a passing Army company that famine and wars among the tribes will keep the Indians far off our trail. But with almost every returning wagon come reports of fearsome atrocities. One man spoke of being held prisoner by the Sioux for five days before he made his escape. Another reported that two of his company were killed, and 16 wagons burned by Indians. We hear of horses and cattle stolen or shot.

Some men of our company, excited to frenzy by these doubtful reports, vow to put a rifle ball through the first Indian they see. They insist that Uncle Sam must exterminate the entire race of red men in order to make this land safe for Christian civilization.

James, I am sorry to say, defends this position. He regards the Indians as lesser beings than us, creatures of a perverse and vicious nature whose innate tendency is towards rapine and slaughter.

I cannot agree, but like not to dispute in such matters, which, as they are in large part political, are properly the province of men.

* * *

We have endured two more days of the most atrocious storms. Truly the elements conspire against us. Tents have been blown down, pots, pans, bedding, and clothing strewn about the prairie by gales. Men and animals were pelted for an hour this afternoon by hailstones the size of robins' eggs. The teamsters had to pull blankets over their heads.

Last night I was awakened by the sound of a heavy rain upon the wagon cover. I saw a flash of lightning, followed by a strange, rushing sound, which quickly became loud as thunder. The wagon began to shake violently, then to move as if pushed sideways by a great hand. It was lifted and thrown over on its side, us within it. There was a crash of breaking wheels and chains. The rapid tramp of cattle became distinct for a minute, then was lost in the distance.

We picked ourselves up, managed to get out, and found, praise be to God, that no one was hurt. We began to try to account for the catastrophe, and to examine its extent. The cattle must have been frightened by the lightning. Those near the entrance of the corral instinctively tried to escape. Others near pressed upon them. The panic grew, till in their frantic struggles they overturned the two chained wagons. At that moment, the chains must have broken and cleared a passageway for them, or they would have trampled us to death. The only serious calamity was the breaking of three wheels.

The cattle had "stampeded," as they say, and were gone, every one. How could they be got back? Often in such cases, we were told, they ran themselves to death. Even while we thus questioned, some of the men had mounted horses and were gaining upon the swiftest fugitives; others on foot had already succeeded in turning back some of the gentler ones. As for the broken wheels, two families had brought with them wide, hard-wood boards, two or three feet long, which they had used for tables while camping. These were freely contributed to the necessity of the occasion; and, as some of the spokes of the broken wheels were still whole, as well as parts of the rims, it was soon determined that, even though we were 50 miles from the nearest timber, enough material for repairs was at hand. In a few hours, the lost cattle were recovered. They had plenty of time to rest and feed while James, in his role of company smith, mended the wagons.

Today we met other emigrants wandering in search of cattle lost in the storm. One Ohio company lost 72 head out of 100. Another 9 of 18. Some cattle were found at a distance of 25 miles from their camps. Surely no situation can be more deplorable than that of being abandoned on a broad prairie, hundreds of miles from aid, without means of locomotion. For travelers in such a case, this storm has been like a shipwreck on dry land. Yet which of our numerous passing craft can afford them the least assistance?

By now our brave hunters had expected to find great herds of the fabled buffalo of the plains. Traces of them are everywhere, in the shape of dried white skulls and skeletons along the trail, and the large cakes of hardened buffalo excrement which we now use for fuel, all wood being absent. Even these were of little use today, soaked and softened to mud by the storm. We managed to start a fire of sage roots last evening, but had to breakfast this morning without fire, chewing on dried fruit and biscuits hard as millstones. Oh, for my kitchen in Vermont!

One party espied what they thought was a buffalo herd at a great distance, looking and sounding like the rolling earth itself; but their horses refused to give chase.

Another entry for my log of funerary inscriptions: Samuel Hake, aged 24, of Clinton Co., Illinois. Member of our company. From the time his first spasms and fever last night, to the time of his expiring was less than six hours. The grave was dug as best as it could be done in the rain.

This time, James did not take his share in the sad work, or his place in the procession. He is himself unwell. I tell myself that work as arduous as his, in weather so foul, would be sufficient cause of illness at any time and place. But I cannot keep from my heart the dread of what may be. Until midday he kept pace, but his pallor and perspiration were an ominous sign. At our noon halt, he agreed to lie in the wagon, and has not been able to leave it since. He ate no dinner, suffering as he was from vomitings and purgings, by turns throwing off all coverings and pulling them tight around him. I administer calomel and morphia from the captain's stock, renew the damp cloths on his forehead, and pray for him with all my heart.

Dear God, if it by Thy will to take my James, pray Thee take me as well. Do not leave me alone among strangers and savages in this wilderness.

May 27, 1849

James remains weak, but is spared. The fever is passed. Thanks be to God.

On this, our second heathen Sunday, I joined with a handful of other Christian folk after dinner to offer prayers and hymns, thanking our gracious Savior for His mercy and begging His continued protection. Our group includes the three other women of the party, Ellen Dawson, Patience Greenough, her mother Mrs. Garner; Mr. Greenough; several of the older men; and two dear boys from Missouri who have joined our mess, Henry and Hector Williams, sons of a Methodist preacher who works as a missionary among the savages (white and Indian) of the western frontier. They have come to look on me, if not as a mother—for I am scarcely older than they—then as a kind of elder sister. They are as disgusted as I am by the coarseness of the men, and find it more comforting to pass their hours of leisure in my company than in that of their own sex, among whom their piety only attracts scorn.

James was unable to join our humble service, because of the lingering effects of his fever. But he was surely with us in spirit, thanking and praising the Lord for His mercy.

We continue to pass emigrants searching for cattle lost in Friday's storm. They will not be able to continue westward—or return eastward—until their animals are found.

This day's travel was our most difficult so far. At daybreak, we piled on all the wood we could find, and filled extra kegs with water. From the guide books we knew that we had a drive of at least 25 dry miles. We climbed the whole day, from the valley of the Little Blue across the bleak prairie to the bluffs over the Platte, then down to our camp site in view of the river. We did not make camp until 10 o'clock. I write on the edge of exhaustion.

The view below is of an immensely wide river, turbid, shoaly, and sluggish, split in the middle by the wooded wedge of Grand Island. The green valley, level as a floor, stretches perhaps five miles from the rise of our camp to the steep sand ridges of the opposite shore.

Having reached this river, which serves as a kind of thoroughfare across the continent, we may feel ourselves fairly launched out on the plains.

The setting sun draws myriads of ravenous mosquitoes from the grasses that grow along the river. It is impossible to escape them. They are larger and more determined that any I have ever seen, and almost invulnerable to slaps. Their bites leave welts painful as beestings. The poor animals are tormented to death. Staked and corralled, they twitch and stamp in a kind of frantic futility, and bellow in their pain.

Fort Kearny
May 30, 1849

In the twenty-one hundred miles between the Missouri border and the California mines, there are three oases of "civilization." This is the first.

The Carthage Company passed the entire day here—our first day of rest in two weeks. The time was spent visiting the fort (a collection of mud-brick sheds); wandering about talking to other residents of this fair; washing, mending, repairing wagons; and driving the cattle off in search of grass.

The thousand-tongued babble of rumor about us has once again stirred up confusion among the headstrong of our company, always ready to seize on any opportunity for dissent. The result is that our party is to be divided. One faction, led by Lieutenant Calkins, is now persuaded that ox-drawn wagons can never finish the journey across the great desert and the mountains of California. They plan to trade their animals for Mexican mules recently brought to the fort for sale. A smaller group, led by a perpetual trouble-maker named James D. Hart, has determined to pack in on mules entirely, and is trying to find purchasers for its wagons.

Unfortunately for them all, every traveler at Fort Kearny seems to be trying to disencumber himself of superfluous weight; to trade jaded animals for fresh, to trade tools and even wagons for provisions, which are here priced exorbitantly. Both bacon and flour are sold by the sutler for two dollars the hundredweight. Those in need try to bargain with those who find themselves overburdened. Sugar is 50 cents a pound.

In any case, Captain McClellan's group—among whom we are still proud to number ourselves—is reduced to a faithful flock of 12 wagons and 70 people. The group includes, I am pleased to note, my entire small circle of Christians.

It is pleasing to mingle in such a varied assembly, after 19 long days on the trail. I felt my spirits elated at the appearance of an inhabited community again, even one so nomadic and rude as this. I wonder if Moses and the Chosen People, at their encampments in the desert, did not bear some resemblance to us. It is estimated that there are more than 600 wagons camped hereabouts; reckoning four people to a wagon would give our canvas city a population of 2,400 people—a town half the size of Burlington. At the fort, James was told that more than 4,000 wagons had already passed this way.

I look for the bonnets and gowns of respectable-looking females, which stand out vividly in this masculine world. One is always received with modest hospitality by a sister. Our common troubles, both remembered and expected, lighten as they are shared. Amidst the boisterous noise of men arguing, bragging, and bargaining, the hammering and sawing, the shooting and loud laughter—as well as the braying and bellowing of thousands of beasts—small corners of domesticity gladden the eye and lift up the heart. I encountered, quite unexpectedly, a group of young children playing at hide and seek among the cottonwoods at the river's edge, and felt I was back among the stone fences and orchards of Chittenden County.

An unhealthy element is infused into our encampment by several groups of travelers who have determined to abandon the journey and return home. James has spoken with members of two of these groups; I visited today with a Missouri woman from another. They insist that the journey is too harsh for men or animals, and that no one but a villain would subject women and children to such an ordeal. All three of these parties started ahead of us, and are now returning from points considerably farther west. They tell tales of lost stock, impassable terrain, trail accidents, deaths from cholera, and long dry marches without water or grass. So vivid are their descriptions that several companies and individuals camped at the fort have elected to follow them home.

They were particularly eloquent on the subject of Indians. We are told that a hundred emigrants, including women and children, were set upon and slaughtered within a day's drive of Fort Laramie. The U.S. dragoons, insists James, "will make these devils pay for their depradations."

Much of their passion has been invalidated by one irresistible argument. A Mormon gentleman, returning from California to his church's outpost at Kanesville, is displaying for all to see a sock full of gold. Against such evidence, all the Indians in the world cannot persuade us. No one in the three groups of the Carthage party has voted to turn back. Even in our dissent, this remains a source of pride.

The fort, which was only established a year ago, is still in the process of construction. The sod-roofed quarters are as yet unprotected by any surrounding wall. A frame hospital is being built. In the meanwhile, the seriously ill and wounded are cared for in large tents. Yesterday, a man who had fallen under a wagon had a leg amputated. Another, poisoned from a rattlesnake bite, lost an arm.

The river grows wider and shallower past the tip of Grand Island. Men roll their pantaloons to the knee and wade across, a distance of two or three miles. Behind us, the northern bluffs begin to assume picturesque formations. The barren sand hills across the river look like beehives, or madcaps.

I am told that the new commander of Fort Laramie, a Captain Bonneville, is a gentleman and a scholar, but that the men under his charge leave much to be desired. They pester the emigrants for whisky. A deserter from their number was returned last week in bonds by outraged Indians, who accused him of murdering the chief's son, when the boy caught him in the act of ravishing an Indian maid. He will be judged by his commander next Tuesday. There is much talk of his plight among the emigrants. If he is judged guilty, the commander may order him to be either returned to Fort Leavenworth, hanged on the spot, or turned over to the Indians to punish as they see fit—an appalling prospect for even the vilest of sinners.

June 1, 1849

The little fort is far behind us. The great gathering-together of wagons and travelers is once again dispersed into a thin thread along this increasingly barren valley. Our road is now all sand, quite steep. Wheels spin hub-deep in it, and booted feet drag. The mid-day temperature rarely falls below 90 degrees. Men and animals grow dry and exhausted. Lips become sore in the heat and wind. Decent water is rare. The wood of our wheels contracts in the heat. They must be unfastened and left in water overnight if they are to remain fitted to the tires.

We pass the bodies of many dead oxen and mules, abandoned where they fell. Surely men might by this learn the wisdom of a measured pace, a lighter load—above all, of Sunday rests! How many of these poor dead beasts might still breathe and work on had they been granted one day of rest and refreshment a week!

We have had to adopt the strange practice of making boots for our stock, when their hooves grew cracked and sore from the hot ground. Their tender extremities are first smeared with tar and grease, then wrapped in skins to keep out the sand and dirt.

The exotic landscape on the Mormon side of the river continues to grow stranger as we pass. It forms a panorama of broken banks and strangely sculpted mounds, peculiar columns that rise suddenly out of empty land. Vegetation is now reduced to the artemesia, or wild sage, which seems able to live without the least water or nourishing soil. (I have also identified something called a "soap plant," with pointed leaves like a pine apple; and a kind of prickly pear, or "cactus," with bright yellow blooms.)

The river remains broad and shallow, foul and brackish. Water for drinking must be fetched from small feeder streams. Even these are often charged with alkali and salt, and in places crusted over with a strange white crystalline substance. To gather wood for our fires, men have to wade out to one of the islets that dot the River Platte, which resembles more a bog or swamp than a

135

running river. I had looked forward to joining the course of this great highway to the Pacific, which seemed on the maps designed to ease and guide the journey west. I had no idea it would prove so stale and unrewarding.

Two events of more than usual interest helped to relieve the tedium of the march. Yesterday two men who had gone off hunting, after being expected for several hours, returned to camp on foot and perfectly naked. Their feet were very painfully burned, and they carried bunches of sage before them, like Adam's apron of fig leaves. Looking for buffalo high in a ravine south of the river, they had been surrounded by a band of armed Pawnees, who forced them to dismount and disrobe. Seizing their horses, weapons, and clothing, the Indians obliged them to make their own way to camp in the condition I described. James and the other men listened avidly to their account. The only way to Christianize such brutes, he insists in heat, is with powder and lead.

Other hunters had better luck. Today they finally encountered a herd of several hundred buffalo, followed them for four hours, and managed in the end to kill eight, at the price of what appears to be a wagon load of shot. On the advice of an old hunter, they selected only the hump meat, "marrow gut," tender loins, liver, heart, and tongue, and left the remains to the wolves. We all feasted on their trophies tonight. Although coarser-grained and not as tender as domestic beef, I found the meat succulent and of decent flavor. James is quite put out to have missed the adventure, which all travelers seem to regard as a test of manliness on the plains. He vows to join the next expedition.

The other fauna of the Platte Valley are less imposing. We continue to be set upon, night and morning, by mosquitoes as large as horseflies, and now by a plague of large flying beetles, resembling what we at home called "June bugs." They rush tumbling into everything. I have spooned a dozen out of one pot of coffee, and wakened to find handfuls of the creatures pulling my hair. We have passed two villages of small, fat ferret-like rodents called prairie dogs. They live by the hundreds in underground colonies, marked by 20-foot wide streets of cone-shaped mounds, laid out with the most wonderful rectilinearity. Unfortunately, as some of our party learned, the dear creatures' holes are also used by rattlesnakes. One man was bitten, but sucked out the venom in time to survive. Six of these evil reptiles were seen in one half-acre plot, and three of them killed.

June 3, 1849

Today we forded the River Platte. It took the entire day, even for our reduced party, partly because of the crowds at the ford, partly because it rained most of the day; but mainly because of the treacherous bed and great width of the river. Large hailstones fell for more than two hours. It felt strange to be a passenger on a wagon that trembled beneath one, the wheels settling by short jerks in the treacherous sand, as the rain poured down in torrents.

We were obliged to leave one wagon stuck in the sand. We could only retrieve it when all the rest had crossed, and we could spare the men and animals to pull it loose. Unfortunately, it was the wagon bearing lawyer

Eleazar Grant, who was ill with dysentery. It looked queer to see one of his mess-mates wading downstream, waist deep in the rapid river, with a pot of coffee in one hand and a plate of bread and meat in the other, going to the relief of his comrade. On the opposite shore stood a pointer dog at the water's edge, howling for his lost master.

Through the day, many wagons found themselves in a similar position. Several (not ours) overturned, and several animals were lost. So slick and shifting was the treacherous bed that only by keeping the teams constantly moving, under a pelting of rain and hail, could one prevent them from sinking fast in the sands. Although the water was never deeper than a man's height, and usually much less, it was more than a thousand yards across. There were pits and snags at the bottom. The rain only hastened the current, and swept dangerous flotsam into the way of passing wagons.

By the time all were across—including poor Mr. Grant—horses, oxen, and men alike were covered with mud, soaked to the skin, and wearied to death. Yet so jolly was the crowd over its successful day's work, that we joined two other companies on the north shore for a feast of brandy, beans, rice, bread, coffee, and crackers. The men cavorted like children, singing and dancing around the fires, slapping strangers on the back, and trading tales of the trail.

It *was* a relief to be quit of the ugly river—though we move tomorrow to its northern fork—and I felt myself stirred by all the merriment around. Fiddles and flutes sang as I have not heard them since St. Joseph. James and I danced several reels. The great favorites of this season on the plains seem to be "Dearest Mae" (which one hears much too often), "Oh! Susannah," "Carry Me Back to Old Virginny," and a number of new songs, composed to old tunes, which celebrate the emigration itself.

June 7, 1849

After an overland pull up high and dry hills, we crossed the steep ridge that lies between the south and north forks of the Platte, and made our precipitous descent down Ash Hollow on the North Fork. Our own animals were more chafed and jaded than I have seen them so far. These four days have taken their toll.

It came as a shock to reach the edge of the bluff, and realize that we had to get all 15 wagons down what appeared an almost perpendicular ravine, with perhaps 500 feet difference in elevation between top and bottom. The cliffside is wooded with vegetation that would have been a welcome sight under other circumstances, and the descent was made by means of a windlass devised from the wheels of one stationary wagon at the top. Each wagon had its wheels double-locked. Men strained at the anchor ropes holding them back. Several burst free nevertheless, their owners stumbling helter-skelter alongside them. One wagon began plummeting with such gusto that the driver leapt out for his own safety and let team and wagon fall where they might. The wagon was smashed to pieces against a tree, and two of the animals hurt so badly they had to be destroyed. We are now eleven. I shall not complain again of the flatness of the plains.

A Mormon traveler we encountered at the bottom expressed scorn for travelers so selfish and impetuous that they never took the trouble to cut a better road. The Mormon custom, it appears (their well-maintained trail lies along the opposite shore), is not simply to hurry on regardless, but to take pains to create the best possible road for future travelers to follow.

The hollow itself is a place of considerable interest. We found dense and useful plantings, including wild roses, currants, chokecherries, and gooseberries; a fine spring of water set among romantic rocks and boulders; a great number of emigrant camps; a small log store used as a "post office;" and, most interesting of all, an encampment of perhaps a thousand Sioux Indians. After so many weeks of anxiety, and so many dire reports of their savage behavior, I felt quite awkward coming into the presence of this strange race of human beings. These are people who claim as their homeland all the territory through which we are passing.

But we had nothing to fear. Though they seemed proud and aloof, they were not hostile. They are armed and prepared for war; but against the Pawnees, not against us. Their cone-shaped lodges, of which there were perhaps 200, are covered with tanned buffalo skins.

The males are fine muscular specimens, although in indecently abbreviated dress. The older men go about modestly wrapped in blankets, but the majority of the male Sioux wear little more than a deerskin apron about the waist. A few of the young warriors, like heroes of the Trojan wars, walk about quite naked.

Some of the women were dressed in robes of the finest white skin curiously embroidered with colored beads. I was told that there are men in their tribe so desperate for strong liquors that they had offered their women in exchange. But such tales are hardly credible.

On invitation of their chief, Captain McClellan sat on the ground with the leaders of several other companies and smoked a long pipe that was passed from hand to hand. This is apparently a token of good faith and pacific intentions. Let us hope they keep to *their* side of the bargain better than we have kept to ours—for surely we despoil their land, and rob them of sustenance, in cropping so much grass and wantonly destroying their herds.

I can keep neither my eyes nor my mind off these noble people. I find myself wondering what their lives must be like, and what they must think of these hordes of white men from the East who roll like a flood through their lands. As far as James is concerned, they are little more than animals, with no rights whatever; to be petted or hunted down as it suits our needs. But surely, baptized or not, they must also be regarded as children of God. Did Christ not die for their salvation, as well as ours?

Observing this handsome and dignified people, moving with such simplicity and assurance among our disheveled lot, a stranger from another world might well err in distinguishing the educated and genteel from the savage.

17

The search for shelter in North Platte ended at Scout Creek Lodge, a restaurant and bar which had cabins for rent, out by Buffalo Bill's Ranch north of town.

In the summer after his junior year in high school, Timmy and a friend had been hired to drive a new Chevy pickup from Sacramento to New Jersey, where the truck's owner had been visiting his daughter. They had followed U.S. 40 to Rocky Mountain National Park, turned north to Cheyenne, then taken U.S. 30 the rest of the way. In North Platte, Nebraska, they had stopped at an old-fashioned restaurant and bar a block down from the rodeo arena. Now, twenty-three years later, Timmy spotted the same lariat of green neon encircling the neon script letters.

The patrons on the barstools, men and women both, wore boots and jeans and denim shirts. They turned around and called "Howdy" at them as they entered. Timmy walked up to the bar and pulled back a stool for his wife as naturally as if he'd been doing it for years. In fact, Audrey had been inside a bar three times in her life; and she had *never* sat on a bar stool. Decent ladies didn't sit on bar stools, her mother told her. (Decent ladies in Dedham didn't go to bars in the first place, except to drag their drunken menfolk home.)

This particular place, though, looked not only harmless but downright homey: high cobwebby rafters, dim hanging lamps, deer and buffalo heads on the walls. The bartender slapped down a paper napkin before her. "What's yours, ma'am?" "Ginger ale?" she whispered. Timmy gave her a critical-quizzical look, but the bartender seemed to think it a perfectly natural request. He filled a tall glass with ice and ginger ale, dropped in a maraschino cherry, and presented it to her as if it were champagne, along with a bowl full of peanuts. Timmy ordered Jim Beam, straight, and ate most of her peanuts. He punched three old Hank Williams songs on the jukebox, and spent the

139

time they were playing telling the folks around them how he had been here twenty-three years ago, and how nothing had changed.

Timmy was talking different, she noticed. He had started dropping the g's from his ing's, rubbing edges off consonants, drawling and slanging in a broad, easy roll. When she first heard it, she thought he was drunk. But then she realized what was happening. He was blending back into his natural setting.

The setting may have been natural to him, but it wasn't to her. She felt peculiar, perched on a stool trading life stories with these loud and open-faced strangers. They all talked in that same flat-braying, cowlike, prairie-roll drawl Timmy was beginning to use. They downed beers and whiskeys like water, one after another, with no noticeable effect.

Why, yes, said the bartender politely. He *did* think he remembered Timmy. And yes, dinner was still on. And sure enough, they still had cabins to rent. Ten bucks a night, with kitchenette. No television, though. That O.K. with you folks?

"Television? Are you kidding? We're on our honeymoon."

"Hey! Hear that, folks? We got a couple of honeymooners here. I'd say that calls for a round on the house."

Trying to enter more into the spirit of things, Audrey ordered a manhattan this time, but in these parts that was almost as ladylike as a ginger ale. Timmy got up and fed the jukebox enough quarters for another hour of Nashville nostalgia. Either someone in North Platte shared his antiquated tastes, or else the records hadn't been changed much since his last visit.

This discovery only heightened the magical time-warp quality he felt about the lodge. It was as if twenty-three years had been an overnight dream. He knew all these twangy, tub-thumping, sad simple songs by heart, every last one.

The Scout Creek bar agreed with him that the new crop of singers just couldn't hold a candle to the old-timers—which, it turned out, was why the bartender had never bothered to change the records. He talked with them of country music, and baseball, and highways, and fishing, while Audrey listened politely, until finally the bartender said they better eat if they were planning to.

The dining room next door was nearly empty, but a fire was blazing away, lighting up deerheads and rifles and Buffalo Bill posters. A freckled waitress talked them into vegetable-noodle soup, buffalo steak (which wasn't bad), huge baked potatoes, and homemade peach and pumpkin pie.

When they were finished, the girl led them through the kitchen, out a screen door, and, with the help of an umbrella and a flashlight, guided them through the rain and puddles out to a log cabin under the trees.

While Audrey explored the Calvin Coolidge-era bathroom, tried the bedsprings (a little dippy), and looked into the kitchen cupboard, Timmy borrowed the girl's umbrella and flashlight, and went back to the car for their suitcases.

He returned, and sat beside her on the bed.

140

"Happy?" he asked.

"Yes," Audrey answered. They kissed, a long contented kiss.

She *was* happy, under a roof and sheltered from the rain. It was nice, she thought, to be in a cozy cottage of their own, instead of a motel cubicle with sanitized plastic glasses and a color TV. The knotty pine walls, the rafters, the tiny sink and stove and frig, the old quilt and bouncy metal springs; the very smell of the place (a little musty, a little moldy; just like her aunts' houses, her grandmother's, her *own* house)—all of these things made the little cabin under the trees in western Nebraska the nearest thing to a home she had known since she was married. Now that they were safe from it, she even loved the sound of the battering rain.

The sun came out the next morning. North Platte was clean and fresh from its shower. Timmy and Audrey liked their little cabin so much they decided to stay over an extra day, most of which they spent in bed.

Other than some new entries for *The Joy of Sex*, the only exceptional events of the day were a pair of small, secret discoveries. Both came after dinner.

Timmy fixed and served the steak, salad vegetables, and fresh corn he had bought the day before for the campfire dinner that never took place. He had also bought a bottle of red wine, which they finished, and a sweet honeydew melon, which they had for dessert. After doing the dishes, they played gin rummy for a while, then sat out on the porch, Audrey in Timmy's lap, listening to the creek.

Afterwards, Timmy took a long shower. Audrey used the time to write a letter to her mother.

She was folding it and putting it in an envelope just as he started his second shave of the day, which was always a sign of amorous designs. She looked in her purse for a stamp. Not finding one, she took Timmy's wallet out of his pants pocket. He usually kept a few stamps tucked somewhere inside. She dumped out the credit cards on the bed, and reached her fingers back into a worn leather pocket. It was then that she discovered the picture.

It had been hidden behind a leather flap in a compartment intended to keep large bills folded out of sight: a much-fingered snapshot of a little boy. It was hard to tell how old the boy was—five or six, perhaps, though he might have been younger. He was thin, almost emaciated looking, and quite white. He was standing alongside the blue water of a swimming pool in red trunks much too big for him, with plastic water wings on his matchstick arms. He had obviously been told to smile by the person whose long shadow loomed diagonally across the picture, but the look on his face wasn't happy. In fact, Audrey found the picture inexpressibly sad. She wanted to know all about the little boy. She presumed he was related to Timmy, since he too had red curly hair and green eyes. But why would he keep a picture of a five-year-old relative hidden away in his wallet?

The water had stopped running. She quickly slipped the picture back into its hiding place, slotted in the pile of cards, and put the wallet back in his pocket. She never did find any stamps, so she left the letter as a page marker in her bedtime book (a paperback called *Love Story*), on the little table by her pillow, to remind her to buy some stamps in the morning.

And that's where Timmy found the letter in the middle of the night. If her discovery was unlikely, his was even more so. He *never* read books. The odds against his looking into even so short and so simple a book as Audrey's must have been almost infinitely high.

But he had tried everything else, and still couldn't get to sleep. He made and ate a bologna and cheese sandwich out of what was supposed to be next day's lunch. He ate a leftover ear of corn. He sat out on the porch in his shorts, and drank a beer. He walked down to the creek and back, looked through the treetops at the stars, sorted out the night's constellations. Back inside, he sat on the toilet and read the lodge regulations on the bathroom door.

He lay back down alongside Audrey (who had been blissfully asleep all this time). His nerves were itching. He turned on the night light, half-hoping it would wake her up so they could talk, or make love, or argue, or do *something*. Three hundred and fifty miles to do tomorrow, if they were going to get to Casper by dinnertime.

She didn't budge. "Audrey?" No answer. He leaned over her shoulder to see if her eyes were open.

That's when he saw the book on the table. He reached over her, picked it up, and lay back on his pillow hoping to read himself to sleep. However soppy it was—he presumed it was soppy; it sounded soppy, what else would Audrey read but a soppy book?—it might just bore him unconscious.

As he opened it, the letter to her mother fell out. She had left the envelope unsealed, planning to tuck in a picture postcard of the lodge. Naturally, he read it.

North Platte, Nebraska
July 22

Dear Mother,

I still say you're wrong. If he could tell, he certainly hasn't let on. *I* may tell him myself, one day. But that will have to wait till I feel more sure of myself—and of us.

As I said in my last card, we've had our ups and downs so far on this trip. Right now things seem to be looking up.

Timmy's taking a shower now, in this old lodge we've stopped at in Nebraska. We've got a hideaway house of our own, alongside a brook. I'm writing this on a pine table in the tiny kitchen corner. The bed is a big old-fashioned one just like yours, with a quilt like Aunt Kath's. It takes up half the cabin. I'd like to stay here forever.

Last night, in the dark, Timmy and a cowboy we met played music together on our little porch. Timmy played the harmonica and the cowboy played a banjo. Then we sat out for a long time, the two men drinking whiskey (you were right about that) and talking. Then just sitting. Today we're staying in all day, to practice you-know-what. As I told you on the phone, that part is getting easier.

You *were* right about some things, Mother. But very wrong about others. In any case, I don't think I made a mistake—at least not yet. Do you still believe God intended me to deny myself forever, just because of something that happened four years ago? You thought it a sign, a curse on us all, I know that. You convinced Barb and Cathy that all men were like him. But not me. Now that I can give myself willingly, I feel as if a great weight had been lifted from around my neck.

I hear the shower water stopping, so I must finish. I'll phone again next time I can get away. I miss you terribly, Mother. Pray for me. I managed to get to mass again yesterday. (Timmy wouldn't come with me this time.) But I feel that my prayers just fall flat. They never rise up to heaven, the way they used to. I don't believe God listens to me anymore.

Am I truly cursed? Or have I been forgiven? Have you forgiven me, Mother?

I love you, Mother, and think of you always.

Audrey

Then came a line of Xs.

Timmy put the letter back in the book, lay the book quietly on her nightstand, and turned out the light. He slept a little after that. But he felt sick to his stomach, and bad dreams kept waking him up.

18

―――――――――――――――――――――

*At the eastbound Sutherland rest area along Interstate 80, you can
see the century-old wheel ruts of the Oregon Trail. At this point, known
as O'Fallon's Bluff, the Platte River runs so near to the south cliff that
only a narrow trail, between it and the river, could be used by early
wagons. Many emigrants, particularly in times of Indian-white warfare,
preferred to travel over the high bluff, to avoid being ambushed by war
parties.*

"Yes. I can see them. I told you I could see them. I don't have to *step* in
them to see them, do I?"

. . .

"Well?"

. . .

"I don't know what you want me to say, Timmy! Your great-grandmother's
covered wagon came this way. I know: you told me three times. I would have
taken your word for it without walking all the way over here to look at a
ditch."

"Sorry."

"Oh, *I'm* sorry, dear. But it's just not getting to me. I'm afraid it's going to
take more than wheel ruts."

"Uh huh. Or Fort Kearney."

"I'm afraid so."

"Or Pioneer Village"

*At Ogallala, the terminus of one branch of the great Texas trail, over
which 800,000 head of cattle were driven in 1894, cowboys frequented
the many saloons, and sometimes ended up in "Boot Hill." Today you
can enjoy a buffalo steak and high-kicking dance hall girls in Ogal-*

144

lala's "Main Street," recreated in the style of the late 1880s, a family fun-spot offering entertainment nightly during the summer months.

"I hate stuff like this. It's pure Disneyland."

"Oh, I'd love to see Disneyland."

"They just *built* all these buildings. They're about as authentic as a Hollywood Indian."

"But don't you think they're cute?"

"Cute?"

"I mean they *look* real. Isn't that what matters?"

"Don't be dumb, Audrey. That jail's about the size of an outhouse. The stone wall is probably polyurethane foam. I've seen B-movie sets that looked more real. Hell, I've seen Lionel *train* villages that looked more real."

"Does it matter if it's authentic as long as people are having fun? Look at all the people here, dear. Look at all the kids! It must be a great place for families."

"What do you know about families?"

"What do you mean, what do I know about families? *I* have a family, don't I?"

"Oh, right. Two nuns, the old battle-ax, and you. You guys go to lots of fun places like this?"

"My sisters were girls like anyone else when they were little. And yes, we did go to nice places together!"

"Very close, you all were?"

"Yes. Yes, we were. Once."

"No more?"

"I don't know what you're driving at."

"Let's get out of here."

Ash Hollow, with its tree-covered slopes, was a haven of cool water, flowers, and trees for pioneer travelers. Deep ruts remain to show the visitor where the emigrants had to lock their wagon wheels to make the steep descent down Windlass Hill. Today, Ash Hollow, on U.S. Highway 26 east of Lewellen, is a Nebraska State Historical Park with an information and historical center. A paved nature trail leads to the top of Windlass Hill.

Today's traveler can also visit a pioneer cemetery, an old-time schoolhouse, and an ancient Indian cave. The area is also the site of the historic Blue Water battlefield, where a major early confrontation took place between the Sioux Indians and the U.S. Army.

"Well, that was a little better."

"It *could* have been better, if you'd taken the trouble to look at something. You've got to exert yourself a little bit to get anything out of these places."

"What good would it have done me to climb down a cliff, now? Just tell me that. Or walk half a mile just to see an old cave?"

"Oh, *try*, for Christ's sake, Audrey! I hate people who just pop out of their

145

cars, grab a two-second peek at some fantastic place, pop back in, zoom on—and then think they've done something; think they've *seen* something. You're acting just like those idiots up in Yellowstone. The only reason they go is to take pictures and send postcards so they can prove that they've been there."

"You seem to be picking on me today, no matter what I do. This isn't going to be much fun if you keep on at me like this."

"It's not going to be much fun if you won't *do* anything either. You could at least have walked down the hill with me."

"It wasn't a hill, it was a cliff. I don't happen to like walking down cliffs."

"It *wasn't* a cliff. There was an easy, paved path all the way down. If you'd come with me, maybe you'd have got some feeling for what it was *like* a hundred and twenty years ago."

"I read all about that in the museum."

"Great. Real first-hand exploration."

"Oh dear oh dear oh dear. Am I offending your great-grandmother by not doing this pilgrimage properly? Like on my knees?"

"Great-great-grandmother."

"What?"

"Forget it."

From a distance, Oregon Trail emigrants thought the lone rock formations called Courthouse Rock and Jail Rock (located near Bridgeport, Nebraska, five miles south of U.S. 26 on State Route 88) resembled their namesakes back home. These outcroppings were the first notable rock formations the pioneers observed on their journey west. Courthouse Rock is supposed to have been named by an early group of travelers from St. Louis after the new domed courthouse in that city.

Today, the rocks (which remain essentially unchanged) retain their interest for the traveler, who can observe their changing aspect for many miles as he approaches them across the level plains. A mobile museum display at Seybolt Park (four miles north of Bridgeport, open eight A.M. to seven P.M. daily through the summer) tells the history of these picturesque promontories. Although the ascent of the rocks, once a favorite expedition for more venturesome emigrants, is no longer regarded as practical or safe, there are nature trails around the area.

"You have to use your imagination."

"I still don't see anything."

"Maybe they got eroded down some."

"No. They're supposed to be unchanged. The book says so."

"Well, we can't tell from here. Let's park the car and walk over."

"Please, Timmy, it's just two big rocks. I don't feel like walking through all those weeds just to get a closer look at two rocks."

"You don't feel like doing much of anything today, do you? You're determined not to like anything I want to look at. You know, you're being a real sweetheart, sweetheart."

"Honestly, Tim: a lot of weeds and rocks! It's not as if this was Niagara Falls."

"Oh, I see. We're bringing that up again."

"And you're *not* being very nice to me. You've done nothing all morning but criticize me and make snide remarks. I don't know what's the matter with you."

"Nothing's the matter with *me*, baby. You're acting like a whining little kid on a family vacation."

"Well, I'm tired."

"*You're* tired? I'm the one who does all the driving. I'm the one who hardly got any sleep the last two nights."

"You never told me."

"You never asked. You never do."

"After all your fun and games in the cabin yesterday, I thought you'd sleep like a baby for weeks. 'Whining little kid!' If I wanted to bring things up, I could mention a lot more than Niagara Falls."

"Oh, really? Like what?"

"Like Toledo. Like Chicago. Really, Tim, I've put up with much more than you have this trip, you've got to admit that."

"Oh, that's real nice, baby. Dig it all up."

"Please, Timmy! I don't want to keep fighting like this!"

"You're not trying very hard to stop, I notice."

"*Will* you stop insisting on having the last word all the time?"

. . .

"Anyway, I'm hungry."

Chimney Rock, located three and a half miles southwest of Bayard, Nebraska, on the south side of the North Platte River, was a spire of solitary grandeur, visible for miles to travelers of the onstretching prairie. Of all the curious rock formations along the trail, Chimney Rock received the most space in the emigrants' diaries. It is now a National Historic Site. Gravel roads lead from Nebraska 92 to within half a mile of the rock. Travel from here is by foot only, but a word of warning: to cope with the rough terrain, rattlesnakes, and sword plants, boots and hiking clothes are essential.

Today the column stands 500 feet above the nearby North Platte River. Erosion has reduced its height considerably since the nineteenth century, but the rock's present contours will probably last a good many more centuries. Emigrants referred to it as "marl" or "earthy sandstone." A more accurate description is that the rock is composed of Brule clay, interlaid with volcanic ash and Arickaree sandstone. The presence of this sandstone in the upper strata probably explains why the column resisted the forces of erosion, while the surrounding clay weathered away.

* * *

147

"You want any more potato salad?"

"No, you finish it. I don't like potato salad."

"Neither do I."

"Then why did you buy it?"

"I thought you liked it."

"It was crazy to take that trail, you know. I told you what the guidebook said."

"I didn't see any rattlesnakes. Did you see any rattlesnakes?"

"No. But what if there *had* been some? And there were plenty of rocks. *Look* at my ankle. Just look! My feet are filthy. I'm not used to walking around this kind of country."

"I'm beginning to wonder how much you're going to like California."

"California isn't like this, is it?"

"Some of it."

"We're going to have to climb up rocks to get to our front door?"

"The cottage at my folks' place is up a path like that."

"Is that where we're going to live?"

"I don't know."

"Tell me about your parents' house, Timmy. Tell me about your parents."

"There's nothing to tell."

"Tell me something."

. . .

"Timmy, please! You've just closed off to me completely today. Either you won't say anything, or if you do it's to tell me I'm doing something wrong. I'm sorry I'm such a poor tourist, but this just isn't my idea of good times. I didn't ask to drag around historic rocks and dinky trailer museums. I wanted us to *talk* today."

"We talk every day."

"But never seriously. We haven't once talked about what our life is going to be like when we get to California. I don't even know where we're going to live."

"I don't know, either. If it doesn't bother me, why should it bother you?"

"But couldn't we at least discuss it? You have no idea how empty it all is for me. I have no picture of my future life at all."

"That didn't worry you before we were married."

"That was different. In those days, just being together was enough."

"And now it isn't?"

"And I'd really like to talk about children."

. . .

"About our having them, I mean."

"I know what you mean."

"Well?"

"I told you already. I don't want to talk about that."

"When did you tell me that?"

"Coming back from Provincetown."

"You didn't say that. You just turned on the radio and ended the conversation."

"Well, I *don't* want to, okay? I thought I got that across."

"Not ever?"

"Not yet."

Traveling south of Highway 92 on Highway 71, you will find the North Platte Valley Museum complex in the Oregon Trail Park at South Gering. A sod home of a pioneer family has been moved to this complex and reconstructed with the original sod. In the sod house, log house, and museum, thousands of historical articles which have been donated to the non-tax-supported North Platte Valley Historical Association make up one of the finest collections in the West. Free parking, camping, and picnicking are available.

"Well, that was a total loss."

"Why do you say that?"

"Oh, come on, Timmy. A tin shed full of junk? How can you pretend to despise Olagawa or whatever it was, and not a dump like that?"

"The stuff here was real, that's why."

"It's exactly like all the stuff at Pioneer Village. Except that there they had a hundred times *more* old quilts and spittoons and wagon wheels."

"That doesn't make it necessarily better. When we were there, you didn't like that, either. You thought they had too *much* stuff."

"So did you! Oh, can't we just stop all this history business and go on to your precious friends' house in Casper? I presume they'll offer us dinner."

"You know, Aud: you're beginning to sound just like your mother."

"What's my mother got to do with anything?"

"Never satisfied with anything, bitching, bitching. I used to think, great, at least you weren't like your mother. Now I'm beginning to wonder."

"Of course I'm like my mother! Is that something to be ashamed of? Don't you start insulting my mother!"

"Hell, you insulted her often enough. You used to go on for hours telling me all the things about her you didn't like."

"Well, she's still my mother. And I don't see how she got into this argument anyway."

"Because you're acting more and more like her all the time. Maybe you're more like your mother than I thought."

"Maybe I am!"

The 385-acre Wildcat Hills Wildlife Area, 10 miles south of Gering, Nebraska, on Nebraska 71, is home for a herd of some eight buffalo, the surviving remnant of millions of buffalo that once roamed the plains at will. The State Game Commission tries to preserve this small part of Nebraska wildlife history.

"It's really not fair, Timmy. Your parents never came to the wedding. They didn't send a present. They never wrote to me. They never telephoned. And

149

yet they have to be treated like some kind of sacred paragons. I admit Mother has her faults. But she did everything, paid for everything. And now she's just someone you make fun of."

"The woman I saw in your house was a narrow-minded, evil-minded, superstitious, bigoted gossip; and she hated me. That's all I ever saw. And you never suggested till now there was anything else. You show me something to respect and I'll respect it. For some reason I got this crazy idea that you were dying to get away from her."

"There's a lot more to her than that Timmy, even if you never saw it. She was a good kind loving woman who had to bring up three daughters on her own. Of course, she worried about us. Maybe she got overprotective sometimes, too suspicious of the boys who wanted to take us away. But you can't call someone bigoted and superstitious just because she's a good Catholic. She bought us the nicest toys she could afford, she read stories to us, sang songs to us, made most of our clothes. She offered up her prayers and her masses for us every day. And she took wonderful care of us when we were sick."

"You've got a *husband* now, right? I thought when girls got married, they were supposed to grow up a little. Forget this beautiful mother-and-daughter trip."

"I don't believe that for one minute. Your mother is your mother forever. Don't you believe when we have children of our own we'll love them and care for them all our lives?"

"We weren't going to talk about that."

"Well, *I'm* going to, whether you like it or not! Did it ever occur to you that if I can't start thinking about children, I have absolutely *no* life ahead to imagine? You give me no home to think about, tell me next to nothing about your parents. All right, I'm a big girl now, I've left my family. I'm a married woman. To me, that means I should be able to start thinking of a family of my own. Can't you understand how a woman feels about something like that? No, you probably can't. For all your hundreds of women, I doubt that you ever once thought about *their* feelings."

"All my hundreds of women, huh? I see. I guess I had this marriage all wrong. I thought it was *me* you wanted. I thought 'love' had something to do with it. No, I get it now. I'm just your stud horse, your baby-planter. And when baby comes along, where do I go then? Back to the stable?"

"Oh, go on, get sarcastic, make *me* sound like the selfish one. You're very good at that, aren't you? It's all very well for *you*, Timothy McCue. You can go to work and be busy all day. Then do your basketball or swim or go off mountain climbing or whatever you want. But what about *me*? What do I do? Clean house all day? Darn your ski socks? Watch soap operas? Of course, when you're *here*, you're all I want. But what about the times when you're not around? What do I do then?"

"You think working in the plant all day is such fun? I don't know what *I'm* going to do in California, either, but you don't see me getting all psycho about it."

"Do you mean you're not going back to Aerojet?"

"I don't know."

"Do you want me to get a job?"

"No."
"Why not?"
"I don't like wives who have jobs."
"Then what do you expect me to do?"
"Whatever housewives do. What my mother did."
"Your mother had four sons."
"They weren't always around."
"But you don't want to have children?"
"I told you, I don't know. Period."

The emigrants looked up at picturesque Scotts Bluff, located five miles south of the city of Scottsbluff via U.S. 26, as they made their way through Mitchell Pass. This massive promontory, rising 800 feet above the valley floor, has been preserved as a National Monument since 1919.

Visitors can drive to the top of Scotts Bluff for a spectacular view of the surrounding countryside. From the summit parking area, a self-guiding trail 0.6 miles long, hard-surfaced and of easy grade, extends to north and south overlooks.

Except for intermittent stretches of cultivation, or where modern roads have been superimposed, the wagon ruts of the old trail, ground down by the passage of thousands of emigrants, can still be seen at the monument.

"Back at that buffalo place, you said you had promised your mother you'd spend the rest of your life taking care of her. Did you really promise that?"

"Not in so many words. But she took it as a promise."

"It doesn't make any sense. There's something unnatural about trying to force a kid to stay with you forever. That old bat has some power over you, some power I don't understand."

"All mothers have power over their children."

"Mine doesn't."

"All girls' mothers do, then. Remember, she had to be *both* parents for me, ever since I was five years old."

"Don't you remember your father at all, then? He just doesn't count?"

"I remember him dead. We had the wake in our house, and they put the coffin on the dining room table. My mother held me up to look."

"Nothing else?"

"Some things. But Mother told us so many other things about him after he died. I can't tell the difference anymore between what I really remember, and what I just think I remember. I *think* I saw him hitting her and knocking her down, and her crying. But that may just be because Mother told us things like that so many times. When she thought we were old enough to understand, she told us how he used to come home drunk with vomit still wet on his clothes, and force himself on her, on the bed. Even the floor."

"She probably scared your sisters right into the convent. You know, your whole family seems set against marriage. Or at least against sex."

"My mother thought sex was sheer torture. One more thing to offer up."

"Didn't her horror stories ever bother you? If you wanted so much to break out of the family nunnery and be a full woman or whatever, have all these kids, how were you planning to do it? Immaculate conception? You didn't seem very enthusiastic about the normal approach, back at Provincetown."

"I'm sure most brides feel like that at first. I married you because I loved you, and because I *thought* you loved me. When you fall in love, you don't reason things out."

"You didn't want that part of it, though, did you? Not after your mother's stories."

"I suppose I must have, on one level. I didn't dote on it, though, think about it all the time. Her stories didn't scare me. But I wasn't a frustrated virgin either, out of some romantic novel, waiting to be swept off my feet by a tall, red-headed pirate."

"But you *were* a virgin?"

"I told you I was. Why should you ask?"

"I was just wondering."

"What do you mean, you were just wondering?"

"You've come along very fast, since those first two nights."

"Oh, for goodness *sake*, Timothy! You pick on me when I *don't* want it. So I try and try, I use all my love for you not to mind; I *make* myself enjoy it. I learn to like it to please you. And now you make me sound like some kind of whore!"

"Keep your voice down. People are looking."

"I don't care. You talk about my mother as if she were a witch. You try to make me feel guilty for loving her. You belittle my sisters for their vocation. You drag me around this horrid desert till I nearly sprain my ankle. And now you slap me with these insults and insinuations.

"For heaven's sake, Timmy! You buy me underwear not fit for a tart, as a *present*—and then act disgusted and suspicious when I try to learn to enjoy the sexual part of marriage!

"Yes, I wanted you. I admit it. I *loved* you, if that word still means anything to you. I wanted you so I could free myself, so I could learn what it meant to be a fully alive woman. I wanted to please you, more than anything else in the *world* I wanted to please you—whatever I might have to do. But one thing is absolutely certain. You're going to have to trust me—not tear apart my family or my past, not think the worst you possibly can about me. It means thinking about my life in California, as well as your own. And that will mean *either* I get a job, *or* I have children. One or the other. If this is really a marriage—what I call a marriage—it means having children."

"Let's go."

"Timmy, *please*. We can't go on forever not talking about it. We just can't. What if we have a baby we haven't planned on?"

"We won't."

On a site half a mile north of this marker, Second Lieutenant John L. Grattan and 29 men were killed by Sioux Indians on August 18, 1854. A Mormon train traveling the Oregon Trail had camped 10 miles below

Fort Laramie. After a lame cow belonging to the train was killed by a Sioux Indian, Lieutenant Grattan and his men were sent from the fort to arrest the guilty party. Grattan refused another animal in compensation, and ordered that shots be fired, in which a Sioux chief was killed. In swift retaliation, the Indians killed all 30 soldiers and their interpreter, and mutilated their bodies. The event came to be known as the Grattan Massacre. In a campaign to punish the Sioux for this atrocity, a detachment of 600 men under Brigadier General William S. Harney killed 86 Sioux encamped at Ash Hollow the following year. These two incidents effectively destroyed hopes for peace between the Sioux nation and white Americans for the next 20 years.

"That's horrible. Killing thirty men. And then mutilating their bodies."

"Who fired the first shot?"

"It was an accident, it says. You don't go chopping up thirty innocent people because of an accident. Not if you're civilized."

"Okay. Then we did the same thing at Ash Hollow a year later. With *no* provocation. No warning. And killed eighty-six. And took women and children prisoners. So who's civilized?"

"All right, then we're both horrible. Why are you defending the Indians all of a sudden? What awful people *all* people are."

"Right. And the sooner you learn that the better. Every one of us would kill another person if something that really mattered was at stake. Half of us would kill just for the sport. For kicks. For nothing, even. Just to see what it felt like."

"What a dreadful way to think. No wonder you hate children."

"I never said I hated children."

"But do you?"

"No."

"Do you love them, then?"

"The more you toss that word around, Audrey, the less I know what it means. I could never say I 'loved' any bunch of people like that, across the board. The world is full of rotten kids, just like it's full of rotten grownups. Spoiled brats, bullies, whining little losers."

"But didn't you ever love any *one* child, in particular? Weren't you very fond of one little boy?"

"What do you mean?"

"That boy in the swimsuit. In the picture. It's in your wallet."

"What the hell were you doing going through my wallet? Goddamn it, woman, who the *hell* gave you the right to do that?"

"You don't have to get so mad about it, Timmy. And please don't use language like that."

"I'll use whatever motherfucking language I want. Where else have you been snooping around?"

"I wasn't snooping. I was writing a letter and I ran out of stamps. You were in the bathroom, shaving. I knew you had some stamps in your wallet, and when I was looking for one I saw the picture. That's all. I don't see what that is to get so upset about."

"I just like to keep some things private, that's all. I don't like to think that every time I go to the toilet some goddamn private detective is going through my pants pockets. I've got enough to put up with already, without that!"

"*You've* got enough to put up with? You don't have to put up with someone's drinking problem. You don't have to put up with someone who stays out half the night with no explanation. I don't cause scenes in expensive restaurants. I don't drive the car blind drunk, and smash into other cars. . . ."

"You don't drive the car, period."

"Will you tell me who he is? The little boy in the picture? Or is that one of the deep, dark secrets I'm not supposed to know?"

"He's my brother. My little brother. His name was Peter."

"I thought you had only older brothers."

"Peter died when I was just a kid. That was the last picture anybody ever took of him."

"Oh—I'm sorry. It did seem a sad picture. He didn't look very healthy. Will you tell me about him?"

"I don't like to talk about it. I . . . I liked him a lot, and he got sick and died."

"I am sorry, Timmy. I really am. I'm sorry I saw the picture, if you didn't want me to."

"So am I."

On the level land near the junction of the Laramie and North Platte Rivers stands Fort Laramie, long a landmark and symbol of the Old West. Situated at a strategic point on a natural route of travel, the site early attracted the attention of trail-blazing fur trappers, who established the first fort here in 1834. It was purchased by the United States government in 1849, and for many years it offered protection and refreshment to the throngs who made the great western migrations over the Oregon Trail. It served as an important base in the conquest of the Plains Indians, and it witnessed the development of the open range cattle industry, the coming of the homesteaders, and the final settlement which marked the closing of the frontier. The fort was given up by the U.S. Army in 1890, and became a National Monument in 1938. Perhaps no other single site is so intimately connected with the history of the Old West in all its phases.

"Do you think your little brother dying has something to do with the way you feel about having children now?"

"No, there's no connection. It upset me at the time, but I got over it. I just keep his picture with me for good luck, sort of. I didn't like you finding it that way, that's all."

"I'm sorry I did, Timmy. But I love you more now for knowing about it, about little Peter and you. I know *you* better, and that means a lot to me. Loving your family is nothing to be ashamed of. That's what I was trying to say about mine. You don't have to be hard as a rock about everything, dear."

"Yeah. Well. I'm sorry I got so mad. I just don't like losing my privacy, I guess. Some things I want to keep mine, still."

"But if we keep secrets from each other, how can we feel truly married?"

"Oh, I'm sure you've got a secret or two in your past you wouldn't want me finding out."

"Don't be silly. *My* past? My life's an open, boring book. With blank pages."

"Are you sure?"

"Of course I'm sure."

"Well. Please don't ever look through my pockets again, okay? Or open my mail, or go through my drawers. And don't ask me about my little brother."

"Peter."

"Right. Peter. Anyway, he's got nothing to do with whether or not we ever have kids. Right now, I'm not even sure about us."

"What do you mean?"

"We seem to be going off in such different directions today. There's no point in our thinking about children until we're sure we make sense as husband and wife."

"Timmy! What an awful thing to say. Of course we do."

"Do you really think so? Do you think today proves that we're the perfect man and wife?"

"Well, I don't know about perfect. But . . . we're still in love, aren't we?"

"Are we?"

"Of course we are!"

"How long will that last, do you think?"

"Forever! Or else it isn't love."

"Maybe we didn't know what we were getting into."

"No one ever does, that's the whole point! It's a big jump in the dark. It's an act of faith. You risk everything, *because* you believe. That's what love is. That's the way I feel. Isn't that the way you feel?"

"I'm not sure."

"You don't need me anymore."

"I didn't say that."

"Because I need you, Timmy. You may hurt me any way you like, but from now on, I need you absolutely. If you left me, I'd die. I mean it. I'd kill myself."

Timmy glanced at Register Cliffs across the river. His thoughts were elsewhere.

Twenty miles past Guernsey, he got caught up again in the Interstate web, and joined it without a murmur. It was well after six o'clock; he had told Gerry on the phone they would be there by six. The effortlessness of a four-lane divided highway with wide shoulders allowed him to subtract driving from his log of concerns. I-25 to Casper demanded nothing more than a steady foot on the pedal, for 96 miles, and slight adjustments of the wheel. For 96 miles, the voice of KVOC-Casper, and the suffering engine, were the only noises inside the car.

It was the longest period of total silence they had endured, while awake in one another's company. Each kept thinking of fresh remarks, then decided not to make them, which prolonged the silence a bit more. The longer it lasted, the harder it was to break. Any remark would only have extended the day's hostilities, which neither really wanted; or sounded more placating and pleasant than they felt.

So they drove on in silence. Audrey felt winded from all the arguing, like a boxer after a difficult bout. It had been terribly unpleasant, but she felt intoxicated from the heady risk of having said out at last what she thought. Her pulse was beating fast.

For Timmy, there was nothing novel or intoxicating about it. Quarrels with his women always left him sullen and sick, sore in the gut. It was dismally familiar.

As the first buildings came into view from behind Casper Mountain, he lay his right hand down on the car seat, palm up, halfway between them. Audrey looked at it, thought about it, then lay her left hand inside it. As a gesture of reconciliation, it was cheap. But it was better than the cold apartness of the last 96 miles. He closed his fingers around hers, and risked a smile. When all else fails, some marriages survive through cheap gestures. Like holding hands.

The Gleasons took a little while to find. Timmy took the wrong exit from the freeway, so they had to drive the lengths of both Center Street (banks, motels, cafés) and East Yellowstone (car dealers, gas stations) to get to the eastern edge of town.

There were no numbers on the houses, no names on the mailboxes. They asked around, and were directed to a white pocked-plaster bungalow with a flat roof in the middle of a patch of weeds. From one sick tree hung a swing made out of a sliced tire casing, attached to a rope. In the front yard stood, among other things, a teardrop trailer, three eviscerated cars, bikes, trikes, wagons, a dog, some cats, children, washtubs, cans, pieces of machinery, a sand pile, toys, and tools. A woman with her hair wrapped in a bandana stood on the front porch, half-hidden behind a screen door. Two booted feet stuck out from under one of the cars.

Timmy parked. They both got out.

"Gerry. Gerry Gleason?"

The feet moved. A large man scrambled out from under the car. He unbent, stood erect; wiped his face.

"Hey! Big Timmy!"

"Gerry baby!"

The two men ran together and grasped each other's hands. They hugged, slapped backs, grasped hands again. Both were well over six feet tall. The

156

red-headed one was lean and strong-looking, barefoot, dressed in jeans and a T-shirt. His friend was paunchy and almost bald, and wore dirty striped overalls and boots.

The woman at the porch stared at the woman by the car. Then she opened the front door and went back inside.

19

Along the Platte
June 9, 1849

Since arriving at Ash Hollow two days hence, we have made our way through the most uninhabitable country fancy could conceive. The river continues shallow and repellent, if somewhat more narrow than before. It is turbid in consistency, fetid of odor, and foul to the taste. The trail itself is nearly pure sand, into which our wheels sink to a depth of eight inches. We reach mule trains that have been forced to stop altogether. Our oxen drag past them. Then, a few miles farther along, the mules overtake us. Despite the terrible slowness, there is a kind of frenzy to keep one's animals moving, however great the strain.

Hot winds drive the sand over the plain, coating all things with fine gray-white dust. It fills the air, drifting like desiccated snow. More of it is roused by each passing train, until the very air becomes blinding. The drivers shroud their faces in kerchiefs and apply court plaster to their lips.

On both sides, the river valley is now walled in by sterile bluffs and vertical ledges of rock eroded with deep ravines. From time to time the junction of land and water grows abrupt and precipitous, leaving no room for a wagon trail on the bank: then we must climb the bluffs and make our way over them. It is, at least, a respite from flatness.

A few stunted cedars have been spied on the ridges. Other than those, the only flora of this wilderness are the ubiquitous sage, prickly-pear in full bloom, and scatterings of small sunflowers with black centers. The few pools we have passed are either stagnant or alkali-poisoned, and resemble in color and taste the lye of ashes. The wiser cattle will not touch them.

The brutality of beast and man are stimulated rather than softened by the omnipresent fact of death. Driving among the graves of cholera victims, we passed several that had been torn open by wolves. The blankets shrouding the corpses had been pulled away, the remains devoured. We saw human bones that had been pulled apart and scattered by the beasts.

These wolves are fearsome creatures. They have great fangs, and enormous heads which they lift to emit long howls that disturb the soul. It is as if they were inhabited by demons. They venture quite near to our fires at night.

Today we came upon one of the high funeral platforms used by the Sioux Indians, and saw evidence of the work of human ghouls. We have passed several of these platforms. (In fact, the only Sioux we have seen since Ash Hollow have been dead Sioux.) In the limbs of a tree, about 20 feet from the ground, they make a kind of wooden rack, and place there the body of a departed brother wrapped in his blanket and a tanned buffalo skin. Upon the body they place his tin cup, moccasins, and various other articles which he had used in his life, to aid him in the land of spirits.

This practice at first struck me as atrocious, leaving the remains exposed as it does to wind and rain. But in these regions it is perhaps more prudent than sepulture, since it protects the body from bestial desecration.

Towards evening today we came upon one of these "burial platforms" of which the limbs had been wantonly chopped away, apparently by some Indian-haters from Missouri. The cadaver, of course, fell to the ground, and became food for beasts. This journey has exposed me to more of man's unregenerate nature than most people witness in a lifetime.

We are passing an extraordinary number of buffalo skeletons, in various stages of decomposition. Of live buffalo, we have seen none (save at a great distance) since our first view three weeks ago. The number of white hunters has driven them from the road. We met one clever fellow who had set up a stall along the trail, where he is making a living selling buffalo meat to his compatriots. Were there not millions of these beasts roaming the plains, the practice of removing only the choicest parts would seem a criminal waste.

We camp this day at Smith's Creek, cool and clear after the waters of the "slews" and the muddy and insipid Platte. Praise be to the Lord from whom all blessings flow, the waters of Whose grace are more refreshing than the coolest of springs.

Chimney Rock
June 12, 1849

We have, these past days, first seen and then attained two long-awaited landmarks of the trail. It comes as a relief to receive any reminder of progress, after travail so apparently "stale, flat, and unprofitable." These landmarks are certainly noteworthy and instructive.

To my disappointment, though, I did not experience the anticipated rapture that previous travelers claim to have felt. Mighty cliffs and pinnacles, standing solitary in a desert, appear to me more as ominous warnings than as cheering oases. True, they are a signal that one-third of our journey is done; but also that two-thirds—and surely the more difficult portion—of the journey remains.

The more distant landmark, known as "Chimney Rock," came first into view. I recognized it from a plate in Captain Frémont's report. It is like a high needle on the plain, and could be seen from two days' drive away. When the nearer landmark ("Courthouse Rock") was first seen, it appeared to be no more than two or three miles away. But distances are very deceptive in this strange land, where one has no trees or other familiar objects with which to judge scale. Those who set out on foot for Courthouse Rock found it to be more nearly twelve miles away than two, and returned quite exhausted from their excursion. James later climbed to the top. The view, he reported, is unrewarding.

The leaders of our party had been eagerly awaiting the first glimpse of these "sights," which they greeted with appropriate whoops and halloos. Courthouse Rock appears square, white, and regular from a distance, with a kind of flat dome on top: hence the name. Seen closer to, it is quite rough and immense, perhaps 200 feet high, and looks considerably less like a building. Except for a bluntly pointed companion rock to the east, it rises solitary and precipitous from this arid plateau. It is identified in one of our guidebooks as a "vanguard" of the Rocky Mountains ahead.

We traveled the next day in clear view of Chimney Rock, a vivid symbol of the region we are about to enter. From a distance, I would have avowed it man-made, the tall chimney of a mill or manufactory. Bluffs of similar height can be seen afar off, so this lonely spire of the plains must once have been connected to them. Over the centuries since the Creation, the fierce storms which rage in this region have worn away whole mountains of softer stone, leaving this solitary core of sandstone and marl. At present, the lofty spire, perhaps 20 feet through at its base, rises 100 feet from a steep pyramid or cone somewhat taller than that. According to the guidebooks, it was once a good deal higher. In a few decades, even this column will crumble to dust. Travelers who come after us will have little or no idea of this celebrated phenomenon, except from our words and sketches, and may well wonder at the exclamations of their ancestors.

Both these notable wayposts are composed of stone that may easily be cut by a knife. The established emigrant custom is to enscribe one's name or initials thereon, with the date and one's place of origin. Already thousands have done so. (James rode up to the rock to add his signature.) I do not understand this compulsion, a form of vanity which has been in evidence all along our route. Nothing escapes the pencil or the knife: buffalo skulls, stumps, logs, trees, rocks, even grave markers are marred by this propensity to signify one's passage. Most singlular is the custom of marking initials— "J.G.B.," for instance—as if everyone should know who J.G.B. was. Others chip off bits of the rocks for curiosities. This can only add to the burden of their animals, and hasten the day when these landmarks will be no more.

Neither these great rocks, nor the country from which they rise, can by the widest application of the term be called beautiful. We accommodate ourselves, as necessity obliges, to whatever terrain lies in our path. But this portion of America seems to me as inhospitable as the surface of the moon, and I for one will be glad to see the last of it. I can feel little admiration for mere geological curiosity, however grand: far more for the cool spring which

160

lies nearby, and alongside which we are now camped, together with far too many others.

Scott's Bluff
June 13, 1849

I had thought myself secure against the supposed seductions of desert landscape, but the soul must be made of cold metal indeed that can calmly view such wonders as lie about us. We are in the midst of a veritable city of fantastic ruins. The colossal central promontory, which rises (according to Captain Frémont) more than 800 feet above the riverbed, stands like a castle for a dead race of giants. Beyond it stretch miles of earth eroded into the shapes of ancient palaces, pyramids, and temples. One shudders in awe, so persuasive is the phantasy of a titanic civilization long disappeared, in whose immense footsteps we are marching. Winds, storms, and frosts have filed down these ramparts over the ages, until there are left only these soul-stirring ruins.

Although the ascent was steep and laborious (Mrs. G. objected that it was no fit excursion for a female!), I joined the Williams boys for the climb to the top, the better to experience the sublimity of the spectacle. James was confined to camp by his duties.

As the sun began to set, a narrow line of lurid light extended along the western horizon beneath a dark mass of vapor, casting lengthened shadows over the plain. The fairy city glistened as if gilded, from the scales of mica intermingled with their softer stone. From the top, we could see the Rocky Mountains towering towards the sky; Laramie's Peak frowning in the plain in lofty pride among his fellows; and the Platte River winding far below. The traveler from the Atlantic shore stands amazed to think that at last he is in the presence of that lofty chain of peaks which divides this continent in twain. The boys and I fell to our knees for a prayer of praise and thanksgiving.

The day was darkened by one ominous encounter. At the spring behind Scott's Bluff, we met a peculiar group of five men heading east, who professed themselves to be Mormons from the city of the Great Salt Lake. They were dressed in buckskins with huge spurs, and rode small Spanish mules. They carried large knives and pistols as well as guns, and were on the whole decidedly rough-looking fellows, with matted hair, long beards, slouch hats, and a distinctly criminal manner. They implied, quite savagely, that there were some folks on the trail from Illinois and Missouri "who would not live to see California."

Not only is our train from Illinois; it is also led by two men who were directly engaged in the expulsion of the Mormons from that state. So these threats occasioned no little consternation. There had been some talk of our traveling by way of the new Mormon city in order to recruit and reprovision. I must admit I welcomed the prospect of seeing homes and gardens again, whatever the faith of their owners. But since Captain McClellan and Lieutenant Briggs could be readily identified as former persecutors of these latter-day "saints," that course now appears dangerous and unwise.

* * *

161

June 14, 1849

I have nothing of interest to write, because nothing of interest occurs. My life at home is made up no less of sameness and scarce-varied routine. But there the sweet air, the flowers, the green trees, the easy security of one's own house, all the daily delights of intercourse with friends and family leaven the weight of tediousness. Here I grow weary not only of the sameness and routine, but also of the meager prairie fare—salt pork, day after day, cooked over dried buffalo excrement; of the inability to keep properly clean; of our incessant traveling; and above all of this devilish country of sagebrush and cactus, mosquitoes and gnats, dust and foul water. One looks into sand hills forever, white as winter frost and dazzling in the sun.

Fort Laramie
June 16, 1849

If we do *not* go by way of the Mormon city—and the company has been debating this question for several days—then this dilapidated post will be the last evidence of settled white civilization we shall see before Sutter's Fort, some 1,350 miles to the west.

We arrived in a violent thunderstorm, which only increased the lugubrious aspect of this "fort." We forded the Laramie River a mile to the east, after waiting in line several hours. The fort, property of a fur trading company, is a simple square enclosure made of whitewashed adobe (sun-baked mud), with defensive walls propped up by timbers, square towers at the corners, and a strong planked gate to the south, over which projects a balcony. From it, I suppose, one could hurl or fire missiles at a foe. Although it has suffered much from time and neglect, it is supposedly proof against Indian attack. ("Friendly" Indians are allowed inside by day.) It is soon to be converted to a United States Army post.

It is surrounded by emigrant parties, all relieved to have reached this frail haven. More astonishing than the numbers of people are the mountains of debris. Everyone grows apprehensive of the mountains distinctly visible to the west, and hastens to disencumber himself of all but essentials.

The waste of property and provisions is wonderful. We saw a mound of about 3,000 pounds of iron in one place. Wagons bought a month or two ago for 75 to 100 dollars cannot be sold here for five or ten. They are broken up for firewood, sawed into two-wheeled carts, or abandoned altogether. Chains and harness, saddles, large quantities of scarcely worn clothing lie about on the ground, all the way from the ford to the fort. Here huge piles of discarded bacon; in another place some 300 pounds of good flour; pilot bread in quantity. Anything that might impede progress, anything not absolutely necessary to life, is cast away as worthless. Costly trunks are torn to pieces. Wagon tires and irons of every sort are strewn along the road. For there is GOLD ahead! Men have grown reckless of all save that.

Tomorrow we begin to climb what are called the "Black Hills." The name, according to Captain McClellan, derives from the dark stunted evergreens on their upper slopes. But it has the sound of one of those dire moral obstacles through which Christian had to pass, on his way to the Celestial City.

20

The inside of the Gleasons' house in East Casper was even more of a mess than the outside. It was more of a mess than any home Audrey had ever been in. It was overflowing with manufactured objects, with a sick superfluity of mess. Whoever kept house here was what her mother would call a "slut," by which she meant a slob.

The Chief Slut was not in sight as they entered. Their host welcomed them by collapsing on a greasy couch from which the upholstery wadding oozed, and made it instantly greasier by wiping his hands on the arm. Timmy sat down, carefully, on the other end. Nobody asked, and nobody offered, so Audrey pulled back a chrome-and-plastic chair from the dinette set in the corner, and sat down facing the two men. The torn seat had been taped to its pad with a black X of electrician's tape. Evidence of decay was visible wherever she looked: cracked plaster, peeling paper, a missing board in the floor.

The men were off in a noisy chain of recollections, none of which they completed or bothered to share with her. Audrey sat up in her chair with a fixed smile on her face, a thin fiction of sociability. Surely the wife would come back soon. She would bring them something to eat and drink. Then they could talk, too.

On the top of the table under Audrey's elbow was a pile of unsorted laundry, a full ashtray, and a magazine dealing with the private lives of television celebrities. A dung-colored shag rug collected crumbs and pieces of puzzles in its wrinkles. Two half-full beer glasses, with cigarettes disintegrating in their contents, stood on the floor alongside the couch. More glasses were lined up on the mantel, along with a row of empty cans of Buffalo Ale. Against a crayon-scribbled yellow wall with great chunks gouged out of its plaster, a mammoth color TV set talked to itself, until a gawky girl in shorts and a Batman T-shirt, tiny breast-buds beneath, walked in, stared at the newcomers, then sat down on the floor inches from the screen and began turning from channel to channel. As she flicked, she kept stuffing her mouth with handfuls of Sugar Smacks from a box she held on her lap.

A little later a boy, a few years younger than the girl, ran in shouting, and began hitting his father's knee.

"Arnie's bothering me."

What's he doing?"

"He keeps coming in my room."

"So what?"

"He's *bothering* me. Make him stop."

"Make him stop yourself. I'm talking. Hey Andy, go bring a six-pack out of the refrigerator."

"I want to watch TV."

The boy forgot instantly about Arnie, walked up to the set, and changed the channel. The girl pinched him in the leg.

"Stop it!"

"I was *watching* that."

"Well, you don't have to pinch!" He kicked her, hard.

"Well, don't kick! Daddy!"

"Cut that out or I'll turn it off! Just cut it out, goddamn it. Anybody do any kicking around here, it's gonna be me."

The two kept bickering and shoving, but finally settled on a program they both could watch. They turned up the volume so they could hear it more clearly over the men's talk. The men just talked that much louder, ignoring the TV except during commercials, which for some reason they watched. In another room, someone was crying. Someone else, somewhere else, was yelling. Audrey felt trapped, to say the least.

"Excuse me." she said.

. . .

"I said, EXCUSE ME."

"Huh?"

"Could you tell me where the bathroom is?"

"Oh, sure. Down that hall there. Second on the left. I think Edith Ann's on the potty now. She usually cries like that when she wants to be wiped. Don't pay any attention to her, though, just go on in."

"Is . . . is there another bathroom?"

"Yeah, but the toilet's plugged up. Overflowed last week all over the hall and I haven't been able to fix it yet. Don't mind Edith Ann.

"Oh hey, look out for the bikes in the hall."

Sure enough, a red-faced little girl was sitting on a potty chair alongside the toilet, her underpants around her ankles, wailing a bored ugly wail between each breath. When she saw Audrey at the door, she stopped.

"*Wipe* me," she ordered.

"I'm sure your mommy will be here in a minute."

"Who are you?"

"I'm, ah, a friend of your mommy's."

164

"*You* wipe me then."

"No, dear. I have to go potty, too."

"No! *Wipe* me!"

Audrey ignored the child's command and sat down on the toilet. The girl started wailing again, louder than before. Suddenly the door opened, and the woman in the bandana looked in.

" 'Scuse me. I have to wipe Edith Ann."

Audrey finished and flushed as quickly as she could.

"I'm sorry. I just . . . Your husband said the other bathroom was . . . "

"Yeah, plugged up. Hell of a mess with four kids. I wish the old fart'd get off his ass and fix it." The woman kept scraping shit out of the toddler's rear end with a wad of toilet paper as she talked.

"I'm Audrey McCue. Timmy's wife."

"I figgered." She dropped the paper in the potty, then dumped the whole load into the toilet and flushed it again. "I'm Lois. Don't mind if I don't shake hands." The woman left, holding the little girl under one arm, and shut the door.

Audrey stood staring in the mirror. She opened the mirrored door, found an aspirin bottle. She shook out four vinegary tablets, swallowed them with water held in her cupped hands: there was no glass.

The bathroom was as foul as any back-country gas station's. Along the tub, around the basin, over the edge of the curling linoleum, the plaster had rotted away in a ragged filthy line of crud, rotted back to the lath and chicken wire behind. Cartoon decals were stuck on the walls. A bushel basket of dirty laundry was jammed behind the door. On the window sill stood jars and tubes of half-used unguents and greasy ointments. The tub was rust-colored under the dripping tap, a tired piss-yellow up to the ring. There were no towels Audrey dared touch, so after she washed her face and hands, she patted herself dry on her skirt, said a prayer, and went back into the front room.

Now there were three kids in front of the television set, and all three were arguing. Lois, still holding Edith Ann on her hip, brought in a six-pack of Buffalo Ale with her free hand—but no glasses. No food.

"I've gotta put Edith to bed."

"When do these guys get to eat, then?"

"Soon's you fix it. They're your friends."

"What kinda shit is that?"

"I've made one dinner tonight and I'm not making another. You want something more, you can cook it."

"Well, for Christ's sake, Lois! Why the hell didn't you tell me that before?"

"You said they'd be here at six. If they'da come at six, I'da had something. Now it's after eight and it's Edith Ann's bedtime. I'm not going to spend all night in the goddamn kitchen."

"Well, fuck you, sweetheart."

She walked out of the room with Edith Ann.

"Tell you what, Timmy. Lois being so lazy and inhospitable, whyn'chyou and me run out and get us a bucket of Kentucky Fried Chicken? That suit you two? That and beer?"

"Suit me fine, Gerry. You, darling?"

"Oh. Anything. Please don't make a fuss."

"No fuss. Be good to get out of this place for a while. You women can talk in peace."

After a few minutes, the strain of solitude in the midst of pandemonium grew insane-making. With the men gone, she was left sitting like Miss Invisible, ignored by three constantly bickering children, watching what seemed to be mostly commercials for feminine hygiene products and beer. But Audrey couldn't bring herself to go in search of a rude, crude woman who hadn't yet made the least gesture of welcome. Instead, she went out the front door, and stood on the porch.

The sun had gone down over Emigrant Gap, but the lights of Casper were too bright for early stars to be seen. It should have felt a comfort to have arrived at a real home, after all these days of free-fall. But this wasn't a home. She would rather be back in the battered red car.

Why had Timmy decided to stop? She couldn't figure that out. What were these people to him? If a boor like that could be one of her husband's best friends—a man who could live in a pigsty, treat his wife so disgustingly, raise a litter of such brats—what did that say about Timmy?

She looked at the rubber tire swing, the teardrop trailer, the hulks of cars spilling their guts on the lawn. Four metal garden chairs, one tipped over, one in pieces, stood against the porch. There were more bicycles and tricycles than there were children in the house. Some of them were in pieces, too. Further away, she could make out a sandpile, a cement mixer, concrete blocks, a metal horse on springs, what looked like a refrigerator.

A sudden howl of pain, a high E-string screech came from under the porch where she was standing. A child ran out past her and began throwing rocks, toys, a broom, under the steps at the noise.

"Is that your kitties fighting?"

"No. There's a family of skunks under the house. We can't get 'em out. My Dad tried to gas 'em, but it didn't work. Our big cat keeps trying to kill the baby skunks. A coyote got one last week."

As they were talking, the cat ran off. The night air filled with the dense stink of skunk. Audrey went back inside.

"Skunk chased you back in, huh?" The woman in the bandana was back.

"Yes. That's quite an odor."

"You get used to it. C'mon in the kitchen. Get away from this racket." The two boys were now spinning around and around to see who would get dizzy and fall down first. They made rising and falling siren noises as they spun. Since the men had left, their sister had taken over the couch. She was lying flat out on her stomach, still watching TV, still eating Sugar Smacks.

Some of the cabinets in the kitchen were painted a glossy pale green and some were not painted at all. The woman pushed the dinner dishes out of the way to make room for her ashtray and beer. Two damp brown paper bags of garbage sagged under the table.

"You want a beer?"

"No, thank you. Beer makes me sick to my stomach."

"Gerry gets that way, too. After he's had about forty."

"Would you have a soft drink of some kind?"

"Sure. You name it." She shoved an ironing board out from in front of the refrigerator.

"We got: Tab, Sprite, Creme Soda, Orange Shasta, and Doctor Pepper." She pushed things around on the shelves as she looked. "And a gallon jug of A & W. Kids drink this stuff by the tank car."

"A bottle of Sprite will be fine."

The woman opened a can of Sprite, reached down a bottle of gin for herself. This time she found glasses.

They sat at a table crowded with dishes and newspapers in a corner of the room. Audrey could look out the window, beyond the junk-mountain of an auto wrecker's yard, to the moonlit Wyoming plains. She sipped her Sprite. Lois sipped her gin. Both women smoked.

"So you're Timmy's new wife."

"Yes."

"When were you married?"

"Two weeks ago. Two weeks ago tomorrow."

"Gerry and I been married ten years."

"Have you known Timmy long?"

"Gerry has. They were in the Air Force together. Trying to drink all the beer in Germany, to hear them tell it."

Audrey smiled politely.

"And fuck all the frauleins."

She choked on a mouthful of Sprite. She had never heard a woman use that word before.

"When I met Big Timmy in Palo Alto, the two of them were trying to lead the same kind of life there they did in the Air Force, far as I could tell. It's taken me all these years to whip the old fart into line." She poured herself another gin. "You're gonna have your hands full, I promise you that." She lit a fresh cigarette off the butt of the last.

"How much do you know about your husband?" Lois asked after a while. "About his life before?"

"Not much, really. He doesn't tell me much."

"I'm not surprised."

"We got into a kind of fight about that on our way here today. About that and other things. It was our first real argument."

"Congratulations."

"No. It wasn't very nice."

"Learn to love 'em. There'll be plenty more."

"I hope not. I feel just sick about it. I should probably apologize."

"Rule number one: never apologize."

167

"It started when I told him I wanted to know more about what we'll be doing in California. He leaves me totally in the dark."

"What did he say to that?"

"He says he doesn't know yet himself."

"Then why go to California?"

"He doesn't like Massachusetts. My family, mostly. I think he wants to be near his own family."

"Is that what he said?"

"Not exactly. But he's obviously very fond of them. He keeps a picture in his wallet of his little brother, the one who died when he was still young. Did you know about that? He was very upset when I found it. But I was pleased to learn even that little bit about his past."

"Jesus Christ. The same bastard as ever."

"What do you mean?"

"Oh, never mind. You'll find out. Oh, my *God*, what a prick."

"Listen . . . if you know something I . . . "

"No, sweetie. Old Lois don't know nothin'." Gulp. She looked at her closely. "How old *are* you, anyway?"

"Twenty-two."

"Jesus, you poor kid. You know how old *he* is?"

"Yes. I don't mind. I never met anyone my own age I liked as much as Timmy." She looked nervously around. "Shouldn't they be back by now?"

She laughed, a laugh like dry cracking. "They're at a bar. I knew all along Gerry wanted to go out and get drunk. That's what they always used to do after *we* got married. Go out and get drunk somewhere, the two of them, so they could replay all their old basketball games and talk about cunts. Oh, they were a rare pair, Gerry and Tim."

"You mean they won't be bringing back any fried chicken?"

"Oh, eventually. Sure. Stays open till eleven. Why, you hungry?"

"Well . . . yes, sort of."

"Help yourself. Make a sandwich or something. Open a can. Potato chips. There's some leftover chile, I think."

"No. On second thought, I think I'll wait."

"Suit yourself."

Two of the children ran in, one crying, the other trying to out-volume her by yelling over and over that It Wasn't My Fault. Lois inspected the bite mark. Unable to determine who started it, she slapped them both in the face. That made them yell all the louder. The older girl started cursing her mother to her face in four-, six-, and ten-letter words. Lois tried to slap them again, but this time they both ducked away and were out of the room. She poured herself another gin, but as they started to talk again, Edith Ann, who was supposed to be asleep, banged in on a little push-trike, which she kept bumping against Audrey's shin. "Go away, dear," Audrey said each time she was bumped. "*You* go away," Edith Ann answered. Lois dropped cigarette ash on the little girl's hair, but otherwise ignored her.

"You gonna have kids?"

"I want to. Timmy doesn't seem to be sure."

"I'll bet he doesn't."

"I wish you wouldn't . . . "

"What?"

"Nothing. I wish he'd come back."

"This lot is it for me. Dierdre is thirteen. She's already sleeping around. Wants to get pregnant so she can get out of the house. Arnie's teacher thinks he's a retard. Andrew has undescended testicles and an overbite so gross he can't chew his food. I was eight hours in labor with Edith Ann, and in absolute torture the whole time. In the end I lost so much blood the doctor said I couldn't take another scene like that. It just came gushing out with the fluid. So I had 'em tied off. The old fart still doesn't know. I told him the doctor said too much sex isn't good for me anymore. Keeps him off my back. Belly, rather. Twenty-one, huh?" She touched Audrey's cheek, fingered her hair.

"Twenty-two." She tried not to wince.

"Timmy used to like big tits."

"He hasn't complained."

"You get much before?"

"Pardon?"

"Much sex."

"I . . . I'd rather not talk about that, if you don't mind."

"I offend you."

"No."

"Don't lie. I offend everybody. That's why I drink. So I can be sure of offending everybody." She reached out and cupped her hands around Audrey's small breasts.

"I'm really surprised at Big Timmy. He used to have such a thing about tits. Like a nursing baby, he was. You must have hidden talents."

"Why are you being like this?"

"Hey, hey. Don't cry, sweetie. It's all a joke. A big joke: two old married ladies trading secrets. Our husbands are old drinking buddies. But we can outdrink them, though, can't we?

"What you say your name was? Have another Squirt, squirt. Sprite, I mean."

"Excuse me. I . . . I have to go to the bathroom."

"So soon? I could have sworn you just went. Well. You know the way."

The two men came back, a bit woozy, about ten o'clock, and then they all sat around the living room, emptied at last of kids, and ate cold fried franchise chicken with their fingers out of a common waxed cardboard bin. They kept adding empty Buffalo Ale and Sprite cans to the collection on the mantel. The three of them (Audrey used her hanky) kept licking their fingers, and then wiping them on their clothes or on the couch. Lois had seated herself close to Timmy, very close to Timmy, and was feeding him bits of the Colonel's crust with her well-licked fingers. Gerry sat on his other side, still babbling on about athletic triumphs or rowdy adventures they had shared. Audrey sat on her chrome-and-plastic chair, one against three, sipping Sprite and feeling sick to her stomach.

Gerry asked how the two of them had met, which led to talk of jobs and plants and bills and money. Lois berated Gerry (whom she never called anything but "the old fart") for his fiscal stupidity and his lack of success, which dragged into a general row between them over money.

"Who paid for the TV, then? And the new trailer? The new refrigerator and freezer?"

"Who got us eight thousand dollars in debt to do it? Who can't afford to have the toilet fixed now? Idiot!"

"Then why did you whine and fuss all those years to get a color TV and a trailer?"

"*Me* whine and fuss? *I* didn't ask for them. *I* didn't want them here. You got the TV for 'Monday Night Football,' and the goddamn trailer to go fishing."

"Don't give me that shit. Day after day, you bitch that we don't have the things all your daddy's friends have up at the fucking country club. Then when I give in and buy them for you, you bitch about our being in debt."

"No big deal, being in debt." Timmy broke in, playing pacifier. "I *live* in debt. You got to, these days. Only way to fly."

Lois slapped his cheek gently, then kissed it.

"Now, don't you go giving him any more of your naughty ideas. The old fart's got enough of his own."

"Do you really believe that, Timmy?" Audrey asked quietly. She hoped it was an act.

"Sure. You got to let go. Take chances, fall free. Getting in debt's like getting drunk: you know there'll be a morning after. But it's still worth it at the time."

After that detour, they got back to more gossip and reminiscences, from which Audrey was totally walled off. She was growing to dislike Timmy's Munich and Palo Alto past with a passion.

Finally, Gerry realized she was still there. He grinned at her and patted her leg.

"How'ja like being married to a blue-ribbon stud, then?"

"Hey, Ger. None of that."

"I'm . . . I'm very happy."

"Ever seen him on one of his real toots?"

Yes, she thought, I have. But she smiled, and shook her head no.

"We did have a little accident in Chicago," Timmy confessed.

"A *little* accident? You never have little accidents. How'd you get him out of jail, cutie?"

Audrey just kept smiling.

"How are things in Chicago, then? We been watching all that on TV."

"Pretty bad."

"You guys catch any of that?"

170

"We were in Toledo when it broke there. Got held up by a National Guard roadblock out of Cleveland. Nothing since, though."

"I hear they burned the whole South Side clear down to the ground."

This led to a half-hour's round table discussion on welfare Cadillacs, black prostitutes and their pimps, the new scientific proof of Negroes' genetic inferiority (there was an article about it in the Casper *Star-Tribune*), the inherent flaws of One Man-One Vote democracy, their old basketball rivals in Germany, and finally (of course) Some of My Best Friends. Lois seemed to make a point of disagreeing with her husband and agreeing with Timmy. Audrey contributed the story of her grandmother's mugging.

"What did your family think of this hunk, then?" Lois asked her.

"Oh. Well!" She laughed nervously. "They thought he was too old for me."

"Ha. He's not too old for anyone. Are ya, Timmy old cock?" She flicked her tongue over her lips, and squeezed his inner thigh. Gerry popped open three more beers. Two and a half packs so far: five each that made, since ten o'clock, not counting what they had before.

"But they were pleased he was a Catholic."

This time it was Lois who gagged.

"You got to be kidding. Are *you* a Catholic?" she asked Timmy.

"Well, you know. Baptized. Irish-Italian family and all."

"*You* a fish eater! Now that is a good one. I can just see you curtsying and doing Hail Marys and all that. Did you have your wedding in a Catholic church?" she asked Audrey.

"Yes. A nuptial mass. It was very nice."

"Bride in white and all?"

"Yes. We have some pictures in the car, if you'd like to look."

"Another time, sweetie. But don't they check up or anything? I thought Catholics didn't allow . . . "

"Shut up, Lois."

"Don't allow what?"

"Forget it."

"The priest knew that Timmy wasn't exactly . . . devout. But once you're baptized, you're a Catholic forever. That's all they need to know."

"Were your mommy and daddy at the wedding, Timmy dearest?"

"No."

"That's too bad. I'm sure they're dying to meet Amy."

"Audrey."

"Whoever."

This sort of thing went on till after one, Gerry playing the high school reunion boozer, Timmy holding his own, occasionally giving Audrey little quizzical looks. Audrey just suffered. Lois appeared to enjoy the moral chaos she was creating—insulting her husband, all but mounting Timmy, throwing a poisoned dart every so often at Audrey.

It was Timmy who declared the festivities over, by standing up and yawning loudly, and then going down the hall for a loud, long, half-gallon piss. When he came back, Lois showed him how the couch made into a bed, and told them to sleep in as long as they liked. Gerry promised to look over the car in the morning, and shook hands with them both, but Lois gave goodnight kisses: a dry brush on the cheek for Audrey, for Timmy a wet smack on the lips.

"Wasn't that *awful?*"

"Wasn't what awful?"

"Everything! This house. The children. The food. The way they treat each other. The way they treated *us*. I don't know how you could stand it."

The stuffing-leaking couch opened into a kind of bed. In a hall closet they had found sheets and blankets, and spread them over it. Audrey had changed into her nightie. She was already under the covers and being eaten by giant Wyoming fleas. Timmy was sitting on the side of the bed, finishing a last beer while he took off his clothes.

"It's no palace. But it's comfortable. It's what they want, I suppose. They've got an acre."

"But it's *filthy!* What did you think of that bathroom?"

"I've seen worse."

"I certainly haven't. And the other one's stopped up. She must never clean anything. And she lets the children do whatever they want. I've never seen such horrid little brats."

"Lots of people's kids are like that. Just ignore them."

"How *can* you ignore them? The way they yell at each other all the time, pinching and kicking, talking back to their parents, walking right in when we're talking and causing a scene. While you were gone, the little one, who was supposed to be in bed, kept riding her scooter into my leg. On *purpose*. They never wash, they eat total junk, they watch whatever they want on TV. That thirteen-year-old swears worse than you do. And she's apparently already having sex!"

"Don't let it get to you. They're not yours."

In deference to the alien household, he had left on his underpants. He slipped under the blanket and sheet, and rolled up against her side.

"I wish you'd wear pajamas. You never know who might walk in, in a house like this. What if you have to get up to go to the bathroom?"

"What if I do? I'm decent."

"Timmy, I don't like being here."

"I guessed that."

"Is Gerry really that close a friend?"

"Not really close, not like Paul. But I wanted us to be able to stop at *somebody*'s house on the way across. Country can get pretty bleak if you don't.

"He's more an old friend than a close one. There aren't many people from that far back I've kept in touch with. We spent six years together in Germany, then we both worked in the same plant in Palo Alto."

"You seem to have had quite a time in those days."

172

"Gerry talks a lot. And Lois was just trying to get a rise out of you. He was a good friend when I needed a good friend. But he's kind of pathetic now."

"How do you mean?"

"He feels trapped up here. Dead-ended at forty. He was spilling it all out to me at the bar. We stopped at a bar on our way to the Kentucky Fried Chicken."

"Lois said you'd stop at a bar."

"He needed it. He's really in bad shape."

"Why did they ever get married? They sure don't seem to love each other."

"They once did. She was visiting some relations in California, and bang: love at first sight. I tried to talk him out of it. She knows that, and still holds it against me. Her daddy's a big wheel here in Casper—oil well exploration. They had to move to Wyoming if they wanted any of his money. Or so Lois says. Gerry hates the place."

"Do they have a lot of money?"

"Not now, apparently. But she *expects* a lot, when the old man dies. Over two million, she says. Unfortunately, her father's healthy as a horse. And he thinks Gerry's a loser."

"Is he?"

"Well, not completely. He's got his own garage in town. And that wrecking yard out back."

"Then why do they live like this?"

"This property is worth plenty, mess or no mess. You heard them talking about the new TV and trailer and stuff."

"That's borrowed money, she said."

"Well, they spend a lot. They've got a cabin somewhere in the mountains. They're just not too fanatic about neat."

"You're telling me."

"Hell, that's no big deal. I'm not, either. Lots of things matter more than neat."

"They could at least have the holes filled up. Clean up the yard. Call a plumber for the toilet. Get a decent couch."

"He just doesn't care about all that. It is pretty depressing, I admit, seeing him like this. He was a real powerhouse, a few years ago. Now he feels like . . . like this place looks."

"What do you think happened to him?"

"Her."

"How do you mean?"

"They don't get along at all anymore. I hate married guys who tell you all their private problems in bars, but he thinks she's seeing someone else. I told him he ought to just pack up and go, but he can't. Four kids, this idea they're going to be rich someday. In the meantime, she puts him down all the time, kicks him out of bed when she's in a bad mood, or has had enough from this other stud, which is apparently most of the time. He just lays there and takes it. She's wrecked him."

"Don't you think he was partly to blame?"

173

"I suppose. He really seemed to be going places once, though. Would you believe that guy was our star center in Germany? With that gut? We went surfing together in Mexico. He could outrun me just ten years ago, beat me at tennis. Now he's a fat lazy slob who drinks beer, complains about his kids, and argues with his wife."

"Maybe that's how we'll end up."

"Not a chance. I don't make those kinds of mistakes. Anymore." He snuggled closer, kissed the back of her neck.

"Why does his wife hate me?"

"What makes you think she hates you?"

"She wouldn't even look at me, when we first got here. Then when you guys were out, she turned really vicious, like she was accusing me of something. And all the time in the living room she kept giving me these looks, making nasty cracks about everything I said. You must have noticed."

"No, I didn't. I was sitting alongside her. I couldn't see her face. Maybe she envies you." He tried reaching under her nightie, but she moved his hand away. "You're younger, you're prettier . . . "

"She certainly seemed interested in *you*, crawling all over your lap, always taking your side against her husband. That big, gooey goodnight kiss. You didn't need to let her do *that*."

He rolled heavily onto his back. He had long ago learned never to try making love to a jealous woman.

"She was a little high, and trying to annoy Gerry. She didn't mean anything. Maybe *she* feels trapped. I mean, here we are, you and me, sailing free across the country, going to California. All she has to think about is her kids' learning disabilities and how much they're in debt. If I'd known they were getting along so badly, I never would have come."

"It's not exactly a dream marriage."

"No, it's not."

"I suppose you don't think ours is anymore, either."

"Hell, don't compare us to them. We got problems, like anybody else. But we'll sort them out better than that."

"How will we?" She was starting to cry.

"I know one way."

"No. Please don't. Just keep holding me the way you are now."

"You're sure you wouldn't like a little more?" He was rubbing himself up against her.

"No, please. And don't do that, either. Just hold me tight."

"If I hold you tight, that happens."

"Don't be difficult, Timmy. All I want to do is get to sleep as fast as possible. Anyway, they'd hear us."

"So *what*? We're supposed to be on a honeymoon. They'd be surprised if they *didn't* hear something."

A dull mumble from the next room reminded them that their hosts' bedroom was just one wall away. They must have just gone to bed. Even as Timmy and Audrey were talking, the mumble rose in volume and pitch. Phrases began to detach themselves.

"I think they're having an argument."

"Shhh!"

"About us?"

"Probably."

"What are they saying?"

"I can't tell."

The shouts grew to shrieks, then shriveled into hisses, but all muted, like noises from the waking world we hear when we're half-asleep. Audrey put her hands over her ears, and tried to close up tight in Timmy's arms like a seashell. She wept silently for a while. Timmy stroked her hair, her shoulder, her back, tried to ease her to sleep.

The muffled argument went on and on, rising, subsiding, halting, starting over again. Timmy knew very well what they were arguing about. He lay on the sprung springs and lumpy padding, with Audrey's weight and warmth in his arms, tempting, frustrating.

Christ! Now the baby was yelling, too. Fresh shouts from next door; a door slammed, feet stomped angrily down the hall, the feet of whichever one of them had lost the argument, and had to go shut up Edith Ann.

God, there *were* fleas! He tried to itch without disturbing Audrey. She was now sound asleep and snoring gently. The last tears were still wet on her face.

I wish I could cry myself to sleep as easy as that, he thought. Sometimes I just wish I could cry. Only cure I know for insomnia is fucking. One quick piece and I'd be out like a light.

But not tonight. *Or* last night, come to think of it. When baby's not sick, she's discontent. Some honeymoon, fella.

Now the bedsprings in the *next* room were going. Good for you, Gerry baby. At least one of us is getting some.

He looked at the sleeping child in his arms, and suddenly felt something like the pure glow of their first days in Massachusetts. I *do* love you, baby; goddamn it, I do. It's just that I get so locked up in myself sometimes that I don't know what to do about it. There are times in my life when anyone from outside is an intruder. That's just the way it is.

I still fight you too much. For no reason. I resist you, just because you're not me. I fight to win, I do, don't know why I do. Damn it, I ought to be strong enough not to have to keep hitting a sweet baby like you just to prove it.

I'm sorry, sweetheart. He kissed her softly in her sleep, like the prince kissing Sleeping Beauty: forehead, eyelid, ear, cheek, lips, five gentle touches he hoped her unconscious mind would register as love.

What I've got to start doing is making her worries and pleasure mine, he told himself, not keep bristling because they're different. She's bored with the West: maybe some of it *is* boring, you idiot. She's scared of lots of things: understand how that feels.

These things matter to her, can't you see that? Even if she's wrong about them, it makes no difference. Give in. Give her more. She's saving you, fella, saving you from a life like these slobs'. Saving you from all the Loises and Dees of the world. You can never give her enough.

I've been such a selfish bastard.
I don't deserve her.

Audrey woke to bright sunlight and the noise of people shouting. Timmy was gone. She sat up in panic. She could hear his voice coming from the kitchen. It wasn't a dream, then: he was arguing loudly with his friend Gerry. Then someone hit someone else.

Quickly she got up, put on her slippers and ran to the kitchen door. She saw Gerry's face, wide-eyed, his nose bleeding. Timmy turned on her with eyes like fire.

"Keep out! Just get out. Please. Pack our things. Right now."

She closed the door behind her, dressed without thinking, and shoved everything into their one overnight bag. Timmy was already dressed; his things were packed. The argument in the kitchen went on for a few minutes more. Then he came back into the living room. He hugged her once, tight, and said only, "Don't ask. We've got to go." They went out, put their bags in the car, and drove away from the Gleasons' about 7:45.

Audrey presumed that Gerry had made some unspeakably rude remark, and that Timmy had done the only honorable thing. He said no more about it, so neither did she. Only after they had been on the road for an hour did she remember that she had left behind the jewel box in which she kept the objects that mattered most to her in the world: her mother's letters, her old photos, her great-grandmother's jewels.

But she didn't tell Timmy, since they obviously couldn't go back. Maybe they'll send them on.

Then again, perhaps it's just as well for me to give them up, she suggested to herself, unconvincingly. Those things belonged to a different me.

There was a time in her life when Audrey Hunter had taken almost passionate pleasure in making sacrifices. She tried to will back that attitude now, but the effort was too much.

She wanted back that box of things. Those awful people had stolen her past.

176

21

Five days we have been marching through these dismal hills, with foul or no water. Our company now forms part of a sad army which strains up steep ridges, only to plunge directly into dry beds of creeks. The land grows more sterile the farther west we move. Daily we ascend towards the Rockies. We are now, by Captain McClellan's calculations, nearly 5,000 feet above sea level, and must climb another 2,300 feet before we reach the pass.

This constant movement up and downhill is exhausting the cattle and damaging the wagons. Since quitting the fort, we have had very little level going. It is one precipitous ravine after another, all carved out by spring creeks long since dried; then up the tedious ascent to the next ridge, wave after tiresome wave. On the downward slopes, women and children run alongside the wagons and try to catch at rocks and shrubs, slipping and sliding along, while the men drag against the wagons, toss obstacles out of the path, and try to keep the oxen from falling. Many of our descents end up in a perfect plummet of panic and confusion.

The absence of grass is becoming a matter of concern. At each day's stopping place, the men must drive the cattle farther and farther from the trail in order to find land that has not yet been grazed to bare earth. Near the road, every bit of green has been eaten off. All trails west have converged into one now, and the traffic is too heavy for the natural supply.

The earth is the color of fired brick. The stone is either calcined or black. In places where there is no vegetation, the earth's surface may be covered with a pumice-gray stone. I am sitting apart from the camp now to write. As I raise my eyes, the ridges in every direction are bare. A little thin grass is all that relieves the sight.

These steep ridges south of the river are threaded by its tributary creeks in the spring, but now most of them are dry. What water we do encounter away from the river can be dangerous to drink. In some places, signs have been posted alerting travelers to avoid innocent-looking springs. Through these hills the trail twists tediously on, lined to the far distance with the weary wagons, men, and animals of this great migration. The animals' hooves stir up fine white dust.

Beyond the trail lie more hills, identical to those on which we move. As the terrain becomes more rocky, it also becomes more strange, less like any region of civilized earth. We pass granitic towers, strange spiring formations, the tumbled debris of ancient volcanoes. Man could never master such a hostile and alien land. It is a hideous country, resembling one's conceit of the primordial chaos. Except for the need to maintain this one trail across it, the land should be left to the Indians in perpetuity, savage land for a savage race.

We passed the northern foot of Laramie's Peak today, and saw a grand thunderstorm circling about its snow-covered brow. But I can no longer take delight in the grandeur of prospects.

Twice we have suffered broken wagons from overturning. One was lost altogether, with its contents and team, when the right side wheels ran off the road at a precipitous turn. In an instant all was pulled headlong down, the wagon smashed, the oxen dragged to their death. Enough was salvaged from the second wreck to convert into a two-wheeled cart, but half the contents had to be abandoned.

The trail continues to look like the route of a fleeing and desperate army, which has left behind all manner of goods in its flight. The Black Hills are littered with heavy mining equipment, mountains of white beans (which were having an unpleasant effect on men's bowels, in any case), expensive furniture, and whole wagons, either intact or in pieces. Some of the debris is left for the use of any needy comer, with a small placard to make clear the invitation. In other cases, men have rendered their discarded possessions unfit for others' use, by breaking utensils, chopping up trunks, pouring turpentine in sugar, etc. It is regarded as unmanly to assist one's competitors in the race to the gold fields. The injunctions of our blessed Savior are scorned.

June 23, 1849

We are forced inland from the North Fork of the Platte. Those who risk drinking from the salt- and sulphur-fouled springs, or from ponds encrusted with saleratus, inevitably become ill. In fact, no day passes without someone among or near us falling ill, although we are at last beyond the reach of cholera. The current spate of chills and fever, of gasping and general weakness is apparently due to what is called "camp" or "mountain" fever. No one knows precisely whence this malady comes, or how to treat it; but it seems not to be fatal.

In country as arid as this, marching over terrain so broken and rough, one craves drink of some kind every hour of the day. (I now walk all day, to spare the animals.) But we have gone as long as eight hours without it. At the end of

178

a long day's march over sage-hills, one rushes to a stream, fills one's cup—only to discover a noxious, bitter brew. It is heartbreaking. Pure water, when it is discovered, has become more precious than gold. In general, it is dangerous to drink *any* water in this region, except that of the Platte. But frequently the rough terrain obliges us to move from that river for days at a time, and men must then travel miles from camp in search of a tolerable spring. The directions of the guidebooks are of no use whatever, as the sheer numbers of this migration have dried up what were once sufficient springs—just as our cattle have devastated the rich meadows promised by the books.

The whole company now covers its lips with court plaster. The drivers' noses and eyes have become as red as blood—all the effect of this vicious alkaline dust.

We have lost another wagon, and two oxen. I do not see how we can survive if we do not reprovision among the Mormons, but Captain McClellan remains adamantly opposed to any intercourse with these people, whom he still regards as treacherous and immoral.

James is growing more and more disrespectful of our companions. He retreats into the solitary and sullen silence I know so well. He now speaks of McClellan as a fool, and of the Carthaginians as "Mississippi River scum." Were I not here, I am certain that he would have packed in on muleback long before now. I fear he blames his slow progress on me as much as on the company. He has not spoken out in anger to me yet; instead he wounds me by making cruel insinuations about Henry and Hector Williams, whom he talks of as "girls"—as if decent manners and a lively Christian faith were not proper to a man! Surely they are doing their share and more of the work. Although they are 10 and 12 years his juniors, they seem wonderfully strong and sagacious, always willing to assist in good cheer. I would be quite wretched by now without the comfort of their company, since James has withdrawn so, and Mrs. Garner appears to have poisoned her own mind, and those of her daughter and Ellen Dawson, against me.

The sour hostility of man against man on this expedition continues and grows worse. At the least provocation now men set upon one another with harsh words, fists, even weapons. I do not think our small party can survive intact another thousand miles, whether James grows reconciled or not. Mr. Parkinson refused to part with an elaborate iron auger he has brought along, as well as a diving bell and all its apparatus which he insists are required to obtain gold from the streams of California—even though the weight so burdens his poor oxen that they are on the point of failing. The captain has asked each mess to discard another 300 pounds of goods. All but Mr. Parkinson, and two others who carry prizes similar to his, have agreed. There is, of course, no way to enforce such "orders" in this lawless limbo, where the very landscape is a model of chaos. We left off flour, beans, salt, and a quantity of iron chain.

Guard duty has been abandoned by all but a few men, and the order of march falls into disarray. Cattle are dreadfully abused. The presence of women no longer offers any guarantee of decent speech or civilized behavior.

Men will bloody one another's noses over the amount of pork on a plate, or a scant patch of grass "claimed" by some first comer. People tend to their personal wants in full view of strangers of either sex.

Twice we have encountered weak and elderly emigrants abandoned to "make it on their own" by companies whose progress they had retarded. Our leaders had enough conscience left to share with them some of our provisions; but each time the vote went against accepting them as members of our group. "Verily I say unto you, inasmuch as ye have done it unto one of the least of these my brethren, ye have done it unto me."

The nights grow colder as we ascend. Each is filled with the mournful dirge of wolves. Yesterday one of our hunters shot an antelope in the rocky uplands, but before he could drag it away it had been half-devoured by these hungry beasts. By day, we come across anthills a foot and a half high, and great ugly toads with horns. Underfoot, we crunch the shells of thousands of crickets. The ground, in some places, is black with them. They cannot be avoided. The Indians, we are told, eat them.

Deer Creek
June 24, 1849

The last eight miles to Deer Creek were a trial. The wind blew so hard that men and animals were blinded and suffocated by the dust. After four hours' march, we had to lie flat on the ground for an hour in order to breathe; then drove on again through the dust.

After such an ordeal, this small cluster of stunted ash and willow, on the banks of a quite ordinary stream, seems a perfect oasis. How little one thought of water back home, where it was as fresh and abundant as air!

I have found a quiet spot under some trees, a little distance from the wagons, where I am seated on a stone with notebook and pencil in hand.

The grassland around Deer Creek is filled with hundreds of wagon parties, recruiting their stock and debating where to cross. The river is perhaps 20 feet broad here, clear and fresh; but 10 to 15 feet deep and dangerously rapid, with steep and sandy banks. The grass is the best we are likely to see for many days. Unfortunately, it is being cropped so rapidly that companies one or two weeks behind us may find the place as barren as the hills before. In order to have another topic to dispute, our men now argue over whether to rest a day or two at Deer Creek. It is obvious that we should (in any case, today is Sunday). But the impetuous are, as always, likely to win the day. The Williams boys and I read from the gospel according to Saint Matthew, and discoursed on the implications of the text: "Come unto me, all ye that labor and are heavy laden, and I will give you rest."

However wearying the day, sleep is made difficult by mosquitoes and what are called "buffalo gnats." These swarm into one's eyes, mouth, nose, and ears, and their bite raises a welt the size and painfulness of a boil. They torment the poor animals.

Hundreds of wagons are jostling for space. The major ferry is 30 miles farther upriver. Captain McClellan is disposed, for security's sake, to continue until we reach it. But the press of numbers is much too great here for any

180

single vessel to carry us all. Many parties are trying to make seaworthy craft of their wagon beds, or building their own rafts, or buying those made by others—which they in turn resell to the next in line. Still others risk a ford, which is foolhardy in water so rapid and full. Six men have drowned already.

Among the litter of heavy goods jettisoned hereabouts—the usual cook stoves, mining tools, chain, lead, bar iron, anvils and crowbars, axes and ploughs—I spied with a sudden pang a walnut bedstead, a quilt, and a rocking chair. These I recognized at once as the "household" of Emma Cluett, which had so warmed my heart at St. Joseph. All of that now seems centuries ago. God grant she is well, and her sorrows abated. How sad it must be to lose so much of one's past in this wilderness of waste.

June 26, 1849

In a state of discord and confusion, the company made its way upriver to the main ferry over the Platte, only to discover that its chief operator, a Mr. Shumway, was a Nauvoo Mormon who not only recognized certain men of our party, but refused them passage on any terms. Harsh words were exchanged, which might have led to still more serious hostilities, had not James and two other non-Carthaginians persuaded Captain McClellan to descend four miles to another ferry. This one is built and maintained by two emigrants from Illinois, who have decided to pause a few days from their own rush for gold in order to grow rich from other men's impatience. We crossed on rafts made from lashed-together canoes, pulled back and forth by means of a rope stretched across the river. The cost was five dollars a wagon. They accept only gold.

Once across, a meeting was ordered by Captain McClellan in an attempt to reestablish some discipline. The result is as I predicted: we are reduced once again. Four wagons voted to go off on their own, or to join a better company. James insists this is all to the good, as it will be easier to find grass in any place for 12 yoke of oxen than for 24, and we are now quit of the worst of the factioneers. I shrink with faint-heartedness, however, at any reduction of our numbers. We once enjoyed the security of a small but self-sufficient village; now it is all we can do to double-team up hills. Were I a man, I hope I should not be such a coward.

June 28, 1849

The last two days were our most strenuous so far. As the country between the Platte ferry and the Sweetwater River is nothing but sulphurous dust, and its water all poisonous, the company voted to make a forced march through the night. We stopped only once, at midnight, when the oxen were on the edge of collapse. We saw our first patch of green grass about seven A.M., having covered 44 miles in 24 hours. Every hour of the way, under sunlight or starlight, we saw other trains on the same undertaking. This bit of grass, with its small spring, was the campground of an army. (The actual river lay 16 miles further on.)

At each stream or spring, we encounter dead or dying oxen, poisoned by their own thirst. What appear to be huge ice ponds turn out to be water totally crusted over with saleratus—or else visual phantasies occasioned by the heat. The effect of the alkali in the sand is so strong that the soles of wagon drivers' boots are eaten away.

Although it is for many a symbol of aridity, since it grows where naught else can survive, I have developed a peculiar affection for the western sage. It is as if God felt the need for some form of visible life even on the desert, and created this hardy little fellow to keep the American plains from assuming the total emptiness of an African Sahara. There is something heroic in the way these round, grayish-green balls spread over and colonize the most desolate landscapes, offering in their endless speckling of the land, the stubble with which they darken and fur over the farthest hills, a presence for the imagination to hold onto, a trace, at least, of life like one's own. If *you* can eke out a living here, dear little plant, perhaps we shall survive as well.

In the meantime, we burn their dry stems for our fuel, and crop their bitter branches for our stock. When even the sagebrush died out on our march to the Sweetwater, I felt we had touched the planet's driest bones.

If not totally clear and pure, the Sweetwater is so much more so than the Platte that it warrants its name. It is only two feet deep here, and perhaps 40 feet wide. But its water is so deliciously welcome one thanks Heaven for directing it into our path. We have only to follow its course now to reach the crest of the Rocky Mountains.

July 1, 1849

Rain fell this afternoon in a perfect sheet, accompanied by lightning and thunder. A few seconds after the commencement of this storm, hail hurled down upon us like immense quantities of gravel. Stones of an extraordinary size followed, which cut and bruised men and oxen.

The day had been very sultry before the storm, and James was in his shirt sleeves when it hit. When it was over, his back was as sore as if it had been thrashed with a stick. As we were in a perilous position, on the edge of a cliff, men had to stand out in the storm half an hour to hold the oxen steady. James was holding to the reins of one yoke, blinded by the vivid lightning and the avalanche of hailstones and rain, when the animals broke free and dragged him 20 paces. He lost hold, and was struck in the back, as the wagon went over him. He had been hit by the water keg hanging to a coupling pole, but was fortunately no worse hurt. In a brief period, the temperature had fallen about 40 degrees. The mountain top was ankle-deep in ice and ice water, which stood in pools and ran down in cataracts through every crevice and gulch.

As we climb higher towards the Rockies, the ordeal of freezing nights is added to the strain of scorching days. We wake to find our blankets and buffalo robes rimed with frost. The ice does not melt until eight or nine A.M., at which time the weather turns very hot, almost at once.

The further we go, the more extraordinary are the individuals we pass: a solitary traveler who journeys only by night, and lives (so he claims) off nothing but berries and roast prairie dogs, which he shoots with bow and arrow; an ancient Swiss, pushing his earthly possessions before him in a handcart; a lone Indian—the first we have seen since Ash Hollow—dressed only in a plug hat and satin waistcoat, which he retrieved from some wealthy emigrant's cast-off belongings.

Dead oxen pile up along the trail. The most wretched are those who stop, footsore and unable to work, where their owners unhitch them and leave them by the side of the road. Almost immediately the ravens and wolves begin to worry them, pursuing them remorselessly 10 or 20 miles through the desert until they fall. The poor creatures have no defense against the persistence of these scavengers.

July 2, 1849

The surface of the Sweetwater valley is white with an alkaline efflorescence. The river has declined to a mere brook.

Today we had our first view of the Wind River Mountains, as the nearest wing or wall of the Rocky Mountains is named. What at first I took for clouds turned out to be their snow-covered peaks, 20 or 30 miles away—snow in July! The tallest among them is named for Captain Frémont.

Stranger still, we came upon an ice field five or six inches thick just under the turf below our feet—a natural ice-house, 6,000 feet in the sky, in the midst of this sandy plain. It has already been half-excavated by curious travelers like ourselves.

Pacific Spring
July 5, 1849

Yesterday at two P.M. we accomplished the most significant intermediate goal of this expedition: we crossed over the "backbone of the continent," to begin our long descent towards the Pacific. From now on, we follow waters that make their way to warm western seas.

Were it not for the guidebooks, which point out precise trail marks by which South Pass may be identified, no one would have known that this great moment had been reached. The gap is many miles wide, and the final ascent so gradual that the crest is indiscernible. It is simply a space between low ridges of granite and sand. One would prefer a more dramatic setting, in order to feel something more in keeping with the sublimity of the occasion. But it would be foolish to rail against ease.

Two miles past this "summit," between low slopes of sand and dry grass, we came to Pacific Spring. From here, in the midst of a muddy swamp, the waters flow west to the Colorado, and south to the Gulf of California. We made camp in company with a great many others.

Fortuitously, our ascent of South Pass fell on the anniversary of our nation's independence. In honor of these two happy events, we joined with two other Illinois companies, from Marion and Centralia, and a number of individual wagons, for a feast of wild peas, stewed gooseberries, peach and apple pies, smoking biscuits, honey, rich milk, cream, venison steaks, tea, and coffee. Could any great eastern hotel offer finer fare?

After supper, the men gave a salute of small arms, and paraded around the

183

corral. Captain McClellan and the two other captains recited what little they could remember of the Declaration of Independence, and gave toasts, which were drunk in whiskey and cordials, to the United States of America, and the California Territory in particular, a discharge of musketry accompanying each. To the music of violin and jew's harp, patriotic and sentimental songs rose into the night, all the more spirited for our remoteness from our fellow citizens. Men danced (of necessity with one another) until after midnight. I did not join, as James declined. His increasing remoteness and taciturnity are to me a source of constant pain, so I could not freely share the joy of this occasion. But it is good to see any instance of patriotism, and of generous, open, neighborly sharing. I have seen far too much of man's baser instincts of late.

22

The route from Casper to Moran Junction, which is the east entrance to · Grand Teton National Park, runs slightly north of west across the state of Wyoming. Through a region of the earth crumpled and broken into high mountain ranges, it follows the path of the Wind River Valley. The road climbs gradually from just over five thousand feet at Casper to just under ten thousand feet at Togwotee Pass and the Continental Divide, then descends rapidly another three thousand feet down the west side of the Wind River Mountains. These are high, jagged mountains, snow-covered the year round and difficult of access. Six peaks of the range, which is a spur of the Rockies, rise to over thirteen thousand feet.

Slightly less than halfway across the state, the road crosses the Wind River Indian Reservation. Although not as large as the vast Apache nation in Arizona, the Sioux holdings in Dakota, or the native lands in Alaska, this reservation—shared by the Shoshone and Arapaho tribes—carves out a sizeable chunk of west-central Wyoming.

Timmy and Audrey reached the eastern boundary of the reservation when it was still mid-morning. Conversation during the day's first hundred miles had been a little surreal, since both avoided any mention of the stopover in Casper.

When they got to the reservation, they agreed to look around for a while before Timmy went in search of his next friend. A little apprehensive after the last visit, he was marking time before making another.

So they detoured up Big Horn Canyon to Thermopolis, then came back on reservation roads to Fort Washakie. There they made the rounds: historical markers and graves, the mission and blockhouse, the new tribal offices, the new post office, the new school.

Of the few people about, only their faces distinguished the residents from the tourists and passers-through. Native faces were dark and high-boned, rounded at the cheeks and chins. They had hawk noses and deep cheek lines and unsmiling, Oriental eyes, which still seemed to carry a flame of defiance or at least disrespect.

The Indians, to Audrey's disappointment, were dressed like everyone else in western Wyoming. ("What did you expect?" Timmy asked. "Feathers?") They drove dirty cars and trucks, or simply stood about the dusty streets. The buildings could have been lifted whole from Casper, Wyoming. It looked strange to see them here, far from any supporting civilization.

For all their bluejeaned normalcy, Audrey was intimidated by the reservation Indians. Their sullen gazes reminded her of the blacks in Chicago. If she bought a few cheap souvenirs at the trading post, it was mainly to escape the evil squint of the woman behind the counter, with her squashed nose and fat cheeks and greasy braids. She lingered in Hines' General Store picking out groceries, trying to hear what Timmy was saying to the beer-bellied man who wore a turquoise and silver buckle on his belt, and had a face like wrinkled leather.

"It's okay. He told me how to get to Paul's place. Have you got everything?"

"I guess so. Enough for lunch and dinner today, anyway. And breakfast tomorrow."

Back in the car, Audrey confessed her anxiety.

"Are you sure this is the right thing to do, just dropping in like this?"

"Sure, I'm sure. Paul's the best friend I ever had."

"So was Gerry Gleason."

"That's not true. I never said that. This will be different, I promise you. Paul is the best *person* I've ever known. He's totally straight."

"I'm sure he is, darling. But I'm feeling very uncomfortable. This place looks like a concentration camp. People keep staring at us like we're prison guards, like they've got a secret plan to murder us and escape."

"Don't be silly, Audrey. They live here. This is their home. It's no concentration camp. They must be used to tourists like us by now, going through to Yellowstone. Nobody's staring at us."

"Was it like this before?"

"I've never been here before."

"Then where did you meet your friend?"

"In Dubois. It's a little town on the west side of the reservation, where the outfit he worked for was located. We started all our trips from there."

They drove out of the village, over a log bridge, off on a bumpy road heading north. At first, the countryside was thickly wooded, but then it grew barren and dry. Small houses were scattered about the hills.

"When did you see him last?"

"Nine, maybe ten years ago. Before I moved to Boston."

186

"How do you know he's still here? Ten years is a long time."

"That old man in the store. He knew the name right away. Anyway, I knew he was here. Guys like Paul never move. His whole life is in these mountains. He used to tell me stories of what the mountains meant to Shoshone. They're supposed to be sacred ancestral homes, he said, the home of their spirits.

"He did go away once, just before I first met him. To a junior college up in Sheridan. The tribe had given him a scholarship. Their idea was for him to go on to the university in Laramie, and then to law school, and come back a whiz lawyer who would make everybody on the reservation rich by suing the U.S. government. That's one of their big dreams, apparently; making the government pay them back for the last hundred years.

"But Paul gave it up after one semester. Couldn't stand being so far away from his mountains.

"Really pissed off his dad, he told me. The tribal council had to pick someone else."

"What does he do now?"

"He got to know these mountains so well that the pack train people up in Dubois hired him as a guide. He had all the old skills down pat. Then he learned European-style climbing from an old German mountaineer when he was a kid. When I last saw him, Paul's plan was to build up his own clientele—climbers, hunters, fishermen; and then save up enough money to buy his own animals and gear. What he wanted to do was break away from Shorter and McHenry, and start up his own outfit. If all the people he'd done well by over the years would stick with him, he'd have the competition out of business within a year. I bet he's done it."

"Why didn't you ever write and find out?"

"We never wrote much. A postcard maybe. I hardly ever write letters."

"But you think you're still friends?"

"I sure hope so. I never had a friend like Paul. You get to know someone really well, climbing with them year after year."

"Is he single?"

"He got married a few years ago. That was the last postcard I got. Must have a house full of kids by now. All he wanted in life, he told me, was a good wife, a healthy family, and his own outfit in Dubois. He was going to sell mountain gear and teach climbing and run pack trips, and get other Shoshone to work for him as guides."

The house he had been directed to was a simple cottage of whitewashed concrete, set far back in a vegetable garden. Two beds of flowers, geraniums bordered by marigolds, bloomed in front of the house. There was a television antenna on top of the house, and a butane tank alongside it. They pulled up behind a pickup truck.

They stood on the front doorstep. Timmy knocked. The door was answered by a young woman dressed in jeans and a workshirt. Two small children stood behind her.

"Yes?"

"I'm looking for Paul Denio. They told me at the store the way to this house. I used to know him about ten years ago. My name's McCue. Timmy McCue."

The woman said nothing, but went off to the back of the house. The children followed her. Timmy and Audrey were left standing on the step, outside the screen door.

An old man, walking with a cane, came to the door. He held open the screen door and gestured them to come in.

"Hello," he said. "I'm Paul Denio. You wanted to see me?"

"Oh. I'm sorry. The Paul Denio I'm looking for would be about thirty. Your son, maybe?"

There was a pause. The man turned and looked at the young woman, who stood in a corner of the room.

"Yes. My son was called Paul, too. Did you know him?"

"I sure did. We used to go backpacking and climbing together here every summer. But that was ten, fifteen years ago. I was hoping to see him again, have him meet my new wife . . ."

"Your name is . . . Tim?"

"Right! Right. Timmy McCue. Did Paul tell you about me? Oh, this is my wife, Audrey. I just wanted to see how he's doing, ask about the business and all. Were those his kids? If he's up in Dubois, we can stop by there on our way out. We're going to the Tetons."

"I'm sorry. Paul is dead."

"Dead?"

"Yes."

"I don't believe it."

"He died two years ago."

"Climbing? In the mountains? Did he fall?"

"No, he was run over. Run over by a car. Here in Lander."

"I don't believe it."

"It's true. Come in. Please sit down."

The woman had been staring at them all this time in silence from her corner. Now she left the room, slamming the door loudly behind her.

"No, perhaps it's best you don't. Would you mind going outside with me, instead? We can talk in the yard." He looked around the empty room. "My daughter-in-law does not like people . . . white people in the house. I'm sorry. She does not like white people at all. But I would be happy to talk to an old friend of my son's."

Audrey held the door. Timmy helped the old man down the steps.

How old was Paul's father? Both of them wondered, but neither could tell. He had broad shoulders, and what looked like strong arms, and no fat at the waist. His gray hair was worn long, and tied at the back. But he walked bent, and leaned heavily on his stick. His face was wrinkled like a topographical map. His eyes were coated over with a kind of film, like small pools in a desert. They looked warily out of weary folds of flesh.

He led them to a distant part of the garden, where a dirt path led between rows of corn. They walked as they talked. He was wearing slippers, and dark shapeless trousers held up by suspenders over a collarless white shirt. He looked like someone's ancestor in a black and white photograph from another decade.

"Sarah does not like to hear talk of Paul's death, or of his life as a boy. She is very jealous of people who knew him before she did."

"I can understand that," said Timmy.

So can I, thought his wife.

"You knew him in the mountains?"

"Yes."

Timmy felt as if he had just lost something private and important. He felt as if he had been told that his house had burned down, or that his leg had been amputated while he was unconscious.

"I remember. He told me about you."

"Yes."

"How did you meet my son?"

"I used to go rock climbing with a friend in California. One year my friend read an article about the Wind River Mountains, so we decided to come out here. Paul led our horses into camp and showed us the trails. He couldn't have been more than eighteen or nineteen then. He had just dropped out of college."

"Did he tell you about that?"

"Not that year. The next year, and the next, and the next I came back on my own. I liked climbing in the Rockies more than in the Sierra. I especially liked going with Paul. It was on our second trip that he started telling me more about himself. He didn't like college."

"Did he tell you why?"

Timmy looked at the old man. He wondered how well he could see, with his eyes filmed over so badly.

"He said it was too much a white man's school. He refused to live anywhere where he had to obey white men all the time, put up with their insults and their sneers."

"What did you say to that?"

"I argued with him. I told him he couldn't hate white men without hating me. He was working for white men, driving their cars, wearing their clothes. If he tried to live his life without them, he'd just be locking himself up on the reservation forever.

"I never went to college myself, but I thought he should go. He was too smart a kid not to."

"Do you know why we sent him?"

"So he could come back and help his people. Become a lawyer for the tribe. He respected you for thinking he could do that, and he was grateful for the money. He was afraid you didn't believe him when he told you that."

They turned and walked back down the row of corn.

"How long had he been married when he died?"

"Six years. He must have married soon after your last summer together."

189

Timmy nodded. "He told me about Sarah."

"Are those his children?" Audrey asked.

"Yes. Two little girls. She is still full of bitterness, Sarah. I think she would like to be free of them. Free of the memory of their father."

They turned, retraced their steps, like nuns pacing white gravel paths in a convent garden.

"He was hit by a car?"

"Yes. In Lander, just over the reservation border. The police called it an accident. When we protested, the coroner called it an accident as well. There were three white men in the car, all of them drunk. The coroner said Paul was drunk, too. There was alcohol in his blood, we were told. There were witnesses who said he had run out in front of the car."

"But Paul never drank."

"Yes, he did. He must have started after you knew him. After he got married."

"Was his marriage so terrible?" Audrey asked.

The man stopped, turned, touched her arm.

"I didn't mean it that way. Sarah was a good woman for him. He took to drinking for the same reason most of our young men do. He could find no way out."

"But what about the business? In Dubois?"

"He never got his business in Dubois. They wouldn't let him. Or rather, he lost it as soon as he got it. He thought he had it all arranged, you know. That's why he got married. He even started buying a house, not far behind this one. Then Mr. McHenry accused him of stealing some equipment. That took several months to settle. In the end the judge ruled against Paul. McHenry talked the bank into canceling his credit. McHenry spread the word about the judgment among visitors, merchants, even people who had been his friends. He lost the house, and had to move back in here. Two small bedrooms we have, my wife in bed with cancer, the first baby. For two years, he tried to fight. But there was never a chance. McHenry knew if he let Paul get started, Paul would win. He knew the Wind River Mountains better than anyone else. He was the only certified alpine guide in Dubois. So they saw to it he never got started.

"The first season, he got a few of his old customers. But there were some accidents, food poisoning. Two of his horses were killed. The second season, he would go to Dubois each day and wait, but no one came. Then he would drive the truck home, to this house, with his mother dying and the baby crying and poor Sarah not knowing what to do or what to say. That's when he started drinking."

"Was there nothing he could do? He used to brag about the Shoshone's lawyers, how good they were winning lawsuits in Washington."

"In Washington, yes. In Washington we have had friends. Ever since Washakie's time. But not here. In Lander, in Riverton, in Casper, even in Cheyenne, we are all lazy drunkards to them. Every time we go off the reservation, they find a way to cheat us and put us in jail."

"Paul used to tell me they cheat you in Washington, too."

"Oh, don't start him on that. He knew the whole story backwards, broken promises, lies, land grabs back to the first treaty. According to him, everything from Casper to the Snake River Valley in Idaho should have been ours. Forty million acres, all of it Shoshone. He used to argue that Salt Lake City should be ours, because it was built on Shoshone land. He wanted it all back. The U.S. Cavalry had just rounded up all the Shoshone left and penned them in this corral, then pushed the Arapaho in with us and shut the gate behind. He dreamed about a time when our people roamed free from the California desert across the Rockies out onto the plains, from Canada down to the southwest."

"Was there a time like that?" Audrey asked.

"No. I don't think so, anyway. What my father told me, when I was a boy, was that the only reason the tribe had moved back here was that all the buffalo had been killed off beyond the Rockies. He said Washakie agreed to accept the reservation in sixty-three because he knew there weren't going to be any buffalo left anywhere, very soon. For many years before that, we had been driven out of this same territory by the plains Indians, the Crow and the Sioux. We lived like rats in the desert, my father said, digging up roots and eating insects. I didn't see anything glorious about our past.

"But Paul knew more about the past than my father or I did. He read everything he could get his hands on about the history of the tribe. After he lost his business, that's about all he did, except drink. Read Indian Movement propaganda, and argue with people about taking back the country."

The old man stopped walking. "Do you mind if we sit down? I can only stand on this leg for about an hour."

"No. No, please. I'm sorry. I don't want you to wear yourself out."

"I won't. I like to talk about Paul, and Sarah won't permit it. It's not easy for her, you know," he said, speaking to Audrey in particular, "having both me and the girls to put up with. But it's not easy for me, either. She won't even let me put a picture of my son up on the wall!"

They sat on the ground, crosslegged in a little circle, hidden by the corn. Audrey felt a consoling energy in the sound of the old man's voice.

"He began taking instructions from Indian Movement headquarters in South Dakota, some young Sioux I believe. He tried to start a boycott of the stores in Lander that he knew had cheated Indians. It was just getting started when he was killed. He made one furniture and appliance store in town his particular target. They depended on sales to Indians for most of their profits, on contracts of a hundred percent interest a year. Paul tried to get our council's lawyer to sue them for fraud. It turned out the lawyer owned part of the store. The son of the store manager was driving the car that ran over him."

"Do you think they did it on purpose? Do you think that Paul was murdered?"

"I don't know. He did drink, I have to admit that. He could have walked into them. He made many enemies, even before the boycott, with all his talk about revolution and killing. Sarah is sure it was murder. That's why she won't have white people in the house."

191

"Did he stop going to the mountains, after all this?"

"No, he went by himself, though. He just took a bedroll, and lived off the land."

"He used to tell me he believed there were spirits in these mountains."

"That's right. He did." The old man looked long and close at Timmy, then at Audrey, through the lenses of his fogged-over eyes. "So do I." They wondered what it could be like, the image of them he perceived. "Do you?"

When Timmy answered, he chose his words carefully. He paused so long after every phrase that he seemed to have stopped talking several times. But the old man waited him out.

"I'll tell you the truth, Mr. Denio. I can't feel what he did. These aren't my mountains. There's no special spirit up there for me.

"But I wish there was. I envied Paul that. I envied Paul lots of things. When I was a little kid in California, I used to dream of being an Indian, before I had any idea what being an Indian really meant. Then when I met Paul, I . . . Oh, hell. I don't know."

He was playing in the dirt with a stick. He broke the stick, kept his eyes down. Audrey was watching him closely.

"He belonged to the mountains the way I wanted to. He was completely at home there. It was impossible to imagine him losing his way, or falling. That's why I couldn't believe it at first when you said he was dead. For some reason, I thought you meant he had fallen. He was always doing things that seemed to me incredibly dangerous. But he knew he was safe.

"The last year we went out, we took off the first week to go up climbing in the Tetons, because I asked if we could, and that was great. But I could tell that Paul wanted to get back to the Wind Rivers. There were better ascents in the Tetons. The scenery was more spectacular. But the place was too crowded for him, even the high country. The mountains weren't his. There may have been spirits there. But they weren't Shoshone spirits. They wouldn't help him.

"So we came back. We made four major ascents that year, all in the same week: Gannett, Fremont, Squaretop, Desolation. I remember it perfectly. It was the best time we ever had."

Audrey had never heard Timmy talk this way about anyone, not even his father. She felt confused as Timmy's recollections, obviously drawn from the heart, shaped themselves out of his careful words. More than once he had told her he couldn't *talk* about love, his love for her, however much it would have pleased her to hear him do it. But what was he doing now, if not talking about love?

He was not crying, of course; he never cried. But she felt that these memories, dropped out quietly and slowly as he stared at the ground, were like tears. In one way, it pleased her to know that he had in him this tenderness, susceptibility to pain. In another way, she felt embarrassed to see him reveal it. She was superfluous, unwanted; a voyeur. This was a private moment that had nothing to do with her.

That bothered her a great deal. Never had he shown toward her the degree of emotion, the sense of closeness and need he seemed to feel for a dead Indian he had only camped out with and climbed with on four occasions, and never for more than two weeks at a time.

Paul's father stood up. The two others rose with him. He lay a hand on Timmy's shoulder.

"I think my son was wrong, you know. About white men. I could never say this in front of Sarah."

Audrey looked from one man to another, frightened for no reason.

"He talked about you. But he never brought you to our home. Why was that?"

"I don't know."

"It's sad. Now he's dead, and you've come, but you're not welcome. His wife runs the house, not me."

"I understand."

"In the end, when his business was ruined, and he had to admit that he was beaten by the merchants, he went almost crazy, I think. It wasn't just the drink. That came after. He could seem almost more crazy when he was sober than when he was drunk."

"How do you mean, crazy?"

They were walking back toward the house. Audrey saw a face, staring at them from a curtained window: the young widow, spying, suspicious. Audrey's heart went out to her.

"He began to have visions. Do you know about peyote?"

"Yes."

"It's more a religion to some people nowadays than a drug. But Paul began to mix up his political ideas with his visions. He talked about them as if they were real, as real as the three of us standing here."

"What sort of visions?"

"The usual things. A new empire. Indians ruling over the whole continent again, from sea to sea. Tear up every deed and every treaty ever written, resurrect forty million buffalo from the dead for his children and his children's children to hunt, season after season. Kill off white men the way our ancestors were killed, or else drive them back to where they came from."

"How was this going to happen?"

"He didn't care. It didn't matter. He had seen it in his visions, so he knew it was coming. Soon, he said, it would be perfectly just for an Indian to steal from white men, to kill white men. You see how crazy he got? Maybe they were right to stop him when they did."

"What did you say to him, when he talked like this?"

"What I tell you: that he was crazy. This was Sitting Bull talk, I said, all over again. 'Sitting Bull was right,' he would say. 'Look what happened to him,' I would answer. 'It doesn't matter,' said Paul. 'He was still right.'

"It bothered me to see him so full of hatred. He had things so much better than his mother and I ever had. I tried to explain to him how much easier life was now, even on the reservation. When I was a boy, the Shoshone were being destroyed by diseases, all kinds of diseases. The tribe was down to eight hundred people. The water was bad, there were no toilets, no irrigation. Most families lived in tipis, or in freezing shacks with dirt floors and tarpaper roofs. One starving couple, neighbors of my parents, had to eat their own dead baby to live. For that, the white agent put them in jail.

"When the government annuities ended, we had to sell off the northern half of the reservation in order to survive. The state of Wyoming wouldn't let us off the reservation. There were no jobs. No one would hire an Indian. Crops went bad. Cattle died. People died. That was the childhood I remember.

"By the time Paul was born, the reparation claim had been won, four and a half million dollars. People had something to live on again. We got paved roads, and a decent school. Movies in the auditorium. We bought back the land north of the river. A few years ago we won another settlement, and built the swimming pool, and the tribal center, and the new gymnasium. New houses, like this one. People got trucks, and TV, and decent toilets. I told Paul that he hadn't lived through what we had, so he couldn't appreciate how much more he had now."

"What did he say to that?"

" 'The hell with the reservation,' he would say, yell it at me, yell at anyone who would listen. 'The whole country is ours!' He despised Washakie for giving in so easily, selling out to Grant for a few trinkets—a silver saddle, a pension, this tiny patch of land."

"Is it so tiny?"

"Two and a quarter million acres. I suppose it's not. But Paul was thinking of a land with no boundaries, you understand? No government; no tribes even. No time, except the seasons. Wide open country, like before the Europeans.

"But you can't bring that back." He turned again to Timmy, stopped in his tracks. "Can you?"

"I guess you can't."

"In some ways, that may be sad. But even these ideas he had, these visions of his: where did he get them? From books, that's where, books and papers printed on white men's machines! If he went off to work for the Movement, it was in this truck—made in Detroit! Him wearing the white man's jeans, drinking the white man's whiskey: I argued with him just the way you did. His family name, Denio—a word some white agent had given to my father sixty years ago. It means nothing. There was no possible way that boy was going to undo three hundred years of white civilization in America. Why, he couldn't even get it out of himself!

"I told him all that, told him it was impossible. But that didn't bother him. He still believed it was going to happen, and he would have died to make it happen. He thought every Indian in America should be willing to die for his dream."

"Did he?" asked Audrey. "Did he die for it?"

"No." They were back at the front steps. "His death was no use to anything at all."

"How old was he?"

194

"Twenty-eight."

"How sad," she said. "What a short life."

My life, she thought; my life, six years more, and then nothing.

"I think that, too." He climbed the step, leaned against the door. "He was my only son."

"He was my best friend."

The two men hugged each other gravely, then shook hands. Mr. Denio did the same with Audrey.

"I hope I wasn't wrong to tell you this. Sarah won't hear of it anymore. No one else around wants to be reminded of Paul's craziness. He caused much trouble, at the end, made many enemies. It would have been better for you to remember him as you knew him, in the mountains."

"No. I'm glad you told me. It makes him seem larger. Someone who fought. Someone who tried to break out."

"But his crazy ideas?"

"I don't think his ideas were so crazy."

The man looked at him, took his hand again. "Thank you for saying that." He took Audrey's hand too, one of their hands in each of his. "Goodbye," they all said.

On the drive out of the reservation, climbing up in the lee of the Wind River Mountains, Timmy realized how alone he had become. He had lost his father, possibly forever. One of his two best friends was worse than a wreck. The other was dead.

That left Audrey. He looked at her, she looked at him. At the moment, she was feeling uncomfortably uncertain of her place in his heart, or his plans.

23

Little Sandy Creek
July 7, 1849

The die is cast, as the saying goes. We are once more on our own.

After a day of private wrangling, and a public debate that lasted three hours, a vote was taken of the whole Carthage Company, or what remains of it. Every wagon except ours is to take the right-hand road at the fork, towards Soda Springs and Fort Hall. Only James and I, in our wagon, accompanied by Henry and Hector Williams, will head south to Fort Bridger and the Great Salt Lake. We are camped near the fork today, on the east bank of the Little Sandy. Tomorrow morning we shall go our separate ways.

Captain McClellan agreed to return half of our "stake." With that, and whatever he is able to earn hiring out his labor to the Mormons for a short time, James hopes to be able to replace our worn-out oxen with better, while resting and recruiting those that still seem fit; strengthen the wagon against the rigors ahead; and replenish our diminishing stock of provisions. The great danger for us, of course, is delay. The road by the Great Salt Lake appears from the maps to be between 80 and 120 miles longer than the road by Fort Hall. Add to that whatever time we spend in Great Salt Lake city, and it is clearly seen that we may be putting ourselves to considerable risk.

James insists that we are sufficiently in advance of the main body of the emigration to be able to afford this detour, which he now regards as essential. He has cited, both privately and publicly, a dozen sound arguments for his choice. But I believe that he is primarily determined to be quit of the society of men he has come to regard as contemptible—if for no other reason than that they reject his advice!

He is unenthusiastic about continuing in the company of the Williams boys as well, whom he continues to insult in subtle ways. But he is obliged to admit

196

the usefulness of additional hands, to one who will be driving a solitary wagon over unfamiliar roads.

I had thought the counsel of Mr. Vasquez, the veteran trader whom we encountered just east of the pass, might prevail on others to accompany us. But it seems he is a partner with Captain Bridger in a trading establishment between here and the Mormon city, which depends for its custom wholly on emigrants taking that route. He is therefore no more to be trusted than the various "runners" from Independence and St. Joseph, who met our boat with such boastful and specious claims at St. Louis.

Not everyone in our band is as deeply imbued with anti-Mormon sentiments as are our three leaders. But all are persuaded that the southern route would add from five to ten needless days to their journey. There are two ferries operated by the Mormons between here and their city, no doubt at their usual exorbitant rates, both at river crossings (we are told) too high to ford. In the city itself, even "friendly" Gentiles (as Christians are termed!) must expect to submit to avaricious terms for whatever they buy. It was argued that there would be no jobs available there for any but Latter-Day Saints; and that the citizens would reserve for themselves whatever crops they had managed to grow.

However dry and difficult the route to Fort Hall, Captain McClellan assured his flock that they could as readily recruit and reprovision there as among the Saints (or, as he calls them, the "devils"). We were reminded that the Reed & Donner Company chose the Fort Bridger-Great Salt Lake Road on their expedition three years ago, with what tragic results the world knows.

This is, I think, a fair account of the arguments put forward this afternoon on behalf of the right hand, or "Sublett's" road. Even though about two wagons in every five seem to be turning south here, James alone rose to speak on behalf of the alternative. He argued the lame condition of the company's oxen, all of whom are sadly wasted from the long dry pull up from Fort Laramie, and obviously suffering from the thin air and cold nights of these elevations. We now pass each day from 30 to 40 carcasses of dead animals, greatly bloated from the sun and putrescence, and a feast for screaming ravens. This, James warned the others, will be the fate of our animals as well, if we do not rest them in some place of sure and extensive pastures, or exchange them for better. And that can be done nowhere except at the Mormon city. The last and most difficult part of the journey, he reminded them, is still to be made.

Captain McClellan rose and swore that he would have us all at Sutter's Fort within 30 days. James offered to wager him any sum he named that it would take at least twice that time, whichever route they chose. Few wagons among us have food left for 30 days, let alone 60, he insisted; and there was no more game to be expected from this point west.

Whereupon there ensued great shouting and hullabaloo, with loud offers to take up James's wager, to double the stakes, curses, insults, shaking of fists, waving of maps. It took the captain several minutes to obtain order.

Then James resumed his argument for the Fort Bridger road. As the company blacksmith (and now, perforce, carpenter and wheelwright as well), he reminded us of the sad shape of most of our wagons. The heat and dry air of the mountains have so shrunk the woodwork of our wheels that many are on the point of falling to pieces, and are held together only by patch-work expedients. He dismissed the reference to the Reeds and Donners as unworthy panic-mongering, by reminding the assembly that several thousand diligent Mormons—whose trail-making skills we had already witnessed—have since followed them on the route, and doubtless improved the trail. He sees no reason to doubt Mr. Vasquez's claim that the Mormons wholeheartedly accept the laws of our nation and the articles of its Constitution. Only last week, we have been told, they elected a delegate to petition the U.S. Congress for admission of their Territory as a full state of the union. He also takes seriously Mr. Vasquez's insistence that the waterless stretch at the start of Sublett's cut-off is much longer and more difficult than Mr. Ware pretends in his "Emigrant's Guide," and that it will be the dying-ground of many of the oxen in their present condition.

Most eloquently, I thought, he cited the ill health and ill feeling from which all of us are suffering, and suggested that a week's sojourn among civilized and settled families, provided with fresh milk and vegetables, would be a tonic for our spirits as well as our bodies, and enable us to cross the great American desert and mount the high Sierra renewed and refreshed.

At this point, Lieutenant Calkins rose to dispute the term "civilized."

"These," he said, "are no civilized men. They are lawless and Godless murderers, who have willfully declared themselves outside the protection of the United States Constitution and the Ten Commandments of God, and who know no law but that of the mad and bloodthirsty lecher Brigham Young. It was not without reason," he declared, "that these people were driven out of the states of Missouri and Illinois by God-fearing men and women like ourselves. Anyone who ventures among them puts himself at the mercy of the vengeful and vicious Young and his band of brutes."

James was about to reply, when Capt. McClennan rose from his place and insisted that a vote be taken straightaway, with the result that I have described. We were left (women, of course, do not vote) a minority of three—James and the two boys.

Of course, I firmly believe in the rectitude of James's position, and look forward to a recuperative interval among the good people of Great Salt Lake. But it is difficult not to be moved by the fiery speeches of the men of Carthage. I am still uninformed as to the nature of the Mormon's beliefs or practices, or what monstrosity they committed that has earned them their exile in the desert. I have been told that their founder and chief prophet, one Joseph Smith, died or was killed in prison in Illinois. It is for this as much as for anything else that their vengeance is said to be sworn against the Gentiles. But however perverted their doctrines may be, or however dark their desires for revenge, I believe them to be followers of Christ Jesus the Lord, as their official name implies. Surely this must imply a respect for the commandments of God and the divine example and precepts of His only begotten Son.

The drive from Pacific Springs to this creek was totally barren, frequently even of the friendly gray sage. It is difficult to imagine a landscape more desolate. At times, the entire western half of this continent seems to serve no purpose whatsoever except that of a bridge to California. The trail runs straight as an arrow over a sterile, undulating, interminable plain of sand, broken only by occasional rock outcrops or solitary buttes. The intervening creek beds we crossed were dry as ash, their waters having been absorbed into the sand. In the distance to our right rose the bleak, broken towers of the Wind River Mountains; to our left the majestic peaks of the Colorado Rockies, their snowy tops shining in the sun. The contrast between distant splendor and immediate desolation is almost too vast for the heart to encompass.

At the fork itself, a split stick has been driven into the ground, with a broad board nailed to the top. This serves as an emigrants' post office. A notice requests travelers to throw stones up against the base, to maintain the stick upright. Onto the board are stuck messages from travelers ahead, informing acquaintances which route they have taken, and when they passed this way. I counted about forty, with a slight preponderance taking the northern route. Like everyone else who passes this way, I stopped to read each one. The men of our party were considerably chagrined to learn that the obstreperous James D. Hart and his mules are already five days in our lead.

At camp yesterday, we were visited by a whole tribe of nomadic Indians on the march, bearing with them not only all their earthly possessions, but also supplies of dried buffalo meat and dressed skins, the fruits of a hunting expedition on the eastern slopes of these mountains.

These are the Snake, or Sho-Sho-Nie, a most civil and trustworthy band, according to Mr. Bryant. Their hunting grounds have traditionally been located on this side of the Rocky Mountains, but the emigration of the last few years has so depleted their game that they are forced into enemy territory on the east. Both game and supplies—including the poles and skins of their lodges—are carried either pack-fashion on horseback (or on "squaw-back"); or dragged behind the beasts on a kind of broad sledge made of sticks. Naked children, and the sick, are also carried on these. The band included a number of domesticated wolf dogs, some of which are also obliged to drag a smaller form of these unusual sledges. The chief hunters wear leggings and breech cloths, and paint their upper bodies. They are well proportioned, and of excellent bearing. They ride horses superior to any we have seen. They love to display their skill on horseback by riding across the desert at a terrific rate, staffs erect and feathers flying, then pulling their horses to and round within inches of a chosen spot. One beautiful young woman in their midst, no doubt a princess, wore a buckskin robe, pantaloons, and mocassins even finer than those of the Sioux maiden we saw at Ash Hollow. She sat with aristocratic grace on a handsome bay horse. But most of their women are poor, tired, ugly creatures, who seem to be used only as additional beasts of burden.

Their chief, a man of strong features wearing a much-decorated coat and carrying a long staff of office, came over to parley with Capt. McClellan. He offered to trade buffalo skins and hides for ammunition, goods, and tobacco. The captain accommodated him as best he could, obtaining at the same time useful information concerning the trail and the Indians ahead. The tribe was on the march to Fort Bridger, which is their traditional trading post, but the chief knew the Fort Hall road as well.

He advises that we have nothing to fear of open attack from the tribes to the west; but that their destitution may lead them to risk stealing our horses or provisions, at which crimes they are considerably adept. He recommended a careful guard in certain portions of the desert, which he described with a stick in the sand. He spoke passable English—a rare thing among red men.

A tale was later told around the campfire of the exceptional sense of honor of this chief, who is a personage of some distinction among residents of the far-west, both white and red. An emigrant was out hunting, at no great distance from his camp, when he was beset by a party of Snake Indians. They took his rifle from him, tied him to a tree, shot him in the back, and killed him. His comrades, wondering at his long absence, went on a search, and discovered his corpse tied to the tree. They found the Indians' trail, located their encampment, and demanded redress. This same chief, who is called Was-Ah-Kie, held a council, detected the murderer, and had him tied to a tree. He then told the emigrants that the man was at their disposal, to do with as they wished. They replied that it was for his fellow tribesmen to punish him in such manner as they should determine. The chief then called the brother of the culprit, and ordered him to cut the offender's throat, which was instantly done.

It is astonishing to see snowdrifts on the trail as late as July. Last night was our coldest so far. By morning, our buffalo robes were white with frost, and a coating of ice a quarter of an inch thick lay atop the water in our buckets. The sun, however, rises quickly and soon dispels all evidence of winter with its rays. Although the limpid purity of the air and the directness of the sun's rays should be conducive to health, I feel something unnatural in the atmosphere of a region so close to the sun.

Despite the cold, I lay awake for some time after dark, looking at the stars from the opening of our tent, and was blessed with a singular vision. About two o'clock a magnificent meteor broke nearly overhead and shot away to the horizon. The report was like the crack of a whip. The first sight I perceived was that of a ball of fire, brilliant as the sun and lighting up the whole plain. As it began to move, the light changed to a beautiful color, decreasing in brilliance as it neared the horizon, leaving behind a trail of sparks of fire. When the first explosion took place, the ball appeared nearly as large as the sun. By the time it had disappeared, it was about the size of Venus. The changes of color were almost equal to those of the rainbow. Never have I witnessed Fourth of July fireworks to compare with this heavenly display.

It would appear to be a sign; but I have no means to interpret it. As James was snoring loudly, I did not waken him.

After their long meeting today, our erstwhile companions of the trail are building up courage for tomorrow's long dry run by songs and carousing. James went off with his rifle, and brought back two fat sage hens which I am now boiling in a soup with dumplings, for a quiet feast of our own. This should help warm us for what promises to be another icy night, under clear and brilliant stars.

O Lord, who protected the people of Israel in the desert, be with us in whatever trials may lie ahead. Give us the fortitude to persevere, even in suffering and solitude, and to place our faith in Thee. Wrap us in the blanket of Thy protection as we pass among unbelievers, and see us safely to the end of this long and difficult road. Amen.

24

When, for however short a time, life seems to be perfect, there is very little words can do to represent that state.

Timmy and Audrey McCue spent the last five days in July at a campground in Grand Teton National Park. For those five days, they were in a state so near to harmony that they dared not try to analyze or explain it. For those five days, their Rocky Mountain high dazzled into shadow all the preceding lows: the family friction in Dedham; the dryness of Cape Cod; Toledo; Chicago; the drive to Casper; Casper.

Writers pretend that good love affairs (sometimes even good marriages) are full of times like this, are one unending blissful sequence of them: a daisy chain of golden-glowing days, the stem of each slipped into a tiny slit in the green stem of the next.

But the lives of real people in love never mesh as neatly as we would like them to. The best we can usually hope for in real life is the tranquility of compromise, almost willing, mostly silent. The social smiles that we try to make warm. The acceptable lies we both know to be lies. If we keep the wounds bandaged, and the throbbing ego down, leave a good deal unsaid and *try* not to hurt—things just may work.

Still, the good times do come. For Timmy and Audrey, the Tetons were one of them. After that, it got rough.

Audrey had been mellowing ever since Dubois, where they crossed the Wind River reservation boundary. By the time they stopped for lunch, in a grove of pine and blue lupin, Timmy had put his private griefs behind him, and decided that a wife might be enough. After lunch, they looked in silence at a herd of deer, feeding in a lime-green meadow.

Just beyond the Divide, Timmy slowed down and pulled into a turnout on the edge of a cliff. He knew what lay ahead, and hoped it would please her. Partly because she couldn't read maps, Audrey was unprepared for what suddenly lay before her eyes. She actually gasped, the way people do in novels; stopped the pace of her breathing. A first, unexpected view of the Grand Teton range of the Rocky Mountains, opening up in full panorama as you come out of a tunnel of trees, is as near as you get to heaven in the American West.

Far below the road lay a broad valley dotted with blue lakes and cut through by rivers and streams. At its far edge lay a perfect mirror of lake. Over the lake rose mountains out of a child's fantasy of mountain: dark forested at the base, turning to gray blue rock as they climbed, crested in snow of an ethereal white. The snow defined sharp peaks and sawtooth ridges, folded one over another, fitted into crevices other snow had carved centuries ago.

Never had she imagined there existed mountains so high, so steep, and so beautiful. The rock rose sheer and abrupt from the mirroring lake, a mile, more, into the blue sky. From this distance one could see the whole of it, like an ice sculpture, a flawless centerpiece in the rich tableland of green.

The spectacular *massif*, an uplifted 40-mile long crack in the earth's crust, kept returning to view as they wound their way down to the Buffalo Fork of the Snake River. Timmy assured her that they would be living with these mountains all day, every day, as long as they stayed in the park. But still she asked him to stop at every viewpoint. She was trying to find space in her heart, compartments in her mind for the wonder. Timmy was so pleased at her pleasure that, instead of looking at the landscape himself, he watched it reflected in her face.

They descended past Forest Service campgrounds, then wide valley ranches. The ranches were marked by fences made of slim, silver-gray logs laid horizontally in X-shaped log cradles.

Timmy had his heart set on a particular campsite, which he had stayed in twice before. It was hidden by trees from the road and other campers, yet still commanded a full view of the sharp parallel ridges of four of the six highest peaks. But at the Moran Junction entrance station, a brown board marked "FULL" had been hung alongside the name of his own special lake.

"What's the story on Jenny Lake?" he asked the ranger.

"Like that all summer long."

"But that's where I've always stayed."

"When was the last time?"

"Ten, eleven years ago. Have things changed all that much?"

"You better believe it. We get two million visitors through a year now. Half of them in campers. Park Service had to helicopter the bears into the high country at Yellowstone, to keep them from mauling all the idiots who wanted to feed them. You have to reserve ahead now even to climb."

"Can you reserve for Jenny Lake?"

"Not any more. We tried reservations a few years, but it didn't work. Too many no-shows."

"So how do you get in?"

"First come, first serve. What most folks do who want to get into Jenny is to stay in some other campground overnight. Then they line up here about six or seven the next morning, and wait for people to check out. The alternative is to cruise around the campground looking for folks about to leave, and make a deal with them to take over their spot. It gets pretty nasty sometimes."

Timmy's heart sank.

"How about Signal Mountain?"

The ranger pointed to another "FULL" sign. "Lots of places at Colter Bay, still." He looked on his list. "She doesn't usually fill up till late afternoon. After that, we send people back to Gros Ventre, the overflow campground at the south end of the park. Holds about two hundred."

"What happened to the Jackson Lake camp?"

"Park Service decided to close it down. Concentrate the damage at Colter Bay." Timmy could feel cars lining up behind him, restless drivers inside them.

"What'll it be?"

"Well. I guess Colter Bay."

He traded three dollars for a windshield ticket and a handful of maps and announcements, mostly warnings about not fishing and not feeding the bears, and drove into the park. The road was aimed straight at Mount Moran, which rises abrupt and symmetrical out of Jackson Lake, defying you not to stare at the glacier in its heart. They turned right at the junction, passed the lodge, drove through pine forests and broad meadows to the Colter Bay turn.

It was unlike anything he remembered. Just off the park road was the village center, where a constant jam of campers and trailers bearing the license plates of all North America circled in front of the stores. Swarms of tourists gathered on the sidewalks, buying groceries and beer and souvenirs, float trip tickets, pack trip tickets. Teenagers sprawled on the steps of the laundromat-and-shower building.

Timmy drove on out to the campsite they had been assigned. It was located off one of a complicated network of loop roads. When they found their number, it signified a treeless parking place, close in among hundreds of others. Already half of them were filled with ugly metal houses on wheels. His heart sank deeper.

"We can't stay here. It's a big empty lot."

"It is depressing. But what else can we do?"

"We can get our money back." After that, he wasn't sure. Hell, maybe they'd have to stay under a roof. He tried to convince himself that wouldn't be so bad.

"I'm sorry," he told the ranger. "It was all those people. No privacy, hardly any trees. I didn't know it was going to be like that."

"I couldn't agree with you more, bud," said the ranger, giving him a clipboard sheet to sign for his receipt. "You couldn't pay me to camp in a place like Colter Bay."

"Where *would* you stay, then? I always camped at Jenny Lake before, but they told us at Moran Junction that it's full up by dawn. Jackson is closed. Gros Ventre sounds worse than Colter."

"Ever heard of Lizard Creek?"

"Where's that?"

"Six miles up. It's usually one of the last to fill, because it's listed as 'Primitive,' which scares away the saps, and because it's away from all the action. That's what folks want nowadays. Action. Half the places up there are walk-in camps, which keeps out the Winnebago crowd. And people who can't stand pit toilets. But it's on the lake. I think it's the place most rangers would choose."

So they drove six more miles through forests of lodgepole pine. Here and there, through a clearing, they caught a view of the narrowing lake, and the mountains across it. At the Lizard Creek sign, they turned onto a quiet forest road, totally in shade. After half an hour of exploring, they chose a campsite off the road, walled in by tall trees. The westering sun, reflecting on slivers of silver-blue lake, found its way through needles and branches.

After another half hour, and a few trips to the car, camp was made: tent, sleeping bags, stove, ice chest, food box. They were sitting close to one another on the picnic table bench, backs against the table edge, facing the sun, the sparkling fragments of lake, a forest full of shadow. Timmy had opened a jug of red wine and filled two tin cups. He opened a can of peanuts, brought warm sweaters from the car. Once the sun had set, he would start a fire and begin dinner. But peace, he believed, was what camping was all about; peace like they had right now. Never hurrying to, never worrying about the *next* chore, the next pleasure. Sitting still, simplifying, becoming quiet like the forest; letting it move into you as you moved into it.

Once she learned how to keep warm—or how to tolerate cold—Audrey learned the right way to do things in Timmy's mountains. Even on that first evening, she knew not to talk. She understood that they were just to sit there, breathing in the piney air, sipping their wine, and wait for the sun to go down. That was all. The world was preternaturally still, despite the sounds of chipmunks and birds and honking lake fowl afar off. She sucked the salt off her peanuts one at a time, then crunched them up quietly, mixing the flavor with that of the wine in a kind of communion. She took hold of Timmy's elbow with both hands, leaned her head against his arm. He touched the top of her head with his lips. But still no words.

Natural beauty, peace, and a sense of sheltering security surrounded them and filled them. The goodness was as palpable as skin.

The screen of evergreens had something to do with it; the separation from cars and other people; the cozy assurance of the tent there, the sleeping bags, the chest and carton full of food, the stove, the lantern, the jug of wine.

The heart of their satisfaction, though, came from something more than the sum of all these. It did not depend on any secret knowledge of all the things they could do and see the next day, and the next and the next, just through those trees, just down that trail.

What felt so like harmony came mainly from their being wholly alone together, away from the car, away from other people, with very few of the props of civilization; dependent on no more than the few things they could carry. In a funny way (pit toilets or no), Audrey felt that this was the place they had been heading for ever since they met.

"Everything's pure and clean and healthy and wholesome over five thousand feet." It was half an old Sierra joke, which he and his brothers had used in their youth to justify hanky-panky in the hills; but half not a joke. His woodland code included all kinds of unusual rules. Perfect tidiness, for one thing, tidiness of a sort he would never have defended back in the concrete city. No scrap of theirs could be left on the forest floor.

One went to bed soon after sunset, arose soon after the animals and birds. The car was there, at the end of the trail, to use when you had to get long distances quickly. But it was better to walk. So too with the stove and the lantern. If a campfire of down wood (he nearly hit her when he heard her breaking a branch off a living tree) could serve for heat, light, and cooking, so much the better. If an animal appeared—and many did, chipmunks, deer, a badger, a marmot, a small brown bear—one stopped what one was doing and remained absolutely still so as not to disturb it. "It's their park, not ours."

It got very cold the instant the sun's rays were blocked by the trees. But one never complained. He approved of, and she bore courageously, the reeking toilets. With great largeness of spirit, he tolerated the clean water, piped in by the Park Service. But he bathed by swimming in the ice water of Jackson Lake. Never never never would he stand in line with the lower-caste campers who dwelt in metal boxes, or under roofs, to take a coin-in-the-slot shower at Colter Bay village. Towards the end of their stay, Audrey begged to be allowed to do their laundry and take a hot shower herself. Timmy drove her down to the village. Then he walked out under the trees and sat reading trail maps till she was done, pretending he wasn't there.

She never understood how or why he drew up his rules of the mountain. But they did seem to fit. Jugs of cheap wine were O.K., but hard liquor wasn't. You could read a book, but not buy a newspaper. The sound of a guitar from someone else's campsite, filtered and softened by distance and the trees—that was fine. That was lovely. But the sound, no less mellowed, no less distant, of a portable radio put him into a rage.

Wild animals, of course, belonged. This was their home more than man's. But bringing domestic pets to the mountains he regarded as a crime. Rowboats, yes; outboards, no. Trucks he respected more than campers or house trailers. However noisy, filthy, or huge they were, trucks were work horses, not toys; they were needed. They "made sense." Campers and trailers were decadent chunks of flatland civilization that had no business up here at all.

And she accepted it all, because he said so.

Timmy-of-the-Mountains was a different creature, and on the whole a nicer one, from Timmy-down-Below. Even when his rules seemed over-strict, she was enjoying herself too much to quarrel or question. On their third day, when she asked whether they might drive into Jackson for the evening—a restaurant dinner, the evening rodeo, one of the old-time nightclub shows everybody was going to—he utterly balked. He, the town drinker, the party boy, the wild man of Boston and Chicago and (by all accounts) Munich and Palo Alto: *not* while we're here.

But he was feeling almost as much in love with Audrey as he was with the mountains, so he compromised. He agreed to put on a clean sweatshirt, and buy her one dinner at the Jackson Lake Lodge.

Even if the water in their bucket froze every morning, (just like the blood in her veins), she was happy; even if she had to get used to making love to scratchy whiskers. Not shaving was another of Timmy's mountain rules.

They filled up the days away from camp in moderately adventurous ways. They bought groceries at the little log store at Jenny Lake, in order to avoid Colter Bay. The second day, they played tourist. With thirty other people, they went for a pack ride out to Hermitage Point, under pine trees and willows, through early morning meadows where moose and elk were feeding, and coyote trotted through the damp grass. When their horses arrived at the lake, college students dressed like ranch hands had huge skillets of bacon, eggs, and pancakes ready for them all, along with giant pots of hot coffee and pitchers of juice. They compared travel notes with their fellow tourists as they ate, in a setting too beautiful to be true: on the edge of the lake, ducks and pelicans feeding in the shallows, with the morning-lit mountains shimmering in the water.

That afternoon they drove to a dude ranch in the valley, where more college-kid cowboys took them for a trip down the river in a fat red rubber boat. Along the way, they saw beaver dams, moose, flying osprey. A single bald eagle perched high in an almost branchless tree. Audrey expected to be frightened; she was frightened of most new adventures. But although the trip was bouncy, although they raced through rapid stretches and got stuck on pebbly shoals, although she had to bend flat to escape overhanging branches, and spray soaked her hair and her clothes, she had a much better time than she expected. Every so often, the river coiled east or west, and another vista of the mountains emerged, recomposed and domesticated. Most of the time they traveled below steep banks and tall trees, all quite jungle-like and private: alders and cottonwood, aspen and willow to the valley side; mixed evergreens towards the mountains. Audrey felt she was getting a chance to explore the heart and veins of the valley. From the river, one could imagine oneself a thousand miles away from roads and buildings.

Timmy was hoping to persuade Audrey into a day-long hike on one of the back-country trails. She didn't cycle, or they might have rented bikes and toured the park that way. She obviously didn't know how to fish, and would not enjoy sitting still for two or three hours watching him. Backpacking was out of the question: no shoes, no packs, no gear; in her case, no endurance.

But having got his new wife to his favorite place in the whole world, he was determined not to waste it by letting her wheedle him into an escape back into civilization. Jackson was civilization. Even Yellowstone was civilization: too many hotels, too many stores, too many of the wrong kind of people.

She liked the campsite, and she had adapted surprisingly well to the evening and morning cold, the pit toilets, sleeping on the ground, the long hike to the car. There were no near neighbors and, so far, no mosquitoes. Sex in the open air, which was one of his favorite pastimes, remained a possibility.

By day two, he had used up the only two tourist diversions he could stand, the pack ride and the float trip, in an effort to keep her contented. She kept mentioning things she read about in brochures, or heard about from other tourists, like the bars and restaurants of Jackson, souvenir shops at the lodge, the chairlift at Teton Village. He scrambled about for legitimate options, all the while hoping to soften her up for his proposal of a hike.

The morning of day three they spent looking over the museum displays at Moose and Colter Bay, learning about trappers and Indians. Audrey got hooked into a four-hour class in Indian beadworking with a real-live Shoshone. That give Timmy a chance to go off fishing for the afternoon, in a rented boat. Afterwards he snuck over to the store and bought a pair of lightweight hiking boots and socks in her size. When they met again at five-thirty, she showed him her partly-beaded mocassin. In return, he showed her their dinner: two handsome trout. Back at camp, he cleaned them and cooked them in foil on the coals of their fire, wrapped up with onions and bacon and butter. (Timmy did all the cooking in camp. It was a bonus she hadn't expected.) After dinner, they took a hike to the lake, then heard a ranger talk about the stars.

Day four they made the great effort. When he showed her the new boots, she could hardly say no. During lunch the day before, he looked over the trail guide, and recalled the first hike he had ever taken into the Teton back country: from String Lake up the canyon to Lake Solitude, then over the divide to Paintbrush Canyon, and back to String Lake. In memory, it was an easy escape that an eighteen-year-old boy in tennis shoes, still pretending he was an Indian, had taken into the wilds, before the valley was part of the park, before the lodge existed. He remembered a trail intimate with wildlife, edging along creeks, sheltered by the north walls of the Cathedrals.

But the current guidebook seem designed to frighten people off. It insisted, quite against his recollection, that this simple hike involved a 4,000-foot climb, an easy-to-lose trail, one traverse over a possibly snow-covered slope ("an ice axe and knowledge of its use may be required"), and an estimated total of almost 20 miles.

He debated for a long time whether it would be fair to ask Audrey to risk it. He ended up convincing himself that it would, which is why he bought her boots. They wouldn't be properly broken in, but better stiff boots than one beaded Indian mocassin, or those Mexican sandals she was always wearing. He would pack a lunch in his knapsack, salami and cheese and fruit and chocolate. They could stop as often as she wanted. She could cool her feet in the creeks, and have a swim at the end.

They quit camp early, and were on the trail at the String Lake footbridge by eight o'clock. He stripped a great pole which she fancied into a *Sound of Music* alpenstock. The trail was crowded with a large number of fellow hikers, who were amused by Audrey's long pole and jolly air.

Along the east shore of Jenny Lake they walked on soft, springy humus, up and down little mounds. Gray jays whistled in and out of the damp pines and Engleman spruce. The steepest of the Tetons rose a sheer mile over the tips of the trees, looking all the more arrowlike and unapproachable the closer they came.

As they neared Cascade Creek, the traffic on the trail increased, thanks to the motor launch crowd from Jenny Lake—fat grandmas, babies in backpacks. Everyone was out today. Timmy wanted to hurry on, but as the trail began to slope a few undetectable fractions of a degree above horizontal, Audrey started to pant and slow pace. Half a mile from the boat dock, they crossed a log bridge and came upon the high white-water rush of Hidden Falls, totally hidden by tourists taking pictures. Audrey collapsed on a rock. (Distance traveled, 2.2 miles.)

"Hey, c'mon, babe. We've just started."

"Timmy. I'm not sure this was a good idea."

" 'Course it was. It's the only way you'll ever get into the mountains, short of climbing. We follow the creek all the way from here on. It's mostly level." (That's a lie.) "I swear, honey. It'll be easier once we get away from this crowd."

She rose from her rock, with the help of her alpenstock, only to have to start climbing in earnest, as the trail made a triple switchback in the next half mile. The crowds were a little thinner here—some of the grandmas and babies had come just for the falls—but only a little. The view east from the top was wide and satisfying. It was agreeable, for a change, to look at a prospect of something less forbidding than the Tetons. They rested at the lookout, nibbled raisins, shared swigs of cold water from Timmy's canteen.

"How much further, did you say?"

"Hey, Audrey! It's not even ten o'clock."

"Oh, Timmy, I *do* want to do this, I really do. But I'm so afraid I'm not going to be able to. And then you'll be mad at me."

"If you give out, I swear to God I'll carry you. Okay?" He gave her a kiss, and helped her on up.

The trail leveled out after that, and ran through the valley of a wonderfully steep canyon. Huge boulders, and great slides of smaller rock, had settled at almost 45 degrees on the lower slopes of the mountains at either side. The creek ran rapid and clear, its banks abloom with wild flowers, yellows, some blues, a few purples and reds. Fellow hikers were fewer, now, and further between. If the great cliffs on her left were discomfiting—she kept feeling as if Timmy or God or someone were about to order her to climb them—the continuing presence of the wide and grassy creek bottom, with the water meandering through, was a comfort. By 11:30, they reached the forks of the creek. Her feet hurt, but not as much as they had at the start. They rested again, dipped into the knapsack, and looked back down the canyon they had already climbed. Audrey took off her boots and socks, and soaked her feet in rushing water.

"Where will we stop for lunch?"

"Lake Solitude, I guess."

"How much further is that?"

"Oh, two and a half miles. Two and three-quarters, maybe."

"And how far have we come?"

"Six. Six and a quarter."

Well, she thought. I guess I can handle that. Beyond lunch, she dared not think. She dried off her feet in the sun, which was already rather fierce, and put back on her socks and boots.

* * *

She made it, but only just, to Lake Solitude. Before they got there, Timmy mentally cancelled the Paintbrush Canyon return.

After the fork, the trail ascended a thousand feet. They came out of the spruce and fir, and began climbing up talus slopes and flower-speckled meadows, until they reached the steep moraine that dams the south end of Lake Solitude. The climb had been very painful for Audrey; at that point, she began scrambling on all fours. She slipped and fell, cutting her knee on the rocks. As Timmy helped her up, and half-carried her over the last mound of gravel and stones, the sky overhead turned suddenly dark. Within a minute, rain was falling; within two minutes, hail. She started crying.

"Don't worry. It's just a summer storm."

"*Just*? Look at me, I'm soaked!"

"They never last very long."

Trapped halfway up a sliding hill of rocks, as buckets of rain and hail poured on her head, she felt as if the mountains had got her, swallowed her up.

"The lake's just over that ridge. Then we can wait under a tree till the storm passes, and dry out in the sun after lunch."

"But the trail gets worse after the lake, doesn't it?"

"We're not going any further."

"We're not?" Sun was breaking through cracks in the black overhead.

"No. I'm sorry, babe. I bit off too much. We'll rest at the lake for an hour or so, then go back the way we came. It'll be easier downhill, and we can take the boat back across Jenny Lake."

She threw her arms around him and cried some more, then kissed him in thanksgiving.

Having decided to cut their losses, they fussed over the perfect place to have lunch, which involved an extra mile's hike around to the north shore of the lake. Relieved of the thought of any more climbing, Audrey fairly skipped along. They picked a cozy lookout high up under some trees, face to face with Teewinot, Owen, and the Grand, only this time they were looking at the mountains' backsides instead of their fronts. They ate their lunch greedily, drank cold water from the creek, had their nap and nuzzle in the sun, splashed a bit in the water, and headed back a little after two.

Downhill or not, the seven-mile return to the boat dock was a trial. Audrey had never walked seven consecutive miles in one day in her life, let alone sixteen. Her feet were blistered, her legs were scratched and aching, her breath and strength were almost gone. Returning home from a new place, though, always seems shorter than going. You recognize the route in reverse, and have at least some idea when it will end. By taking the motor launch, they spared themselves the last two miles' hike. At the Jenny Lake ranger station, they hitched a ride back to their car.

The couple who picked them up were astonishingly good-looking youngsters in an orange Karmann Ghia, who turned out to be students from the University of Colorado. They were up for the week taking mountain climbing lessons. They planned to spend all day Friday and Saturday climbing the North Face of the Grand. Audrey was shamed by the greater audacity of this girl exactly her own age, who was also so much prettier. She wondered, with jealous apprehension, what Timmy was thinking. In a way that was unlike him, he was bragging to the youngsters about the peaks he had climbed ten years before, and talking a lot of mountain climber's lingo. He seemed to be showing off, as if he were afraid they would think an easy 16-mile hike was the best he could do.

Back at String Lake they changed into swimsuits, and went for a late afternoon swim. Audrey couldn't believe how quickly and completely her aches and pains disappeared. Dirty feet, blisters, sore muscles, scratches, all the fatigue of the day, all the memory of entrapment by the wilderness washed away as she floated dead on her back, or frolicked with Timmy among the reeds.

That was the evening Timmy kept his earlier promise, and took Audrey to dinner at the lodge.

She could hardly believe that so elegant an establishment existed in the same world as their tent. For all the times she had seen the Tetons, she was astonished by them all over again, seeing them framed by Mr. Rockefeller's huge window in the Hall. Roaring fires, costly rugs, Indian jewelry in glass cases, the hum and tinkle of luxury bars: back and forth over the polished floors walked obviously rich people in obviously expensive, vaguely western clothes; silver-tipped ladies in suede pants suits with French neck scarves, arm-in-arm with tall men in tailored leather and cavalry twill, around whose necks hung tiny cord ties with gold slides. She felt hopelessly shabby, and wished Timmy had broken his rule about shaving.

But the headwaiter in the Mural Room seemed not to mind. He even gave them a table by the window when Audrey asked. They ate steaks and drank wine and held hands and watched the moon light up the Skillet Glacier, and the stars come out in a purple sky over the cut-out profile of Mount Moran and its neighboring peaks. As Audrey started to pick a French pastry off the trolley, two golden youths came in, dressed with elegant western ease, and walked over to their table.

"Hi there!" said the girl, fringed vest over silk blouse, yards of silver chain. "Remember us?"

Their drivers from Jenny Lake. The boy was dressed in Levi's, tooled cowboy boots, a reddish leather jacket. He shook Timmy's hand with gusto.

"Seems we have the same taste in food as in mountains."

"Well," said Timmy, explaining away their presence, "I prefer to cook in camp, myself. But I promised Audrey we'd try the lodge once."

"Oh, we always stay here," said the girl. In the car, her golden hair had been braided and coiled up with pins. Now it fell shining and free to her shoulders, like a shampoo commercial. "My family's been coming to the lodge since I was in fourth grade."

"Are they here with you now?"

"No. We came with a gang from school. That's them over there." She waved to a big table in the middle of the room. It was surrounded by more gilded youth, all handsome and well-dressed.

211

"Well. Enjoy your meal," said the boy. "Fun seeing you again."

"You, too. Enjoy the climb Friday."

Timmy stared after them. Audrey wished all the more he had shaved. Maybe even worn a jacket. Of course, there was no point in even thinking about what *her* hair looked like.

"Kids like that piss me off."

"Why?" she asked in genuine surprise.

" 'Oh, we *always* stay here. Mumsy and Dadsy have been taking me to the lodge since I was just a puking little brat.' Shit. This place must cost thirty bucks a day."

"It's a beautiful hotel."

"Fucking college kids."

"But if you had the money, wouldn't you like to stay in places like this?" She adored the idea of luxury hotels, luxury resorts, luxury restaurants, luxury liners, luxury anything.

"Not in the Tetons. Places like this don't belong here. Neither do people like that."

For four days, Timmy had been watching the younger people in camp, on the roads and trails, around Jenny Lake. As he looked at all these college kids, park workers, campers, hikers, climbers in their 50-dollar Vibram-soled hiking boots and thick socks and flap-pocket khaki shorts and lots and lots of hair, fresh and limber boys and girls—in his day, the backpackers and climbers had been almost all male—he felt a caged eagle's surge against the bars.

A raucous "Happy Birthday" sang out from the Colorado kids' table: it was golden girl's day. Everyone in the room stopped staring at Mount Moran, and turned to watch the center table instead. A waiter brought out a cake with candles. Blondie blew them all out. The dining room applauded.

"Isn't that sweet?" Audrey was captivated by the festivity.

"You know another thing about them that bothers me?" Timmy had turned his back to the party. "They're so goddamn young. Everybody around Jenny Lake today looked about sixteen."

"Why should that bother you? You can do anything they can."

"I can't have their next twenty years. All the time they've still got to live through, I've finished. I've used it up."

"But you've done so much, Timmy. I thought you'd be *pleased* to have done so much, happy to have the memories of all those years."

"Memories? I want it now, Audrey, alive, I want it in my hands." He turned back. "Look at them!" His eyes were red-rimmed, a little crazy. He glared at the gang at the center table, fresh-faced and bright-eyed, bouncing around like puppies, handing out presents.

"I was there, once. I belonged there. Oh, not at some fancy college. Not with parents rich enough to let me stay at a place like this. But when I was their age I had all my *life* still to lead, all the good things still to do. Total strength. Zero responsibility. Enough knowledge to cope.

"And now I'm forty. I don't *belong* at Jenny Lake anymore, and that bothers me. It's like a club I can't join. My lungs aren't as strong, I can't eat and drink what I want without suffering for it. I run out of energy, my nerves go all foul. I have moods—God, you must know that by now! Ups and downs, high ups, low downs. I keep crawling into myself like some kind of cave. I know too much. The world isn't all mine any more. Not even a tiny piece of it." End of tirade.

"And now you've got responsibilities, too: huh? Responsibilities like me. That bothers you too, doesn't it?"

You have to tell the truth over five thousand feet. It was one of the rules.

"Yes. I'm afraid it does. When I was twenty, I wanted a woman of my own desperately. I envied my brothers, and friends who were married. But I wanted the whole world even more."

"Do you envy me as much as you envy them?" She nodded in the direction of Colorado. "I'm almost the same age they are."

He looked at her again, but didn't touch her. He thought for a long time, looked out at the glacier.

"No."

"Why not?"

"You're young, and that's beautiful. You're beautiful." She was. He kissed her hand. "But you're not as free as they are. Not as free as I was at your age."

"That's because I'm married. I married you."

"No, it's not. You were never that free. You never will be. You've never had the kind of feeling I'm talking about—the feeling that there's nothing you couldn't do, nowhere you couldn't go. Have you?"

"No. But I still feel . . . young." She wanted to cry, why she didn't know. For him, maybe. For eighteen years she'd never know.

"You *are* young." He held their hands together over the candle. "Look at the skin on the back of your hands, and look at mine." He stared up at her. "Look at my eyes, look at my neck. I snore like an old man, I know I do. People tell me I do. My knee gives out, my hair is going, I've got a permanent crick in my neck I've been told is arthritis. At *forty*, goddamn it. Arthritis! I've got scars and stitches all over. I'm just fucking getting *old*. And sometimes it gets to me."

"You never told me this before."

"I shouldn't be telling you now."

By their fifth and last day, he had half-decided to offer to drive the lower Yellowstone loop, if she really wanted it.

But as it turned out, they spent the day just puttering and lolling around their own National Park, doing little of anything much. After another of Timmy's spectacular breakfasts (sausage, eggs, fried potatoes, toast, juice, coffee: they got ravenous up here), they walked down to the pebbly beach at the end of Lizard Creek. There they sat for a while and talked, trying to commit it all to memory. They walked the long way round back to the car. After driving out to look for trumpeter swans at Oxbow Bend, they took a gravel and dirt road up to Two Ocean Lake, which the car just barely made.

There was an easy trail around the lake; but Timmy guessed, rightly, that Audrey had had enough of hiking. They ate lunch there. Then they discovered another beach, hidden down a steep footpath just over the bridge. This one they had all to themselves. They swam for a little while in the cold water of the lake. Afterwards they explored a little Catholic chapel nearby. Only then did the fact that another Sunday had come around register on Audrey, so completely had she yielded to the pagan pantheism of Timmy-of-the-Mountains. She knelt for a moment to explain to God why she hadn't gone to mass.

From the top of the twisting road up Signal Mountain, they could follow the whole course of the river as it wound its way through the valley.

Letting his mind run with the river, Timmy came up with a new idea of how they might spend their last day. It was even better than driving up to Yellowstone. When they got to the car, he drove straight to their campsite. There, he pulled the air mattresses and the double sleeping bags out of the tent. He spread them out carefully on a soft pine-needled space of ground out under the sky.

"In the afternoon?" asked Audrey. "I mean, out here in the open?"

"What better time? You afraid the chipmunks will see us?"

"But I thought we were going to . . ."

Before she could say it, he had scooped her up in his arms; laid her down on the sleeping bags; then laid himself down beside her, and began kissing her deeply. Full of five days of bliss, she could hardly resist. She hugged him every bit as tightly as he hugged her, and kissed back with fierce and loving force.

He undressed her completely, then undressed himself, rolled on his side and pressed himself against her. He fitted his bent knees behind hers, his loins against her rear, his chest against her back, eased one arm under her soft bare waist, and reached the other over her side so that he could move his hand up and down her, feel her breast, her belly, her thighs, her pubic hair. Under the blue mountain sky, among the pines, the deep smells, the small woodland sounds, it had only wanted this to be perfect.

It was strange, this need of his flesh for her flesh, the irresistible impulse he felt to touch it *all*. Only rarely, or only at climactic intervals, was his lust focused on this part of her body or that; only very rarely on the specific piston-in-cylinder fitting that obsesses so many men. What he loved most was skin, tenderly stretched over a whole body. And since it covered and contained all of her, he felt that in loving it he loved *all* of her, by which he meant all he could feel, palpate, squeeze, lick, press against, finger, and kiss.

What was it about skin that excited him so? The thinness, softness, warmth of it, the blood and fat under it, veins that throb through it, perhaps the *give* of soft skin, its contour-continuations, the changes in texture as you moved to ridged and hard places, nipples, lips, ears; hairy places, the underarms, the neck, the vulva; to areas moist with natural secretions: the inside of the mouth, the vagina, the rectum. He liked the dryness of hands and fingers, which could also warm and turn damp; the inlaid enamel of nails; the wonder of eye jellies. But above all, he loved the *run* of it, the flow under his fingers, his palms, then under his own skin surface. He loved to rub gently the fur of his arm or chest a fraction of an inch away from the sort surface of her skin; to rub back and forth the soft yielding fat of her waist, the full-fruited roundness of her hips, thighs, buttocks. He adored a female ass, the soft thickening below the waist, the way the skin of some parts would give at the touch, as if created to be squeezed, moved, kneaded. These small, boyish breasts were too wonderful even to think of: they fitted so beautifully to a cupped hand, waited to be cupped, to be kissed, to be sucked with a wide open mouth.

To press it all hard now, twist it, squash the breasts against his chest, press her stomach and crotch, to feel them with as much of his own body as possible. Then to do the same with her belly, hips, buttocks, crotch, legs, writhe and roll and wrestle about until he had intimately introduced every square inch of her skin surface to every square inch of his, as if to absorb her, make her into him, or at least his: flash, weld, meld and melt the two surfaces together in some voluptuous and ecstatic union. It was as if the very body heat, the pulses and sweat their writhing engendered would end up by sealing them together into one creature: a four-armed, four-legged, bisexual devil of pure lust.

For the moment, he was as happy to tongue or finger her openings as to prod them with a prick. He was obsessed, perhaps: but with her body, not with the simple idea of fucking it. He wanted to swallow her up, and not miss an inch.

In order to savor his tour of her mounds and valleys, her inlets and forests, he pulled away now and then to slow down his rod, keep it out of her reach and away from her tempting tunnels.

Then, holding the poker with one hand to keep it ready, he knelt back up and started slowly again: started kissing toes, ankles, instep, kneading his way up one calf and down the other, licking the small of her back, the fragile bumps of her spine, letting his nose or little finger play about her ear or neck, touching his elbow or the hair of his arm to her sides so gently the muscles beneath her skin would ripple in involuntary little shocks. Only then did he drag the tip of his penis slowly and gently up her stomach, between her breasts, let it rub over her cheeks to her lips. Hers, then, first, to suck for a while. Then his again, for the final fitting-together of part to part.

It was only the second time in her life she had done it out of doors. And Timmy was right: it *was* better and cleaner and healthier and more wholesome, above 5,000 feet.

25

This is a mean excuse for a fort. It is nothing but an enclosure for horses surrounding three rude cabins erected some years ago by Captain Bridger, a grizzled and apparently unprincipled mountaineer, who operates the place together with his untrustworthy Mexican partner. This Vasquez is the same man we encountered ten days ago, near South Pass. It is now obvious that his sole purpose in camping there was to entice as much custom as possible to this isolated post.

It has, I must confess, a beautiful situation. After five days' travel through forsaken barrens and dreary desert (during most of which I was disabled with a digestive disorder), we came upon handsomely wooded country out of English romance—in some respects, out of dear New England. Captain Bridger's establishment is situated on a damp and fertile bottom between four separate forks of the Bear River. The waters run clear and cold. They are full of large spotted trout, on which we have feasted.

But the thievery of these traders is a scandal. They ask up to 150 dollars for a horse or a mule, and charge 12 dollars to shoe a single ox. For a small box of matches, the price is 25 cents. Bad whisky, which appears to be the major item of sale, costs two dollars a pint.

Despite the presence of many white-topped wagons and emigrant parties, this compound gives off the stench of half-breed degeneracy, surrounded as it is by innumerable domestic animals; by great numbers of transient Shoshone; and by 20 or 30 French mountaineers with their squaw brides and mongrel children. They all live in filthy skin tents, and appear to do nothing but gamble, drink, and fight. Some appear more barbarian than the Indians. Captain Bridger himself is "married" to a dirty Indian girl perhaps half his age.

216

I recorded nothing of the six days' progress we have made since parting company with the Carthage Company, because there is so little to report. Without the distraction of fellow travelers, driving through country in which each day's terrain is much like the last's, and in a state of debility oneself, one passes the hours plodding mindlessly on. I began to feel like an ox, or a mule. James has settled into driving the animals with a grim and distant taciturnity—doubtless the effect of his own wearying labors of the last two months, and the new strain of undivided responsibility. I fall back more and more on the company and conversation of the good preacher's sons, and the solace of my well-worn Bible.

It is interesting to note how remarkably different the two boys are, for children born to the same parents. Henry, who is twenty, is sandy-haired and ruddy complected, with broad shoulders and strong arms. He seems afraid of nothing, and can quite hoist an axle on his back. Hector, who is eighteen, is quite timid, although he tries to hide it. He is as fair as his brother is brown, and as slender as a reed.

Their affection for one another is unashamed and open, a model of brotherly love. Watching Hector's sunny and sudden smile on seeing his elder brother arrive, or seeing how readily they share chores, in an effort to lighten one another's burdens (as well as mine, of course, and James's); seeing the ease with which they embrace in manly fashion; or shove and josh about like young schoolboys, one is minded more of some deep soul-brotherhood out of the Bible, like that of David and Jonathan, or of John, the beloved disciple for the Master, than of the usual bickering and rivalry between kin. Would that the men of my own family, or of James's, had half their tender grace. They have had great sport at this "fort," pushing one another into the creek. Hector dunked his brother unawares, and was then able to escape by running more swiftly (he flies like an antelope). But once caught, he was helpless. Henry simply fetched him up in his arms like a baby and deposited him without ceremony into the stream. I laughed till I wept at their foolish sport. How I treasure such diversions!

It is clear from the way he looks at him, rushes to assist him, and tries to imitate his speech and his manner that Hector idolizes his elder brother. It is no less clear that Henry would die himself rather than allow harm to come to Hector. Along the Sweetwater, he cared for him through three days of fever as any nurse or anxious mother; for once, I felt totally superfluous. How proud their parents must be of two such youths, now as playful as puppies, now industrious as oxen. I wanted to post a letter to that man of God, their father, from this place, telling him of my admiration for his sons, and letting him know of their good health and progress. But Henry insists that Reverend Williams's movements as an itinerant preacher are so irregular that is is impossible for one to know where to direct a letter. Their mother, whom they adore, lives at home, but alas she cannot read. How I envy their parents the years of joy they have had, nurturing and observing the growth of such bright and brave young men!

Hector, who did all their cooking before joining the Carthage party, is a deft hand at a stewpot, and is now sharing with me the labors of the morning and evening fire. This does not endear him to James, who seems to think it unnatural that a man should trouble himself with kitchen matters when a woman is about.

Since the dark clouds and wet weather seem to have passed, James and I sleep once more in the wagon, the interior of which is more spacious since we have abandoned or consumed so much of our load. The boys pitch their small tent nearby.

The only "adventure" (if I may call it that) this side of Mr. Sublett's cut-off was the exorbitant and unsafe ferry we were obliged to take Tuesday over the Green River, which was (by my guess) 300 feet across, and much too high to ford. The boat, owned and operated by three smug latter-day Saints, was as seaworthy as a washtub full of holes, and threatened to capsize more than once. A lamer excuse for a river-crossing craft I have never seen. It required one man to bail all the time, whilst another at every crossing kept stuffing bits of rag into the leaks. For this, we were obliged to part with four dollars.

City of the Great Salt Lake
July 19, 1849

After the three most difficult days' travel of our expedition so far, we reached the opening of Emigrant Cañon (as the Mormons call it) at three o'clock in the afternoon. There we saw before us a true miracle of the desert. Past the lower slopes and across a wide river a trim, tidy city lay like a vision, with broad avenues laid out at right angles, verdant gardens about each dwelling place, and extensive farms to the north and the south. It cannot be called either handsome or rich; but in these dry latitudes, it is like a mirage of paradise itself.

One comes upon this prospect with startling suddenness. From narrow mountain gorges and rough crooked turns, our road abruptly led us through an opening like an immense doorway, unarched at the top. Here we were on a small plateau some hundreds of feet above the valley, with nothing to obstruct our view for many miles. There was the Great Salt Lake itself with its background of mountains, and in its foreground the well-ordered, miniature city of snug cottages and thrifty gardens set within a level oblong. It is impossible to describe how, in the transparent atmosphere, everything was brought out with a distinctness that belied distance. From here the road, which the Mormons have widened and leveled in order to use it for fetching wood, winds gradually down the mountainside to the plain, then becomes a broad avenue leading into the city.

After watering our stock at the river (to fit their conceit of a Promised Land, the Mormons have honored their little stream with the name of Jordan), James drove our wagon into the city. Following the advice of others we have met, he drove up to a respectable-looking log house and knocked at the door. He enquired of the woman who answered if a party of four California emigrants could find shelter and entertainment under her roof. She declared that we were most welcome, but that owing to the size of her household, there was sleeping space only for two, on the floor of their summer kitchen. The house was surrounded by an acre and a quarter of garden, however, in which the boys were welcome to pitch their tent. Her husband, upon his return, could direct us where to leave our animals.

That evening this good woman, whose name is Hannah Samuelsen, laid before us a feast of fresh vegetables from her garden such as I have not seen these many weeks. There were green peas, runner beans, new potatoes, sweet corn, as well as rich sweet milk, butter, and fresh-baked bread. The memory of this delicate feast will live with me forever.

City of the Great Salt Lake
July 20, 1849

The Samuelsen household is made up of the husband, Mr. Ezra Samuelsen, a gruff and bony old Dansker, late a Lutheran farmer from Chautauqua, New York; his wife, Hannah, who is, I would guess, about my age—gentle, quite illiterate, and an absolute slave to her husband; her younger sisters, Thelma and Miriam, who also attend their master hand and foot, and who have the low wit and high spirits of Irish servant girls just off the boat. There are three small children, one just a babe, forever squawling and tumbling about. All these, fancy, in one log house of two rooms and a pantry!

Or so it at first appeared. Mr. Samuelsen seems also to own a second house adjacent to this, in which Hannah's two sisters and two of her children reside, doubtless to ease the strain of such limited quarters. If this arrangement is in some ways convenient, it is in other ways bizarre, as it obliges the master and mistress of both houses to travel back and forth a good deal. One would have thought it more sensible to expand the original dwelling than to have built a second, but for some reason this appears contrary to the code laid down by President Young. Since our arrival, in any case, the entire family has gathered here each evening for supper, the two younger sisters bringing over both the children, as well as cooked and covered dishes which they prepare. It makes for a full and festive board, and causes me (as the sight of happy families always does) to long for babes of my own.

Most of the emigrants arriving in this valley, to the number of about 150 or 200 a day, come with the intent of obtaining fresh provisions and trading old stock for new, heavy wagons for light. Although the Mormon residents, thanks to their irrigations and their industry, are well-supplied with all manner of farm produce, they have no wheat or flour to spare, and no use whatever for United States money—indeed, they have instituted a currency of their own, guaranteed against deposits of gold already brought hither from the California mines by the faithful. They will, if pressed, sell from their scant stocks sugar or coffee at exorbitant prices (50 cents a pound for coffee!); but flour is unobtainable at any price, while they wait for their new crop. They will happily exchange fresh garden produce, however, for such of these staples as we have left; many among the emigration are depleting their stocks of dry groceries for the luxury of vegetables, fruit, eggs, milk, and butter.

They have no great need of lame oxen or large covered wagons, with which we of course are oversupplied. But like sharp Yankee traders, they realize that the former may be rejuvenated here, and then resold; and the latter made over into vehicles more useful to them. So they purchase our animals and wagons for next to nothing, or trade them against the fresh horses and mules and small wagons that are becoming as precious as the gold they are to enable us to find.

This morning James took what seems to me a very dangerous risk, but he insists it is the only way we can be sure of arriving safely and soon at the mines. He traded our large wagon against a smaller, and sold our three yoke of oxen—for one-third what they cost in St. Louis! With half the sum obtained, he has bought from a Cincinnati emigrant desirous of lightening his load enough additional metal-working supplies to equip a complete black-smithing shop. This he has set up in the midst of the large emigrant camp along the River Jordan. From Mormon merchants he has been able to purchase what was wanting to complete his equipment. With the help of the Williams boys, he built a small shed and enclosure for animals out of lumber and hardware left from broken-up wagons.

His plan is to work until he is able to purchase six sturdy Mexican mules, animals he now believes to be far abler than oxen to manage the desert and mountains ahead.

Already he is busily at work. The line of animals and wagons grows longer by the hour at his hand-painted shingle—JAS. McCUE, PROP. ALL BLACKSMITHING DONE CHEAP. Henry and Hector offered to help this afternoon, but James prefers to work alone. So they accompanied me instead on my explorations of the town.

City of the Great Salt Lake
July 22, 1849

James works from morning to night at his makeshift smithy, shoeing animals, repairing wheels and wagons. He suffers some hostility from the Mormon smiths in town, who had anticipated having all this work to them-selves, and set their prices accordingly. But the extraordinary numbers of emigrants pouring into the valley each day (and almost all in need of repairs) assure more than enough work for all. He charges somewhat less than his local rivals—three dollars to shoe a mule instead of four, for example—so that despite the costs of equipment and supplies, he reckons that in two days he has already earned the price of a span of mules.

I hinted that, today being Sunday, he might take a respite from his labors in thanksgiving to the Lord, but he did not respond favorably to the sugges-tion.

So instead Hector and Henry and I accompanied the entire Samuelsen clan (Ezra, Hannah, her three children and two sisters) to their own regular Sunday service, which is held in a vast open shed known as the Bowery. This place is to serve the community until a proper temple, which is to be enclosed and built of stone, can be completed. This edifice will rise just north of the Bowery, on a ten-acre square in the center of town already identified as Temple Block.

At 9:45 A.M., we entered the Bowery. It is advisable to go early if seats within hearing are required. The place was a rude shed about 100 feet square, with a roof of bushes and boughs supported by rough circular posts, and open at the sides. It can contain about 3,000 souls, I was told—perhaps half the population of this valley. The congregation is accommodated upon long rows of benches opposite the rostrum for dignitaries. Between the people and the dignitaries was a sort of pen allocated to the brass band and a "choir" of six persons, who sang the songs of Zion in an unmusical manner.

We took our seats on the benches allotted to Mr. Samuelsen's "ward," or parish, and continued to observe the congregation flocking in, some from considerable distances. The men were attired decently enough, although the weather being hot some of them had left their coats at home, and even opened their vests. The relaxed costume looked natural to such hardworking men; their posture and demeanor were evidence enough of their propriety. The women wore the customary long-sided sun bonnet, and gowns of sober color and neat stuff. The elders, on the platform, all wore coats of black broadcloth, and kept on their tall, steeple-crowned straw hats until the address began. There were numbers of very old persons, vivid testimony to the strength of the Mormon faith—each of these aged souls has made a journey that has destroyed younger and hardier folk. Almost every female seemed to carry or escort a child, more often several children. Never have I seen so many of the young at divine service. Many faces bore an aspect of grim severity. Fanatic devotion to an unpopular faith seems to lengthen noses, foreheads, and chins, and to narrow the space between the eyes. The rigors of two years building this desert kingdom showed in angular limbs and a sunburned skin.

The meeting began with a hymn, followed by prayers and exhortations, including one imploring the blessing of heaven on President Young. One Phelps then rose to deliver a violent philippic against all Gentiles, and the United States government in particular. Another elder or bishop by name of Smoot then delivered a foolish and un-Biblical exhortation on religious matters, in nasal tones and execrable English.

Then their great apostle and prophet, Brigham Young, arose and came to the lectern. He is a tall, sturdy, bull-like gentleman with a large bent nose and hair worn full to the collar. He wears a silk vest with a gold chain, and a black silk tie. For half an hour, he pronounced the most extraordinary tirade I have ever heard. First, he lauded the Saints for their zeal in supporting the church, obeying its decrees, paying their tithes, and observing the ceremonies established by the elders and bishops. He assured them of a certainty that they were God's chosen people and sure of a seat in Paradise. These simple farmer-saints were informed that they had a glorious destiny before them, and that their morality was as remarkable as the beauty of the Promised Land. The soft breeze blowing over the Bowery, and the glorious sunshine outside, rendered the allusion most appropriate.

He then whipped the idle drones who hung about street corners and prayer meetings when they should be building roads, cutting timber, and harvesting crops in order to increase the revenues of Zion. He came down most savagely on female saints who indulged in extravagance and love of dress (although I must say I have seen no evidence of any such follies!). They could better advance the cause of God's people by self-denial, milking cows, and making bread.

I was so shocked by what followed I would have left the assembly, had it been possible. But by now, people were pressed in so close it would have been most difficult, as well as embarrassing to my hosts.

President Young proceeded to curse the Gentiles bitterly as the evil persecutors of his people, and called on God to consume them root and branch. "Do you know, brethren," he asked—I reconstruct his words from memory—"do you know that some of the murderers of the prophet Joseph have been among us? If I had known it, what do you think I would have done to them? Would I have hurt them? No! I would not have hurt them. I would have killed them so quick they wouldn't have known what hurt them!"

I inwardly uttered a prayer of thanksgiving to God that Captain McClellan and his band were not amongst us at the moment. A week ago, I refused to credit the fears of the men of Carthage regarding these their erstwhile adversaries of Illinois. As of yesternight, in fact, so impressed had I become by the generosity and piety of these modest but deluded folk, that I was convinced the company's fears of Mormon vengeance were mere chimerae, and they could have traveled this route as safely as we.

Alas, this "divine service" proved their apprehensions all too dreadfully just. The "Prophet" Young appears a latter-day type not of the gentle saints and apostles of Jesus, but of such fanatics as Mahomet or Cromwell. He is a shrewd and cunning egotist who can easily control the weak and superstitious who have followed him hither. The rough congregation of farmers, mechanics, and their womenfolk gazed at him as if he were the Apostle Paul himself. They attended in fascinated silence to his coarse ranting and curses, which grew progressively more forcible, more degrading, and even blasphemous as he continued.

He warned the Saints that all who passed through the city lusting after gold were crazed and an abomination. "God almighty will give the United States a pill that will puke them to death," was one sample of his elevated style. "I am prophet enough to prophesy the downfall of the government that has driven us out. Woe to you, United States! I see you going to death and destruction. Indeed, I *pray* for your death and destruction, and order you my brethren to do the same. Missouri and Illinois will either make atonement for all their sins against us, or sink disgraced, degraded, and damned into hell, where the worm dieth not, and the fire is not quenched."

Never at a supposed Christian service have I heard anything less resembling Christianity. I was well pleased that James had not come. I was careful on departing to commend only the singing and attendance. I made no mention of President Young's address, and winked at the boys as a signal to do the same. In point of fact, I believe that Hannah was as embarrassed as I was by the performance.

She has been explaining to me something of the building of this oasis. Yesterday and today, I was able to explore it myself, first in her company, then escorted by young Hector.

It is plotted with the most wonderful regularity, like the prairie dog villages we saw on the plains, precisely as President Young directed two years ago. At the outset, their "pioneers" all lived in small adobe rooms inside a single walled enclosure farther up the hill. Then, when it appeared that the local Indian tribes were not likely to be belligerent, each family drew numbers in a lottery for a piece of land of its own. Many—like the Samuelsens—have already built or begun to build houses of their own. With each dwelling house goes an acre and a quarter for a garden. The plots are laid out eight to a block, eight blocks to a ward (the wards are fenced separately), and twenty wards to the city, which covers exactly eight square miles, with Temple Block at its center. The wards are divided by extravagantly wide avenues and sidewalks, numbered by direction from the Temple Block. Along each meridional street are dug courses for little streams or ditches, from which pure water for irrigation is directed from the main circumferential ditch. This is in turn fed out of City Creek and other mountain water courses to the east. Were it not for this system of artificial watering—which has clearly required an immense amount of collective labor to build—nothing would grow in this dry and desert waste. Each household is permitted to tap these ditches only once every four days during the dry months. In this season, one can enjoy in every home garden the sight of a rich crop of beans, peas, potatoes, and corn. The yield appears to be far richer than one is accustomed to in the East, for all our months of rain.

The Samuelsens came to this country from Mormon winter quarters on the Missouri last summer, in company with two or 3,000 others, persuaded hither by the promise of free land and a tabernacle of their own in Zion, as well as their unquenchable faith in President Young. Of course, they had no idea of the rigors of the journey, nor the barrenness and heavy labor which awaited them at the end. Their first season, before a crop could be harvested, was apparently one of extreme hardship, and they were utterly at the mercy of Young and the pioneers of '47 for their survival. After what little had been grown was shared out, no miracle came to multiply their loaves and fishes, so all were forced to feed on roots, wild hawks, and the like. It is clear that this hard charity, and the loss of all other ties, has bound them with iron chains to the orders and ideals of their masters. It is inconceivable otherwise that free Americans would subject themselves to such tyranny.

The city is full of illiterate and dependent immigrants willing not only to work but also to die—some would say kill—for their outlandish religion. Hannah confessed to me that, upon their arrival, they were ordered by Pres. Young and Mr. Kimball to have no intercourse whatever with Gentiles and strangers, for fear of corrupting the purity of their faith and the single minded necessity of their industry. On learning of the discovery of gold in California (a company of their own happened to be there at the time), the church leaders were at first delighted at the fortunes it brought to their coffers; then dismayed at the news of Gentile mobs heading west, likely to intrude on their isolation and tranquillity. Finally, Pres. Young has come to regard our passage as providential, a miracle akin to the flock of heavenly seagulls which ate up the plague of locusts which was about to destroy their first crops. Mr. Heber Kimball, another high church dignitary (I am not sure of his exact title) is said to have prophesied that just such a "miracle" as our passage would come to pass.

From our discards, our surplus oxen, machinery, and St. Louis groceries, they are enabled to build their empire much more rapidly and cheaply than would otherwise have been possible. Young continues to denounce the greed of all black-hearted, gold-seeking Gentiles. But he now encourages the Mormon brethren to make good use of our passage. The Lord, as we know, can convert even the deeds of the wicked into good. His only restriction is that they hold back from selling or trading wheat and flour too cheaply (which injunction they have certainly obeyed.), as their crops will be required o feed the thousands of fresh Saints due to arrive in this valley next fall.

City of the Great Salt Lake
July 24, 1849

Today was the festive day. It is two years ago this day that the first of the Mormon pioneers arrived in this valley, after the expulsion from the States and their long trip across the plains.

We were invited as guests of the Samuelsens to a grand picnic at the Bowery, which was conducted along the lines of a Fourth of July celebration back home. (The Fourth, as a matter of fact, they ignore completely, to demonstrate their contempt for the federal government.) Owing to the need to conserve provisions, each family provides its own food for the feast that follows the celebration, and on this occasion the Samuelsens were kind enough to include us in their "family." Hector and I helped the women prepare the viands last night. James, having purchased the last of his mules yesterday, celebrated by taking the day off, and assisted young Thelma in carrying food and drink to the Temple Square.

Very early, we heard a clarion call of trumpets and drums, and the thunder of an old iron field piece brought back by Mormon soldiers from the Mexican War.

A procession was formed, led by the brass band we heard on Sunday, followed by a uniformed military contingent, then an array of family wagons bearing each a banner announcing the ward or other locality from which it had come. In one large wagon stood twenty-four virgins dressed in white, each bearing a Bible and one other book symbolical of some of their peculiar tenets. Behind them marched twenty-four youths, each carrying a sheathed sword in his right hand and a copy of the Declaration of Independence and the Constitution in his left. This was, I suppose, intended as a show of their patriotism; but it was not very persuasive. Then came the bishops or elders, each carrying the banner of his ward. Citizens from that locality followed after.

The procession ended at the Bowery, which was quickly filled with a motley concourse which seemed far to exceed three thousand. It included, as before, a great number of children. We were entertained by loud if discordant music from the band, then some songs by the choir. A historical address was given by President Young, recalling the heroic band of 1847, not without a few of his usual gratuitous blows at their persecutors. Innumerable toasts followed, all quite according to program. (There were no voluntary toasts, and no responses.) These were singularly "lyrical" and old-fashioned. One, which I copied in my notebook, was raised "To the Mothers in Israel, fruitful as the vine, you have crowned Zion with your jewels."

The formal part of the ceremony lasted perhaps three hours, and was followed by our sumptuous *al fresco* repast. It is quite wonderful to see so much joyful hilarity and enthusiasm aroused without the use of spirits. (Although spiritous liquors may be sold in the Kingdom of the Saints, they are taxed so heavily that they might as well be forbidden. I believe no Mormon uses them.)

James was in unusually fine fettle. He seems quite charmed by the girlish manners of the younger of Hannah's sisters, and joined her in the strenuous and joyful dancing on the green. I had thought to promote some interest in her or her sister Miriam on the part of Henry or Hector, who are much nearer their ages. But my dear boys become great shy boobies around any other female but myself!

After the band played "Home, Sweet Home," the square and the streets were rapidly deserted, every family having returned to its abode. It is heavenly to witness so much real harmony and brotherly love, so much earnest industry and thrift, without the least hint of scandal or bickering.

City of the Great Salt Lake
July 26, 1849

I do not understand what has happened.

This afternoon two sergeants of the Mormon police—for church and state are one in this place—came to the Samuelsens' house in search of James. Mr. Samuelsen, who seemed to be expecting them, directed the men, who were large and blackguardy looking, to the place of his smithy in the emigrant camp. I ran about the house asking what had happened, but everyone pretended not to know, and the officers refused to tell me. Hannah was cold to the point of insult, saying things like "I am sure I don't know, *Mrs.* McCue," and, "Excuse me, *ma'am*, I must get on with these peas," when until now we had used one another's Christian names, and been as close as kin.

I ran after the officers, and came up just as they were seizing James at his forge. There was a great hullaballoo among the Californians, who resent any Mormon interference with one of their own. But the men were armed and fierce, and had the power of the city and its rulers behind them. James seemed almost to expect their arrival, though he demanded to know the cause of his arrest. He was told only that he must come along.

Held tight by the arms, he was paraded through the camp and into the town before the gaze of hundreds of passers-by. I ran along beside him in a perfect fit of frenzy. At the home of the magistrate, he was led in the door and up to the desk. There, to my astonishment, stood Mr. Samuelsen and two of his neighbors.

The upshot is that James is accused of allowing his new mules to wantonly destroy the gardens of Samuelsen and his neighbors; and of "blasphemy against the institutions of the Church and the person of its President." He is to be fined three hundred dollars, including "costs"—exactly the value of the mules!

Allowed to speak on his own behalf, he stated that Samuelsen had knowingly allowed him to pasture his mules in his garden, that we had been living there as paying guests for a week; and that if he uttered some careless or disrespectful opinions concerning the church of Jesus Christ of Latter Day Saints, or of its president and prophet Brigham Young, it was in heat and under severe provocation from Mr. Samuelsen.

The magistrate, a Mr. Stout, disallowed or disregarded this perfectly reasonable defense, and went into a harangue against the greedy gold-seeking Gentiles who murder their prophets and drive them from their homes. Allowing stock to eat up the sustenance of the Saints had been specifically outlawed by the Deseret legislature two months previous, and mocking the sainted Brigham is apparently an offense that cries to heaven for vengeance.

James made bold to interrupt, and insisted that he was none of these, but had always spoken and believed fairly of the Saints.

The judge, who is obviously a creature of the Church, grew more heated, and said he knew upon sworn testimony that James had been one of the party of murderers from Carthage, Illinois; that he had traveled with the most notorious villains McClellan and Lewis, who had seized Joseph Smith in prison and pushed him out a window to his death. If he had since separated himself from their company, it was evidently in order to spy, or for some foul purpose, and that Brother Samuelsen's sworn accusations of blasphemy and the wanton destruction of property were proof of the blackness of his heart.

So it is because of our joining of the Carthage Company in St. Joseph—which was purely a matter of chance (and seemed at the time such a stroke of good fortune!)—that we are here to be persecuted so unjustly.

James tried a few more times to deny these accusations, but to no avail. He was warned that further "outbursts" would lead to additional fines for contempt of the court. His mules are to be seized and sold to pay the charges. He was offered the alternatives of either paying the fines and costs, or of working them off on public roads and buildings of the city at two dollars a day, which option he indignantly refused.

In this haven of refreshment, we are left without shelter or succor. We must of course quit the Samuelsens' roof at once, and do what we can with a small wagon, a single horse, and a very small purse. All of Capt. McClellan's warnings about the injustice of these people, and their settled design to rob and torment Christian travelers who fall into their trap, prove to be true as Gospel. We are wholly at their mercy, and must pay dearly for the wrongs others have done them.

It is destructive to the soul, and harmful to one's faith, to be abandoned and cast down at a time full of hope. I find myself utterly unable to pray, and have asked Henry and Hector to petition heaven on my behalf.

26

City of the Great Salt Lake
July 27, 1849

I can hardly hold the pencil to write; but I must attempt to perform some rational act, to convince myself that I am sane, and dwell in a world of religion and order. I have learned more of evil this day than I can bear: evil in the Samuelsen house, evil in my own husband's heart; evil, perhaps, even on the part of Henry and Hector Williams.

Truly, Satan is amongst us. I have been dwelling amidst corruption of the most unspeakable sort, and all the while blind as an infant newborn.

None of this would I have learned—and how happily I would have abided in ignorance!—had James and I not begun to quarrel over Henry and Hector. After we had moved out of the Samuelsens' house and up to the river encampment, Hector came to me with an idea that seemed inspired. He begged me to plead with James to let him and his brother contribute towards the repurchasing of our oxen, at the very least, so that we might all continue together to California. Their welfare was every bit as much at stake in this matter as ours, he declared, quite reasonably I thought. They had depended for many days on our wagon, provisions, and support. They had some money, he declared, and only pleaded for the right to assist us with it now, in our hour of need.

This struck me not only as legitimate, but indeed as a blessed means of release. I kissed Hector for his generous offer, and flew to convey it to James at his "shop." I knew he might prove resistant, because of the difficulty he has in accepting aid from any one, and especially from two young men of whom he is not overly fond. But I certainly did not expect him to fly into such an extravagant rage.

At first, what he was shouting made no sense to me at all. He spoke as if the boys and I were responsible for his difficulties with Samuelsen, and the straits we were in now! He accused them of vileness and filth, and me of being a fool. I pleaded with him to speak more calmly, so that I might understand of what they and I were being accused.

In the case of the brothers, he said, he could not with decency tell me what he knew. It was not fit for a woman to hear. Imagining that they might have fallen prey to one of the pretty Mormon girls in town (as several susceptible young emigrants appear to have done), I insisted that I was no child to be spoken to thus, and that in justice to me and them he must explain his words. He said that he knew what he knew. He had had his suspicions all along, but they had been confirmed a week ago when he met a border emigrant who knew the boys in Missouri. He was not going to bandy words about such matters with a woman, and I must simply take him on his word.

I protested that I knew them to be Christian young men of a superior sort, as susceptible to the temptations of the flesh, no doubt, as any man born of woman; but in no way debauched; and that he ought to be ashamed to believe vile calumnies of a passing stranger. I had surely seen and spoken with the boys enough to understand their true character.

Once more he flew into a rage. He swore that if I had not abandoned him (which of course I would never dream of doing!) in order to "play the flirt" with Henry and Hector Williams, all our present troubles would never have occurred.

Unable to reply for my sobs, yet unable to bear such abuse, I ran to the shelter of our wagon. I cannot describe the confusion of my feelings.

After about an hour, James came in and sat beside me on the wagon bed. He put his arm around me, and apologized for his temper and his language. Unpleasant as it was to face, he insisted that what he had heard of the boys was true. He had more evidence than the stranger's word, but would spare me any further revelations. He had asked them to pack their things and leave. If he felt sorry, it was for my sake.

I turned away and wept. I realized I might only anger him more, by making him think that I *had* been unnaturally fond of the Williams brothers, and that I was weeping more for their departure than for his own discomfiture, or our present sorry state. But one's feelings cannot always be controlled.

Horrible as this was, there was unfortunately more to be told. James had grown so jealous of what appeared to be my preference for the company of these boys, that he determined to have his revenge.

The reason for Ezra Samuelsen's cruel harrassment of James was not simply a fit of Mormon prejudice or pique, and had nothing to do with our having traveled with McClellan. Samuelsen openly accused James of alienating the affections of, to put it more bluntly of seducing, not his "wife"—but his wife's sister Thelma! When confronted by this accusation, James did not deny it. That is now my cross to bear.

Instead, he counter-accused Mr. Samuelsen of living in lecherous concubinage with all three sisters, a fact that was revealed to him by young Thelma.

Samuelsen denounced the girl for betraying family matters to a stranger, which seemed to him more culpable than her promiscuity. But he also insisted that plural marriages are not only permitted but encouraged by the elders of his church, for the greater populating of their kingdom. President Young, he declared, claims *27* different women as his wives.

James, who was in no position to cast stones, told Samuelsen what he thought of so abominable and heathen a practice, and of President Young in particular. Whereupon Mr. Samuelsen went to the city officials and asked that James be arrested for blaspheming and lechery. He later agreed, in order to prevent my learning of it, to substitute for the charge of lechery the lesser offense of the animals' trespass.

The enormity of all this information destroys me quite. To learn, within an afternoon, that my beloved husband has been unfaithful with a young girl; that she and her sisters abided willingly in a kind of pagan harem; and that the two kind boys who have been such a comfort to me during this ordeal dwell in the shadow of some unpronounceable suspicion: this is to be awakened from a dream of paradise, and find oneself in hell.

In our mutual guilt and confusion, James and I have grown a bit closer towards each other. He begged my forgiveness, which I of course granted him at once. This is the only consolation I can draw from what otherwise appears a moral disaster. He had been industriously repairing wheels and wagons for fellow emigrants since early morning, but he shut up shop early this evening and prepared supper himself, so that I might try to rest, and recover some of my spirits and failing strength.

City of the Great Salt Lake
July 29, 1849

We sat gloomily over our fire last night, wondering what we could do. James suggested, and I half-agreed, that we might find ourselves forced to stop in this place until spring, when he will have earned enough to purchase new mules and continue our trip. Attractive as the town once seemed to me, this was now a dark prospect, because of all that has happened to us here.

By mid-evening, James repented of all his earlier accusations, and blamed himself entirely for our situation. Had it not been for his thoughtless vengeance and lust, Samuelsen would never have had occasion to hail him into court; he would never have been so outrageously fined; we would still have our mules; and could by now be on our way.

I held his hand and asked him to join me in prayer. As we were bent by the firelight, who should come up but Henry and Hector. James saw them first, but said nothing. He was too cast down by his own griefs to express anything of either anger or distrust.

Henry asked if he might speak. James looked up and nodded. The boys remained on their feet. None of us looked at one another. Speaking carefully and with obvious pain, Henry confessed that what James had been told of them was true. He and Hector wanted to go to California not so much for the gold, as to start life anew in a place where they were unknown. Jesus, he

229

believed, understood and forgave them. They were ill-equipped by temperament, training, or provisions to travel to California alone. They were afraid to travel among rough and suspicious men like those of Carthage, who might torment or even kill them for what they knew, or believed they knew, of their past. They dared not risk subjecting themselves much longer to the harsh moral government of the Mormons. They admired James above all other men in McClellan's party for his honesty and integrity, no less than for his strength and skill. They greatly respected the speech he made at the end, and vowed to join their fates to his, despite what they knew of his disaffection. They admired me, they said, as a Christian woman of intelligence and good spirit, and a kind and trusted friend.

Having recited all this as if rehearsed, without pause or interruption, Henry repeated their offer. Although the mules are now lost, and they could not afford the cost of six more, they would like at least to invest in our continuing journey the sum required to buy back the oxen, and begged that they be allowed to continue to the California mines in our company.

James stood and turned his back to us, and walked some distance away. I feared that Henry's fine words, so carefully prepared, had been in vain. I dared not raise my eyes from the fire. James came back, walked over to where the boys were still standing, and very soberly shook the hand of each.

With no word about all that has passed, he accepted their offer, and agreed to share with them the trials of the journey ahead. I rose and shook their hands as well, then retired to the wagon while they discussed our future plans. James came to bed soon after. I did not ask, and never shall ask, the crime of which they stand self-accused.

James is off with the boys this morning to recover our oxen. I have been up since dawn, putting our belongings in order. The sun is warm now, the camp full of motion. James has elected to follow the trail to the north around Great Salt Lake, on which he expects to rejoin the main emigration from Fort Hall within five days. The more direct route across the salt desert itself is denounced by all as unsafe, despite the claims of Mr. Hastings' guide book.

From the wagon seat where I am writing this, I can see the houses and streets of the city of saints, which once appeared so welcoming and decent, and now stands revealed as a pit of foulness and corruption. I only wait the return of the men for us to be on our way.

27

The latter-day McCues, who were certainly not saints, came down from their magic mountain. There was no reason for staying five nights rather than three, or seven. They weren't in any hurry. It wasn't one of the rules. Five just seemed to be enough.

They're fragile things, perfect times: you blow a glass ball as thin as you possibly can, but then you stop. Otherwise, you end up with slivers of glass all over the floor.

They were supposed to be out of their campsite by eleven. But Monday mornings were slow in the Tetons, and very slow at Lizard Creek.

By the time they had cooked and eaten breakfast, washed the pans and silver, closed up and packed the stove, unstaked and folded the tent, unzipped apart the two sleeping bags, rolled them up and stuffed them in their carry-bags, stowed away the food, and gathered up their clothes and other bits, it was noon.

They drove out along the park road instead of the highway, so they could have a last close-up look at their mountains, and the shore of Jenny Lake. From Moose Junction, Timmy took the unpaved road to Teton Village, which he had known before it got developed. Now a vast parking lot, with room for a thousand cars, stretched in front of a crescent of expensive looking lodges and step-pyramids of condominiums. In the middle of the crescent, the red and blue cars of the aerial tram floated up and down on sagging cables.

Jackson was hoked-up and touristical, but Audrey liked it. If not the perfect tourist, she was the perfect audience for the staged effects of traveler's kitsch; the sort of person on whom memorial arches made out of hundreds of elk antlers jammed all bristling together were never wasted. She liked the imitation-early western stores around the square, and wished they'd been able to come to town earlier to see a show at one of the honky-tonk saloons.

After Jackson, they followed the north bank of the Snake River Canyon; the road twists about in order to stay with the river on its serpentining way. Far below, canoes and red rubber floats bobbed in its foam.

South from Alpine Junction, the road ran through a valley of western Wyoming farms. Fat cows stood knee-deep in green grass, ignoring the mountains all around them. Sprinkler pipes on wheels poured out fountains of water.

They stopped at a dairy to buy a chunk of local cheese, which they ate with French rolls under an oak tree.

As they neared the Idaho border, the road climbed back into pine forests. Timmy felt the old rush of satisfaction he always experienced driving on good mountain roads, well-banked roads that kept curving up and down, right and left, through a vertical evergreen world.

A banner flapped over the main street of Montpelier, Idaho, advertising a rodeo that was already over. After that, they drove past collapsing log barns in empty farms and near-deserted villages.

Timmy decided to end the day's drive at Bear Lake, on the Idaho-Utah border. They edged its western shore, which was almost barren of trees. The lake was vast and steely-blue. Further west, on the other side of the road, the hills climbed suddenly. In every other direction, the earth sloped gently away.

They started looking for a place to camp. The most attractive campsites, under evergreens, were on the far shore, inaccessible by car. The state park was bleak: paved spaces for fishermen who slept in their trailers. Finally, they found a row of campsites just off a wide beach at the south end of the lake. They swam, and walked on the beach, and slept out on the sand.

Next day they drove up to the pass on Beaver Mountain, then down through the forests of Cache Valley. They emerged from the mountains at the Utah State campus above Logan. There civilization recommenced, and they started following the signs to Salt Lake City.

They debated whether to look in on the city. Timmy had never liked the place much. If you have to mess up mountains with cities, he thought, better the crass gusto of a Reno or a Denver. Here the state package stores, the eerie absence of bars, the religioso-freako tourist attractions, the family farmhouses set along wide, empty streets marked the holy city as something puritanical and un-western. The Utah capital seemed to him an alien, church-ridden place.

But Audrey wanted to see it.

So he turned off on 184, and they eyeballed the capitol on its hill, and then drove around Temple Square to look at that. They headed out to the east end of town, to see the pioneer monument that overlooked the city, and get a sample of the Wasatch Mountain view. They got out of the car to read the inscriptions, then sat through a tape recording of the Mormon emigrants' story, which played over and over in a little building next to the monument.

232

Three walls of the room were painted with a heroic mural, in which the artist had managed to fit a thousand miles of legendary suffering onto about fifty square yards.

The detour took an hour and a half. But it was enough to put Timmy in a mood, if not bad, exactly, then not good either: edgy, defensive, prickly-selfish. He had relaxed into a nice country-western detachment up in the mountains. Now, fighting the traffic and tourist crap of an inhospitable city, with its tabernacle choirs and beehives and gold angels and *dumb* liquor laws, he was rapidly losing hold of his whiskery mountain mellow. In proper conjugal fashion, he began to blame Audrey for his discontent. I mean, she was the one who wanted to stop here, wasn't she?

He didn't say it out loud, of course. But the thin wedge was back, the old impulse away; the call of the self.

Which was a pity, because everything had been going so well. Just talking had become easier, since the Tetons. They knew each other better. They had more to talk about. They were beginning to know one another's instincts, anticipate responses. They balked less at differences, avoided the quicksands, played the games more willingly. They knew how to feed lines, when to offer the desired answer in place of the true one. Either one, now, could start a conversation about any one of a thousand common reference points, then play it along with a fairly good sense of what the other might be thinking.

Audrey tried that as they drove out of Salt Lake. The first topic she ventured was the Mormons. Timmy didn't want to talk about them. O.K. She thought for a bit, then tried the funny people at the amusement park where they had stopped for lunch.

"Mmmm."

Nothing there. Bear Lake, maybe.

No.

She tried the Cache Valley road. He had been ecstatic about it the day before.

"You're right. It was a nice road."

She gave up.

Actually, Audrey didn't mind silences as much as she had at the start of their trip. She just hated to think that the least grit of friction might have entered the blissful rapport of the past perfect week, now that they were back below 5,000 feet.

At this point, a more experienced wife might have berated him for his monosyllabic answers. Audrey settled for an obvious sigh, slid her head back on the headrest, and looked out the window.

The holy state of Utah obviously had plans to build something better—yellow trucks and earth movers were all over the place—but for now the road out of town was just two chewed-up lanes sheared off in clifflike drops at the side, over which Timmy twice drove in frightening jolts, scraping his under-carriage and doing heaven knows what to his tires and shocks. The road surface was badly cracked, and pitted with unfilled holes. Behind the yellow bulldozers were salt processing works coated with dust. As they came nearer to the inland sea, one of the most uninviting bodies of water in the world, Audrey could see gruesome little resorts out in the glop.

She wanted to look at the lake from closer to. Timmy, quietly resenting another detour, took what he thought was a turn towards the south shore, but ended up in the middle of a sprawling copper company town, heavily guarded. He kept driving the wrong way, among prisonlike smelters and piles of mineral waste. A factory guard finally pointed them towards the lake. Timmy parked in front of a souvenir and refreshment shack on the shore.

Audrey got out and walked two hundred yards to where the water began, then took off her sandals and waded. The shallow brine seemed to stretch listlessly on to the ends of the earth. On the walk back, she collected a handful of salt crystals, then threw them away and bought a little cloth sack of salt marked "Great Salt Lake" at the souvenir stand. Timmy asked what she wanted that for, and she didn't know, so she threw it away too.

He had sat in the car the whole time, with the doors open and the radio going. He put his bare feet up on the dashboard. As Audrey walked out to the lake, he watched her grow smaller and smaller. He imagined her disappearing altogether.

Salt Lake City brought Timmy down from the mountains. The desert that followed had the same effect on his wife.

At a last little town in a curdled swamp—a tin café, a tin house, a broken-window gas station—Timmy gave in to her pleas and the intimidating signs: "LAST GAS AND WATER BEFORE DESERT." He filled up everything that needed filling: ominously, everything did. It was not good to need that much water. It was not good to need that much oil. The old lady who pumped their gas looked like a desert reptile herself, a creature that could live off the sun's heat and the water of salt marshes.

At first, the desert was just like any other western desert: sandy hills speckled with sagebrush, odd rock formations, dry gulch cracks. Along the road, there were even a few scatterings of purple candleflowers and bright yellow black-eyed daisies.

Then came the salt swamps; then the salt. Gradually all vegetation died, elevations flattened to zero, colors drained to one dazzling white.

The silence between them lasted unbroken for twenty miles. Timmy would never admit to being afraid, anywhere. But crossing this place always put him slightly on edge. He liked to have other cars or trucks in sight. Today miles went by in which no one else came in view. He drove down the ever-straight line of narrow road, etched across ever-widening spaces of white. His eyes pinched into headache, then vertigo, envisioning faint mirages. Sparkling whiteness kept tempting the car to swerve off the edge. The road became a tightrope stretched high in the sky, the white desert only empty space below. It grew hard just to keep driving in a straight line.

He wanted to stop, refocus, clear his head of these fantasies. But as he watched, the car's temperature needle settled in the red, moved past the H, kept moving up.

234

The road shoulders looked like quickmud. They passed a dead truck off the road, sunk to the tops of its tires, trapped in a slurping muck that lay just under the crust of salt.

"Look."

"I see it."

Twenty miles, four words. Back to silence.

Audrey's will was concentrated on one single wish: that this desert would end. Looking at the empty spaces on Timmy's road map back in Indiana, she had feared the worst. But this was worse than the worst. The lack of life or variation was appalling, and the sheer whiteness was driving her bats. She felt they had left the world entirely, and were cruising the surface of an uninhabited moon.

"How much farther?"

"About thirty miles."

She thought about that.

"Timmy, I'd like to stop."

"We can't."

"What do you mean, we can't? Why can't we?"

"The radiator would blow."

"Timmy, I'm serious. This is making me sick."

"See that needle? If we keep driving, it stays where it is. If we stop, it goes over the top. Boils over, destroys the seals and gaskets, even the engine maybe. Then we really are stuck."

"But what will you do?"

"Keep driving. When we get to Wendover, I can pull straight into a gas station. If we get to Wendover."

He tried to sympathize. "I'm sorry, babe. I just wouldn't want to risk stopping out here and not be able to get started again." He pulled his gaze away from the hypnotizing line, looked at her, patted her bare thigh. She shrunk as if from a leper's touch, clutched onto the door handle, double-checked to be sure it was locked.

A sign appeared, warning drivers not to leave the road. She could see the tracks of people who had dared; another abandoned car-carcass, lost in the mud. Timmy pointed to a miniature whirlwind far off in the desert. Soon it was crossing their path. The great wind in its wake blurred out the road, scattering fine salt and sand against their windshield, roof, doors, under their tires. The car caught, swerved, spun its wheels in the sand, then pushed on in pain. The wind and pelting salt beat against walls inside her skull. Timmy turned on the wipers and the lights, fixed his hands to the wheel. A truck tore on past, honking wildly, nearly blowing them off the road with the suction of its passage.

Past the time-warp of wind, blur and terror past, they settled back on the flat sea of white. Now distant islands appeared, far mountains broke the level line of the moon's surface. A lone hitchhiker: how did he get here? A miniature freight train two hundred cars long crawled across endless space, far away to the left. The needle stayed just beyond H on the red. Both of them

235

glanced at it every few seconds. They pushed on through the glittering moon-desert, cleaving to their pencil line of security, happy for the company of a passing car every couple of miles.

At last, two shaded picnic shelters appeared, one on either side of the road, at the Bonneville Speedway exit.

The mountain-islands grew larger, began to cluster into continuous uplands. One high pyramid detached itself far to the right.

"That's Pilot Peak. It's not far now."

"How far is not far?"

"Twelve more miles. You just try to relax."

She closed her eyes, and tried to think of other times and nicer places, in which there were trees and houses and gardens. Neither had thought to turn on the radio after Great Salt Lake. The desert and the dry radiator had taken whatever space there was in her imagination. She tried to pull free of them now, and imagine something from the world she had quit. Before long, she was back on the cool lawns of Holy Rosary Convent.

She opened her eyes. Like one more mirage, the buildings of a little town broke the far horizon on a rise of land. On a cliff to the right she could make out a white W.

"That's Wendover. Half in Utah, half in Nevada. One more state to go, baby, and we're home."

She smiled as best she could, and reached for his hand.

236

28

When things start to fall apart, they often crumble at the edges first. All that happens then is that the sides aren't quite as straight as they used to be. So you scarcely even notice.

Wendover, Utah (population 700-something) is of no particular interest to anyone, except for anxious westbound travelers on Interstate 80 (or old U.S. 40). To them, it signifies that the Great Salt Desert is over. And except that you can lay down your money there legally (for the first time in 2,500 miles), in the odds-against hope of instantly winning more money, the west edge of town, which is just over the Nevada line, would still be desert.

That's where Timmy headed, past any number of gas stations, both major brands and the cheesy local brews—Pit Stop, Oil City, Husky, Stinky—right to the Nevada line. At slower speed, you could hear the engine water bubbling, protesting. He pulled the car in to a Chevron station alongside a thirty-foot-tall neon cowboy, and left the engine running. A young muscle-bound attendant, whose name (would you believe Rocky?) was stitched to the breast of his black form-fitted T-shirt, came up to chat.

"Radiator?"

"You guessed."

"Lucky you made it acrost."

"It's not that bad."

"Wanna open it up?"

"Opens from the grille. Left-hand side."

The sculpted creature took a pile of rags to protect his hairy hands. As soon as the hood sprung up, you could hear, feel, everything but see the agony of the engine. Timmy got out to look.

"Don't turn if off," he shouted to Audrey.

237

Rocky pulled up a hose, and started spraying water on the suffering metal, which sent it back in hissing clouds of steam. The engine sounded as if it wanted to crack.

"Wow. That's really hot."

After a couple of minutes' spraying, Timmy took a rag himself, and risked unscrewing the cap, little by little. It hissed more. Standing to one side, he kept turning, until the cap was hurled into the air by a geyser of steam. Rocky flopped his hose around and began pouring water into the car's thirsty hole. At first, whatever he poured in seemed to evaporate at once.

"That's more'n just dry, buddy. You want that radiator seen to."

"It's brand-new."

The guy shrugged, kept on filling.

"You do it tonight?"

"Shop closes at six."

"Anybody else here work nights?"

"Nope."

"You guys got some deal with the motel owners?"

"Huh?"

"I hate wasting time in nowhere places." He looked at his watch. "Tell you what. Flush it out and test it now. Check out my hoses, seals, thermostat, freeze plugs. If you spot any leaks, see what you can do about 'em. If you don't find anything, put in some Stop-leak. Okay?"

"I guess we could do that. You wanna wait here?"

"No. I'll be next door." He looked at the casino-motel up the hill, for which the bowlegged neon cowboy served as a shill.

"Give me one good reason we shouldn't stay here. It's obviously the best place in town. It's new, to begin with. It's got its own restaurant, its own pool . . ."

"And it probably costs the moon. I don't want to stay in the middle of all *this*." She waved her arm at the scene in front of them. At twenty past five on a Tuesday afternoon, in the absolute middle of nowhere, several dozen adult Americans were ramming away at silver slot machines lined up in rows, in a darkness lit up by fluorescent tubes and blinking bulbs in primary colors. There were two colossal machines, each the size of a small garage, which accepted only paper bills. They had to be maneuvered by metal levers the size of seesaws. People stood in line to play them. Beyond the machines and the blinking lights, more people were clustered around green topped tables. Each spill of coins from the slots added to the general racket, over a grinding bass of rock-Muzak and babble. Major jackpots set off electric alarms, and an infection of envious squeals.

"I can't *stand* this, Timmy."

"Listen. Our room will be up behind the pool. You won't even know the casino is here. You can stay in the room or out by the pool and pretend you're in . . . Honolulu. Or in Massachusetts.

"We drove past some perfectly nice hotels on the Utah side. I don't see any reason to waste our money on a gambling joint."

"One reason," he shouted—they were both shouting, now, you had to shout to be heard over the din—"one reason is that our car is next door."

"It won't be for very long. The shop closes at six, that boy said."

"He won't be finished tonight. So we might as well stay where we are."

"We could easily walk back to the Utah Side. It's just a couple of blocks. And stop yelling at me."

"What do you mean, stop yelling at you?" he yelled. "You're yelling, too, for Christ's sake!"

"That's one of the things I don't *like* about this place," she yelled back. "It's so loud you can't hear yourself think."

"Let's go in the bar and get away from the noise. I think we could both use a drink."

What Timmy had forgotten was that in even minor Nevada casinos, you never get away from the noise. The bar was a raised platform in the middle of the gaming room, placed as close as possible to the tables and machines. The coffee shop, which they tried next, was an extension of the lobby-casino-bar, with the same bright orange carpeting and flashing red blue and yellow lights. Keno boards blinked at you wherever you looked. A waitress the size of a mattress rolled up sideways, with improbable orange hair, tried to herd them into the nearest vacant booth. When Timmy said no, they wanted to get away from the noise, she became indignant and refused to seat them. Instead, she went back to the bar and fed some of her change into a juke box (which played *over* the Muzak). Soon all the Tijuana Brass came blasting out of a speaker right over the far corner table they had picked.

"What do you want?" Timmy asked.

"What do I *want*? Earplugs and blinders. Six giant Bufferin."

"To drink, I mean. Don't you want a drink?"

"Of *course* I want a drink! What do you think I want, a pack of Life Savers? Worrying myself to death half the day driving across a desert in a car about to blow up! I . . ."

"Right. One drink. Do you want to tell me what, or shall I choose something for you?"

"Where's our waitress?"

"Ignoring us. We didn't sit where she wanted us to, so she's sulking. Some women," he smiled, italicizing, "are like that. I'll go and order."

"All right, then. A gin and tonic. I'm breaking my rule because of that drive." She was fishing for her cigarettes. "But don't you go having too much, now. You know your problem."

He thought about busting her one in the nose, but decided against it. She was so busy trying to click her lighter into flame, and look in her mirror at the same time, that she missed his evil eye.

At the bar, he had another offended female to confront.

"Sit in there, you gotta eat."

"Okay, sweetheart. I'll have a cherry. You can pop it in my drink."

"Don't smartass me, cowboy, I'll have you out of this place in two seconds. You gonna eat or not? Anyway, that back section is closed."

239

"Look, sweetheart. My wife got a terrible headache driving across the desert, and the noise out here is making it worse."

"Your wife my ass. What noise you talking about?" She looked around, as if he were referring to a buzzing fly she may not have noticed. She was shouting over what sounded like the crashing of sixty cars at once, taped for replaying.

"Take my word for it, sweetheart, it's noisy. All we want is a quiet corner to sit in. You bring us a menu and we'll order something, I promise. Okay? Can we stay where we are? Pretty please?" He pulled out a couple of bucks and left them near her elbow on the bar. State Gaming Rules.

She slipped the money in her apron pocket, sniffed what he presumed was an O.K., and turned back to her jukebox. The old McCue charm. Timmy patted her on the ass, and paid for their drinks. He got a sympathetic glance from the barman, who looked as misogynist as Timmy was feeling. He carried the drinks back to their corner table, where Audrey was still trying to smoke, repair her face, and learn how to play Keno at the same time.

"I'm sorry, sweetheart," she said. "I didn't mean to be cross." She slipped her compact in her purse, lay down the Keno booklet, and stubbed out her cigarette in the ashtray.

"Me neither, babe." He kissed her cheek, clinked her glass. "Cheers. Let's just relax for a while, okay? That desert does take it out of you. But we're home, now, nearly. How about that?

"I'm sorry about the racket. But I do think this is the most comfortable place we're going to find. Lucille Ball over there promised to bring menus, if you feel like eating."

"I wouldn't mind."

"We have to order something, apparently. House rules."

The gin, the nicotine, eventually a big steak sandwich with French fries eased away some of the wear and tear, tuned out the more extreme vibrations of audio-visual assault. The worst of the journey *was* over, she realized. Perhaps the afternoon's coolness had been only a temporary slip, the sort of thing Great Salt Deserts do to loving couples. Timmy had two beers, to cool down, then a serious Scotch, while swallowing a toasted ham and cheese and a large piece of pie. When the waitress brought Audrey her coffee, Timmy stood up. He wanted to go to the bathroom, he said, and look around a little bit.

"Why don't you just sit here and relax?" He gave her a kiss on the cheek.

He took his drink with him. He gave the old lady another feel as he squeezed past her at the bar. She gave him one back. Welcome to Nevada.

Blackjack was the first card game Timmy's father had taught him; the simplest game in the world and, he believed, the best. He had been away from it so long he had almost forgotten how good a game it was.

His dad had started him and his brothers playing for pennies around the dining room table. He expected his sons to know how to shuffle and deal flawlessly by the time they were six, and understand splitting and doubling by eight. When they played at home, the deal changed every five hands. If you went broke, tough luck: you went broke.

When each boy was in his last year of school, he was allowed in on weekend poker and blackjack games that George McCue ran in a back room of his restaurant. There they learned Reno rules, and how to play for serious stakes. Some of the smaller clubs in Reno didn't worry too much about I.D.s in those days, so Mr. McCue introduced each of his boys to the legal version as soon as he grew reasonably tall. The Reno Trip became a rite of passage almost as important as the annual Fishing Trip, which they were allowed to join as soon as they finished eighth grade.

Timmy still preferred places where one person held, shuffled, and dealt a single deck of cards. He didn't like the dealing boxes they used at fancy places; didn't like fancy places generally. Dealers could still cheat you, he knew, especially in a little place like Wendover. But that was part of the game.

His dad played mostly instinct, along with a few old Basic Strategy rules he had probably picked up from *his* father. Even these he had internalized years ago, which allowed him to ignore them when his gambler's sixth sense started receiving the right signals. In the Air Force, Timmy had learned to count score on dealt-out cards, so that he knew when the odds on a desirable hit increased towards the bottom of a deck. His father sneered at such tactics. Conscious attention, he believed, could only break the flow of mystical information any clean heart could draw out of a deck. He disapproved of Timmy's habit of playing two or three hands at once against a dealer, which struck him as greedy and anti-luck. You were bound to slow up a game that way, and might get yourself booted out.

Actually, old George McCue's sixth sense was only telling him the same things as Timmy's card-counting: what was left in the deck, when the odds were on making a winning hand; when to bet high, or double down, or split; when to bet low; when to quit.

So Timmy McCue, gambler, left his bride in the Wendover, Nevada Casino coffee shop to "look around." After one stop (to change fifty dollars of dirty money into nice clean chips), he perched on a stool in front of a kidney-shaped table.

Half an hour later, he had totally forgotten he was married. He was a hundred sixty dollars ahead. Already people were clustering behind him. Winners give off silent radiations that spread quickly through a casino. Now the pit boss was watching him closely. A waitress was at his elbow with her tray. He nodded at the interruption, Scotch, double, Chivas, concentrated on moving his chips into the three mystical piles of one of his systems, and trying to freeze out the luck of the cowboy at the other end of the table, who was obviously souring his luck. The thing to do now was to play low for a while, he decided, low and safe, then throw in a big dumb bet to confuse them. First time back at the tables in years. Already he was hot. He played his chips alternately from each of the three piles.

"Timmy?"

What the hell, he thought. Who knows me here?

"Sweetheart, I've been waiting for you for almost half an hour."

Oh my God.

"It's after six. Shouldn't we go get the car?"

"Yeah, babe, Right. Just let me play out this stack."

"Goodness, what a lot of chips. Are they worth money?"

The dealer gave him a look. What playground you pick her up at, bub?

Timmy felt chagrined, felt his luck leaking away.

"You in, bub?" the dealer asked. Timmy could feel the table staring at him, pitying him the bad luck that interruptions always meant.

"No. I'm out." He shoved his stool back and stood up. He pocketed his chips and silver dollars, and elbowed his way out of the crowd, leaving Audrey to make her way in his wake. Players and kibitzers closed ranks behind them. The pit boss wandered off. For all the lump of chips and coins in his pocket, he felt beaten, shamed, and angry.

"I didn't know where you were, dear. I was beginning to worry."

"I told you I wanted to look around."

"I know, but half an hour? If you had just told me where you were going, I wouldn't have minded. But not to know . . . I didn't know you gambled."

"Well, now you do."

"Did you win?"

"Mmm."

"A lot?" It looked like a lot. But she didn't know what the different colored chips were worth.

"Enough. A couple of hundred."

"*Dollars*? My goodness. But do we have enough money to risk playing that much?"

We? What's this *we*?

"I wouldn't play it if I didn't have it."

"My mother told me people who gamble always lose in the end. Unless they cheat."

"Your mother doesn't know what the hell she's talking about. As usual. I don't play to lose." (Like all people who gamble, he did lose most of the time. Audrey's mother was right.) He was sore at her for breaking his luck, cracking into his neon escape with her dull gray reality.

The chips and silver added up to $227, $177 more than his stake. No big deal *yet*; but it could have been if he'd been able to play it out. It was almost as if Audrey had robbed him of a hefty chunk of cash.

The car wasn't ready, as Timmy knew it wouldn't be. As he had intended, they spent the night at the casino's motel. After lugging their suitcases up the hill, and settling into a decent room just off the pool (all the rooms were just off the pool), they both went for an early evening swim. Down the hill out of town, you could still see the white desert, reaching to the dark horizon.

Timmy did his laps, fantasizing perfect hands and stacks of green chips. Audrey floated on her back and looked at the sky. Marvelous mountains of cloud were moving, as if in formation, from east to west across the early evening. Her mind was still suffering from the day's whiteness and heat, but her body floated free of cares, her eyes rested on the cloud mountains, and the early stars between them.

They showered, dried, rested, made love, watched a little TV, she in her nightie, he in his shorts. She could feel his restlessness, as one feels an imminent thunderstorm in the air by the way it charges the ether.

"Oh, go ahead, Timmy. I don't mind."

"Go ahead and what?" He could have burst.

"Go back to the casino, I mean. Back to your card game. That is what you're fidgeting about, isn't it? You keep fussing around here like a tiger in a cage. *I* can't relax when you're acting like that."

"You really don't mind, then?"

"Oh," she sighed. "Yes. I do. Of *course* I'd rather you stayed here with me and watched television, or just held me, and showed me you loved me. I hate to think all the good times we had in the Tetons are over so soon."

"They're not! I swear they're not. I *do* love you, baby . . ."

"And it's very depressing to learn you're addicted to something so idiotic as a card game."

"But honey, I told you . . ."

"You *know* you're going to lose in the long run. And now it's my money, *my* future you're risking as well as yours!"

"So you'd really rather I didn't go?"

"No. I *said* go. I'm not your keeper."

"I really don't take any risks."

"When you're in a mood like this, I feel more comfortable with you gone. I suppose it's better we did stay in this place, in the long run. At least I know you're in the same building."

"Sure." He quickly pulled on shirt and pants, put on socks, tied his shoes. "Don't worry, sweetheart." He kissed her on the forehead. She ignored him, kept watching the television, scrunched up on the couch in her nightie. "I'll just be a couple of hours. No later. Promise."

"Go then. Go."

He did stay, as he promised, just a couple of hours. By nine-thirty, he had lost everything he had won on the first round, plus his fifty-dollar stake, plus another fifty, mainly because he got carried away playing five and twenty-five dollar chips instead of silver, out of God knows what urge to look big. He started hitting twelves and thirteens, and doubling down nines (they let you do that in Wendover), no matter what the dealer held. He tried to keep track of the cards, but the count kept getting away from him. When he was absolutely swear-to-Jesus sure that there was nothing left but tens, he bet twenty-five each on three spots, doubled on two, and busted on all. End of game. This was obviously going to take a little more practice.

He didn't mind too much. It was exhilarating just to be taking the risks again, riding that old roller coaster in the sky. He counted up: Wells, Elko, Battle Mountain, Winnemucca—four more practice stops before Reno and Tahoe. When they got there (two more days, say), he'd find some place on the beach, somewhere Audrey would like, and win her a cool thousand bucks. Lay the whole pile in her lap.

He was starving. The casino coffee shop didn't do room service, so he bought two more steak sandwiches and chips, two pieces of angel food cake, and two beers and a coke to go. Audrey was still in exactly the same place, still watching TV; happy to see him, delighted at the pre-midnight snack. It felt very Old Married Couple to have let her husband go off and gamble, and then have him come back home with goodies late at night. They got cozy in bed and made their crumbs there, watching old movies till after two. Snuggling up against him hip-to-hip, staring at the box, she liked the idea of marriage.

It never occurred to her to ask how much he won.

29

The next day got them three-fifths of the way across Nevada. To Audrey, the state seemed little more than a sequence of dry desert drives between casinos.

Against the tan mountains, the smaller casinos of Nevada are planted in the middle of towns that are half-rancher-local, half-tourist-gaud-and-bawd. Between the towns, you drive for an hour through beige flatlands and sage sandhills that grind the mind to powder. The imagination is zonked out by the prospect of breaking down or being lost here, where there is so little.

Timmy filled the gas tank in Wells; they had lunch in Elko. He bought his wife a turquoise ring in Battle Mountain, and they spent the night in Winnemucca. But for him each white-painted initial on a hillside signified mainly another table piled with chips.

I-80 follows the curving course of the Humboldt all the way from Wells to Winnemucca, then past the Rye Patch Reservoir on to Lovelock. But you rarely see the river from the road, and it does little to enrich the terrain. Occasionally, the roadway will veer closer to the dishwater-gray stream, and bring you green weeds and thin trees, maybe a brief valley, a farm house, a cow. Then back to the desert.

Side roads lead off to ranches and mines. Trains rest on sidings next to smelters, gravel mounds, piles of underground refuse. The road passes through tunnels below the Union Pacific tracks, which follow the course of the emigrant trail. Medium-sized billboards announce casinos in Elko or Winnemucca. Large billboards tempt you on to Reno.

The land adjacent to the highway is mostly flat, either dry bottom land or salt plain. But as you keep rolling over transverse mountain ranges, the horizon is closed in by bosomy curves of treeless hills, one folding over another.

Timmy liked the wide-open spaces of Nevada, found something tranquilizing in the great distances, gentle and subtly varied. There was a softness to their contours, a comfort in their powdery-brown hues streaked with ochre sand and dotted with sagebrush. He liked the feel of good tires on good pavement, the force of the engine, the wind at his back, big skies in big country. He liked looking at a great arc of road ahead, curving uphill like a magical river. On long grades, they passed cars with their hoods up, trucks suffering up to the summit; then flew down the other side. Overhead, the clouds marched on in great islands of white, flat on the bottom, explosions of silver on top, precisely ranked in battalions receding in perfect perspective.

What Audrey noticed more were the signs of danger and desolation: fences that fenced nothing in and nothing out; the remnants of a thousand burst tires. The corpses of small animals lay crushed alongside the road, lumps of fur and dried blood for the crows to peck at. Dead trucks rusted in the sand. Timmy paid no attention to the hitchhikers, but Audrey saw them well enough—as common as abandoned cars they were, as common as squashed rabbits and coyotes. Shirtless, careless, escaping from something, going somewhere else.

How did they get where they were? she wondered. And where were they going?

A few places broke the barren pattern: a row of geysers at the Beowawe turnout. West of Elko, Easter Island heads grew out of the earth. They passed evidences of the life processes of the earth: hot springs, uptilted strata, lava beds, outcroppings of rock that looked like towers.

Out of Wells, Timmy felt himself fading early with heat and highway fatigue. He opened the car windows, turned the radio up full-volume. When he stopped for gas, he got the water jug out of his ice chest, and filled it with cold water. That way they could keep a towel soaking in it, and wipe their faces and arms as they drove along. In the gas station toilet, he found a prophylactic dispenser.

New! Not a wet, not a dry. Makes every other prophylactic seem old-fashioned. Exclusively formed for unnoticed protection and maximum natural sensitivity. So different, so modern, you will never again be satisfied with an ordinary prophylactic. Approved by the Nevada State Department of Public Health. Sold only for the prevention of disease.

He bought six.

Timmy decided to have a Scotch while Audrey drank her mid-morning coffee, which meant they had to go in to the Wells Casino. Twenty minutes later, twenty dollars ahead, they drove on. It was the first time she had ever seen him drink before noon.

At first, each town was just a few signs in the desert, then more signs, bigger signs, MORE JACKPOTS, GAS, TWENTY FOUR HOURS, FUN! The letter on the hillside, the water tower, tall lollipop standards over tin shed gas stations. A distant view of toy houses in a pocket of the hills. Out of the sand comes the first auto wrecker, the first trailer court, the first A&W, Gulf, Chevron, Pit Stop, Husky, the bars, the billboards. Kids in T-shirts and jeans with knee patches cut in and out of cars, popping wheelies on dirt bikes. Old men in baseball caps and balloon khaki pants sit wherever there is a place to sit, and stare at the cars passing. Somewhere there must be houses, even churches and schools.

Folks live between the towns, too, in homesteads with dry laundry flapping. Behind fences made of old tires, they park trailers and trucks. Single trailers stand alone on dirt roads off the highway. One ranch, on a little hill all by itself, has an airplane parked in the driveway.

They stopped for lunch at an old hotel in Elko, where the café was presided over by a giant stuffed polar bear. On the way into town they passed banks, a new Safeway, a domed court house, traffic, *two* main streets lined with motels and gas stations, Silver Dollar bars and Dairy Queens. Timmy didn't like the look of the dealers in the hotel casino, so he drove across the train tracks to the town's other old hotel. He went in to play, while Audrey sat in the parking lot and wrote postcards.

At Battle Mountain, she got her new ring. She liked it, even though it was the wages of sin, and outshone her wedding band. When Timmy finally pulled himself away from the Owl Club, he was 180 dollars ahead, even after buying the ring. His system was working. He felt like a member of an outlaw band, hitting bank after bank across the state without a miss.

When they were back on the road, Audrey began dropping hints about a campground at Rye Patch Reservoir she had been reading about in the guide.

"You know how much we enjoyed camping in the Tetons, sweetheart. You said yourself it was the only way to travel in the West. We could buy groceries at Winnemucca."

"How far is it from here?"

"That last sign said 'Winnemucca 54.' After that" (she was doing her best with the map) "it's another two, then twenty-six, and then another twelve. That makes . . . ah . . ."

"Ninety-four. Four o'clock now. Stop in Winnemucca. It'd be after dark."

"I don't care, dear. I think camping out has been the nicest part of the whole trip so far, don't you? Don't you like it more than motels?" It was the only way she could think of to keep him from gambling any more.

"I guess so. It's just that . . . It's just that I got them to cash a big check for me in Elko. I'm feeling really hot right now, honey, and I don't want to break it. I know you must think it's crazy, but I was counting on riding out this streak at Winnemucca. I've come out ahead now each of the last three stops."

"Couldn't we just have one night alone together before we get to California? Just the two of us? One last night under the stars?"

She put her hand on his thigh, and leaned over to kiss him on the lips. He could see a clear straight mile ahead, so he held the wheel still with one hand and seized her with the other, pulled her up against him, kissed her deeply back. He remembered his new condoms, decided his luck would hold till Reno.

"Rye Patch it is."

And then it rained. Just as he downshifted into first to make the last haul over Golconda, it turned very dark overhead and started to rain.

Within a minute, it was more than rain, more than any weather they had experienced so far. Blinding water and driving wind were flying across the mountains like a force out of hell.

They were on a winding downhill slope where they couldn't see. Stalled trucks and cars kept looming up out of the rain. The wind from the north pushed against the car, as if it would tip it over completely. Steering was a joke. He kept his foot hovering between accelerator and brake.

"Timmy, I'm scared."

"So am I. Shut up."

Now hail was shooting like bullets against her side of the car, smashing great pellets against the windshield. Hailstones made their way through the grille, fought against the engine.

"Oh my God," he said under his breath.

"What? What's that?"

"Nothing."

He had felt the engine stall. He jumped his foot on the accelerator, choked, geared up and down.

"Timmy!"

"It's *okay*, I said!"

It wasn't. They were rolling downhill full-force into the storm, blind on a dead engine. The engine caught again.

"We're okay."

Then as quickly it died. Caught, sputtered, died; started, quit. He pounded the gas pedal, skidding back and forth across an invisible road. Insane with frustration, he braked, slowed, pulled off on what felt like the shoulder.

"What are we going to do?"

"Wait."

"Wait for *what*?"

"For this to stop. I told you before: storms out here can be wild, but they never last very long."

"But if the car won't start?"

"I can make it start. You just relax." Rigid as a pipe wrench himself, he managed to unclaw one hand and reach over for hers. She fell shivering into his arms.

They waited. The tempest continued. Ghostly trucks and cars ground past in the gray torrent and the fog, blasting on their horns as they passed. Then for a long time, no one passed.

Timmy turned on the radio.

. . . all traffic is advised by the N.H.P. to avoid Interstate 80 between Elko and Winnemucca. Two trucks have already overturned in the eighty-mile-an-hour winds, causing dangerous road hazards to east-bound traffic near Battle Mountain. One appears to have driven off the road. The highway patrol estimates that anywhere from twenty to thirty cars are now stalled in the vicinity of Golconda Summit, several off the road. No estimate yet on accidents or injuries. Many smaller cars have been unable to make any headway against the winds. All vehicles are in danger of side blasts and water-logged engines.

If you are in the vicinity of Winnemucca, Battle Mountain, or Elko, do not attempt to drive between these cities until an all-clear is given. Repeat: do *not* attempt to drive between these cities. If you are on the road, the Highway Patrol advises you to pull over with caution, stay in your vehicle, and leave on your flasher lights to avoid rear-end collisions.

Now back to country music . . .

They listened to the radio, the wind, and the battering hail. Between records, the station repeated its warning.

Finally the hammering hail reduced to a downpour.

Timmy pried Audrey's arms loose from his neck, and tried the key. Battery, yes; but no spark.

"I'm going to see what I can do."

"But it's still raining!"

"So I'll get wet."

Timmy put on a poncho, and got his tool kit and some rags out of the trunk. He lifted the hood, and eased out the spark plugs one by one. He wrapped them to dry in the rags, then replaced them. That took half an hour. He waved at Audrey through the windshield, signaled her to start the engine. It took. He slammed down the hood, threw tools and rags into the back, and leapt into the driver's seat just as Audrey slid over. They were back on the road.

An hour later, they were spooning up hot soup, as the rain beat on the roof of an old restaurant in Winnemucca.

"I'm sorry about that, honey. It would have been fun to camp out one more time. But I promise you. We'll do it lots in California."

She had given in, of course. They were staying at the Winners Casino and Motel across the highway. She would have said yes to anything with a roof. The dinner was Timmy's way of making amends.

"Oh, that's all right." She sipped from her tumbler of red wine. "It is nice to be in a cozy warm room, I must admit. I just hope you don't catch a cold."

"No fear." He had taken a hot shower as soon as they got into their room, changed out of the wringing wet clothes, and had two Scotches in the bar. Five already today, she counted. Plus all this wine. Two beers at lunch and whatever he had at the second hotel in Elko. He kissed her fingers, she kissed his.

249

Rain kept battering the roof, thunder rolled near and far. This storm had settled in for the night. They were eating a filling, aromatic seven-course dinner at a Basque restaurant he had remembered from expeditions past. Around them, handsome silver-haired ranchers and their wives talked of acres and dollars and heads of cattle. Coffee was served in little glasses wrapped in straw holders.

After dinner, they went back to their upstairs room, over the casino. This time she begged him to stay, pleaded her fear of the storm, took off her blouse and bra and insisted that she wanted him, needed him. He fucked her, fierce, quick, detached, not even taking off his clothes. Then he pulled the cover over her, buttoned up his pants, and kissed her on the cheek.

"So you are going again."

"I'm sorry, babe. I have to."

"Even if I ask you not to."

"Even if you ask me not to."

"Timmy, I'm serious about this. I beg you not to go."

"So am I, babe. I love you as much as I ever did. But I never agreed to give up the things I want to do."

"I see." She turned on her side, her back to him, miserable at her failure.

"No, you don't see. You think it's wrong, you think I'm going to ruin us. You think I don't love you because I want to go back downstairs.

"That's not you talking. That's your mother.

"Listen to me, babe. I'll do everything for you any husband ever could. I'll support you, love you, take care of you, see you have what you need, make sure you have fun. But I'm forty years old, goddamn it, I know who I am, and I'm not going to change because of your mother's lace-curtain-Irish morals. That's something you're just going to have to get used to."

She turned back, sat up in bed, and faced him. "Well, I *don't* like it, and I think you're horrid! Either you care about me, Timmy McCue, or you care about your damn card game, and you're going to have to make up your mind!"

He combed his hair in front of the mirror, put his wallet in his back pocket, and walked out the door.

Bitterly, she wept at the meanness of men.

About two o'clock, down in the casino—he was one of the few players who looked at his watch with any regularity, who kept trying to relate fantasy to reality—about two o'clock, Timmy had in front of him what felt like a healthy pile of chips and silver, including a stack of green chips about two inches high. When playing, he tried to stop thinking in dollars, and to estimate his changing situation in terms of the different-colored piles. In fact, what lay in front of him represented about four hundred dollars, which meant he was two hundred ahead. He had sipped his way carefully through four whiskey sours, resisting extra offers from the miniskirted waitress. He sipped to calm his highs, to blur the ticking sense of time, and to blank out

250

distractions; but not to blunt his instinct for the game. About an hour earlier, a tall bottle blonde in red silk slacks and a red tube top began admiring his play. She had a black scarf tied around her waist. "I'm Irene," she whispered, snuggling up. "Mind if I watch?"

"Not at all." He ordered her a drink, too. Just for luck.

Since then, she had stayed faithful through two more drinks, for richer or poorer, for better or worse. He put an arm around her fanny between plays. She kept her hip pressed against his side.

Half an hour later, on a naughty impulse, Timmy reached up and slipped a green chip down the chute of the lady's red top. He was six hundred more ahead. Giggling, she shook it down inside her pants, licked him in the ear, and tucked a hand under the waistband of his jeans till it tickled bare ass. "Go for it, lover," she whispered. "Double or nothing."

The dealer shuffled up, and in two more hands, to two tidy dealer's blackjacks, Timmy lost five hundred dollars. Irene's hand came back out of his pants. Amazing how much less time it took to lose than to win. He eyeballed the dealer, wondered if he had got the word to start dealing him out.

About five hundred bucks worth left in front of him, he guessed, two hundred of it his stake. An angel whispered to him to put the two hundred in his pocket and leave it there. A devil (who knew more about blackjack) whispered that if he never took risks, Fortune would ignore him. Good things happened to those who bet big. Irene's left hand was back on his ass.

It was too late to go back to nickel-and-diming it. Everybody around the table was watching to see how high he would go. A hundred a crack, he decided; double or split on anything legal. He signaled the waitress for two more drinks, gave her a five-dollar chip tip, and pressed another twenty-five into Irene's warm right palm, which was moving slowly up and down his thigh.

Pair of twos. Split. Twelve, then eighteen on the right. Idiotically, he asked for another: twenty-one! He drew to seventeen on the left, and slid the cards under his chips. Fortune favored a man who played foolish and prudent by turns. Curious, he watched the next card dealt, which would have fallen atop his seventeen. A jack. Ha!

As he sipped his new drink and watched the others' draws, Irene whispered again in his ear. "How long you figure on playing?"

"Why? You got plans?"

"If you do. You're paid in advance." She tucked a card in his shirt pocket, and gave him a quick squeeze in the crotch. "I'm in 206. I stay up late."

He watched her butt as she swung away toward the elevator, wiggling her fingers over her shoulder. By the time he had turned back, the dealer had drawn twenty-one as well. He was out another hundred.

He was itchy-anxious now, thinking of the lady in red. Breaking all his father's rules, he gulped down his fresh whiskey sour, and divided his remaining piles, silver and chips alike, into two. One half he set in front of him; the other he shoved to the dealer to set in front of the last open space, out of his reach to the left.

251

Eight. Two eights. He died a small death when the dealer faced yet another ace, but had no chips left to insure against a third natural. The man looked at his hole card, then left it down. Salvation.

He split the eights, reaching in his wallet for the extra money he needed to do it: just barely enough left. Where the hell had it all gone? The dealer shoved his bills in the slot, counted out the necessary chips, then dealt him a six. "Hit." A three. Seventeen with an ace up: his dad would say stand. "Stand." Goddamn it, Dad: you better be right.

Now, the other eight. Four; two; ace; another fucking two! Slow torture. He reached for Irene's ass, forgetting she had left; then he remembered what she had said before she left: 206. Screw you, Dad. "Hit." The last three in the deck. Home safe at twenty.

After playing around everyone else (he stopped his other hand at sixteen), he and the dealer were face-to-face again. The man drew to six, then sixteen, hit it, and went over. Timmy raked in two handfuls of silver and chips, slid two fives back to the dealer, bade everyone good night, and headed for the cashier to turn all this toy money back into real.

Within five minutes, with eight hundreds and some small bills in his wallet, he was knocking softly on the door of room 206.

When Timmy got back to their own room it was almost four, but Audrey was not asleep. As soon as she heard his key fumbling in the lock, she switched off the bed light, pulled up the covers, rolled over to the wall and buried her head in the pillow.

Since he had last ditched her like this in Toledo, she had done a little growing up. No tears this time, no fears, no wifelet waiting up worrying in fuzzy slippers. She was mad as hell, and got madder the longer he made her wait. But she wasn't going to give him the satisfaction of thinking she gave a damn. She'd find a way to make him pay in the morning.

Anticipating another Toledo reception, Timmy had decided to bulldog this one out. He was more belligerent-drunk than dumb-drunk. His activities of the evening had left a layer of guilt so thick he had to smother it with an even thicker layer of bluster. Mentally, he was daring her to say anything, suspect anything, even hint anything. In the elevator, down the corridor, all the way up from 206, he kept socking his right fist into his left palm. Nobody tells *me* I can't gamble. Nobody tells *me* when I have to be home. Nobody tells *me* I can't . . .

So he was a little disappointed when he finally got the door open, and saw that all the lights were out, saw only the sleeping mound of Audrey's blanketed back.

Jesus Christ, he said to himself, as he tried to shut the door quietly behind him: she doesn't even *care!* Five fucking hours I been gone, and she doesn't *care*. Hot damn. I coulda been dead.

He sat on the edge of the bed, and undressed in the dark. He let his shoes clunk loudly to the floor, thinking that might wake her up, so they could at least argue. Not a budge. Well, screw you, too, baby.

("Will you hurry up and go to sleep?" she was thinking, in fact. "Are you so drunk you have to make noises like an elephant?")

He finished undressing, got under the covers.

Edgy business, climbing into the same bed with someone you've just cheated on, your body still tingling with the memory of another's. It's not easy to lie perfectly still next to someone you feel both mad at and guilty towards, someone you want to fight with and beg forgiveness from all at once.

He lay on his back, then on one side, then another. He pushed the covers down below his pubic hair, then pulled them back up to his chin. He placed his arms at his sides, over his stomach, behind his head, under his pillow. Angry, he threw the pillow on the floor and twisted over onto his stomach.

Next thing he knew, bright sun rays were flooding in through a crack in the curtains. Eleven o'clock. He reached over. No Audrey. He called out. "Audrey?" No answer.

He climbed out of bed, hungover, looked in the bathroom. Not there, either. He looked around, sick in his head, mouth, and stomach, confused. Her suitcase was gone, her small bag, her purse, her clothes from the closet. All gone. Oh, my God: now what have I done? He looked around for a note, for something, anything. He dialed the desk. God, do I feel awful. "This is McCue in 319. Did my wife leave a message for me? Right, for me. McCue. You will? Thanks.

"Nothing, hey? Okay." He hung up, and sat down on the edge of the bed, queasy, not knowing what to do.

She must have known where I went. How did she find out?

Where could she go? How will she get anywhere by herself?

He picked up his pants off the floor, and took out his wallet. A chill passed over him as he touched it: light. Thin. It turned to panic as he looked inside. Empty. Eight hundred dollars. Sick now beyond nausea, he felt eviscerated, totally wiped out. On a thought, he reached in another pocket. The car keys were gone, too.

He picked up the phone, dialed zero again.

"Could you page a Mrs. Audrey McCue? She may be down in the coffee shop, or in the lobby somewhere. That's right, McCue. Me again. Ask her to call 319? Thanks a lot."

He hung up, knowing it was hopeless. So she left first. Son of a bitch! Gradually he got his mind into gear, working on the needful. I should get the highway patrol onto the car. I'll need a lawyer. Christ. Who could you trust around here? Have to phone Dad's lawyer in Grass Valley. No. Ted in San Francisco. I should be able to get this joint to okay another check.

The phone rang.

"Hello?"

"I thought you'd never wake up."

"Audrey? Is that you? Where the hell are you?"

"Downstairs. I finished my breakfast hours ago. I wasn't going to wait all day for you."

253

"Then where's your suitcase and stuff?"

"I decided to save time by putting them in the car myself. Oh, I borrowed your car keys, too. Do you know what *time* it is?"

"Goddamn right I know what time it is. Don't you dare pull a stunt like this again! What'd you do with all my money?"

"All what money?"

"Don't be cute. The money in my wallet."

"I don't know anything about any money in your wallet. I charged my breakfast to our room number, if that's okay with you. Since then I've been playing nickel slot machines. With *my* money. I'm four dollars ahead."

"Listen: do you swear you didn't touch my wallet?"

"Timmy, don't be an ass. Of course I didn't touch your wallet. You came in so drunk last night you're lucky you have a wallet at all."

"How would you know? You were dead to the world when I came in."

"No I wasn't. I pretended I was, so I wouldn't have to tell you what I thought of your behavior. I decided to save that for the morning. It was ten to four, and I know very well where you were. So please get dressed and packed and down here as quickly as you can. I'm going to trade in my nickels and sit in the car, and the sooner we get out of this state, the better it will be for both of us." She hung up.

"Aren't you going to say anything, then? Are you going to keep quiet all the way to California?"

"What would you like me to say?"

"Oh, for Christ's sake, Audrey! I hate it when women act all sanctimonious and frigid. If you think you're making me suffer by this offended silent act of yours, you've got another think coming."

"I'm not 'women.' I'm your wife. I don't care to hear your views about 'women,' thank you, however many millions you've known. Just watch the road, please."

"God, you can be such a bitch, you know that? I don't know what's got you so pissed off, but I'm fed up to here with this act of yours."

. . .

"Listen. I went back to the casino to play blackjack. You *know* that's what I was doing. I don't give a shit what you think about gambling, I like it. I like it and I win at it. Do you know how much I came out with last night?"

. . .

"*Do* you? Do you know how much I won?"

"No, dear. I don't. I don't know how much you won. Show it to me."

"So you *do* know where it is!"

"No, I don't know that, either. Maybe Irene does."

"What?"

"Irene."

"Who's Irene?"

She opened her purse and plucked out a card. " 'Irene,' she read. " 'Relaxing and stimulating massages, French or Scandinavian. Relieve your tension.

Outcalls to your motel by the hour or the night. Try me, you'll be glad you did. 555-9359.'

"I wouldn't have thought the prostitutes were so well-organized in a hole like Winnemucca."

"What do you think you're talking about?"

"About you and your whore. Did you have French or Scandinavian? You not only left her card in the bathroom, you left something else, too! Maybe from now on, I'll have to start charging, since that seems to be what you want. I'll have some cards made up. Give receipts."

"You want to call it all off, then?"

"This would be the right place for that, wouldn't it? I mean, we just drive to Reno, wait around a bit, and poof! There goes marriage. Lovely. No, dearest, I don't want to do that. I decided last night, during all that time you left me to think, that I could probably learn to cope with you and your little weaknesses. But in return I'd have to start asking for a few things of my own."

"Like what?"

"I've got it all written down." She reached in her purse again, and took out a little note pad. "An allowance every month, a car of my own, time to spend as I want to. Either children, *or* a job, or maybe both. We both go to church every Sunday. We invite my mother out every other year, and the years in between I go back and visit her."

"Now look here a minute. We're married, huh? We're staying married. If that's the case, then the wife is subject to her husband. It says so in the Bible. 'Husbands are in charge of their wives.' I am not going to be hogtied and grounded, and ordered around like some teenaged delinquent, just because I got married! Christ, Audrey, I'm forty years old! When did I ever agree to give up the right to do what I want? Do what I want with my money, with my time . . ."

"With your penis?"

. . .

He drove on, furious, struck dumb by her insolence.

"If you had just . . ."

"Don't try, Timmy. Don't you try to justify your trashy habits to me. You left me, on our honeymoon, so you could gamble, get drunk, and commit adultery with a common whore—a whore who advertises! I'm not likely to forget that very soon. You've lived up to all my mother's predictions."

"Then why not call it off? You could go back to your precious mother, who takes so much better care of you than I do."

"For one thing, because I believe in the sacrament of matrimony, whether you do or not. I said for better or worse, and I meant it. Till death us do part. I meant that, too. For another, I still love you, God knows why. Maybe He was punishing me by allowing me to fall in love with so weak and so sinful a man, but whatever the reason, I did. Maybe my prayers can make you better."

"Oh, don't give me that religious crap, Audrey. Okay, I shouldn't have gone off with Irene. That was bad. That was wrong. I'm sorry about that. But

I'm not going to grovel to you and ask for your fucking prayers for the rest of our married life just because I once got carried away—and by a woman who was *nice* to me for an evening, who stood by me, didn't keep sending out disapproving vibes and bitch at me like *my* goddamn mother because I wanted to have a few drinks, wanted to win a little money. *Eight hundred dollars* I won last night. Eight hundred dollars!"

"And where is it now?"

. . .

"She took it, didn't she?"

"Shut up!"

"She *did*, didn't she?"

He flung his right hand off the wheel and hit her hard on the face.

"I said to shut up!"

She was still crying and holding her bruised cheek, when she felt the car slowing down.

"What are you doing?"

"Stopping the car."

"Why? What are you doing that for?"

"I'm going to pick this guy up."

Ahead of them stood a thin young man with his thumb raised to the traffic. He had a sallow, pock-marked face, long blond hair caught in back with a rubber band, and wore an Army jacket over a green T-shirt and fatigues. Alongside him on the ground were a bedroll and pack.

"Timmy, you can't!"

"Who says I can't? It's my car."

"Please! Please, I mean it. You'll ruin everything."

"I thought everything was already ruined." He pulled to a stop alongside the hitchhiker, who opened his mouth in a gap-toothed smile.

30

The Mormon settlements extend two days' travel out of the city. We passed several substantial farmhouses made of logs, at which we obtained fresh milk and other wholesome fare. On our second night's stop, a young housewife named Mrs. Chase (the *only* wife of the household, I assured myself), kindly offered me the use of her spare feather bed—my first proper bed since leaving the States. But my slumbers were not so pleasant as I had anticipated. I have become too accustomed to lying on the ground in our tent, or on straw in a wagon—and I am unused to sleeping alone.

The next morning, Mrs. Chase offered a hearty breakfast to all four of us, and a better morning meal I never sat to. I must not let our misadventures prejudice me against these hardworking and hospitable people.

Along the way, we passed natural springs of water too hot for the hand to touch. Up to the time we reached the Bear River yesterday, we remained in the sheltering lee of the great brown mountains east of the valley, whose names I do not know.

We attempted a ford at the river, but were forced to quit. The current was too rapid, the banks too slippery and steep. The water was about 250 feet wide, and three feet deep. It offended James to have to make use of the Mormons' ferry, as he was determined to contribute no more to the treasury of Zion. But there was no way around it. Scarce had we achieved this crossing when we came upon another, much narrower than the Bear but almost as difficult, as it ran deep and fast, and full of encumbrances. Here there was no ferry. Although a party of pack mules just ahead of us crossed easily enough, it took all of the three men's efforts for more than an hour to conduct our oxen safely down one bank, through the deep torrent, and up another. James roundly cursed the Mormon magistrate who "stole" his new mules. It is at

257

times like these that I fear we shall miss most the support of our friends from Illinois.

This brave independence of ours was the source of no little anxiety when, three days out of the city, a party of mounted red Indians rode up, armed with rifles and painted as for war. One lay his rifle stock across the head of our lead ox, as a sign that we were to stop. The others surrounded our wagon, gesturing and babbling. There were about fifteen in number. While James parleyed, I prayed. After about half an hour, and a donation of gun powder, whisky, and two woolen shirts, they allowed us to pass.

Finding no water after these two streams, we were obliged to drive on into the night. After the rich and fertile valley of the saints, it was disheartening to encounter a desolate plain of sand, varied only by the universal sage. Around us in the dark lay a silence as of death, unbroken by the least chirrup of a cricket. As we followed the trail through hollows and around knobs, there seemed to be moving parallel with us in the moonlight shadowy horsemen as silent as ourselves. We halted after midnight for the sake of the oxen, and turned them out with their yokes on. They passed the night unwatered.

This morning we set out unrefreshed. The beams of the August sun were intensified by their reflection off the dry sandy soil. Men and animals alike began to suffer the agony of thirst. We reached water after six more hours' driving this morning—a spring that gushed clear out of a dozen places. The oxen rushed to it, then backed away. It was sickly-warm and, what is worse, bitter with salt. But the poor beasts were desperate, and drank it. James thinks it will do them no harm. We human animals proved more delicate, and spat it out after the first mouthful. The dregs of our canteen had to suffice.

We have suffered more from want of water these two days than at any time since our journey began. But our week of rest and refreshment among the Mormons seems to have left us more than usually fit, and the deprivation was not as dreadful as I had expected: no fainting, no foaming, none of the wild spectres or swollen tongues one is frighted by in the books of desert travelers. Forty-seven miles we walked between water and water. At the end of this afternoon's drive, four miles into the mountains, we came upon a spring of pure, cold water. No one can fully appreciate the luxury of a good spring who has not crossed a desert plain.

The streams of this country behave most peculiarly. Due, I suppose, to the porosity of the soil, they suddenly sink and disappear into the earth, only to reappear somewhere else.

We are now skirting the northern shore of the Great Salt Lake, although its margins are too marshy to permit of approach. Apparently, a mammoth inland sea once covered the whole of this salt basin, which is now reduced to this smaller sea of concentrated brine. Waters flow into it from many sources. But as it lies at an extremely low elevation, at the bottom of its basin, no water flows out. Instead, it is left to evaporate under the sun, and leaves behind each year its residue of salt.

The desert, off to our left, appears from here as a snow-covered plain, glittering in its whiteness. It appears to go on forever. We were told by the Mormons that the distance between waters in the Great Salt Desert is slightly more than eighty miles. They claim that several parties have crossed it and survived.

Awful as it is, my eyes are drawn irresistably in its direction. This white desert haunts the imagination, whether one looks at it or not, and almost leads one to question the purposes of an all-wise Creator. I cannot understand what good such a piece of earth can serve. As a challenge to foolhardy travelers, it can only result in cruel disasters. Its poisoned surface must forever remain barren and fruitless, insusceptible of cultivation or habitation. Was it placed here to preach some moral lesson? If so, I cannot read it, any more than I could understand the shooting star. Why should Providence so curse this portion of the American continent? Perhaps over aeons of geological time it will be transformed into something more humane. Strange, and at times unfathomable, are the ways of the Lord.

Tonight it glows ghostly under the light of a full moon. The night is still, and strangely sweet.

We seem to have started opportunely from the city, for we have not yet overtaken, or been overtaken by, any other teams on the march. They would only annoy us with their dust, and interfere with our choice of encampment.

My heart remains criminally full of my personal griefs. At times, I would curse the Mormon city and all within it for what they have done to James and to me. I wish we had never gone there, and would gladly see the city reduced to desert dust. The fact that I may have been in part responsible for driving James into serious sin, and from sin into shame and low indigence, torments me without let. I try by means of smiles, soft words, and gentle caresses to knit up our raveled union. He will not talk, or hear me talk, of our experiences in the city, which is perhaps all for the best. But he seems, if not more affectionate than heretofore, at least more considerate.

It is only now, cast off as we are on our own, that I realize how much encouragement one derives, even when happily married, from the surrounding presence of others. From now on, we must be all in all to one another. I quake under the burden of responsibility: can I ever be all in all for James? Is it my fault that God has not granted us a child?

The Williams boys keep their distance, silent and apart. They do their work, share the care of stock and wagon, and speak to me no more than boarders or hired hands. I must choke back my memories of our former sweet intercourse, and try not to look them in the eye, or think upon them lying at night in their own small tent. James's nocturnal embraces have become almost painfully ardent.

August 8, 1849

Today about two o'clock we rejoined the great parade. A billowing cloud of dust to our right announced the convergence of our route with that of the main stream of Argonauts, those who have traveled by way of Fort Hall or the cut-off below it, instead of by Great Salt Lake. We struck the heavily traveled trail near two high masses of rock, which rise out of a single base several hundred feet in the air. Once again we must journey in a floating sea of other men's dust.

Near to us in the line of march was the very same preacher who so lauded us all back at St. Joseph with his erroneous interpretation of a passage from the Book of Job. He seems to have abandoned his sacred calling altogether, along with his party, and now travels with a band of Pike County toughs. I also met Ellen Dawson and her husband, who had quit the Carthage train after a bloody affray at Fort Hall, over what cause I do not know. We traded stories of our respective journeys since last we met. By her account, Captain McClellan's party is only five days in advance of us, notwithstanding our extended detour and long sojourn by the Great Salt Lake. She believes the company will not stay together very much longer, after this unpleasantness at Fort Hall.

Like everyone else we talk to, she was curious to hear our account of the Latter-Day Saints. But nothing I could tell her of their decency and industry would disburden her of a settled conviction that they are some species of bestial savage. I was surprised to learn that their practice of multiple marriage was common knowledge, at least to hear Mrs. Dawson speak of it; I had never heard mention of it before. This tenet, of course, I could neither deny nor defend. But she is also firmly convinced that they practice human sacrifice, murder newborn babes, and have leagued with the most blood thirsty Indian tribes to slaughter those amongst us they regard as their special enemies.

None of this can I credit in the least. But then I would not have believed gossip about multiple marriages either, or the character of Brigham Young, had I not seen these things with my own eyes. I insisted that the Mormons gouged Gentile visitors no worse than good Protestant Christians do at Fort Bridger—or for that matter, at St. Joseph. Of course, the sham trial to which James was subjected belies this, rather. But I could scarcely make mention of that.

Last Sunday, for a change, we rested like proper Christians ourselves, which allowed me to wash clothes, and James to make repairs. He was more than usually pleasant and relaxed. As the moment seemed opportune, I confessed to him, at our noon rest, some of the fears I recorded here last week, concerning our self-sufficiency, and of the likelihood that I would prove inadequate company to him, deprived as he is of other society. He assured me that this was untrue. He also swore most solemnly that he does not hold our childlessness against me. He would welcome a family, and will continue his efforts to sire one, but treasures our union just as it is. It was a great comfort to me to hear him confirm this, as I am tormented by doubts—especially after learning of his dalliance with pretty Thelma Samuelsen. He vows he took no pleasure in his adulterous embraces, and I believe him.

James also explained to me something I had not understood about Henry and Hector. They are, it appears, not brothers at all. They were out hunting much of the day, and brought back a single scrawny duck.

Observing this great processional anew, after a month's separation, I find myself feeling quite distant. It is as if I were no longer part of it myself. I look upon men, animals, and wagons with fresh eyes, and am astonished at how ragged and shabby they all seem. One cannot help but be struck by the contrast between this spectacle and that of the brave, clean-shaven fellows, the prancing steeds and fat oxen, the snowy-white wagons at St. Jo. Now the animals' heads bow low. Their gaunt sides are marred with whip cuts. The men are strung out in a long line, their faces hidden by hair, their clothing in tatters. All of this disfigured with a pale coating of dust.

August 13, 1849

After rejoining the emigration, we climbed steadily for several miles. Looking back from the ridge, I could see to the north a broad valley surrounded by rock walls, in the midst of which rose stone monoliths of all shapes and sizes, some conical, some like loaves, some vertical spires hundreds of feet high split by great cracks or fissures, with hawks' nests at the top; some like a pile of children's blocks. Without understanding in the slightest how this unearthly landscape came to be, one can feel at a glance the volcanic convulsions that must have shaken this place aeons and aeons ago.

Beyond the ridge, we were confronted with a descent so steep it appeared beyond the staying power of anything less than mules or mountain goats. No one but a gold-crazed "Californian" would have ventured it with ox teams. As it was, all wagons had to be rough-locked and held back by ropes. From the cliff top, the descent was frightful to contemplate. From the bottom, the wagons appeared to be tipped over on end. It was inconceivable that the ropes would hold. On the hillside leading to this great slide, the trail was so sideling that men had to push against the wagons to keep them from turning over. It was here that we broke an axletree, and for a short while I was quite anxious. But James was able to purchase a spare from a stranger, for one dollar.

Each of these new obstacles appears insurmountable. Once overcome, they remain in the memory like nightmares, experiences that leave one not so much proud or relieved, as stricken forever after on the recollection with retrospective terror.

For 16 miles we followed Goose Creek, which runs north. There we passed several abandoned wagons and much property, which nobody thought worth picking up. To one wagon was pinned a card: "This vehicle is left for the use of other emigrants. Kindly do not destroy it, for it may be of important service to some poor traveler like yourself." All four of the wheels had been removed.

The traffic along the creek was so thick that every blade of grass anywhere near water was eaten off close. Willow bushes are cropped to the very stump, rushes to their stems. At each halt, cattle had to be driven two or three miles to feed. There is a rumor along the trail (there are so many rumors along the trail!) that some Mormon pioneers found gold along this creek last summer. But the boys could find no sign of either auriferous rock or past mining activity, so this particular rumor may be dismissed.

The next day we took a left fork, and quit the creek. The drive was difficult and dry, 20 mountainous miles without water. One day more brought us into a strange valley of hot springs, where we rested.

Here one could see the remains of frogs and lizards scalded to death in the boiled springs. One could cook directly in them, and many did. A few yards from a source of boiling water ran another spring, as cold as the former was hot. I cannot understand what is going on under the ground. Inasmuch as our guide book is quite defective in its description of this territory, I fear it will serve us ill for the journey ahead.

Once again we are in a region of burning days and freezing nights, where ice forms in buckets and robes are rimed with frost. An August morning here seems as cold as a morning at home in December. By how much would I rather be there!

The strain of four months' travel—bad water, biting dust, unpleasant camps—has put everyone in poor temper, men and animals alike. The nearness of others who press constantly upon you in camp or on the trail, and fight you to get soonest to grass or water, would put an early-day saint out of patience. Crowding close this noon to a thin trickling spring, one bumptious lout pushed his ox full into the basin, muddying it for everyone else. Thereupon his neighbor fell on him with a knife, and was only kept from murdering him by the force of many others dragging him back. Even so, the first was badly slashed about the cheek.

Horses and cattle are become so nervous in their febrility and fatigue that they bolt and run at a shout, or at a dog's bark—sounds that would not have troubled them in the least a fortnight ago. For the safety of their draft animals, some companies have taken to shooting their dogs. I tell myself that this is wise, and that the survival of all depends on the well-being of our teams; that animals are creatures without souls, and are of value only insofar as they can be of service to man, who alone among living creatures is made in the image of God.

But my heart cries out that this is *wrong*. How many kind, decent, long-suffering beasts on this expedition will lose their lives on account of the folly of man?

The great excitement this afternoon was our reaching a south-running creek, which is identified as one of the headwaters of Mary's river. This is to be our "path of salvation" across the Great American Desert.

August 20, 1849

We were forced to ford the south-running creek I mentioned nine times in seven miles, on a cañon road choked with the traffic of hundreds of teams.

Another day's drive brought us to the bank of Mary's River itself, and a welcome camp of excellent grass and good water. The emigration strains every nerve in order to reach this place, impelled hither by Captain Frémont's rapturous description. In actual fact, this river is even less impressive than the Platte.

Mary's River, at this point, or at least at this season, is a relatively small stream. The channel is of moderate depth and about twenty feet wide, with steep, perpendicular banks. In many places, however, it is nearly dry. The water, having been absorbed in the spongy earth, stands in stagnant pools with no flowing current to enliven its sluggishness, cool its offensive warmth, or purge it of the noxious minerals which so thickly impregnate the adjacent soil. Clumps of small willows, at most an inch in diameter, fringe the margin of the river and constitute the only "timber" in the valley, along with a few wild currant bushes. These bear black, red, and yellow berries, of which the yellow are the sweetest. We pass beds of the gaudy western sun flower. The marshy areas house great colonies of horned toads and brightly colored lizards. To north and south rise barren mountains spotted with sage. This river valley is, on the whole, as monotonous as that of the Platte, although not so wide.

Whatever its demerits, it is only the miracle of this wretched watercourse (which Capt. Frémont officiously rechristened the "Humboldt," after some fellow-explorer—no doubt in a fit of anti-popery) that makes possible the overland journey so many have undertaken. Without it, there would be nothing but an impenetrable dry waste hundreds of miles wide between the Great Salt Lake and the Sierra Nevada mountains, and the American continent would forever remain divided in twain, as decisively as if by an ocean. If a railroad is ever built across America (which James thinks unlikely), it will doubtless have to follow the course of this river.

As it is, one must still traverse a waterless desert of fifty miles between the end of this river and the start of the Salmon Trout. But this is a thing many have accomplished. Mary's River runs like a line of life across the dead basin.

After resting briefly at the river, we drove through a narrow and rocky cañon, with a chain of snowy mountains on our left. The trail returned to the river by supper time. Once again, we camped with good grass. Here the water ran rapid and clear, as healthy as any we have tasted since the States. James and Hector gathered crickets to serve as bait, and fished the river to good purpose. We feasted off four excellent salmon trout. For a few miles, at least, the guide books were correct: we did enjoy good water, good grass, good game, and even some wood for the fire. The thought that in less than a month our journeying will be done put all in good spirits.

After that we came upon meadows of blue grass and red-top clover, healthy and high, mingled with mock-timothy and stands of spear mint. One would have thought oneself back in prime farm country in one of the cultivated states. Unfortunately, I spent most of these three days lying in the wagon, quite ill from a bilious attack, I think the effect of poor water. It is a nuisance to be ill in a wagon, traveling under a hot sun. The feelings of those dear to you are so blunted by weariness that they will not take the trouble to administer to your comfort. I took laudanum to sleep.

For a gay diversion during my illness, young Hector showed me a human skull he had found along the trail. He is saving the teeth. The same day James brought me the skin of a long rattlesnake he had beaten to death with his rifle. It leapt out at him while he was gathering currants, and he struck it down at once. He is saving the rattles. I am told that cream of tartar would have served as an antidote against the venom of alkaline springs. But who has cream of tartar? Who, indeed, has anything left but salt pork and hard biscuits—and precious little of that?

The sky here is most extraordinarily pure and clear, purer and clearer than

I have seen it anywhere else. The air is so dry there is not a drop of dew to be seen of a morning. Today, my first day back in health, began with an Indian summer air of the most blissful warmth and limpidity, inviting one to laze or meditate in the shade of a tree, which I might well have done at home, had my chores permitted. Alas, there is naught for it here but to push on. There is no rest for the greedy.

The stars shine in these latitudes with uncommon brilliance, and force one's thoughts to friends distant in space or in time—friends over whom these self-same stars are shining, or once shone. There is a benignity about them.

After our piscatorial interruption, we were forced away from the river again, this time over an arid path of 20 mountain miles, by which a bend in the river was avoided. I saw none of this. I lay the whole while in the wagon, aware only of my entrails. On our return to its banks, the men found the river bottom considerably drier than heretofore, and were forced to drive the oxen across the river, with willow branches laid down for their footing, in order to find anything resembling grass. This was a species of islands or mounds of tough mold, the nearest they could find to edible forage.

I met today a stout old woman from Boston who expressed her impatience with her masculine companions. They are forever complaining, she complains, and making ado of toils and hazards. They grow frightened of shadows, and magnify every sage brush into a bloodthirsty Pie-Ute. She told me she had often wandered off alone in search of plants and herbs (of which, she was pleased to inform me, she is a great *connoisseur*), and met many Indians on her promenades. Not one of them had ever offered to molest her. I inquired whether she was not disturbed (as I confessed I was) by the possibility of the grass running dry, and her team perhaps failing. "Not in the least," she replied, from her great moral height. "I estimate we have no more than four hundred miles to go. Any female of decent hygiene and sound constitution can walk that easily." I felt properly chagrined, which I am sure is the effect she intended.

Next to failure of grass and water, the great fear in this territory is of the thieving Root Digger Indians we were warned of by the chief near Fort Bridger. We have already seen several of these pitiable creatures. It seems they subsist off the very refuse of nature: seeds, roots, insects, lizards, and snakes. They are shrunken from undernourishment to the size of children or pygmies. They come up to beg, filthy and naked, with long matted hair. Like most of the wagon drivers, James refuses to deal with them, and drives them away. They then follow behind us, whining and beseeching in hideous voices.

James's refusal is not a matter of hardness of heart, or his settled prejudice against the aboriginal American. Every emigrant party is growing increasingly sensible of the diminished state of its own provisions. In lands as desolate as these, charity must indeed begin at home.

These same wizened creatures, we are told, creep about at night like hyenas, and steal the white man's cattle for food. What they cannot steal, they shoot arrows into. Then they come down to fetch the dead or disabled animals once their owners have moved on. However much one may sympa-

264

thize with their plight, one's first concern here must be to preserve one's own stock, and thereby oneself.

A company from Illinois claims to have lost 22 head of cattle to these subhuman predators. Discovering their loss, a search party set out at dawn. For 30 miles they tracked the thieves, into the high, snowy reaches of the mountains. When at last they discovered their cattle, the beasts lay either dead or hamstrung by the trail, or had been driven off a ledge into a natural pen surrounded on all sides by rock walls.

Suddenly they heard the sound of ghastly shrieks high over their heads. On a cliff hundreds of feet above them, the naked pygmies were dancing about and jeering, waving tomahawks in menace. As they could not be followed further (nor even shot at with any hope of success), there was nothing for the men to do but turn back, abandoning all hope of recovery or revenge.

We have heard different versions of this story from several people. Portions of it may have been added by subsequent narrators to heighten the romance of the tale.

The day after we first heard this account, we passed our first direct evidence of Indian depradation: a horse and two oxen shot dead with arrows and lying alongside the trail, as if warning passers-by to greater vigilance. A little further yet, we passed an advertisement stuck to a tree, offering a reward of $200 to anyone who apprehended four stolen horses and their thief. Henry believes that the wording of this notice suggests a white-skinned thief, and wonders if other desperate and unscrupulous emigrants may not be responsible for crimes attributed to the Indians.

This evening, as I sit down to write alongside our small wagon, it is impossible not to think of friends at home, relaxing in their snug and comfortable houses. Of late, I have been experiencing the most persuasively realistic dreams. In them, I am once again a child in my parents' house, feasting on roast turkey, fresh greens, cool milk, mounds of bread and butter. How my heart sinks when I come back to consciousness, and find I am only here!

August 26, 1849

The Mary's River is now more a succession of stagnant pools than a stream. It has, in fact, no perceptible current. In it are no fish, no insects; no discernible life. Along its bank grows insufficient timber to construct a snuffbox. When it does deign to run, it twists and meanders like a serpent.

This is a dreary prospect. Immediately about us lie sterile sand and dust; naught in the distance but bare rugged hills. The eye tires, the mind wearies of this tasteless monotony. Surely the deserts of Arabia could not be more unpleasing to the sight than the land that borders this river. There is water, to be sure, but such water as offers little compensation. Contrary to the laws of nature, the river grows narrower, rather than wider, as one proceeds from its source. It will end, we are told, by disappearing altogether at a place called the Sink. The porosity of the desert sucks it down. It is now a surly, turbid watercourse bordered with eaten-away willows at the top of banks as abrupt and steep as those of the Mississippi.

No one living in a fertile land can form a correct idea of this waste, or of what it is like to travel week after week without seeing anything worthy the name of tree. There is no grass away from the river, and little enough alongside it. Today we passed thousands of acres of swamp, filled with bullrushes up to ten feet. The upland, if composed of sand or loam, sinks beneath one's feet, burrowed in all directions by unseen prairie dogs or moles. The very ugliness of the landscape gives the quality of it a curiosity. Perhaps one day people will travel to see it for that reason alone. Sixteen weeks we have been on the road.

A fat and irascible doctor from the city of Rochester, New York, who has kept a considerable library in his wagon all these miles, heaped scorn upon the guide books and memoirs of distinguished travelers for their deceptively pleasing descriptions of this region. According to the celebrated Bryant, whom he quotes, this river bottom should be "highly fertile, and covered with a luxuriant growth of grass and flowers." Nothing, of course could be further from the truth. Captain Frémont's account is almost as misleading. The guide books provide no warning whatsoever regarding the discouraging absence of grass. Acording to Mr. Ware's guide (on which James has been depending ever since we left the city of Great Salt Lake), the valley of Mary's River should be "rich and beautifully clothed with blue grass, herds' grass, clover, and other nutritious grasses." He also tempts the reader with a 300-mile long line of timber on its banks, "furnishing the requisite for the emigrant's comfort in abundance." This is nonsense worse than criminal, since it may well mislead travelers to their death!

It is arguable that there *were* more grasses and trees here when these authors passed, before our ravenous hordes came along, devouring everything in their path. But for whatever reason, the vegetation along Mary's River has been grossly misrepresented.

What the thousands of teams behind *us* are to do, after the animals of our train have scraped these last bits of stubble and furze, God almighty only knows! I pray He will come to their aid—as He did so many times to His chosen people in their desert wanderings. But we have little cause to believe ourselves "chosen," or worthy of his special protection.

The alkaline dust here is different from any I have ever seen, very like ashes or powder of magnesia in its texture and smell. Raised as it is into a constant hovering presence by the passage of so may hooves, feet, and wheels, this all-enveloping atmosphere proves most irritating to eyes, nose, throat, and skin. Some try to protect their faces with hand-made goggles, or bandages, or little aprons designed to cover nose and mouth. It is luxury beyond words, after a day's tramp, to pour water over one's face and clear it at last of its coating of dust of ashes. How refreshed one feels!

I saw today my first "whirl-wind." In this, the dust mounts into a terrifying yet majestic column to the sky. It then spirals on its way with terrific force, knocking anything it encounters with the power of its velocity and vortex.

For several nights our sleep was broken, first by the dreadful howling of wolves, and the explosion of rifles fired in order to disperse them; then by the

266

crunch and clangor of passing wagons whose owners had decided to travel by night, in order to avoid the heat and dust of day. This seemed a bizarre and unnatural choice. But after some discussion, James and the two boys decided to try it as well.

So for the next two nights we traveled under the moon, now in its last quarter, and tried to nap by day in the shade of wagon-top and tents. Our traveling was indeed cool, clear, and free of dust. But when I gathered sufficient resolve to confess to James my unreasonable fears of this mode of travel—fears of Indian attack, fears of wolves, fears of losing our way—it became clear that he had similar misgivings. The experiment was abandoned. We travel by day again, like normal people, and sleep by night.

One can observe the effects of this desolate road on the tempers of men and animals. People are dissatisfied with everything, and disagree about the least trifle. Men run to brutal encounters with a kind of glee. They wrestle in dead earnest, shoot off guns to no purpose, corner one another with whips. Many are afflicted by the scurvy, and suffer from bleeding gums and discolorations of the skin, the skin of the legs in particular. And yet companies with the least surplus of vinegar will not part with it for less than three dollars the pint.

Many of the "packers" we talk to speak of their former companions in wagon companies with childish and disgusting spite. They would sooner starve and die alone, they tell us, than spend another hour in the company of "such fools"—men who, at home in the States, were their dearest friends! Surely it is the height of folly to leave the security of a train, however plodding and slow its progress, with no more than a few days' provisions and a bed roll on one's back, a tin cup at one's belt, and a few dollars in one's pocket—and continue thus equipped for California! How they are to get along I cannot conceive, since few companies have any superfluous provisions to spare for such obstinate beggars.

As we draw nearer to the so-called Sink of Mary's, rumors concerning what lies ahead grow more fanciful and appalling. One popular tale has it that a legion of Root Digger Indians lies in wait for us there, ready to slaughter every last emigrant in revenge for our wanton killing of some of their own kind. We are told that absolute famine reigns in California, and that guerilla bands of starving miners are stopping wagons by force to press provisions.

For almost two hours today, our progress along a narrow portion of the trail was obstructed in a most aggravating manner. The cause, we finally discovered, was a Mormon train heading east, trying to make its way against the line of west-going traffic. As they pushed their way along, many called out curses and rude remarks. Their hostility was aroused, I am certain, not only by the deep-dyed prejudice so many hold against the Saints, but also by the enviable fatness and sleekness of their oxen, and the sturdiness of what, compared to our scarce-rolling wrecks, seem to be almost brand-new wagons.

Leaving Henry and Hector to drive our team for a while, James detached himself from the westbound train and walked along with a respectable looking group of Mormon gentlemen, in the hope of eliciting from them some more substantial information concerning the trail ahead, and conditions in

267

California. Observing several decent women in their wagons, I concluded it would not be unseemly for me to join him, in order to obtain some means of sifting truth from fancy myself.

At first, the men were loathe to talk to James, having been harrassed by questions from gold seekers ever since they left California. But James, in a tricksy ruse that quite surprised me, told them that we came from the State of Vermont, very near to the scene of the Prophet Smith's angelic visitation, and that we were quite sympathetic with the cause of the Saints. Only recently, he told them, we had been visiting with his "very dear friends" Ezra and Hannah Samuelsen, in the city of Great Salt Lake. He also pretended to familiarity with President Young, Elder Smoot, and Magistrate Stout—the very man he has been cursing these past three weeks for robbing him of his precious mules! James pointedly ignored my sharp looks and elbows throughout this charade. The good Mormons were readily taken in, and proceeded to open their hearts to him regarding the world that lies before us.

Of the California mines, they confided that riches were indeed there for the taking. They secretly displayed to us, their new "friends," several bags of dust and nuggets. But they estimate that for every man who makes his fortune there, a dozen others lose whatever fortune they have brought. They described very vividly the hard labor required to sift or pry loose flakes of gold from the rivers and hills of California. They believe, however, that those tested by the overland trail will be better suited to prosper in the mines than those who travel by sea. A wiry little fellow like James, they declared, examining him with approval, should easily be able to earn ten dollars a day.

The storied Sink of Mary's, they informed us, is a most disagreeable place—a sea of slime, a veritable slough of despond. There is no grass for miles about it. Its waters are horrid, unfit for man or beast. The long desert that follows is a region of cinders and volcanic rock, without a trace of vegetation. It is hazardous, and the road through it, when they passed, was already piled with the bodies of hundreds, perhaps thousands of dead oxen, horses, and mules. Hundreds of desperate emigrants, forced to abandon their wagons, are trying to survive there now on the sour meat of these putrefying corpses. Others leave wagon and oxen, walk on to the nearest spring, fill their kegs and canteens, and return for the teams in the cool of the night. Scores of abandoned wagons lie with their canvas tops shrinking in the hot sun, the tires ready to fall from their wheels.

Once arrived at the blessed waters of the Salmon Trout (which these gentlemen call the Trucky), or, by an alternate route, the Carson River, the problem of water and grass disappears. But they warn us that the roads across the California mountains are steeper and more difficult than any we have encountered so far. Animals must be driven up what are, in effect, high granite steps, through oppressively tight cañons; then let down cliffs by ropes and slings; and finally forced over rocks the size of barrels.

The toil and privations of the last 300 miles, they insist, are beyond all bounds of reason for teams not absolutely fresh. Inasmuch as Mormon travelers start at Great Salt Lake on their way west, or, on their return journeys, confront the mountains and desert *first* instead of last, the ordeal is for them considerably reduced. The main problem for us, they declare, will be not so much the height of the mountains or the breadth of the desert, as the debilitated state of our animals as we enter the Sink of Mary's. For beasts that have already been forced to travel 20 or more miles a day, for three or four months, this desert and these mountains will very likely prove more than they can bear.

James's new "friends" did offer one hint as to a possible means of escape. They reported to him news of a new cut-off that permits one to avoid sink, desert, and mountain defiles altogether, and to arrive at the mines a full hundred miles sooner than otherwise. This new route has been in use for only a fortnight, and the Mormon gentlemen had not traveled it themselves. But in passing the fork four days hence, they observed that the bulk of the emigration—including wagons—was now making use of this new northwestern route. It is said to by-pass the higher reaches of the California mountains, and guide one by gentle, well-watered stages to the mining camps of the upper Feather River, where there is still gold aplenty, and not so many miners.

Heaven grant that this prove true! We would then be only a few days from our goal!

The sun is the hottest I have ever felt. My pots and pans are too hot to touch. This dry, unnatural heat presses down from ten o'clock on, and causes me the most agonizing headaches. At such times, I wish California sunk into the sea, along with all its gold.

Every evening for the last three days, the men have had to drive the oxen up into the bluffs in search of bunch grass, or strip what is left of the willows for their leaves. Yesterday, we passed a small Wisconsin company which had lost half its stock to the Indians. They had reached at the same time the bottom of their larder, and the end of their lead animal's strength. They were devouring a soup made from the poor beast's head, having already slaughtered and stripped it, and dried what little meat was left on its bones.

It is foolish and female of me, of course. But I cannot bear the thought of killing one of our own beasts. They have served us so faithfully and uncomplainingly all these hundreds of miles. I was pleased when we were obliged to reclaim them at the city of Great Salt Lake, although of course I said nothing. James makes mock of me for christening them with separate names, and imagining each to have a character different from the others. I think of them, if not as children, at least as beloved family servants who have earned our solicitude. I believe I would share with any one of them my last crust of bread and mouthful of water. As I walk beside them, or sit in the wagon seat behind them, I can clearly perceive their heads hanging lower day by day. I greatly fear we shall lose one or more before our journey's end.

August 29, 1849
At the new cut-off, which we have finally reached, there stands a large water cask half-filled with notices and letters left by our forerunners. Others are posted on sticks and trees nearby. Each argues for or against the new road, by leaving word of the decision made by its author for the enlightenment of acquaintances in the rear. The consensus seems to be that this new road is closer to the mines of the Feather River, but considerably farther to

Sutter's. By it one is spared the desert of Mary's and the steepest reaches of the Sierra Nevada; but obliged to cross another desert almost as difficult, and possibly to spend more time on the trail. After what he heard from the Mormons two days ago, however, James has quite determined in favor of the new turning.

One all-knowing gent from a Cass County train maintains that the advocates of the right hand road make far too fine a thing of it. He declares that the Black Rock Desert (through which this road must pass) is more to be dreaded than the Sink or desert of Mary's. After that, he claims, we shall have to endure 200 more miles of mountain travel than we would have by either the Trucky or Carson River routes; and that the Indians of our northern route are by much the more ferocious.

But considering the large numbers who have followed the new cut-off already—and the clear authority of their predecessors—this seems quite incredible. A 70-wagon train from Jackson County, Missouri, guided by two of the most experienced mountain men in America, elected to take the new road more than two weeks ago. Before them, a company from Ray County, Missouri, voted for the cut-off. It is directed by a Mr. McGee, who has been traveling back and forth to California for several years. And since these two parties made the decision, the signs and notices here posted prove that hundreds, perhaps thousands have followed their example. If we are making a mistake, at least we are making it in company with many others.

Having made our decision, we joined a multitude of hay-makers in the meadow. It is understood from notes left in and around the water barrel that all must provide themselves with three days' provender for the desert road ahead. (How, one wonders, can they know?) There is something very poignant and home-like in the scene: hundreds of men and families scything, tossing, drying, and loading grass. James estimates that this meadow would cut three tons to the acre.

If only one could blot out the awareness that this thousand-acre meadow is an infinitesimal oasis in a world made of sand, and that this busy effort is nothing more than our anxious provisioning against breakdown and death. Like everyone else, we fill our barrels with the foul-smelling sulphur and alkali water of these wells, for further security against the desert. We shall pause here for another day or two, in the hope of bringing our tired cattle up to strength for the final act of this tragedy, or farce. What fools we mortals be!

A certain fresh exhilaration fills our breakaway army with renewed energy and hope. We turn our backs willfully on our former comrades who persist in heading west. It is surely Providence that has opened this Red Sea path to us, and spared us the horrors of a road still marked by the bones of the Donners and the Reeds. To think that the obstacles I have most dreaded, ever since this journey began—the great western desert, the snowy summits of the Sierra Nevada—are now miraculously removed from our path! Already my imagination has placed us in California.

270

31

I was totin' my pack
Along the dusty Winnemucca road,
When along came a semi
With a high and canvas-covered load,
"If you're goin' to Winnemucca, Mack,
With me you can ride."
So I climbed into the cab
And then I settled down inside.

He asked me if I'd seen a road
With so much dust and sand
And I said, "Listen, Bud, I've traveled
Every road in this here land."

I've breathed the mountain air, man.
I've been everywhere, man.
'Cross the deserts bare, man.
I've breathed the mountian air, man.
Of travel I've had my share, man.
I've been everywhere.

Been to Reno, Chicago, Fargo, Minnesota,
Buffalo, Toronto, Winslow, Sarasota;
Wichita, Tulsa, Ottawa, Oklahoma,
Tampa, Panama, Mattawa, La Paloma . . .

The hitchhiker had talked Timmy into taking a detour off the Interstate, so
he could get out to some of his friends who lived by a little town called Jungo.

Always happy to get off an Interstate, and having nothing better to do anyway, Timmy allowed himself to be guided right at the crossroads by this diseased-looking kid, onto a road that rapidly declined into one and a half lanes of gravel over dust.

Been to Boston, Charleston, Dayton, Louisiana,
Washington, Houston, Kingston, Texarkana;
Monterey, Ferriday, Santa Fe, Tallapoosa,
Glen Rock, Black Rock, Little Rock, Oskaloosa;
Tennessee, Hennessey, Chicopee, Spirit Lake,
Grand Lake, Devil's Lake, Crater Lake, for Pete's Sake.

I've been everywhere, man;
I've been everywhere, man.
'Cross the deserts bare, man.
I've breathed the mountain air, man.
Of travel I've had my share, man.
I've been everywhere.

When it became clear that Timmy was actually going to pick up this character, Audrey froze. She stared out her side window, and refused to say a word.

When he let himself be persuaded to detour onto the terrible road, without a word of protest or question, without ever asking her if she minded, she gave him a poke, which he ignored, and an ice-dagger glare, to which he returned a broad smile. After that, she withdrew totally from social existence. Let the creep think I'm crazy. Let him think I'm some deaf-mute half-wit who's being moved from one asylum to another.

The car bumped and wheezed along, scraping rocks, veering around potholes. To a hovering hawk, it looked like nothing but a growing cloud of dust. Swooping down for a closer glance, the hawk could see ahead of the dustball a red critter crawling along the one claw-scratch that disturbed the bare sage plains west of Winnemucca.

The road ran dead-straight and almost unused. One pickup truck passed them after two miles. After four, another. The road before them narrowed in perspective to the next rise, disappeared briefly, continued on to the next rise, narrowing still, dipped again, narrowed on, until it ended in an invisible point on the far horizon. The usual Nevada mountains, soft and bare, rose left and right, hills piled on hills, like forever. During the first twenty minutes on the detour they passed R.F.D. mailboxes every few miles. Audrey looked off past the mailboxes to the trucks and high windrows of ranches in the distance.

Then even those signs of life disappeared. The car clattered along in its dust, farther and farther from the Interstate, and whatever the Interstate represented of civilization. Timmy made small talk with the hitchhiker, as Audrey sat walled in her silence and disgust.

The hitchhiker's name was Norman, and he came from San Francisco. Well, not originally. Originally, he was from Oregon. But now he lived in the

City. He had come back from the war ten months ago, and been living with this "chick" in the Haight. But then she had this kid, see, so they broke up, and now he was going to see these buddies of his, guys he knew from the army who had bought this far-out ranch in the desert. He had been waiting at that turnoff for two days. Almost nobody stopped, except queer truckdrivers, and even they refused to drive off the freeway.

"I didn't know there were any," Timmy said. "How did you know they were queer?"

"They ask you what you'll do for the ride."

"You gotta be kidding."

"Straight shit."

The two talked about that for a while. They were traveling over actual sand, now, sand like on beaches. Fine grains blew in clouds across the road.

"What's it like, this ranch?"

"I don't know. My buddies wrote in a letter they got this place, and that I oughta come. There's five of them: two guys and three chicks. I thought I'd better head out and even things up."

"But I mean what do they do? This doesn't look like very easy country to run a ranch in." The sand began blowing in earnest. He turned on his windshield wipers.

"That I'm not too sure about. They grow stuff, I think—live off the land. Wood fires, horses, chickens, all that shit. It's what we all oughta be doing."

"Not out here we oughta. There's not a hell of lot of water, for one thing."

"Maybe they got wells. Windmills, like that. Do you know this part of the country?"

"Not off the highway. I haven't a clue what's in this part of Nevada." Timmy was beginning to grow exasperated at the younger man's stupidity.

Norman took a folded envelope out of his pocket, and read from the letter inside. " 'There used to be a dirt road out of Lovelock, but it's been closed. So you got to go to Winnemucca. You'll see the turnoff to Jungo a little bit west of town. Our ranch is on a road about twenty miles north.' So all we have to do when we get to Jungo is ask someone the way to the Dead Sea Ranch."

"Is that really what it's called?"

"Yea. Funny, huh?"

Funny as a coffin.

"And those are the only directions you got?"

"They're enough, man. If you knew my buddies you'd dig. By now everybody in Jungo is probably totally freaked."

They hadn't passed a car for a long time, in either direction. Over the pale tan sand, streaked with yellow and gray, was scattered a heathery brush. Crumbling cubic rocks grew in islands. The mountain tops began to turn from rounded to rocky. On the peak of one mountain stood a small white building, tiny at this distance, an observatory, a weather station. Crows, abandoned

273

cars, no shoulder at all to the gravel line that was their road; no signs to indicate anything ahead or behind.

The men talked man-talk about the war, about the Haight-Ashbury "scene," about buying and selling drugs—which apparently was what Norman did for a living. Timmy came down very middle-aged and puritanical on the subject of drugs, but he was sufficiently fascinated by the logistics of the trade to keep asking questions. He couldn't quite get it into his head what these people *did*, what their jobs or relationships were, how they lived. Audrey lay her head against the head-rest, dropped one arm over the back of the seat.

She stared out the window. The landscape felt like the inside of her head. In her life she was going nowhere through a desert, over an unmarked and miserable road. She was too dry to cry, and saw no point in praying.

She felt something touch her hand, dry and slippery like a snake, and she jerked it away. Turning, she saw that the hitchhiker had taken hold of it. When she stared at him, he gave her a smile and a wink. Timmy, engrossed in a story he was telling about his Air Force days, hadn't noticed. She was left more frightened and bewildered than before. Was this person planning to get them lost, to . . . *do* something to her?

What looked like a lake turned out to be nothing but alkali flats. Layers of cloud cast black shadows over the land, dappling and striping the hills, which kept repeating themselves, range behind range, like waves of the sea. Soon they leveled off at the top into long, horizontal buttes, eroded at their bases into red-orange canyons and gullies that cracked their way across the desert, like an earthquake caught in the act. The din of gravel kept rattling onto the bottom of the car, which chunked over rocks and down potholes. As the miles added up, talk died down. Timmy began to look peeved, wrinkled his brow: how far could you drive and find nothing? He was having serious second thoughts about his impulsive gesture back at Winnemucca. Norman touched Audrey's hand again; again she pulled it away, a little less abruptly.

They passed the stone walls and chimney of a roofless house, abandoned to the heat. Timmy tried the radio, but got nothing but static. They were now too far from any town, or any transmitter. On they rattled, bumped, ever-raising the enveloping cloud of dust our floating hawk was using to mark their progress.

JUNGO, 12. The first road sign in almost an hour. Audrey came out of her bleak reverie and spoke to break the vacuum of silence.

"I hope there's a shortcut back to the freeway once we get there."

"I don't know about that for sure. We can ask at a gas station once we get there."

But there wasn't a gas station at Jungo. There never had been. There hadn't been anything in Jungo to speak of for at least fifty years.

Jungo was an abandoned nineteenth-century mining town, what is called in the west a ghost town, at the foot of the Antelope Range. A trail from it once led out to miners' shacks in the hills. Timmy stopped the car in what used to be Main Street.

All three of them got out. They stared at four roofless buildings, with empty window holes and dry weeds growing where the floors used to be. Two other buildings had lost their walls as well as their roofs. On one stone wall Audrey could make out faded letters that had once spelled the name of the town. Knotted planks had gone silvery in places, weathered in death to a rich range of color. Rows of rubble marked the outlines of a few more buildings that no longer existed.

There was something sad in a skeleton of a town that refused to fall to dust altogether, that stood useless in the middle of its sage-spotted plain. Iron tie bars stuck crazily out of walls, attached to nothing. Part of an iron balcony sagged loose from a second floor. Someone had carved deep quoins and decorative moldings in the stone which now only reptiles could admire. For a few moments, the sadness of it all overcame their own predicament.

The three of them explored the little ghost town much longer than they needed to. Each went off in a separate direction, examining privately every corner of the ruins, in search of answers to their separate plights. No one was eager to admit the fix they had gotten themselves in.

"So this is Jungo," Timmy finally said. All three had by this time shuffled back to the steps of the largest hulk. The heat pinned them to the place, like sun focused through a magnifying glass. The world was made of hot dust. Timmy sat down on the steps.

"Do we have anything to drink in the car?" Audrey asked.

"Some warm beer. We never did do our grocery shopping yesterday." Nobody felt like jumping up to get it.

"Your friends didn't suggest anybody in particular we might look up in Jungo?"

"No, that was my idea. All they said was their ranch was about twenty miles north of town."

"Well, I don't know about you people, but I've about had it with this road. It's beating the shit out of my car." They were joined on the steps by a lizard, who appeared out of nowhere and moved close to Timmy. It twitched its way over in quick little spasms.

"I'm glad we got the radiator fixed," Audrey said.

"You and me both."

He turned to the hitchhiker, slapped him on the knee in mock-camaraderie.

"Any ideas, Norm, old buddy? This is your joy ride."

"Well. There may still be some dude living around here. A prospector, like, or a rancher. Can't we look around a little more?"

"You've seen a lot of prospectors and ranchers the last thirty miles, then, have you? Funny, I sure haven't. I'd say we've got a clear view of at least ten miles from here in every direction. You see any signs of life?"

"Well, hell, man. Shouldn't we try?"

In the end, Audrey took Norman's side, so they divided up the last of the melted ice water from the jug and set off again in different directions, looking for some sign of life larger than a lizard, or indications of a road heading north. Audrey found a large arcaded stone wall behind a rise of ground they hadn't seen before, about a mile south of the town. Near it were the remains of a few iron-stained shacks. It had something to do with a mine. But she found no evidence of human passage, and no directions out.

Timmy found what looked like a recent pile of litter, potato chip bags and cupcake wrappers with the labels still readable, Burgermeister beer cans as yet unrusted. This was a northern California brew, and suggested the possibility of a recent passage of Norman's friends—or if not them, at least something human, and from California, with a taste for cupcakes and beer and potato chips. He also found, a half-mile beyond the state historic marker, a milestone pointing east to Winnemucca, and west to a town called Sulphur, 22 miles on. He argued in favor of their continuing to there.

"But that won't get me anywhere, man," Norman complained. "The whole point of coming this way was to get to the ranch."

What *he* had found was a trail heading north at a right angle to the ruins, out past the last foundations. Blown sand had covered a good deal of the tracks, but it definitely looked like a road. He was sure that this was the way to the Dead Sea Ranch.

"I think Norman's right," Audrey risked. "There's not much point in our coming this far into the desert, if all we do now is drive back to the freeway."

"We couldn't do *that* now, even if we wanted to. If the Lovelock road is closed like Norman says, there's no way to the Interstate from here unless we drive back to Winnemucca, which doesn't exactly thrill me. Here, look on the map."

"You know I can't read maps. Why didn't you look at it before you turned off?"

"Because I was trusting our hophead friend here."

"Come off it, you guys," Norman protested. He took Timmy's road map himself, and studied it carefully. His opinion was that their best way out was to continue on across the desert, through Sulphur to a place called Gerlach, 40 miles further on. From there, they could pick up one of two secondary roads into northeastern California. But at first he insisted they at least try to find his friends.

"What if Sulphur turns out to be another ghost town?" said Timmy. "And Gerlach, too? I haven't filled the tank since Wells, and that was more than two hundred miles ago."

"There's gotta be something in Gerlach, man. Look, it's on the railroad line. And anyway Chris and Ozzie are bound to have gas. We can siphon their tank if we need to. All you got to do is another twenty miles."

"I don't like the look of that road."

"*I'll* drive the rest of the way if you want, man. No shit, I don't mind. I drove jeeps over country a lot worse than this the last couple of years."

"This ain't no jeep."

But he was wavering. They had to go in *some* direction. He was feeling wiped out by fatigue, too morally inert to make a decision. The longer they stayed in this place, staring into blank, sunbaked space, the more he felt his will caving in, like the buildings.

"You guys decide."

"I vote to go north," said Audrey, not quite sure why.

"Me, too."

"Okay. North it is."

"Want me to drive?"

"No. I'll do it."

They got back into the car, no longer red but the color of dust. Each of them wiped face and arms with the wet towel from the ice chest, which was warm and smelled of sweat. Norman navigated Timmy onto the tire tracks he had seen earlier, which is really all they were. From time to time even the tracks disappeared under powdery drifts of sand. Then Timmy's intestines would cramp up until the tires found a purchase on something like a road.

Two miles out into the desert, they saw a sign. All three saw it at once, and called out in expectation. They drove till the words were legible. No one read them aloud.

DANGER. ABANDONED ROAD.
TRAVEL AT YOUR OWN RISK.

The sign was pitted with bullet holes.

"Oh, that's just great," said Timmy, all his wanderlust gone.

Out of the heat waves, a high-wheeled truck emerged in the distance, growing larger across the flat, raising its own billowing dust. Relieved beyond words, Timmy slowed down, pulled to a halt, and began waving at the driver.

"What on earth are you doing?" Audrey asked.

"Waving at that truck, idiot. Maybe he knows where the hell this road leads."

"*What* truck?"

"That one! that blue and white one!" he pointed, incredulous at her sheer denseness.

"Do you see a truck, Norman?"

"Mirage, ol' buddy."

"Are you guys shittin' me? You mean you *really* don't see that truck?"

"No, dad. There's no truck. Sorry. Gotta just keep going."

Stupefied, Timmy started up again, with a great clanking of metal parts. Sure enough, the truck disappeared.

The white earth grew gently bumpy, the greasewood bushes large. Heaps of wind-driven sand were blown into geometrical patterns, symmetrical, precise.

The whine of wind grew louder, as loud as the engine. Now they were traveling in a cloud of powder that coated the windshield with dry fog. The car swerved, slowed helplessly. The road was gone. They were driving on pure sand.

Timmy shoved his foot to the floorboard, not daring to stop or shift gears. He tore off his sunglasses and leaned forward like a ship's lookout, straining to find the road. The road, wherever it was, did not run straight, like the gravel line from Winnemucca, but wound around among the dunes, following the contours. Norman opened his window and leaned out, told Audrey to do the same. Timmy kept his hands glued to the wheel, his foot down to the floor, his eyes on the faint shadow on the left side of the road that wasn't quite like the rest of the desert. "Left!" Norman yelled, as the windshield grew thicker with dust. "More left. I think it's turning left!"

"Right, now, I think," Audrey shouted.

The dust-blind Cougar, pushed to full power, was moving at twenty miles an hour; but now even that was dangerously fast. Timmy's gut was tight as steel, agonizing with the pain.

"If we lose this road, man, we've had it."

"Thanks a lot."

They swung along through the drifts for about two more miles, moving with the ferocious slowness of people trapped in dreams, unable for all the force in the universe to pull free of the muck of inertia. In dreams, of course, the only way to escape is to pull with such violence that your very will to move throws you half out of bed, and in waking you tears you out of the fix.

Which is what happened to the car, in a way. The piled sand at last seemed to thin, and the road bed to show through. Little islands of a darker earth became visible through the boiling lake of sand. The wheels caught hold of something firm; the car leapt ahead, rudely awakened from its bad dream.

After the tracks showed clear for some distance ahead, and the wind had died down, Timmy pulled the car to a stop. He opened the door and got out, saying nothing.

"Wow," Norman said to Audrey, placing a hand on her shoulder. "That really freaked me out. You?"

She began to get out of the car.

"Stay inside!" Timmy called.

"What for?"

"I'm being sick."

She got back in, and waited in silence with Norman. He put one hand back on her shoulder. Five minutes, ten minutes they waited, looking into the desert. Neither could think of anything to say.

When Timmy came back, he was deathly pale and damp with perspiration. He leaned in at the driver's window.

"Sorry. My whole guts just gave out."

"Will you be all right?"

"There's nothing left to come out. But I don't think I can drive anymore."

"Hey, man, no sweat. Let me take over. It can't be much farther now."

Too weak to argue, care, do anything, Timmy let Norman take the wheel, and collapsed on the back seat, his knees bent, his feet on the floor, his head against Norman's sleeping bag. His insides felt raped. What an awful way to be sick. He hoped the blowing sand would cover it, quick.

They drove on, grinding in jolts over the winding jeep road. Audrey, in the front seat, talked to Norman, while Timmy rested in the back, hoping to sleep. Nothing but real sleep, he felt, could ease his intestines back to softness, and remove the clamp from his brow.

Winds, wings, swings, sails slipped him away. The jolts and screams of the car blended into his dream.

He was on a ship, a Navy ship. He was a boy, standing on the bridge staring through field glasses into white capped waves. The whole ship was depending on him. Suddenly the ship had sails, and he was high up on a mast, staring forward, shouting unheard instructions to people below. The sea grew more and more rough, he was tossed from side to side, but still he stood firm. The winds grew louder, crying, howling loud, until his hands were torn from the rail and he was thrown down, down . . .

They had stopped. He had fallen off the back seat. The noise was the noise of the engine, the scraping of iron.

"What's the matter?" He scrambled back up, leaned over behind Norman. "What's going on?"

"I don't know, man." He was terror-stricken. "The car started making this noise, man, this awful noise. Then it just sort of ground to a halt."

"Does this little light mean anything?" Audrey asked.

"What little light?"

"This green one here. It went on just before the noise started. At first, it was just blinking every so often. Then it got brighter. It's still on now."

"Oh my God. Oh, my good God."

"What is it?"

"We're out of oil. You've been driving without oil."

"What does that mean, dear?"

"It means we're fucked. Drive more than an hundred yards without oil and your engine seizes up. The parts get so hot they fuse together into one solid block."

"But then what will you do? Can't you put more in?"

"There's nothing you can do. We're stuck."

"But . . . " She looked out at the white dunes. They stretched unvaried in every direction. The horizon was encircled, as at a great distance, by what looked like the craters of the moon. Except for three people and their car, nothing broke the empty space.

The hovering hawk watched as the cloud of blown sand gradually stopped moving and dissolved.

279

32

Timmy, Audrey, and Norman got out of the terminally disabled Cougar. It was two-thirty in the afternoon, Day 23 of their marriage. The sun still ruled in this part of the world.

"You are such an *idiot*," Timmy was screaming. "Didn't it even occur to you to look in the book, or wake me up and ask *me*, when the green light went on?"

"How am I supposed to know it was important?" She was crying. "It's your car."

"What about you, then, smart ass? What about all those jeeps you're supposed to have driven? Don't *you* know what an oil pressure warning light means, either?"

"They don't have 'em in jeeps, Pop. Over there, we checked our own oil. You ever tried that?"

"Of course I have! I checked it in Salt Lake. I checked it in Wendover. I checked it in Wells, when we last filled up. You must have driven straight over a rock, and tore open the crankcase."

"Okay, man. If it makes you feel any better to blame somebody else, you just go right ahead. Fine with me. All I can say is this car is in fucking terrible shape. What I think is that you've been losing oil all along. You had to put oil in, I'll bet, plenty of oil, every fucking time you stopped. Your engine sounded like shit. Didn't you realize what that meant?"

"Of course you did, Timmy. It's been in terrible shape ever since Chicago." She turned back to Norman. "He got drunk and crashed into another car in Chicago. We've had it in garages for repairs three times since then. *You* were the one who decided to risk it!" she spat out at her husband, all sense of faithfulness gone. "You *said* so at that place in Nebraska!"

"What did you want us to do, walk? If it wasn't for this idiotic chase across the desert, looking for a crazy bunch of dopers I don't think even exists, we'd at least have broken down somewhere on the Interstate. And I'd have been the one driving, not some drug addict asshole who couldn't see a green warning light if it bit him on the prick. Jesus H. Christ, *no* one who drives a car keeps going when that light goes on. It's the first thing you learn."

"What would *you* have done, Mister Expert on Everything?"

"I would have *stopped*, first thing. Got a ride to a phone and called Triple-A. If we needed it, there's a quart of oil in the trunk that would have seen us through to the next gas station."

"Hey, man: wait up one fucking minute. I don't remember nobody ordering you to pick me up, with no gun in your back. It was your free choice, right? And I *offered* to drive when you got the runs. Don't go laying this whole trip on my back."

Timmy lunged at him, wanting to pulverize this stupid little creep into the sand: he outweighed him probably sixty pounds, and could have smashed him like a rat along the road.

Audrey ran between them, and started socking Timmy in the stomach.

"*Stop* it! Stop it."

Timmy backed away.

"What would happen if you put that quart of oil in now? Wouldn't that get it going again?"

"Not a chance, if we've run this far without it. The whole engine must be locked in one piece."

"Couldn't we try it, man?"

"And then what? It must be running out like a sieve by now. Do you have any idea on earth where we are?"

"Not for sure. We left that ghost town about an hour ago."

"An *hour?* You said this place was twenty miles away! If we've been driving an hour, we've gone a hell of a lot further than that."

"Well, man, I just followed the road. Same as you. Maybe you took a wrong turn during that sandstorm."

"And maybe you picked the wrong road out of Jungo."

"How about trying the oil anyway, Timmy? Just in case?"

"What about gas?"

"At most, we've got thirty miles' worth," said Timmy. "Hell, give it a try. Nothing else the oil's good for."

He opened the trunk, dug out the can of oil, opened it with a church key. Then he let up the hood. He stared in silence for a minute at his paralyzed engine. He took out the dipstick. Clean. No trace of oil on it at all. He unscrewed the oil cap, and carefully poured in the precious quart. Then he got back behind the wheel, daring not to hope, but still hoping. He turned the key: nothing but the same metallic scream. He shut it off. Poor dead fucking car.

He got back out, slammed the door, kicked the empty can.

"Any other ideas?"

Norman seemed careless and Zen-like, going with the flow. "Wait here for someone?" he suggested.

"Someone like *who?* Have you seen one single car on this wagon track since we left that ghost town? You pisshead. We hardly passed anyone on the road after Winnemucca—and that road was on the map!"

"You mean this road isn't on the map?" The idea of a road that wasn't on a map seemed unthinkable to Audrey.

"Lots of roads aren't on the map," Timmy answered. "Private roads, logging roads, park service roads, ranch roads. But it's not usually too swift to drive on them except in a four-wheel-drive vehicle, like one of Bright Boy's jeeps. Even then it helps if you know where the roads go to. For all we know, this road may have been abandoned the same time as that ghost town. It could be as old as those wagon ruts we saw in Nebraska."

"Take it easy, man. Somebody's bound to come along."

"I sure as hell hope you're right."

First round of blaming over, they proceeded to concoct for themselves elaborate fictions of hope. Sitting in the car with all the doors hanging open, they tried to convince themselves, and secondarily one another, that this was only a temporary mishap.

By blanking out different portions of reality, each wrote a different scenario.

Norman kept insisting that other cars were bound to come along. His friends' ranch was just a mile or two away. His friends *must* go into Sulphur, or Gerlach, or Winnemucca every so often. The tracks they were following, under the shifting sand, didn't look all that old. Presuming the rain washed out the tracks every winter, these must have been made sometime since spring.

Audrey's fantasies were far more elaborate and unlikely, to compensate for fears that were more vivid and atrocious: she kept coming back to her original picture of Norman the Rapist, to dry bones in the desert picked clean by crows.

Thanks to a good Catholic education, she could imagine the most horrible of horrors as real, and easily make blind leaps of faith towards whatever miracle was required. So she left reasoning altogether and spun out wild and crazy dreams, which she uttered in a high staccato pretense of calm.

They would dig into the sand and find springs, from which water would gush. They would be found by the inhabitants of a secret city that lay just between those folds of brown hills, an atomic bomb site they didn't dare put on maps. One of the Army helicopters would fly over and see them, come to save them, drop out a new engine.

Her fantasies of course were useless, except that they helped her to fend off the demons of the probable. They marked the start of her retreat from reality, which aligned her more nearly with the drug-addled hitchhiker than with her husband.

Timmy was no dreamer, no doper. He couldn't escape reality nearly enough. Even his gambling, his compulsions to danger and risk were based on what felt in his veins like a structure of hard-earned skills and reasoned odds.

There was a chance, he conceded, that Norman was right. They had passed that one blue truck, just out of the ghost town. It must have come from somewhere.

Then he remembered. There had been no blue truck. Only he had seen it.

He had given up believing in Norman's maniac friends, airy figments "living off the land" in a land that gave no life. Even if they *had* once come out here, and written him to join them, they must have given up and left, or been killed off by the Nevada sun, long before now. The odds against another car coming by this road within a week—which is what he set as their survival time—were probably fifty-to-one.

Underground wells, then secret atomic test sites? No. They posted clear "KEEP OUT" warnings miles and miles from every bomb site in the desert. So no helicopters, either. And there was no way they could send signals. There was a chance, a hundred-to-one, say, that they might be on the path of some aircraft, private or commercial—though it was hard to imagine where it might be going. Reno to Boise, maybe. Winnemucca to . . . where? Alturas? Why would anyone in Winnemucca want to fly to Alturas? Did people in Winnemucca fly?

O.K., then, what else? He tried very hard to subdivide the problem before them into possibilities, and trace each possibility through all of its ramifications.

All three sat silently, now, speaking only when each had finished shaping another fable of escape.

Except as a storeroom, and a place to sit, lie down, and get out of the sun, the car was as useless as a boulder of its size. They had paralyzed it out of their own carelessness and stupidity.

Which meant that whoever went off in search of help would have to go on foot. Audrey would be of very little use there, he knew from their hiking ventures so far. Norman looked pretty feeble and uncoordinated, and was probably half-wasted by drugs. (I wonder if he has any with him.) I could probably manage a 10-20-mile trek, if I avoid the midday sun, and take along something to eat and drink. We've still got a little left in the food box, a few days' worth, say. There should be one warm six-pack of beer under all that stuff in the back seat. If nothing else, we could drain the radiator water. Oh, Christ, it's got antifreeze in it. Plus that stop-leak. Well, if we need to. Two hundred-to-one.

Sulphur. Say 30 miles back to the ghost town, 22 more after that; 52 miles. He had hiked 50 miles before, twice, once in basic training at McClellan, once on the John Muir Trail to earn a Boy Scout badge. But on both those occasions he had been equipped with everything one could possibly need: he had traveled in a coherent group with trained leaders; and had moved on marked trails that were never far from water. He looked closely at the map, and despaired of the blank space in the midst of which they were lost. He didn't see any way he could possibly make it.

That was as far as careful reasoning could take him. It was not, in the end, much farther than Norman's imaginary ranch or Audrey's imaginary wells.

The sun circled round the southern sky. Timmy forced himself to move, to take what felt like meaningful action. He inventoried the food box and ice chest. Having no plans to camp out again, they had not replenished it since Bear Lake. He came up with one full box of Cheez-Its, a salami, six eggs, some old bread, two tomatoes, salt and pepper, a few carrots, a half-bag of marshmallows, potato chips, and two cans of hash.

But what are they among so many? In the glove compartment were a bag of lemon drops, which Timmy liked to suck while he was driving, and four tubes of mixed LifeSavers, which Audrey cracked with her teeth, the way he cracked ice cubes.

Two, three days' food? He dug the six-pack of warm Coors out from under his sleeping bag. He opened two, gave one to Norman, offered Audrey half of his. It seemed a good omen, finding the beer.

As he was rolling out the sleeping bags, Audrey stopped him and asked if he would mind not zipping them together, but leaving them as singles.

He understood her reasons, but he didn't like them. It hurt him to see the two bags lying like grave mounds, side by side but apart. A body in one could not reach out and touch a body in the other. Norman flopped out his own thin bag on the other side of the car.

To sustain the illusion of domesticity, of life-going-on-as-normal, Timmy brought out the Coleman stove, pumped it up and lit it, and cooked up a can of hash and three of the eggs. They ate the food off paper plates, lone creatures under a darkening sky, scarcely moving specks alongside a motionless car in the middle of the desert. They stuck marshmallows on sticks, like kids at a picnic, and called that dessert. Each commonplace flavor seemed wonderful and exotic. It was as if they would never taste corned beef hash, or scrambled eggs, or toasted marshmallows again.

After eating, Timmy tidied everything up with meticulous care, while Norman and Audrey lay on the two good sleeping bags and talked, watching the first stars overhead. After a little more housekeeping, Timmy sat on the back seat of the car with the door open and his feet on the sand, and played slow, whiny tunes on his harmonica.

It began to get dark, and began to get cold. All three said good-night to each other, and curled tight inside their bags without undressing. Thus ended their first day in Black Rock Desert.

They awoke early the next morning, hit by the first low rays of the sun. The world inside the sleeping bags was better than the world outside, but they were all stiff and uneasy, and Norman was freezing. So they got up.

Breakfast was potato chips. The three remaining eggs were too important to eat yet. Timmy tried to call a kind of meeting, but neither of the others was interested enough to be attentive. They listened for a while, sitting on the ground, but had no suggestions to offer, and no responses to make. Norman seemed uninterested in any form of logic, order, or authority. For Audrey, confronting their situation in a rational manner would force her to acknowledge its existence more than she wished; to acknowledge its seriousness, perhaps even its permanence. Better to play the heedless and unreasoning female, than to face anything so drastic as that.

What Timmy was proposing, gently, tentatively, was a careful exploration of the surrounding terrain. Two of them at a time—preferably Norman and he—could venture greater and greater distances on foot, early or late in the day to avoid the heat. The third person, preferably Audrey, would remain alert at the car, in case another vehicle should pass. In four precise daily sweeps of discrete areas—two surveyors, working twice a day—they should be able to map out this portion of Nevada, and detect whatever traces were to be found of water, food sources, car tracks, buildings, or signs of human passage. It was inconceivable that any circle of the lower 48 states twenty miles in radius—the area he thought they could survey—had not been traveled and settled by man.

Neither Norman nor Audrey could arouse any enthusiasm for his carefully reasoned scheme. They sank, the second day, into a kind of heedless lethargy, feeling much hungrier and thirstier than they should have. Audrey crawled into the back seat of the car and tried to sleep it all away. Norman kept moving his sleeping bag into the side of the car that cast a shadow. He *did* sleep, sleep as if drugged. Which he was.

Timmy could not sleep, so he kept thinking. He walked in small, then larger circles around the base camp of the car. The car was now fixed and still, like a monument to some disaster, a metal joke, a Kienholz assemblage.

What might have been, what *should* have been: a cabin in the woods on the west shore of Tahoe, all of Stateline just minutes away. Sand, yes, but sand and blue water, too. Their own beach, their own lake, the thousand-dollar stake. The chance car might come by, there would be phone calls, tow trucks and garages, delays, costs, a rented car; it *could* still all be, of course. But now he didn't want it.

What *did* he want?

To get out of here, naturally. To feel safe and secure, to feel the hardness of paved road; to be plugged in again to that national network of phone booths and cafés and gas stations that keeps us all alive.

It shouldn't have felt like such a total disaster, he thought, walking in circles around the fixed car. One more breakdown in the wilderness. He had repaired any number of broken-down engines—that had been his job, once. And he had sought out wilderness all over the West. He preferred it. How many times had he not *tried* to get far away from freeways? What was the point of all he had learned from his father, his older brothers, from Scout leaders and ski coaches and climbing instructors in Germany, from Paul, Paul of the Wind Rivers, Paul above everyone else?

At that thought, he sat down in the sand, and lay his head in his arms. What would Paul think of me now? Paul, whose whole tradition was one of survival in just such conditions; whose people had lived in deserts like this, perhaps this very desert, for so many years before they were able to cross the mountains.

He wiped his eyes, ashamed of his weakness, and stood up. What good was all that now? Paul was dead. His problem was not only how to survive himself, but how to help a weak, nervous fusspot of a girl to survive as well, a girl he still loved very much. He had got her into this trap; even if he could walk 52 miles back to civilization, or climb the mountains ahead, live off the dry land—could she? No. Of course not.

And then there was a third. What of him?

There was one thing he would not do. He would not simply stay at the car, and share with them the last of the food, drink with them the last of the beer and the ethanol-poisoned radiator water: wait, sleep, decline, and eventually die.

So he must begin his orienteering circuits, conscientious and, if need be, alone.

The decision was obvious. Reason, Paul, and the life-instinct won.

He would draw up his master map now, begin his first trek later this afternoon, when the worst of the day's heat was over. Already the sun was past the crest. The breath-taking heat had begun to ease.

He turned and walked over a high dune, back in the direction of the car. From far off he heard a faint noise of laughter. It grew louder, wilder as he came within view. Objects of all sorts were strewn around the car. Others were being hurled from it into the air. He began to trot across the sand, to run.

"Oh, Timmy, Timmy." Audrey ran up and hung upon his sunburned neck. She had stripped to a halter and shorts; she would be red as death tomorrow. "Norman's thought of a way out!"

"What the *hell* are you doing?"

"We're going to empty out everything in the car to make it lighter, then build tracks under it with weeds and brush, and push it to start! Look at the pile of branches I collected already!" She was giddy, strangely out of control.

"Stop it!" He grabbed her wrists. "Stop this right now!"

She burst into tears, and spat in his face.

"Let me go! We've got to push the car." She wriggled out of his grasp and ran back to Norman, who was standing by the car trunk, dressed in a pair of green Army undershorts.

"Hey, man," he said, while Audrey cowered at his side. "We're going to push-start it. You never heard of push-starting? The weeds are for traction."

Timmy choked on his fury and frustration. Alone, he could have escaped. With these two idiots, he was doomed. He grabbed Norman by the shoulders, pulled him away from Audrey, and threw him down on the sand.

"Listen to me." His voice was cold fire. "Just listen to me, both of you. This car is never going to start again. Running without oil, the pistons expanded with too much heat, and then locked into the cylinder walls. They may even have melted into one solid piece with the block. I don't suppose you know what pistons are, goddamn it, but that means the engine can't turn over, the sparks cannot fire, the axles cannot turn. It means this car cannot move under its own power. If you want to push it by hand to Winnemucca, that's okay with me. But that's the only way you'll ever get it there from here."

"Man, I started millions of cars that way," said Norman, still lying on the ground, looking more than usually helpless for his baggy green shorts and sunburned skin.

"Well, you're not going to start this one."

Norman got up, went back and took Audrey's hand.

"C'mon, Audrey. This old fart doesn't know what he's talking about."

Timmy watched them walk away. He wondered what had come over Audrey. It couldn't be the heat yet, for Christ's sake. And then he realized: he had fed her some drug, some one of his drugs. That explained her eyes, her jumpiness: the sudden tears, the spitting.

He looked at them again. Norman was proceeding with this insane project, throwing out rags, the jack, the spare, blankets, pans. Audrey kept hanging about him, more subdued now, moaning quietly, touching his bare skin from time to time. Norman paused in his efforts, ordered her to start laying a path of sagebrush and dry grass under the car. She obeyed. Timmy sat some yards off on top of a sand dune and watched them.

After a while, Norman decided the time had come to start. He waved at Timmy to come. Timmy waved back, and stayed where he was. The two pushed and pushed, then undid the emergency brake and pushed some more: with their hands, with their shoulders, with their backs; against the trunk, against the side. Finally, the car began to move. Ecstatic, they hugged one another and leaped up and down, calling again to Timmy. He waved again, and sat still. They pushed some more, the car moved some more. Harder, straining, excited, at last believing in something; until little by little the trail of brush ended and the car nosed back down into the sand, came to a permanent rest twenty feet from where it started.

They tried a while longer, then realized what had happened. Audrey broke into tears. Norman got out two beers from the six-pack. They both joined Timmy on his dune.

"Have a beer?"

"Thanks."

"It didn't work."

"No. Too bad about that."

"We tried something, though. We thought you'd be pleased about that, man. Didn't we, Audrey?" Norman gave her a hug.

"Yes, I thought it was going to work."

"Me, too, Aud. Have a sip?" Norman offered her the warm beer.

"Thanks." She drank and drank, nearly emptied the can.

"Hey. I said a sip."

She handed it back.

"Now what?" Timmy asked.

"You're the boss."

"Oh, am I? I didn't realize that. I sure didn't order that crazy stunt. Look at the mess you guys made. The car's deeper in than it was before."

"Hey. Not our fault, man."

"Right. Well, I say that's enough bright ideas for today. I better sort out some way of dividing up the food we got left."

"We finished the marshmallows, dear." Audrey looked as if she expected to be hit.

"No big deal. Marshmallows wouldn't have kept us going long. You guys better keep covered up more. This sun will burn your skin right off." Already he was unconsciously thinking of them as a pair: him the old man, the two of them kids.

"What about you?"

"I'm covered up. And I'm already more tanned than you are, so I can take more of this sun. But you guys are pure white; you'll be like lobsters by tonight, and I guarantee you'll feel it. There may be some Sea and Ski in the car."

That evening Timmy cooked the last three eggs, sliced some salami and a tomato. Audrey fussed for more. Norman bitched about shells in his egg. But Timmy had determined to make their few provisions last just as long as he could, so he ignored their complaints. He felt more like a Daddy all the time.

They talked a while after dinner, Norman about a Christmas party in Saigon where everybody got stoned, and one guy got shot; Audrey about Christmas dinners at her grandmother's house in Dedham; Timmy, as if to remind her about them, of their wedding, and their honeymoon so far. He asked Audrey privately if he could put their two bags back together. She shook her head, and went over to sit with Norman on his, and share her first-ever joint in the gathering dusk.

After Timmy fell asleep, she moved her bag over to the other side of the car. That night a sandstorm blew, half-burying all three bags, and leaving a slope of sand piled against the right side of the car almost to the handles.

The next morning Audrey felt sick, and threw up what little she had eaten. Her back, shoulders, arms, thighs, and the tops of her feet were badly burned. She huddled under a blanket in the back seat of the car, chilled and feverish by turns.

Norman, too, was bright red. When he went searching through the debris looking for his clothes, he found he had torn his only pants in half. He borrowed a pair of Timmy's, but they were so big on him he decided to stay undressed. He, too, was good for very little that day. He spent most of it sprawled on the front seat, listening to the radio (here, for some reason, you could get Winnemucca), eating LifeSavers and carrots, talking to Audrey, sharing joints with her and telling her about the wonders of LSD and cocaine.

Timmy's burns were crisping as well, especially on the bald spot on top of his head. Stoically, he ignored them. He spent the day building a survival camp the way he had learned in Boy Scouts, existing on lemon drops. First, he salvaged and organized all the jettisoned belongings. Then he drained out a gallon of radiator water into his cookpan, straining it through a towel, and buried it under the car wrapped in cloths in the hope of keeping it cool. He dug a sort of shelter, propping up the walls with sage stumps and dead sticks, and erected a tent roof over it made out of canvas and clothes. In it he lay the three sleeping bags, Audrey's in the middle, each of the others a reasonable distance away. Let her choose. Near his bag, in the shadiest corner, he put the ice chest, the food box, and the stove.

Then he, too, slept through the midday sun, under the hot shade of his shelter. Farther and farther away they were drifting, his careful plans for exploring on foot a circle of twenty-mile radius.

When he woke, Audrey was at his side. She was failing, badly. He dug out the water pan, forced her to drink some of the foul-tasting fluid. She did, but retched again, long minutes of dry heaves, then what was left of her scant meals of the last two days. She lay near him, but not with him, while Norman scraped out giant letters in the sand with his feet, ten-foot high letters spelling H E L P. He then started filling up the letter-ditches with armloads of rocks, but gave up before he finished the E. He, too, came into the new shelter. Neither mentioned it, or commented on Timmy's building it. They acted as if it had been there all along. At dinner—the last of the salami, Cheez-Its, with radiator water—Timmy and Norman argued briefly over Norman's unfinished H E L P letters (intended for airplanes) and his drinking more than his share of the water. Audrey began choking again, as if on purpose to stop them fighting, and they stopped. She said her prayers. Norman rubbed her back, and shared his last joint. Timmy vowed to begin his expeditions the next day.

As soon as he awoke, he took two pieces of the dry bread, some lemon drops, and a canteen of the water, and set off. Audrey and Norman were still asleep, knees bent in parallel and pushed up against one another spoon-fashion, her back to his front. At least they were still zipped up in separate bags. Timmy looked at them thus nearly connected, and was surprised to find he felt nothing. He wrote a note explaining what he was doing, and set off.

He stayed away all day, partly because he had the strength and the food, partly in hope of covering distance he should have covered before; partly to keep clear of the other two, whose very presence was beginning to demoralize him. Norman, he believed, was the most useless and evil person he had ever known. He had seriously affected Audrey, poisoned her, weakened her: changed her.

Timmy climbed dune after dune to the north, then walked up a canyon trail to a high mountain range. There was a chance of finding a spring, he thought, and from the top he might survey many more square miles of land. The canyon trail wound deeper and deeper, till its sides were blood-red cliff walls a hundred feet high. Animal (surely animal?) bones lay along the edges of the walls. The walls declined, crumbled to talus slopes. Timmy scrambled up the rocks on one side, falling back almost more than he ascended, like Audrey at Lake Solitude. At last, he reached the top.

No spring; no visible vegetation. The view before him, perhaps twenty or thirty miles across the desert, looked exactly like the view behind. The only difference was that to the south he could make out the tiny speck that was his car. No human specks were visible.

But he had tried. He drained his canteen. Tomorrow he would go in another direction.

When he got back he found that Audrey and Norman had eaten the last of the Cheez-Its and carrots, and cooked the other can of hash. There was nothing left but some more dried bread. He ate that slowly sitting under the shelter, and wrote out some notes of his travels, while the two of them sat in the car. Norman was now wearing one of his shirts as well as a pair of his trousers, the excess cloth rolled up and cinched in at the waist. He looked like a clown, like a kid playing in his daddy's clothes. Audrey seemed to be feeling better. Timmy neatened up the shelter—the three bags were all in a pile—then went for a walk by himself to look at the stars. When he got back, he saw that the two good sleeping bags had been moved out of the shelter. They were out by the car, zipped into one. They were occupied.

Blood rose, surged, filled his brain with rage. He could feel his body transforming, like some animal whose territory had been invaded, changing under the pressure of proprietorship and lust. His face flushed. His eyeballs opened painfully wide. He looked on the scene through a sheen of red. His forehead, and the bone above his ears, throbbed as if clamped tight in a metal headband. He strode towards them, shoulders squared, taller than ever, his fists already clenched into weapons. He could feel himself dragging them out and beating them, and the feeling was good.

Then a small hand pulled down a corner of the bag. Audrey's white face appeared from under the back of Norman's head. Her eyes locked into Timmy's line of sight. Strange currents passed along that line, from her to him, from him to her. The current paralyzed him in his tracks. He stood there, looking at Norman's squirming bulk inside the bag, at the one visible eye that Audrey kept focused, unblinking, on his. Her look expressed not fright, nor defiance, nor pleasure, nor sadness, nor apology. It said nothing.

The fingers in his fists unclenched. His arms fell loose, like an unstrung marionette's. He turned away, grew a little less tall. His shoulder bones sank; his eyes, half-closed, stared at the horizon.

Gradually, he felt his cheeks grow cool. Soon all that was left of his rage was a faint throbbing under the imaginary metal band around his head.

He opened the remaining bag, and climbed inside it, with his head at the open end of the shelter. That way he could look up and see the stars some more.

It's hard to believe how cold the desert can become, deep on a summer night. For some time after the red edge of the sun disappears, its heat remains in the sand, in the air. But by the time summer stars begin to burn overhead, the warmth has gone, and the temperature of sand and air alike drops to a bone-chilling cold no less hostile and destructive than the evil heat of the day.

This part of the planet is not suitable for man. It has no paths, no landmarks, no dimensions. Its surface is too even and yielding, too grainy and dry. And now it was cold as any moon. All a human being could recognize were the reflected lights of other suns and planets overhead, millions of years away; beautiful, perhaps, but at this distance unable to help.

Timmy lay in Norman's sleeping bag, greasy, smelling of Norman, far too thin for the sub-freezing night. His wife lay in Norman's arms, her legs pressed against his, his foul body against her fair one, in Timmy's down-filled

Arctic double bag, zipped up over their heads. He could make out the serpent-like lump a dozen yards away, next to the impotent car. The mound that was Audrey and Norman moved.

Ice-cold as the night was, Timmy lay with his head and arms outside the thin bag, staring hopelessly into the night, so that he might have some recognizable objects before him. At one point, he lifted up his shivering arms to the stars, wearing out his heart in an effort to make sense of what had happened, of this last defeat: Audrey and Norman.

It didn't matter, he told himself. They were all three on a deathbound course. All they could do now was wait until they died. What did marriage vows, what did love (had they ever really loved?) *matter*, at a time like this? Why should two men not share the one woman?

But the night sky was too clear for such self-deceit. They were not sharing. The bastard had taken Audrey from him, as he had taken everything else.

And it *did* matter, he told the stars. Damn, it mattered! It mattered more than anything else. More than their sand-buried, burnt-out, immobile car, more than their hunger and thirst and fatigue, more than the day's heat, the night's cold. He was abjectly wasted and miserably alone, betrayed beyond his ability to bear it, beyond his ability to fight. He could not find words or even tangible thoughts for his grief, so he stared at the stars, and cried.

The night cold, and the noises from the warm bag near the car grew too cruel, at last. He pulled the sleeping bag over his head, turned on his side, bent his knees up high, and shoved his hands down between his legs. Unwanted they may be, but his genitals were the warmest thing he owned.

If he slept that night, it was never for more than a few minutes at a time. The cold, and his grief, kept shaking him awake. He turned, twisted, sought every which way to find forgetfulness, sleep, enough warmth to stop his body from shaking with the sobbing and the cold.

Lying on her side, Norman's whole body pressed against her back, Audrey slept inside her separate cocoon, and never once looked at the stars.

The next day, for some reason, Norman regained an inexplicable strength. It was as if he had access to a secret cache of food, on which he surreptitiously fed through the night. He asked for more of Timmy's clothes, and he got them. Again, he rolled up the legs and sleeves to make them fit. Now it was Timmy, foolishly, who dragged about in cut-offs, moving things uselessly from here to there and there to here, going over and over his hand-drawn map and the notes from his one pointless hike. He was embarrassed to bother the youngsters with his company, so he took another piece of hard bread and a canteen, and set off nearly naked back in to the hills.

This time the heat, and his general weakness, disoriented him. He walked in circles, fell, slept, got up again, walked in circles some more. Lizards he found, cactus, animal bones, a green puddle encircled by white plants. He scooped foul water from it to wask his face, and to drink. It was salty and putrid, but that didn't seem to matter. He would not tell them where it was. It would be his secret spring.

This time when he got back it was far from dark—only mid-afternoon—

but Norman and Audrey were already in the sack. Timmy sat in the shelter, all his now, and tried to fill in on his map the places he had been today, locate with a secret symbol his precious spring.

He looked up to think, and saw another mirage: a cloud of dust from the south, followed by a truck. He stared at it silently, waiting for it to disappear.

But it wouldn't disappear. It grew larger, kept coming. Now it was making a noise. Did mirages make a noise? Timmy sat like a stone, staring.

Now Norman heard the noise, too. He sat up, stared, jumped out of the blue bag buttoning up Timmy's oversized jeans. He ran towards the road, waving his arms, the pants slipping down his ass. The truck came on, slowed down. It was an old black flatbed, with three words painted crudely on the door: "DEAD SEA RANCH." Audrey sat up, clutching the sleeping bag around her bosom with one arm, waving with the other. Timmy never moved.

Norman was about twenty feet away from the truck, and salvation. Suddenly, with a grinding of gears, it started up and roared away without him. He stopped for a moment on the side of the road, half blotted out in dust. Then he ran down the road after it shouting, until he was quite out of sight.

33

"Well? Aren't you going to do something?"

"About what?"

"About Norman, of course." Audrey was still sitting up in the sleeping bag, clutching it around her bare breast. "You can't just let him run off like that."

He stared at her, unbelieving.

"Why should I care about Norman? Jesus Christ, woman. I hope he runs off the end of the earth!"

"Timmy!" She was scrambling back into her clothes. "How can you be so horrible?"

"For Christ's sake, you little slut!" He walked over and stood above her. "For two days I go off wandering around the desert, looking for water or a road or *some* way to get us out of this. Nobody worries where *I've* gone. Nobody gives a goddamn whether I'm every going to make it back. And when I *do* make it back, what do I find? You, in my sleeping bag, screwing that little turd. Don't talk to me about Norman. I hope he rots." He kicked her as she sat there, kicked her again in fury, hard.

"Stop it! *Stop* it. Please stop."

She collapsed back on the bag, curled on her side, wailing like a mad thing.

"Oh, cry for him now. That's just great. That's really lovely. Bawl your head off for poor Norman."

"I'm not." She sobbed out the words, then went back to her wailing.

"Well, you're sure as shit not crying for me. You don't give a damn about me."

"Yes, I do." She grew quieter, finally. She was shivering all over.

"Don't lie."

"I'm not. I do."

"Then what's with you?" God, how he wanted to believe her. "What the fuck got into you? You start out hating the whole idea of sex, and you end up three weeks later bedding down with this weasel—this useless, ugly, scrawny hophead of a weasel. Does he have you on some kind of drug?"

"He did. A little. But it wasn't that."

"You knew what you were doing, then?"

"Yes."

"Doing to *me?*"

"Yes."

He gave up the posture of master-slave, standing over her bowed and shaking form, and sat down on the sleeping bag, across from her. Here they could parley eye to eye.

"Why did you do it, then?"

"I don't know."

"Did you think you were getting even, or something? Paying me back?"

"No. No." She was still shaking badly, like someone in a fit. He knew she needed to be hugged, but he couldn't bring himself to touch her. He kept his seat a yard away, stared at her face, and waited.

She wiped her eyes, pushed back her hair, and dared to look back at him. Rippling shivers seized her flesh.

"I don't know why I did it."

"I need a better answer than that, Audrey."

"It's just that . . . I don't understand myself."

"You weren't doing it to get even? To make me mad?"

"No. No, I swear it wasn't that."

"And you weren't drugged?"

"Not enough. I wish I were."

"What, then?"

"He said you weren't coming back."

"Did you believe that?"

"No."

"He attracted you. He appealed to you."

She said nothing to that, which nearly pushed him over the brink.

"*Answer* me! You thought that filthy little shit was sexier than me? ANSWER ME. Why? Because he was younger? Because he was better in the sack? *Was he?* I thought that sort of thing made you sick!"

She shook her head, under his attack, back and forth, back and forth.

"Well?" The very idea that she might have preferred Norman to him was unbalancing him, making him morally sick.

Audrey couldn't speak. She lay back, flat out, on the sleeping bag, her head still rocking back and forth on her neck.

He turned away, looked to the direction the truck had taken. After a while, he felt a hand on his shoulder. He shook it off.

"Timmy."

He kept staring into the distance, his back to her.

"Timmy, please?"

"What?"

"Look at me."

He did; hard.

"Not like that."

"What do you want? You all but *admit* you prefer that useless bastard to me. Don't feel you've got to play up to me now, just because I'm the only man left."

"I didn't . . . say that and it's . . . not true." She was looking him in the eye, which made it hard for words to come out. "You asked if he attracted me, and I couldn't answer you easily. Because something about him did. It was ugly, and mean. But it did."

He stared back, unblinking as the sun.

"I was going a little crazy, I think. You've got to try to think how all this feels, to me. I've got nothing, now, Timmy. Not my family, not my home, not my faith, not even my grandmother's jewel case. Not even you, now. Not after Winnemucca. *You* didn't want me any more. I was sure my mother wouldn't take me back. Oh, for a little while I thought I was strong, I could fight you back. I mocked you. I pretended to give you orders.

"But I'm *not* strong. You know that. When you picked up Norman after our argument, it was almost as if you were throwing me out at the same time. First you pay to go sleep with another woman, then you invite a total stranger to take my place in our car. All the way to that ghost town you talked to him, not to me. It wasn't another woman you needed; anyone would do: anyone but me.

"Think how many times already you've left me, Timmy. But it was never like this. What was I supposed to think? In the car, while you were driving and talking to him, Norman touched my shoulder, he did it on purpose. He smiled at me. When you got out to be sick, he put his hand on me again, and I decided to let him. I'm not sure why. From that moment on, I couldn't make myself resist. Or care. Or do anything."

"So you were getting even."

"No! I know it doesn't make sense, but it felt like the only thing to do. We were all going to hell. Since you didn't want me, I was going to go with Norman. When we finally broke down, it seemed . . . planned. It seemed right.

"Partly I wanted to hurt you; maybe that's true. Partly I wanted to break free, do something crazy. Partly I wanted to give up: completely. Partly he *did* attract me, whatever he was, the way the devil attracts people. He seemed to feel closer to the way I was feeling than you did, more like giving up, letting go. All your plans seemed so silly. He had come to get me, I felt, take me away, come like a fate; like a punishment. All I could do was accept it."

"A punishment for what?"

"For my sin."

"What sin? The one you told your mother about, in that letter you wrote in Nebraska?"

She flinched, frightened, afraid he was going to hit her. "When did you read that?"

"You left it open, in a book. It didn't make any sense."

"I thought you'd be able to tell. My mother said you'd be able to tell."

"Tell what?"

"That it wasn't my first time. At Ohio. At that motel. Could you tell? You never said anything."

"That you'd slept with someone before? Jesus, do you think I would care about that? What do you think I am, Audrey? Some great hairy Sicilian who was going to send you back home to your mother because you'd been used once before? There's a difference between doing it then and doing it now. It's your doing it *now* that I'm talking about."

"Then you could tell."

"No, as a matter of fact, I couldn't. Lots of girls tear it before their first time. Riding horseback, exercising, I don't know how. Sometimes doctors even do it for them, one woman told me, to keep it from hurting later. Anyway, you *told* me you hadn't, so I believed you. For two nights, you told me. That's why you were so scared, you said."

"I said that because I didn't want you to find out. My mother swore you'd be able to tell, and then you'd hate me. She said it was God's way of getting even."

"Audrey, let me tell you something. Your mother is a mean, stupid bitch who doesn't know any more about God than she knows about men. I didn't know then, I do know now. And it doesn't make any difference. It wouldn't have made any difference to me then, and it doesn't make any difference now. What wipes me out is what you did the last two days *here!* Here we are—the two of us may very well *die* here, in the middle of nowhere—and you go and sleep with someone else. That's what I still don't understand."

"I haven't told you all of it."

"You guys did something *else*?"

"Not now, I mean. Then. The first time."

"Audrey, baby, listen. Think about us. Think about where we are now, and about what's happened. Let's just try to face that, huh? And forget about the past?"

"Please listen, Timmy. Please let me finish. It's the only way I know how to explain."

Now he lay down, too; alongside her, but not touching her.

"You remember that retreat I told you about once? The one at Holy Rosary Convent in my senior year?"

"Mmm."

"The priest who ran the retreat, who gave sermons in chapel every day, was a young man from Ireland, almost a boy. He was very skinny and pale, with red hair. Redder than yours.

"He taught at a private boys' high school in Williamstown. Father Leonard was his name. He was used to talking to teenaged boys about their problems, I guess, lecturing to them on impure thoughts and deeds. He had this sermon on the Sixth Commandment, and what he did in it was describe in detail some of the most wicked things that boys could do to girls, things he'd heard boys tell him about in the confessional. Once he got going, I think he totally forgot

296

that he was talking to a group of twelfth grade girls from Dedham who had never heard of such things in their lives. He went on and on, getting more and more excited about these dreadful sins.

"He hinted at indecent acts I couldn't even understand. Then he stopped and glared at us and started talking about the way God punishes such sins. Not only in hell, he said, but here on earth, we will be made to suffer dreadfully, and especially in the places where we have sinned. He described some of the most awful diseases, rashes and sores and pus in people's private parts, people becoming paralyzed and going insane and dying horrible deaths. And after they died, he said, it would become even worse: it would be in those same places, the places where we sinned, that the fire would burn worst, forever and ever. And once you started in on sins of the flesh, even as children, even at our age, there was never a chance to turn back. Sex became like a drug, he said, like something you couldn't resist. He had seen it happen. People, young people our own age, people who had been to the best Catholic schools and had the most devout parents, all the best training and examples, just became more foul and promiscuous. They couldn't stop themselves. The devil had taken over their bodies, and hell was the only reward they could expect.

"He ended that sermon by telling us about a horrible car accident he had seen. He was working at a parish in Providence then, just a year or so after he'd come to this country from his seminary in Ireland. A phone call late at night had come from the police, asking for a priest to administer the last rites to some people in a car crash. He was the one on duty, so he got dressed and got his things and drove to the place. It was the first time he had ever administered Extreme Unction.

"A car had apparently made a sudden turn onto the highway, and been rammed into broadside by a huge truck. In it were four high school kids, two boys and two girls, coming back from a dance. They had been drinking, he said. All four were killed. The tow truck and ambulance people were just cutting off the smashed-in doors to get at the bodies when Father arrived. He said he got out of his car, ran through the crowd with his bag of holy oils and things, and identified himself as a priest, when the back door fell open and he could see the dead couple inside. 'They were unclothed,' he said. 'They were coupled together in the instant of lust, covered now by nothing but one another's blood. They had been struck down by God in the very fraction of a second in which their mortal sin was consummated.' Those were the exact words he used.

"There is only one person, he said, other than Christ and His Blessed Mother, we know for sure is in heaven today. All the angels and saints are probably there, but there is only one specific individual we know about for sure: the Good Thief on Mount Calvary, who hung on a cross next to Jesus. Because it says in Saint Luke's Gospel that he asked Jesus, 'Remember me when Thou comest into Thy kingdom,' and Jesus promised him, 'Today shalt thou be with me in Paradise.'

" 'Those two young people,' he said to us, 'are the only people I know for certain are burning in hell, this moment and forever. Judas may have

297

repented as the rope tightened about his neck. For all we know Hitler and Stalin may have gained the grace to beg pardon for all their multitude of sins in their final moments. But that young Catholic boy and that young Catholic girl from Providence, Rhode Island, were committing a willful mortal sin at the very moment they were killed, and they could not possibly have had the chance to make a perfect Act of Contrition.'

"That sermon had the weirdest effect on me. It was supposed to terrify us, terrify us for all time out of committing indecent acts. But more than anything, after I heard him, I wanted to commit that sin. I didn't care about hell, about burning forever and ever. I went back up to my room, and all I did was think about it. I prayed every prayer I knew, I got down on my knees and said a whole rosary, but all I was thinking about was that naked boy and girl in the back seat of that car, just one second before the truck had hit them—and I wanted to be that girl!

"First I played with myself, but that wasn't enough. I went downstairs to the hall, where there was a shrine to the Infant of Prague, and took a big white candle out of a candelabra. I took it back to my room and used it to pretend I was that girl in the back seat of that car, used it till I bled.

"Then I didn't know what I would say about the sheet. So I stayed in bed the next morning, till Sister Agnes Julie came up to see if I was sick. I told her I thought I was. She took my temperature and washed my face, and arranged to have my breakfast and lunch sent up. At lunchtime, she asked if I wanted to see a doctor, or be sent home, and I said no, I thought I'd be all right. Then when she came up about six o'clock with my dinner, I told her that this was the first day in my life I'd missed daily communion since my First Holy Communion, that my two sisters were Sisters of Mercy and that my whole family always went to daily communion and offered it up for the poor souls in Purgatory. That was a lie of course, but she believed me. Nuns always believe stories like that. I asked if there was any chance, as a special favor, of Father Leonard coming up to my room to hear my confession and allowing me to receive communion in private.

"After about half an hour, there was a knock on my door. I said come in, and he did, and closed the door behind him. He left his little mass kit in my dresser. Then he came and sat down on the chair by my bed. I was on fire, I couldn't talk. He thought it was the sickness, and tried to smooth the hair off my forehead. He picked up the wet cloth Sister Agnes Julie had left in a saucer by my bed, and rubbed my face and neck with it. I wanted to die.

"He asked if I wanted him to hear my confession first, and I nodded. He got a little purple cloth out of his bag and put it around his neck, made the sign of the cross, and waited. At first, I couldn't say anything at all, so he began trying to help by asking questions about this little venial sin and that, had I missed my morning or evening prayers, had I lost my temper, had I committed any sins of envy. I just kept shaking my head no.

"Then he asked me very quietly about impure thoughts, and my voice came back. I began pretending I had commited every filthy thing I could imagine, confessing to all those things he had been hinting about, everything I'd ever heard of, everything I'd dreamed of doing that day, lying there in my bed. He looked appalled, I could tell he didn't believe me, didn't know what to say. I had taken off my nightgown, and still held that candle grasped tight in one hand, under the covers. I had to prove to him that I *was* as bad as that girl he had seen killed, so I threw back the blanket and sheet and pointed to the blood marks, and started to put the candle back in. He reached to take it away, and I held on to him, held as tight as I could."

"That night I washed out the sheet myself with a bar of toilet soap, and left it to dry overnight in the bathroom. I told Sister I felt better the next morning when she came in, and went to mass and communion along with everyone else. Father didn't even pause, or look at me, when he put the host on my tongue. The Mother Superior called me aside before our Stations of the Cross in the garden to ask how I was. They had all been talking about me, it seems. She said they were very proud to have a young woman with them with such devotion to Our Lord in the Holy Eucharist, to the Body and Blood of Christ. I think she believed there was still a chance of talking me into joining the order.

"Father Leonard finished out his retreat sermons and masses on schedule, and we never looked one another in the eye. I never heard what happened to him. Maybe he's still at the school in Williamstown.

"I *did* get very sick, after I got back home, so sick I stayed in bed most of that summer. I thought I was pregnant, I even wished I was; I pretended to my mother that a boy at school had seduced me. But I wasn't. I hardly ate anything at all. I got so moody and depressed my mother started sending me to different doctors, there were long family consultations about ruined little Audrey. They offered up novenas.

"What bothered me that summer, what nearly wrecked me, were two things. First, I had learned what sex was like, and I decided it was awful. I didn't ever want to do that again. And second, I was living with a mortal sin I never dared to confess, never to anyone until this minute. I began to wonder more and more whether God would ever listen to my prayers again, ever care about me or love me after what I had done. I kept on praying, hoping, pretending, going to mass and communion, confessing all my other sins. But this one was always there, like an ulcer, like a great rock inside me.

"Now when I need to pray most, I can't."

She looked up at the perfect sky, luminous, not black, brilliant with stars. "There's no one there anymore."

Timmy broke into her reverie.

"What's all that got to do with Norman?"

She turned her head back from the sky, and looked at him in surprise. Enraptured by the sound of her own confession, she had completely forgotten why she began it. It had left her purged and purified. She felt as if he had been her confessor, and this her last confession. It had left her truly prepared for death.

Had she wasted it then, given up her most precious secret for no reason? She sat up and looked into his worldly, wondering eyes.

"I don't get the point, Audrey. That's ancient history. A lot of teenaged girls get mixed up like that. You bring religion into it, you just mess up your head worse than ever. Anyway, it was probably just what the guy needed. It was his fault for turning you on in the first place, him and his horny sermons."

"Then you *don't* understand!"

"What's to understand? Okay, it bothered you, it upset you: first time, mortal sin, I understand that; I've heard the whole routine. It screwed you up for a while. But no harm done, huh? You got over it. Obviously. I don't see any connection between that whole story and what I thought we were talking about now. We got married; we were fighting a little bit—married people do that, you know? We get led out into the desert by some hitchhiker, our car breaks down, we're stuck. And just about the time I think maybe this predicament is going to pull us back together, you and this hitchhiker throw me out and take over our sleeping bag. Like you can trade off partners whenever you feel like it. You let that runt do it to you like it's the most natural thing in the world. And why? Because something about him attracts you.

"Think about it, huh? At that convent or wherever, nobody got hurt. You had to lie, you embarrassed the poor mick, you broke a commandment or two: but nobody knows, so nobody's hurt. Here you destroy me, destroy our marriage, foul up every blessed thing we've got just when both of us are at our lowest-ever point, when we ought to need each other, support each other most. There's just no comparison."

"Timmy, I can't explain any better. If you still don't understand, I can't explain. Hit me, lose me. I don't care. Some part of me must still feel diseased, I guess. About sex. I began to think I was over that, that I really could enjoy it because at last I was really in love; because I might even be a mother; because you cared for me, you were helping me. But when I thought our marriage was over, after just three and a half weeks, that it was dead like this car, then we were no better than those two dirty kids in the back seat of the car covered with blood. It was ugly, it was wrong. Norman brought all that back. If I wanted him, it was the same way I wanted . . ."

Timmy started to interrupt. "I *know*," she said. "I know it makes no sense! I didn't want it with you, because we weren't in love anymore. I had to prove to myself how bad it was. I'm sorry, but I can't explain it any better."

Let it be, he said to himself. There was nothing he could do now but pretend he understood, and hold her in his arms. He felt afraid of, intimidated by this strange creature he had married. "My poor baby," he said, and kept smoothing her hair, over and over, as a mother would do to a child who had just awakened screaming from a nightmare she couldn't describe.

34

The earth is round, we are told, and it moves; it's the *sun* that stays still. But things are so contrived that we never feel the earth as round, or in motion; and our senses assure us that the sun's bright-burning disk does not stay still. In midsummer, in the middle latitudes, it first rises above the flat earth's eastern horizon some time around five A.M., dispelling darkness slowly with tender hues; gradually moves higher up the southern sky, to reach its apogee around noon; then curves down toward the western edge of land or sea, where it disappears, occasionally in a splendor of cloud- or haze-reflected color, a little after seven P.M.

In deserts, this imaginary cycle of the sun takes on a striking reality. There is so little else to attend to; so little else that changes or moves. In the absence of shelter or distraction, the apparent presence or absence of the sun, its height, its heat, its light come to dominate all one's motions and thoughts. They become matters of life and death.

For six days, they had followed the cycle of the midsummer sun over Black Rock Desert. For the two days that Norman had been gone, they did little else. The last of the beer and rusty radiator water were gone. The Cheez-Its were gone, the salami was gone, the lemon drops were gone, the LifeSavers were gone. Audrey walked as far from the car as she dared, and brought back sage leaves, rye grass, and pieces of cactus. They chewed these, and tried to pretend they were food. The cactus, at least, was moist. Timmy crushed and cut up a few small lizards that ventured near their encampment, but they could not bring themselves to eat them. He never even bothered to light the stove. When the winds blew, fine grains of ashy sand filled the air, settled, shifted the dunes by a few inches this way or that, coated their skin with gray-white dust, and piled up against the sides of the buried car. Timmy ran all the parts of the car around in his mind, thought and rethought everything

301

he had ever known about engines. He even fantasized taking the engine out (without a hoist?), taking it entirely to pieces (without tools?), magically making it work just by doing the job with minute care, fitting each part back in so precisely that the very intensity of his dedication—a mechanical act of faith—would take the place of oil.

But he knew it would do no good. He left the hood closed, tried not to look at the dead car, tried to blank it out of his mind.

By day they lay on, by night in, their sleeping bags, under the tarp that served for shade. They talked, or didn't talk, suffered, tried to sleep, sometimes slept, as they watched the rise, ascent, peaking, descent, and fall of the sun.

"Do you think he'll ever come back?"

It was the third evening since Norman had left. The sun was very low, almost gone, a circle of flame surrounded by crimson streaks. Tiny objects cast long shadows, soon to disappear in the all-over dark.

"I don't know."

Timmy lay flat on his back. His burnt skin was grayed all over with desert dust. His eyes were as red as if they had been bleeding. Between unshaven cheeks and jaws, his lips were puffed and cracked, erupting in sores. It hurt to open them to talk.

"I tried to work out the chances yesterday. But today I just can't think about it anymore. He doesn't exist. There's just us."

"I like it better that way."

"Do you?"

Audrey was sitting up cross-legged, brushing her hair and staring into the red circle of sun.

"Do you think we're going to die here, then?"

Timmy said nothing. He let his tired eyelids drop over the blood-red eyes. Then he opened his eyes again, and he looked up at the makeshift roof.

"Yes."

"You mustn't say that."

The sun was a half-circle now, and going fast. The streaks around it were brighter, flame-orange, many colors. They spread for miles.

"It's not fair."

"It's what is. I don't mind dying. I just hate doing it this way." There were pauses between every remark.

"What will it be like?"

"Like this, only worse. Choking, harder to breathe, getting weaker and weaker. Like being strangled, I suppose, only very slowly. If we're lucky, we'll pass out."

"Well, *I* mind." The sun was gone. "Dying doesn't make any sense."

"I can say that, you can't. You're supposed to be the believer."

"Oh, Timmy," she looked at him, and touched him softly on the leg. "I don't believe anything anymore."

"Because of this?"

"No. Not because of this. I've been faking it for years. I don't think I've

302

really believed since high school. Since Father Leonard." She started to cry.

He sat up, put one arm around her.

"Hey. Hey, baby. I'm here."

That just made her cry more.

Audrey moved away from his arm, laid down his hand. She tried to compose herself, stop crying, rubbed her eyes and cheeks. She stood up and went outside the shelter. In the sand, she walked a few yards, looked at the buried car, took a visual circuit of the whole horizon, turning slowly on one spot, stopping when she got to the place where the sun had been.

Already the brightest stars were starting to come out. Timmy sat in the shelter and watched her. She walked further away, past the car, still looking west, until she became very small. Then she came back.

The temperature was dropping. She lay on her back with her arms straight at her sides, like a corpse in a coffin, looking up at the canvas roof.

He bent over her, touched his lips to hers, then lay back down by her side. They lay like two tomb figures, like stone statues of a medieval knight and his lady.

She stood up, and walked outside once more. She stood by the dark mound of the car, and stared again at the place where the sun had gone down. Timmy got up, and stood just outside the shelter. It had grown very cold. He watched as Audrey opened the right front door of the car, got in, sat in her regular place, and shut the door. It was as if she were just waiting for him to come and drive off.

After a while, Timmy walked out, away from the car, onto the dry grass of the slope where Norman had dug the letter trenches of his pitiful H E L P sign, now buried again and level with the rest of the darkening land. Deep into the land he looked, a wrecked sailor in search of a sail. Things moved, night birds, coyotes. Soon their evening chorus would begin, unearthly hoots and howls. It was a frightening noise, an alien noise, but it was better than the silence, a silence that was only magnified by the static of unseen bugs, the rasp of the windblown sand.

Above, the usual mocking display of every star in the summer sky, with pools and streams of stardust in between to represent those too dim or far away to stand out on their own. At six thousand feet, the air pure as pure, with no early light around to distract, no earthly machine to foul or fog the air, and, tonight, no moon to rival their luster, the sky above was as rich as the earth below was poor. There was a kind of stoic, naming-the-parts satisfaction in simply spotting this star and that, tracing from constellation to constellation. Norman was gone, the car was dead, their marriage was a joke, their lives were running out. With all that disorder, Timmy felt vaguely pleased to see that all the night stars were still where they belonged.

Polaris dead-center north, the Little Dipper upside down, the Big Dipper rightside up, around it the lines of the Great Bear. The Dragon, Cepheus, the W of Cassiopeia. Highest and brightest in the sky tonight: Vega. The planet

Venus and orange Arcturus glowed high in the west. The Milky Way, the very rim of the galaxy, flowed pale through the southern sky, sparkling with the bright points of the Swan, the Eagle, the Archer, the cat's eyes and red Antares in Scorpio. He looked with deep longing at Berenice's Hair, the cluster of the Dolphin. He went on till his neck was stiff, sorting out the sky, until he had placed every notable light into a pattern, naming names as if he were reciting some magic litany that would lend coherence to his own small, incoherent fate.

When had he first learned to do this? At Scout camp, finding ten constellations to get his astronomy merit badge? No: he knew them all before he got there, passed his test the first night. He must have been eleven then, so he had learned the stars earlier than that. From Joe, then? His father? On the fishing trip? It must have been his father: he knew everything there was to know about the outdoors.

Then it clicked. Blood drained from his face at the uninvited miracle of recollection: time disappeared, the land changed, his very limbs grew small. Only the sky was the same, and he was on Grandma Portale's lap, in a big wicker chair on the front porch at the Deer Creek farm, five, six years old he could have been, and she was making him see lions and bears and archers in the summer sky.

He looked back toward the car. Through the frame of the windshield, he could make out the fragile silhouette of Audrey's head. He walked back. By pulling hard against the sand piled up against it, he managed to open the driver's-side door. He got in beside her and shut the door.

"Shall we go, then?"

"Yes. Let's."

The car key was still inserted in its slot under the steering wheel, his other keys dangling below it on a ring. Timmy turned it one notch. To the surprise of them both, the radio came on, as loud and clear as if a third person were sitting with them in the car.

Hello out there, Nightpeople. This is Deanna Crow, your Midnight Dream Lady from KWA, 'mucca, with music for dancin' and romancin' through the night. Comin' up this next hour we got Merle-baby, and Tammy, and Buck and all the Buckaroos singin' all your requests, Nightpeople. But first this message from the good folks at Winners' . . .

He switched it off.

For minutes they sat silent. Then Audrey began again.

"Timmy?"

"What?"

"Who was that little boy in the picture?"

"My son."

She had guessed right.

"Is he still alive?"

"Yes."

304

There, she had guessed wrong: thank God.

"Would I have been able to meet him, if . . . if we got to California?"

"No. I'm not allowed to see him anymore."

She leaned on his shoulder. More than ever, now, she wanted to help him: to warm him, thaw him, open him up, release him.

"I knew it couldn't be your brother, the more I got to thinking about that picture. If you really had a younger brother who died when he was five, the picture would have to be more than thirty-five years old. It wasn't that old. They didn't even *have* color pictures then, I bet. And if you'd had a little brother you loved so much, you would have mentioned him before, I thought, when you told me about those fishing trips and all. There weren't any other pictures in your wallet. None of your parents, none of your other brothers.

"I *knew* it was your son, Timmy. The way you wouldn't talk about having kids, the way you got so upset whenever I mentioned it.

"I didn't care that you had a son, sweetheart. I could have loved him, too. That's what you and your friend in Casper were fighting about, wasn't it?"

"Yeah. Gerry knew about the kid. He threatened to tell you, let you know what you were in for, what sort of a bastard you had married. Lois put him up to it, I think. She hates me."

"She hated me, too. Why did she hate us?"

"She was Dee's best friend. And she knew what happened to Patrick."

"Patrick's the little boy?"

"Yes."

"How old is he now?"

"Nine. His birthday was June sixteenth."

"Did you write him, or send him a present?"

"No."

"Who's Dee?"

"His mother."

"Does he live with her now?"

"No. With my folks."

"But when we got to Deer Creek, wouldn't we have seen him there?"

"We weren't going to Deer Creek. My father wouldn't have seen me if we did go there. He hasn't written or spoken to me for over four years. He swore never to see me again. That's why I went to Boston."

She didn't know what to say. If what he was saying was true, it was one of the saddest things she had ever heard. Timmy kept his arm tight around her, but his eyes looked straight ahead, into the desert. She pulled his head down and around with both her hands and kissed his dry lips, as hard as she could, licked them, kissed them again. But they wouldn't open up.

She leaned her head back on his shoulder.

In his head, he was trying to sort out the pros and cons of telling Audrey the whole story. He had vowed when he first met her never to do it. It was all so brutal, so banal. It showed him up as such a foul, cruel, selfish human being.

In those days, of course, he had lived in a world made of foulness, of cruelty and selfishness. He had been no worse than the rest.

305

But that was no excuse. If he had been no worse than the rest, he had been no better, either—and a whole lot more unlucky. In the end, he had lost the only things in the world he cared about at all. Now it looked like he was doing it again.

Oh, what the hell. He cut the debate, closed his eyes, and started to talk.

She moved her head off his shoulder so she could watch him as he talked. He left his arm around her.

"Let me tell you a story."

"It's a story about a kid who grew up in a little town in the West."

No. That wasn't the way to begin. She already knew that part.

"No, let's start in . . ."

When? When did it start?

"Fifty-two. Nineteen fifty-two. I got to the end of my time in Germany when the Berlin blockade started. My C.O. talked me into re-enlisting. So I stayed, for two more years.

"Then in fifty-two, my mother wrote me that my dad had taken sick, had to go into the hospital in Auburn with some blood disease. That's when I finally came home. Dad had been writing for the last two years telling me to get the hell back, the war was over, I'd served my time, and what was I doing hanging around in Germany anyway? It was almost like he got sick so as to force me to come home.

"He was eight weeks in the hospital, and when he came out he was healthy again, but he had suddenly turned into an old man. He was still tall and strong, but all his hair had fallen out. He turned over most of the running of the restaurant to my brother, Mark, and moved out to his place fifteen miles up the road in Deer Creek. He was pleased to have all four of his boys home around him again, not just the three."

Timmy paused in his story, took his arm from around his wife. He leaned his elbows on the steering wheel, and rested his chin in his hands. A crying wind was blowing across the desert, lifting ghostly trails of sand in the night. Were those wolves howling into the wind, or distant winds crying louder? The shell of the car seemed very fragile—a vulnerable shelter from the noise and creatures of the night.

How could he ever explain to her what happened next?

"I tried to settle back down in Grass Valley, but I just couldn't make a go of anything. It was like all that time away had spoiled me for all the things my father and brothers were doing. We tried one more fishing trip together to the Warners, except Joe, whose wife wouldn't let him go, but it wasn't any fun. I wasn't the same person I had been when I left, couldn't find a place to rest even in my own family. I even talked different from the rest of them, dumb Army slang mixed up with bastard German, sloppy, dirty, simpleminded talk. No real sentences even. I began to annoy everyone in town with my foul mouth. High school boys started to imitate me when I hung around the courts

306

playing basketball with them, and that made their parents mad. I mean, this was a pretty free and easy town, okay. But nobody was going to put up with my dirty Munich stories and Air Force filth nonstop—and I didn't know anything else to talk about. My father walloped me a few times for getting stupid-drunk and breaking things, like smashing up the family truck. My mom got most upset when I started messing around with one of the high school girls whose folks went to St. Patrick's.

"I'd take a job somewhere, some friend of the family's place, then get arrested or crash a company car or screw up somehow, and that was the end of that.

"After less than a year, I cleared out. First I moved into a room in Sacramento. Because of my Air Force work, I was able to get a job as an aircraft technician there. Sacramento seemed small-time after Munich, so I moved down to San Francisco, and went to work for United at the airport. But in those days the big money, the heavy action, was down in the suburbs further south. So after a while I moved again, and got another job as an R and D technician at a new electronics plant down by Stanford."

He lifted his chin from his hands, and looked at Audrey.

"It was a little like Route 128, the scene in the foothills around Stanford, west of El Camino. Same kind of plants, same kind of work mostly. But the way people lived there, you just can't compare. Oh, it looked good. It looked great, in fact. In those days, the boom was fantastic. People thought it would never end, it would go on forever. The University leased out hundreds of acres to electronics companies, old ones like G.E. and Sylvania, new ones like H-P, Varian, Fairchild, Itel, they built these modern plants all over the foothills, their stocks went zooming, seven points, fifty, three hundred. They kept advertising for engineers and technicians all over the country at higher and higher salaries, stole ideas and top people at the big Wescon conference each year in San Francisco. Developers kept chopping down the peach trees for new housing tracts and poolside apartments. Fancy restaurants and motels and bars filled up the empty spaces up and down El Camino.

"It all looked very good. I had money, now; more money coming in each month than I ever seen before. I had this hot-shit job, I could swim laps in the apartment pool every morning before work, go skiing or climbing on weekends with my buddies, booze it up after work at places up and down 101, from Menlo Park to Sunnyvale. The place was crawling with women.

"I bought an orange Kharmann Ghia; racked it up; a silver Porsche; totaled that; a blue Alfa. That's the way it went. I went through half a dozen roommates. One would take a job in Texas or L.A., or get married, or just clear out, after some drunken argument. Once I lived for six months with two Stanford grads, electrical engineers, suit-and-tie boys on their way up the company ladder. That got kind of sticky. Without a college degree, you could just go so far and no further in those places, and these two guys could really make me feel like an uneducated slob. I was probably worth ten times more to the company than they were. But they wore their dumb Stanford crewcuts, and had old fraternity brothers over for brews, and it just got to be too much.

307

So I moved again. This time it was to a big apartment complex off of Alma in Palo Alto that had two pools, a sauna, its own tennis court, and a reputation for super action.

"Which was no lie. The place was built in the shape of an E, one pool between each wing. The tennis court and sauna were behind the pools, next to the parking lot. There were about sixty units on two floors, all connected by patios or balconies—and there was a lot of traffic between them, let me tell you. They all had sliding glass doors and the same kind of cheap modern furniture. Sometimes you could hardly tell if you were home or next door. It was like that Holiday Inn at Council Bluffs, only fancier, you know, sundeck on the roof, banana trees out in front lit up at night by big yellow spots.

"The parking lot was full of sports cars, and the poolside action was incredible. Available, good-looking young California people with money and energy to burn. Great bodies, great tans.

"It looked good. Damn, it looked good. Life was packed from morning to night. Every weekend the place was one giant party, and the sun was always shining; all you had to do was bring your share of drinks to the pool, or to follow the barbecue smells and music at night and slide open the door to whatever apartment seemed to swing the loudest, mingle in with all these sun-tanned honeys and hustlers, cool clothes and warm skins, till you found what you liked. Then you'd head off to the El Camino bars, or back to your place, or hers—or, what the hell, up to Tahoe or Squaw: two hundred, two hundred fifty miles, four-five hours up the pike in your Alfa for more of the same, higher up. That's what the mountains were for: it was just the Peninsula scene, pushed a little higher. Everything's good and pure and wholesome and healthy, remember, over five thousand feet.

"People dropped out, but they kept being replaced. They moved on, or died, or got married—although some of the ones who got married kept on with the scene just the same. They usually got divorced after a while, and took up right where they left off. If they ever left off.

"You've got to picture me then, pushing thirty, no longer a kid. Playing the south Peninsula scene heavily for five or six years, heading up my own R and D shop now at RVC, earning more than I could spend, drinking more than I could hold. I was beginning to freak a little about my age, since the crowd around me kept getting younger, my old roommates and girlfriends kept marrying off and moving out. I was beginning to lose out to teenage punks, on the courts, or the slopes. But I just kept working out all that much more fanatically, swimming, running, playing tennis, lifting weights, working on my tan, watching out for the first wrinkles, the first sign of flab. Each summer, I could get my back-to-nature fix climbing in the Wind Rivers with Paul. I might drink like any fat old boozer, but I was *not* going to let myself go to pot. Too many guys I knew did that after thirty. It was depressing to look at them, fat bellies, soft double chins, broad behinds, all packed into the same clothes they'd been wearing when they were twenty. That ruined the whole game.

"On my thirtieth birthday, my roomates threw this giant party for the whole crew, and it spilled over into four different places, onto the pool deck

308

outside. It got really gross. People were throwing up in the oleanders, jumping in the pool, fucking in the showers. I ended up sleeping with a Pan Am stewardess named Dee in the living room of the place upstairs she shared on and off with four other stews. Dee and old birthday boy had rolled off the couch during the night, and we were both flaked out on the rug when the sun shone through the glass, naked for all the world to see. We only woke up when one of my roommates brought a gang of friends upstairs onto her balcony and started pounding on the window and singing 'Happy Birthday.'

"In some ways, Dee was no better or worse than a dozen other girls I'd taken up with since I got out of the Air Force, but I liked her. She was my kind of woman, I thought. She had spirit, independence. She was about the same age I was, a Laguna Beach girl who had been around a lot: long legs, dyed blonde hair, fiery temper, great sense of humor. She snow skied, water skied, played tennis like a man, wrote the book on sexual tricks. Two things I really admired: she drove a classic, pure white MG-TC, ten years old but in absolutely mint condition; and she could drink me under the table. I'd never known a woman who could do that before. Flying for Pan Am, she had about one week off for every week on, which meant I could still play around while she was away, and settle back into keeping house with Dee when she was home. It seemed a perfect arrangement."

"She's the boy's mother, then?"

"I'm getting to that. After a couple of months of this, sleeping together when she was in town, Dee tells me she's pregnant. No big deal, ordinarily, though it was a first for me. Abortions weren't legal in those days, but they were still pretty easy to get. Everybody seemed to know a doctor somewhere who'd take care of it for four or five hundred bucks. Dee had already had two abortions herself, but she didn't tell me that till much later. Instead, she said she couldn't possibly do a thing like that to our own child, kill an unborn human being. Which was pure bullshit. She just wanted to get married and quit her job.

"One Friday we stayed at the bar at L'Ommie's after work arguing about this until closing time, then drove straight on up to Reno in her car and got married."

"You mean . . . you've been married before?"

"You guessed it."

"But why didn't you tell me? The priest wouldn't have . . . Timmy, our marriage may not even be legitimate in the eyes of the Church!"

"Let me finish my story.

"So we drove up to Reno and got married. I mean, why the hell not? All my brothers were married. All my old Air Force buddies. Most of my ex-roommates. Some of my Peninsula friends were already on marriage two, marriage three even. Marrying was just what you did, eventually. After ten or twelve years of it, some of the novelty starts wearing off of boozing and empty freedom and one-night stands. One time, I might have wanted a solid, sensible country girl like my brothers' wives; but I was much too far gone for that now. All things considered, Dee Ryan seemed about as good as I was likely to do.

309

"After this, the story gets bad. There's really no way to explain a marriage that goes totally wrong. There are some situations you get into that are so bad you think even dying couldn't be any worse. 'It was like hell,' is what we say. It's the constant burning of it, the incredible nonstop pain you insist on causing each other—and you're locked in, like people are in hell: there's no way to get out. You keep creating your own torture, day after day and night after night, until you need it, you feed on it: both the million and one mean little ways you dream up to hurt the other person, and the million and one ways she dreams up to hurt you.

"It's not the punching and biting and throwing things—though God knows it came to that, too, often enough. Twice we had to move because of neighbors' complaints, even before the last big mess. Once she had to go to the hospital to get her face sewn up. More times than I could remember, the cops had to come to shut us up, pull us apart, sometimes take whichever one of us was more obviously drunk, or had hold of the more dangerous weapon off for a night in jail. Some neighbor usually ended up taking the poor kid out crying in his sleeper or PJs to spend the night with them, away from this screaming, bloodthirsty pair of parents who seemed to get off on scenes like this.

"I *did* need it, after a while. I think I did. I mean why else would I have kept it up? So did she, really. It was like the other side of sex, some nights. I'd come home from work, she'd start bitching about some trivial thing, I'd make some nasty crack back, both of us would start drinking, dinner got forgotten, the kid got sent next door, louder, nastier, both of us digging up and raking over every selfish act of the other's, every dirty mistake we could remember, cutting closer and closer to bone. We could fight till we were black and blue inside if not outside, but then almost without knowing how it happened we'd be in bed or on the floor fucking, kissing instead of cursing, squeezing instead of scratching, and then we'd keep at *that* till we were totally wiped out, both of us. Only then could we go to sleep.

"Once we got going, we didn't have too far to search to come up with things to throw at each other. Dee had quit work as soon as we were married. She was fed up with the regulations and weird hours and long-haul lechers on Pan Am. But after she quit, all she had to fill up her days were things like watching TV and reading movie magazines, belting down gin, screwing up the poor kid's head trying to play mother according to Spock and Gesell, gossiping around the pool or out at lunch somewhere with the other shabby discontented wives in the place who were no better then she was, writing checks for twice my salary before the first goddamn week of a new month was over. She bought all kinds of useless shit for the apartment, new drapes, new appliances, a five-hundred-dollar piano neither one of us knew how to play, two hundred bucks worth of baby pictures from some door-to-door salesman, dumb prints for the walls, junk sculptures we had no room for, long dresses for parties we never got invited to, enough gigantic turquoise and silver Indian jewelry for some Navajo hag with a sixteen arms and eight necks.

"I got pissed, naturally, and tried to stop her checks, make her take stuff back. But that only drove her to spend more—she hated the idea that all the money was mine and not hers, but still she wouldn't go back to work—not that I wanted her to. We were always in this hopeless hole of debt, refinancing, begging from sleazy Finance Plan crooks, borrowing from my parents. After three years, some sharp lawyer in the apartment talked us into declaring bankruptcy, so we could move out and start spending all over again.

"We hadn't been married a year before both of us started sleeping around again—not so much because we needed or wanted to, I think, just to hurt each other as much as we could. I think I caved in first—just broke out one night in the middle of one of our usual ring-dings, walked over to an old girlfriend's place in the same apartment building and didn't come back till morning.

"Her response to that was something totally new. And it worked. She gave me the long, silent Freeze, and it broke me. Noise, insults, screaming, slaps, all that I could handle; I thrived on it. But the Freeze was too much. Finally I groveled, licked dirt, cried even, begged her forgiveness. She had her new weapon, her magic whip. And boy, did she use it.

"That didn't stop the slanging and slamming; we could both still get off anytime on that, just by some crack about her mishandling the boy, or her warning me about the third drink, or me asking about some new bill—or about *nothing*, even: the wrong brand of breakfast cereal! 'You know I hate Cheerios: who do you buy them for?' 'You never told me you hated them.' 'Yes I have. Millions of times.' 'You ate them happily enough two weeks ago.' 'I ate 'em, but not happily. I just thought you forgot again. And anyway those were Kix.' 'Kix my ass. Those were Cheerios.' 'Don't give me that. I know what I eat.' And so on, and so on, another whole day screwed.

"But after that first night away, whenever I hit her, or slept with someone else, or stayed out all night for whatever reason, she'd pull the icy Freeze, the death mask face: look right through me, pretend not to hear me, walk about the place like I didn't exist. Come nighttime, she'd either sleep on the couch, or lock me out of the bedroom; or if I really got belligerent, she'd take the kid and go and sleep over at a friend's. In those days, we still had some friends. Then only in her own sweet time would she decide when to admit I was still alive, allow me the privilege of begging her pardon and fixing the meals and doing all the household chores. Maybe a day or two later, she'd permit me the thrill of a little kiss on her dry, turned cheek, to which she'd reply "Mmm," and go on reading her magazine or watching TV. That was the sign that I could start pretending to be a human being again, and not a dog.

"She slept around some too, for a while. She never bothered to hide it. She told me what she was doing. But I didn't hide my other women, either. Both of us really only did it after a while to wound the other, so there wasn't much point to it unless we let the other know.

"That could get really nasty, too: comparing performances in bed can become a real hand-to-hand knife fight. The way some other chick looked versus the way you do, her tenderness, her tricks, his size, his stamina, a hundred ways of trying to rub someone else's nose in the mess of your own infidelity.

"After a while, though, she readjusted the terms of combat by giving up other men, except to talk to, to tell her side of their story to: she loved to do that. It was as if she realized that as long as she could pretend that she didn't *need* sex, that she could take it or leave it, she would have this terrific new power over me—because I obviously *did* need it. I had to have it. So I either had to get it from her, on her terms, when she felt like offering it—which left her on top. Or else rape her, or get tricked into believing I was raping her, and then be made to feel rotten about doing *that*. Or else go out and get it somewhere else—and then suffer the deep freeze for two or three days, play the cringing whipped little cur, the kid who wets his bed and then gets spanked and locked in a closet for doing it.

"It was no-win. It was hell, if the word means anything at all this side of the grave. And yet, goddamn: we held out for five fucking years.

"No, I'm not telling this story right. It wasn't all hell. It couldn't have been. There were still good times, quiet times, loving times even, though we hardly ever used the word. Good sex. In fact, it was better, sometimes, for all the aggravation, the yelling and red-hot hate that came before it. We got to know each other's bodies like, like . . . like a scientist gets to know every speck, every living cell of some minute organism he spends years dissecting and studying under his microscope. Every mole, every body hair, every fold and wrinkle, we memorized them, like U.S.G.S. topo maps, got to know just where each pressure point was, every hard bone edge, the ticklish spots, the curves where soft turned to hard, patterns of freckles, the crack in a nail. It was like exploring a whole world: you could spend a lifetime just getting to know well one other body.

"Out of bed, during cease-fires, we could share other good times. We bought a sailboat and went out together on the bay: that was good. We played tennis doubles, in tournaments even, and still skied every winter, leaving the kid with my folks on the way up to the mountains—although ski weeks and weekends often ended up with me getting drunk in the lodge after a race and trying to make it with some other woman, followed by the long drive home without either one talking for two hundred miles, that whole bit again.

"Little things still worked, sometimes. I'd do her Sunday breakfast in bed, or we'd drive out to San Gregorio and pitch rocks into the surf. Presents. Presents got double-edged, though. We kept trying to make up for some nasty scene by buying each other some expensive thing, a watch for her, a leather jacket for me, stuff we couldn't afford, which just sucked us back into the well of debt and tenseness and blame all over again.

"It was really pathetic. After a few years, the biggest gestures of loving-ness, of being nice we ever risked—giant investments designed to please the other, in the hope of rubbing out the past and starting over again happy—every fucking one ended up a dud. A fiasco. I arranged this huge expensive surprise birthday party for her on a chartered yacht in Sausalito. Half the guests didn't show. The other half got either seasick or nasty-drunk. Then it rained, and big waves came up. We took all day getting back to port. We ended up totally miserable. There were big dream Second Honeymoon proj-ects like a cruise to Acapulco one year, a weekend at Vegas; but something always happened to poison it, ruin it, make life worse afterwards than it had been before, because now we also had to live with the memory of one more giant effort gone sour, until even the efforts began to look as desperate as they

312

were—hopeless, last-ditch attempts to pretend we could still be happy together. Once, after a three-*week* Freeze, a record, which I earned by taking off to L.A. for three days with another guy's wife, I decided I had to make some really super gesture to bring us back together. So I went another four thousand bucks into debt and bought her a new Triumph TR-2—we had had to sell her precious MG to the lawyer-friend when we declared bankruptcy. And she *was* pleased. She said so, and she showed it. But of course it turned out to be a lemon, stalled on the highway, refused to start in the mornings, spent half of its life in the shop. It was all paid for under warranty, of course, but the whole point of the big gesture was wrecked. All I did was prove myself an irresponsible, childish ass once again, at a cost of four thousand bucks.

"After that, she decided she hated being dependent on me financially, and told everybody that I was responsible for her quitting the job she had hated all along, and half-married me to get free of. She spent two months doing the employment agency bit, dumping the kid wherever she could, and ended up getting a rotten-pay receptionist's job at an office of manufacturers' reps on Page Mill Road, because the boss liked her body and wanted to make her. Which he did. That really helped a lot.

"When we got moaning about our lot to our separate friends, both of us used to say we were only staying together for the sake of the boy, which was a lie. We stayed together because we were sick. We needed this kind of a hell to live in. We hated it, but we needed it. We flourished in it.

"We sure weren't doing the kid any good, staying together. If he stayed sane at all, it was thanks to his grandparents, not to us. We used him, used him as one more weapon to try to bash each other's skull with, blamed each other over and over for the rotten way he was turning out.

"He was really a mess. Everything he did he did later than all the books said he should. He didn't talk till months after every other kid we knew, and then he mushed up his words like a retard. Dee would scream and scream at him about wetting, spank him, send him to bed, take away toys, make him wear a diaper over his pants in public to embarrass him, but none of it did any good. Goddamn, he was always stumbling around like a clown with this big wet stain in his pants, at four, five years old, always another pile of urine-soaked sheets in the bathtub. She couldn't send him to nursery school, even, since he was the only five-year-old in the neighborhood who wasn't potty-trained. He broke every toy he ever had that he liked, and never learned to tie his shoes, or drink without spilling. He fell off everything. God, did he cry: nonstop, it sometimes seemed. Night after night, he'd wake up screaming bloody murder from some nightmare, the same one every time, except he could never describe it after he woke up. We ended up leaving all the lights in his room blazing away all night long to keep away the monsters.

"You try to be sympathetic about that kind of thing, but in the end you just crack, some nights, and give the little bastard a whack for wrecking your sleep, or worse: you torment him on purpose to get even—take away his teddy, turn out the lights, lock his door, until he's choking in hysterical terror, banging on the other side of the door, sobbing out 'Mommy! Daddy!' like a gibbering idiot. And then where were you?

"He was a cute kid. Well; he would have been a cute kid, with any other parents. He was thin, short, puny-looking, which was odd considering how tall and strong both of us were. But then he'd been a very picky eater ever since he was born. Freckled, redheaded: great little smile, when he smiled. He tried to make friends with other kids, mostly kids younger than he was, but never had much luck. They usually ended up sharing his toys but not sharing theirs, or ganging up on him the way kids do, and then he'd cry, and wet his pants. He was such a baby, always, scared, bed-wetting, talking his mushy baby talk with half the consonants wrong.

"One place he was happy: up at his grandma and grandpa's house in the country. We got to leaving him there lots on weekends, whole weeks, a month or more more in the summer, so we could take off skiing or sailing, or just to get the little brat out of the house and off of our consciences. My folks disapproved like thunder of Dee, although they never said anything in front of her. But she wasn't their kind of person at all, a woman drinking and smoking and cursing like that, no fit wife for their son, no fit mother for their grandson. In fact, they didn't think too much of their own son anymore, either, from what they could tell of the life I led down in the Bay Area. But they'd still take me in when I drove up some days to get clear of Dee, to try to clear Peninsula living out of my head for a day or two, and sit around the porch talking old times.

"The old farmhouse mattered a lot to me, the idea of it, at least. I held on to it like a rock through all five years of that miserable marriage.

"The little boy, though, the two old folks loved like crazy. They adored him. They had seven other grandchildren, healthy normal kids all of them, but this little runt was their favorite, and they gave him the run of the farm when he came up to stay. Up there, only up there, he smiled a lot, he talked more clearly. He stopped wetting. He slept through the night.

"We wanted to love him, the way his grandparents did. But damn, he was hard to love. We both felt so strong, so independent, so proud of our strength. It was just plain embarrassing, sometimes, to have this sniveling, stuttering loser for a kid. At our worst, we'd take out our own griefs on him, as if he were the one responsible for our hell of a marriage. And in a way, of course, he was.

"That's . . . that's how it all came to an end.

"We were living in another of those plastic apartments—we never did get a house—another of the palm tree-balcony-swimming pool jobs, fourth or fifth one in five years. We had damn few friends left by now, except some divorced rejects and a few couples as far gone as we were. It happened about two, three o'clock in the morning. The usual. Both of us drunk, mud-slinging back and forth, over and over, God knows about what. She makes some crack, I'm not gonna take *that*. I call her a filthy cunt or something equally sweet, she slaps my face hard, I hit her back, knock her down, start kicking her between the legs, she screams and crawls over by the sliding glass doors, neighbors hear her and start bellowing at us to shut up; I keep her down, keep kicking her, yell at the neighbors to mind their own fucking business. Then there's this kid pulling at my leg, this idiot midget in his wet pajamas blubbering over and over, 'You leave my mommy alone, you leave my mommy alone,' and that does it: no dumb little bed-wetting kid is going to blame *me* when it's all her fault, take this bitch's part against his own father. I shake him off my leg and give the boy an almighty swat. And the skinny little kid in his Snoopy pajamas runs screaming out the door onto the patio. Except the door's closed. He crashes right through the glass.

"God looks out for some people, I guess. Not us, but some people. Like little kids. We hear this awful noise of the glass, cracking in huge pieces, crashing down in splinters. Then one scream. Just one, and an evil thud. And then nothing.

"We run outside, and he's lying on the patio with his teddy, his face cut up, blood and glass all over the place: passed out, but he's still breathing. Neighbors are running out of their apartments. I call an ambulance pronto, and Dee holds the boy's body in her arms, there on the patio, until it comes. She won't let me touch him, won't speak one word to me. In fact, that swat was the last time I ever touched my own son.

"Well. They stitched up the cuts in Emergency, kept him in the hospital for about a week. Mild concussion. Nothing broken. No permanent damage, they said.

"Which is more than you can say for his parents. A lot of neighbors had heard and seen the whole thing, neighbors who hated us already by that time. Police came, there was a court hearing, testimony from all these enemies around the pool who had put up with our fights night after night, taken care of the kid when we were past caring. With the help of the same lawyer who got us into bankruptcy, we were able to persuade doctors and a judge that the whole thing was an accident.

"Which it was, when you think about it. It was nobody's fault. It's just that it's hard to convince yourself of that afterwards, seeing your kid in a hospital bed with all these bandages on his face.

"But so much had come out at the hearing about our run-of-the-mill violence, our unfitness as parents, that the judge ordered the county welfare people to remove the boy from our control. My parents had come down from the country as soon as they heard of the accident, booked into a little motel in Menlo Park and stayed with the kid at the hospital each day until he was released; then sat out the hearings after. On their own petition, the boy was turned over to their custody.

"The day the judge issued the order, my dad sent my mom ahead to their truck with the boy, and stopped me in the courthouse lobby. He told me that he was ashamed before heaven, those were his very words, to have a son who could do to his own child what I had done to Patrick. He had never heard of anything so sinful and wicked. From this day on, he said, he never wanted to see me or speak to me again, and he wanted me to keep completely away from the boy. He was going to ask my three brothers not to see or speak to me, either. He looked me straight in the eye as he said this, then left me there and walked out to the truck.

"The old man kept his word. That was the last time, there in the lobby, I ever saw or heard from my own father. My mother was too soft-hearted, too traditional an Italian mama still for a total break like that. She kept making me secret little phone calls from time to time, wrote me sad little notes without return addresses on the envelopes, notes filled with stories about how the boy was doing, little bits of family chat.

"The accident, the hearings, the talk all around the neighborhood and at work—it got to be too much. With the boy gone, it all finally fell apart. We tried to hang on together for a while at a new place in Sunnyvale, but it was no go. Within two months, we were divorced. Within three months, I had quit my job, cut every remaining tie—there weren't very many—sold or stored or gave away almost everything I owned, and moved to the other side of the country."

"To Boston."

"To Boston."

Neither one said anything else the rest of the night. There was nothing else to say. After a long, long wait, as both Timmy and Audrey tried to take the measure of all they now knew for the first time, she lay her head down in his lap, one arm resting on his thigh. Timmy stretched down in the seat, until he could rest his head back against it, and held her right hand in his left hand, trailed his right fingers softly through her dusty hair, across her sunburned cheek, let them come to rest against her shoulder.

They fell asleep, finally. But before they did, Audrey made one last grand effort to send out her soul in search of God.

The sky over Black Rock Desert turned blue black, deeper blue-black. A crescent moon cast strange dim shadows, shadows of sand dunes, sagebrush, outcroppings of rock, a half-buried sedan; then sank in the sky to the east. As it moved, so did the stars sprinkled over the sky; as it descended, they paled away, and the sky grew by infinitesimal degrees less black, a cool smoky gray, a first hint of blue, then rose. The two figures in the sedan lay fixed like plaster models, head against car seat, other head nestled in lap, exactly where they had fallen under the rising moon.

By full morning light, they still had not moved. Only when the car door opened did the man's head twitch, his eyelids lift.

"You people okay?"

Timmy stared unbelieving, uncomprehending, at the wrinkled face. Audrey's head still lay unmoving, a dead weight in his lap.

"I said. You people okay?"

"No. No. I mean, we . . . we broke down here. Our car. A week ago. Engine. Engine seized up. Food . . . all gone. No water. I couldn't find a road."

"Ain't none. I thought you were goners. Scared me when you moved like that. Wouldn't be the first ones."

With a start, Timmy grew aware of the silent weight in his lap. He shook it, slapped it, called its name:

"Audrey! Audrey wake up. It's okay. There's someone here."

She didn't wake up at first; she couldn't. The spark of life was so far, far

316

away from the world inside the car. But she kept breathing, as the slow battle to break through into consciousness went silently on. Finally, it cracked through the thick wall into light, daytime, the world we call real.

"I got a four-wheel truck here," the old man was saying. "I can take you back to Alturas. That's where I'm headed. Looks like you both could do with somethin' to eat and drink first. I'll see what I've got. Then I can get you to a doc in Alturas. Send someone back to tow in this heap."

"Thanks."

"No trouble. Makes my week, finding somethin' like this. 'Cept I thought you were dead. You looked dead, from outside."

Audrey was beginning to take in the dimensions of the miracle, but her limbs, everything below her eyes was still without feeling or strength.

"I'm kind of a desert rat myself," the old man explained, as he helped Timmy carry her into his truck. "Got a shack out on the reservation, Summit Lake. 'Bout forty miles east. That's where I grew up, Summit Lake. Half-Indian, my mother's side. I sort of prospect out here now, fool around, run things back and forth to Cedarville and Alturas for the Indians. Know this desert like my own hand. You'd be surprised how many folks break down, run off the road out here, like you two. Wheels won't turn, engine seizes, folks panic, run around in circles, wear themselves out. Dehydrate, drop. Seen more than a few dead out here, in my times. Coulda swore you were two more."

Moving slowly, still in a kind of dream, Timmy helped the old man load the remnants of their belongings onto the truck. Cheery old soul. Audrey listened to their talk through a heavy haze.

"That's three sleeping bags, I make out. For just two folks?"

"Oh," said Timmy. "Yeah. One's an extra. That dirty one. We just had it for, for the cold."

"The cold. Only the two of you, then?"

"Only the two. This was supposed to be our honeymoon."

"No kiddin'."

In the bull's-eye of a fever dream, Audrey saw him for one last time, fallen face downward somewhere in the sand, fallen as he dragged his feet up one last dune. The hitchhiker. The same patient hawk wheeled beneath a white circle of sun, waiting for him to die. Pretending that Norman never existed became one of the great bonds between them, in the long and difficult game that lay ahead.

35

September 4, 1849

Lord, have mercy on us.

The desert we tried so hard to avoid could not have been worse than the desert we have just crossed. We have lost four of our oxen, while adding to our burdens the care and feeding of two elderly people—an act of charity no Christian could have refused. I have been to the edge, and looked into the abyss. I know what it is like to resign oneself to death, certain that it is imminent. I have even prayed for the *release* of death, though such a prayer may be sacrilegious, a sin, a will to suicide.

We journeyed fifteen miles before we found the first thin spring, then twenty more miles to the next. During all this time we passed not a single spear of grass. The trail was lined with dead oxen, repulsive to smell and frightening to contemplate. With each passing mile, I felt certain that ours were soon to join them.

No one had described to us the true deprivation and horrors of this boasted-of cut. The heat was murderous. Altogether the experience came very close to what I imagined the Great Salt Desert to be, even to the white crust on the plain, and the mirages of tree-fringed lakes that dissolved as one drew near. Walking on, slowly and with effort, one encountered many animals perishing for want of food and water on the plain. Some were gasping. Others, unable to stand, issued low moans as we came up, in a most distressing manner. Still others, unable to walk, seemed to brace themselves on their legs to keep from falling. Here and there a poor ox or horse would stagger towards us, emitting a weak growl or rattle, as if begging for water.

We tried to sleep at Rabbit Springs, but the stench and low moans were appalling. The next day offered more of the same. We traveled almost thirty

318

miles to a miserable trickle of water, hot, unpleasant water surrounded by dead and half-dead animals, and abandoned wagon wrecks. Scores of wretched travelers fought over a few threads of grass. Some of the basins were stopped up by dead animals who had fallen into them, and whose hind quarters and rear legs projected from the holes. Evil hawks hover over us constantly, and settle in black possession on the carcasses of the dead. For thirty hours many of these beasts have had to march without food or water (those whose masters failed to make hay and fill kegs at the meadow). This is the cause of all these swollen cadavers.

It was on this day's march that the first of our own oxen gave out. He seemed, after he fell, to look back at us over his shoulders, asking for release from suffering and slow death. Weeping for old Tom, I could only nod when James offered to shoot him in the head, to spare him the final agonies, and whatever an animal feels of despair. I turned my back. At the blast, I felt as if I had been shot myself.

It was at this hot spring that we came upon an aged and emaciated pair from Rhode Island, whose two oxen had failed, and who were trapped in the middle of the desert, unable to move forward or back. It took no great persuasion for us to offer them protection. They bring with them a decent supply of flour, and an iron box of money. So now we are six, with five oxen and Henry Williams's horse.

Unfortunately, our new companions can do little to lift our spirits or expectations. Old Mr. Bissell seems as near to death himself as his oxen were a day ago. He breathes with great difficulty. His wife sits with him in the wagon, moaning more in self-pity, I believe, than in sympathy. She is anxious of what is to become of her when her husband passes on, and fearful of the gold in his box.

For several miles before the hot spring, men and animals alike collapsed, unable to complete the dry march. Some were saved by returning companions, who filled kegs and canteens at the spring and went back to their aid. A Captain Bayley of Wisconsin made two trips on foot with pails of water, each day for two days, in an attempt to revive his cattle, collapsed four miles out in the desert.

At least four men died while waiting thus for help. Before now we had seen the graves of many for whom this expedition proved fatal—victims of cholera, dysentery, fevers, gunshot wounds purposeful and accidental. But these are the first we have seen who have been destroyed by the rigors of travel itself: by thirst, exposure, and exhaustion.

The next day's drive was shorter, but we traveled again on burning sand, under a scorching sun, watching our oxen fail. Instead of avoiding the awful desert of the Mary's, and finding (as we were promised) water, grass, and a better road, we were in fact upon a more dreary and a wider waste, without the least trace of grass or water, inveigled into this purgatory by lying or foolish reports. But how were any of us to know?

Today, in order to effect our escape from the Black Rock Desert, we were obliged to travel over rugged mountains, down sideling slides of loose stones, and between narrow defiles. Many animals driven to exhaustion by the desert crossing succumbed to the strain. Their dead and dying bodies line the trail.

As the sun set this evening, we descended into a valley richly clothed with grass. We are camped here with the others with whom we have shared the miseries of the last four days, deluded like us onto this diabolical route. Although this appears to mark the end of the worst desert, the hills ahead look as barren as the plains behind.

Instead of escaping a 45-mile stretch of sand, as we had fondly anticipated when we left the Mary's, we have actually crossed the Black Rock Desert where it is nearly 100 miles broad. All curse the hour in which we were first tempted to quit the main trail, and the lying men who induced us to do it. We are told by new-comers to camp that many wagons returned to the old route after driving to the first spring of the Black Rock Desert, convinced that the sand plains west of the Sink could not possibly be as dreadful as these. I believe they were right.

Even after drinking, my mouth remains dry. Even after resting, my body aches. I feel that my soul has shriveled into something hard and small.

September 9, 1849

You think that you have touched the bottom of suffering and grief. But then there is worse.

For a few days, our journeys, however difficult, led us by each noon rest and each sunset to grass and water. We rode past and over masses of rock glazed and fused as if by the heat of a furnace. There were dry stretches enough, but also wild black cherries, nectarines, and tall shading pines. The trail followed dry gulches and gullies carved in the sand by winter storms. There were rattlesnakes under the sage. An eastbound Oregon party told us that a feasible wagon road had been opened last season from Goose Lake, which is just over the mountains, down to the Feather River diggings, a distance of not more than 100 miles. There is, we were told, good grass and water all the way. I said a prayer of thanksgiving. One hundred miles more seemed so little, after all we have been through.

But today we discovered, nailed to a tree in a meadow at the foot of the trail up the Sierra Nevada, a clearly painted placard written by a U.S. Army lieutenant for the direction of emigrants on this route. It informs us for the first time of the *actual* distance that remains to be traveled. We now learn, from Lieutenant Williams' placard, that it is 248 miles from here to Lassen's Rancho—the first settlement in the Sacramento Valley; 288 miles to the nearest diggings; and 403 miles to Sutter's!

We have been living in a dream. We have made the most atrocious mistake, and may pay for it with our lives. Only yesterday, men were talking of shouldering packs and striking directly across the mountains to the mines, supposing the Feather River diggings to be no more than 50 miles away. They would have died of starvation had they done so—and so may we all yet. We have at least another three weeks' travel ahead, and food for less than half of ınat! We lost a second ox last night to thieves. The boys endeavored to track the culprits—the ropes were clearly cut by hand—but without success.

All along, James was under the impression that we were moving directly towards the Sacramento River Valley by means of a trail described by Captain Frémont, which passes by Pyramid Lake. Now this seems not to be the case.

I must admit to having been seduced by what appeared to be favorable omens. The sight of our first trees in many weeks, near the salt-encrusted expanse of Mud Lake, was a cheering treat after so much desert. At about the same time, we caught our first glimpse of the bold but unthreatening line of the northern Sierra. Even old Mr. Bissell improved somewhat, although he was still unable to walk, which added to our animal's burden.

He has a miser's fixation to his strong-box, which he will not let out of his hands. So it is unlikely we shall be able to purchase additional food, unless James decides to obtain the money by force, which he is loathe to do. Mrs. B. has taken to unburdening herself to me of the complaints of a lifetime. She is one of those bitter and selfish old souls to whom nothing but evil has ever occurred, one who sours the lives of all she meets by her accounts of what she sees as the world's concerted campaign to thwart her sacred will. She does nothing but whine against others and recriminate against fate. My reserves of charity and good nature are quite used up.

248 more miles!

September 18, 1849

Mr. Bissell has died, and our last oxen have given up. There was nothing we could do to save either.

The ascent of the mountains was rocky and in some places steep, but less strenuous than many we have already climbed, and far easier than my timid fancy had depicted it. It took us past good springs and creeks, and pine trees 200 feet tall. Even so, and although many wagons crossed the pass with no difficulty, the strain of the final pull was too much for two of our last four animals, Arthur and Old Will, who simply sat down in the trail, unable to go further. When no coaxing or prodding had the least effect, James unyoked the pair, and shot each once through the skull. Their eyes remained wide. "What have you done to us?" they seemed to be asking. Then their heads fell slowly down, eyes still staring in death. Poor old friends!

As we were almost to the summit when this tragedy occurred, we were able to persuade a neighbor to lend us two additional yoke to pull our wagon over, then continued down the west side with our single remaining pair. In other circumstances, I might have been aroused to pleasant or romantic reflections by this, our first sight of the fabled land of Gold. It is a broad green valley enclosed by high pine mountains. In the near distance lie the broad blue waters of Goose Lake.

At the summit, I looked back on the eastern slope. In the center of a broad sandy road were men urging their heavy trains up the hill with lashes and imprecations, some riding up on horses and mules, amidst clouds of blinding dust. One old man rode up on a wasted horse. A mattress covered the horse. The sick man rode astride, but fallen over on his breast, with a coverlet thrown over him, a corner trailing in the dust. He had his arms around the neck of the old horse. Another unfortunate followed him, riding on a mule and enveloped in a blue blanket, barely able to retain his seat. Small boys led tired animals up the hill. I saw women occupied at chocking wheels all up the ascent, while the oxen were permitted to blow. One man had a baby in his arms, and in the midst of thick dust kept urging on his team. Some wagons were drawn by as many as twelve yoke of oxen. One wagon, with women and children in it, became uncoupled near the summit, and ran downhill stern foremost with great rapidity. The women screamed. Fortunately, it was brought up against a dead ox just ahead of a heavy team, with no great damage.

By this time Mr. Bissell, who could no longer even stand erect, was coughing horribly in the wagon, and spitting blood. His wife became as if deranged, slapped him in the face and shouted at him to silence his ghastly noises, fearful that James would cast them off.

She had more reason to fear the cruelty of fate than any hardness of heart in dear James. That night, her husband coughed and gasped his way to what we are told is a better world, victim to his own illusions at the age of 83. When James went to dig the grave this morning, he found that one of our two remaining oxen had been shot full of arrows in the night. There was no longer any hope of pulling the wagon. After burying the old man's body, we salvaged from the wagon what little we could carry on our backs, or pack on the one remaining ox and on Henry Williams' horse. Then we bade farewell to our rolling house of the past five months, and left it to rot alongside the road with so many others.

Mrs. Bissell insisted she could not possibly continue on foot, so we persuaded a slightly stronger wagon party from West Virginia to give her board and room and carriage to Lassen's Ranch. For her fare, she dared to unlock her late husband's sacred strong box, and paid the Virginians twenty dollars in gold. She then entrusted the box into James's care, afraid she would only be robbed if she kept it herself. He has promised to return it to her locked and intact in the settlements.

We learned next day that Goose Lake, which had appeared a tranquil sheet of azure from the mountain top, was far less attractive nearer to hand. The beach was a perfect quagmire, which made it impossible for us to get down to the mineral-encrusted shore. Those who managed to reach it, by laying down boards and branches, brought back water nauseating to drink, full of soda and salt.

The California landscape is blessed with pine and fir and spruce, and a variety of mountain shrub. The underbrush is made up mainly of laurel bushes and what the Californians call manzanita, that is "little apple," an evergreen plant with small dark green leaves, a crooked stalk, dark red branches, and bitter black berries.

Another day brought us to a little brook that grew rapidly into a river, from which the men were able to seine out quantities of silver trout.

322

It was noon the next day, along this river, that our last ox gave up and died. This forced us further to reduce our stock of worldly goods. I could scarce carry myself any longer, let alone a pack on my back. James estimates that we can eat for another week, if we limit ourselves to two servings of water thickened with a little pine-nut flour each day. We have totally exhausted our store of all other provisions. The trail is now crowded with weak men and women like ourselves whose oxen or mules have died, and who are struggling forward on foot in a desperate effort to get through.

Much as we dread losing their support and companionship, it was judged prudent for the boys to go ahead with their one horse to Lassen's, to see what provisions could be begged or borrowed there, and return with them to us, along with whatever certain news they can find of the nearest mines. We bade them a terse farewell, and watched them move on out of sight. At the place where we separated, one could look across many miles to the west, to where the cone of Tschastes' Butte rises on the edge of a green horizon. To the south, a similar elevation designates the peak listed in the book as St. Joseph's. Below us, the sparkling river wound its way onward to the great mountain, willow-fringed, a scene at once peaceable and grand, but ill-fitted to our destitute condition.

We talk very little. There is, in fact, little conversation among any of us, fixed as all hearts and minds now are on a single goal—to reach the settlements before every last scrap of food is gone. "How much farther do you think it is to Lassen's?" "Do you think he's got provisions for sale?" "How much do you think he charges?" That is the extent of trail conversation between strangers.

James told me I behaved quite hysterically the morning Mr. Bissell was buried, the same morning we discovered the murdered ox. I have no recollection of this, but can well believe it true. Oftimes I feel myself on the brink of some irrational abandon, as if my very faculty for self-control were eaten away by hunger and fatigue, and all the demons of despair had moved into me body and soul. At such times, it requires a conscious effort of will to perform the simplest tasks correctly, to speak sensibly and to some point; above all, to continue moving steadily on. One feels such a terrific impulse to stop, and go no more.

More and more I find myself clinging to James, both mentally and physically, despairing of my inability to pray or think clearly. We must now lie on the cold hard ground at night, without a tent. Our blankets glisten with frost, and I grapple myself to James like a sick, frightened child clutching its mother, sure that every noise I hear is a bear, and Indian, a marauding emigrant crazed by starvation. Around us are more families with women and children than I have seen throughout this journey. It is as if the trials of this last and most difficult ordeal left the weakest to the rear. Many are utterly lost, without team or wagon. Small children in rags beg and drag their way along, aging in days into little old people. For all my longing for a child, I thank God I have not one to answer for here on the trail. I thank God also that my family in Vermont need never know the state to which we have been reduced. If we are spared, never will I tell them of these days.

We passed a grave marked, "Here lies Mr. Easton of Stourbridge, Conn., killed Sept. 17 by an Indian arrow." Into the mound of earth was planted the feathered stick itself, to which a second card had been attached reading, "Here is the fatal arrow."

Lassen's Rancho
October 2, 1849

Four days from this place, and on the edge of collapse, we were met by the first relief train sent out from Sutter's to provide succor for starving emigrants on the route. Their aid is destined, of course, for the truly desperate, who are still hundreds of miles behind us, and who now run the risk of traveling unprepared into the first winter snows. But we were totally without food, as Henry and Hector had never returned. The military men acknowledged our need, and (on my petitioning) handed over to us 20 pounds of crackers and a large piece of pork. This alone has seen us through; this and the hand of God. It continues to serve as our entire larder here in what passes for civilization, since we cannot afford to purchase anything at Mr. Lassen's prices, and have nothing left to trade. He sells salt at 75 cents a pound, flour and sugar at 50, doubtful pork for a dollar, cheese and butter for two. Blessed are the rich in purse, for they shall be fed. It wounds me to have to live as a beggar, surviving off the charity of others. But it can only be good for the soul to know abasement, as Our Lord did before his crucifixion and earthly death, spat upon and insulted, tormented by men.

The will to assist a neighbor in need persisted, I am pleased to say, among many of the emigrants—primarily among those as destitute of provisions as ourselves. Men who did find themselves with surplus goods were not giving them away, but selling them at prices even higher than Mr. Lassen's—which was no good to us whatsoever. Although James holds fast to Mr. Bissell's strong-box, he refuses to open it as long as any hope remains of our finding his widow in the settlements. We have heard no word of either her or her West Virginia protectors since we arrived.

One cannot view the smoke rising from the chimneys of these small dwellings, surrounded by ragged emigrants, bony beasts, and naked Indians, without considerable confusion of emotions. This is the "estate" of the Danish pioneer and merchant who is responsible for so wickedly deceiving thousands of emigrants. Although we are now dependent on his stores, and at the mercy of his charges, his name is accursed by almost all. There are those who would hang him if they could. "110 miles to the diggings," read his lying advertisement at the Meadows. In fact, we have all journeyed more than 400 miles since then, equipped with scarce sufficient provision for 110.

There is no place in these notes for false shame. I have survived on the flesh of dead mules and ox carrion. I have lived like a dying mule myself, like an Indian dog. Never have I craved flesh so much as when we had none— although the meat of a poor ox who has staggered to his own death after 2,500 miles on the march is totally devoid of fat, and as dry and hard as a bone. I have been reduced to brazen beggary in my rags and my filth. He who exalteth himself shall be humbled, and he who humbleth himself shall be exalted, saith the Lord. The hills along the Feather River and since have abounded with game, but James lost his rifle to the same Indian thieves who stole our ox along the Pit River, and was forced to kill what he could with a Bowie knife. There are grapes and gooseberries to be had for the picking, which I believe helps to ward off disease. As large and fearsome bears were seen along the mountain trails, the lack of a gun was a serious matter.

Even had our poor animals and wagon survived to these last days and miles, we would have had to abandon them before now. Between leaving the Pit River and first sighting the Feather, we traveled 12 miles without water, 14 without grass. It was here we saw our first oak trees, a poignant image of domesticity. Like the sight of drying laundry and the wistful sound of cowbells, they quite brought tears to my eyes.

The descent from the Feather River junction is so rugged, so continually steep—it descends full 5,000 feet in 40 miles—that human pedestrians were hard put to manage, oxen and mules had to be unyoked, and what wagons were left had to be let down by hand—an adventure that would have been quite beyond our strength, without the aid of Henry and Hector.

We found the boys again this day. After trading for some groceries, they had been (they say) on the trail three days without finding us, and so returned here to wait. They argue for breaking into Mr. Bissell's legacy, so that we may buy new animals and head at once for the Yuba River diggings, of which such great stories are told. James is weakening in his resolve to keep the strong-box intact. Already we have seen, in the branches of a creek here, stupendous outcroppings of black slate and white quartz, which are said to be sure signs that we have reached Eldorado. Despite our fatigue, and my sense of having walked the very precipice of mortality, it is good to know that we are at last in the valley of the Sacramento, within a hand's reach of the goal of all our labors.

36

The earth does not always welcome civilized men. The trail guides and the mountain men, the French traders with their Indian wives were a reversion to pre-civilized norms, not a model the emigrants could follow. For a few months, many of the emigrants themselves reverted to pre-civilized norms, despite the brass bedsteads in their wagons, the five-dollar gold pieces, the frontier courts, the Christian crosses staked along the trail. Around their tiny oases—Kearny, Laramie, Bridger, Great Salt Lake City—roared an alien emptiness that could have killed them all if it had wanted to, laid their bodies to dry, rolled flat the skin and bones, blown the motes of their dust indistinguishably into its own.

There are many ways to destroy If you choose not to destroy, you can still hurt so badly that life from then on will fester from the wound. You can twist soft inner places into such a permanent state of derangement that they will wince with pain whenever they are touched. You can brand images out of nightmare on to the moist tissues of the brain, never to wear away, like concentration camp numbers burned onto the skin of a breast. You can pinch off nerves in such a way that certain areas of feeling will never return.

On August 31, 1859, three white men disguised as Indians intercepted a party of nineteen Iowa emigrants on the Lander Cutoff, twenty-five miles west of Fort Hall. After conversing pleasantly with the travelers, they suddenly ordered an attack from both sides of the trail, in which twenty unknown persons took part. Eight of the emigrants were killed, scalped, and butchered. One five-year-old girl had her ears cut off, her eyes gouged out, and both legs cut off at the knee. The three men, who were never apprehended, forced the little girl to walk on her severed stumps until she died.

Some historians say that the survivors who came out healthiest and prospered best in the West were those who had learned the life of the savages, red-skinned and white, and adopted most wholeheartedly their hard and brutal ways. In their mines and saloons, then in their general stores, later in their offices and banks, they spat into their brass cuspidors generation after generation, disdaining the effete scruples of Europe and the East. They were proud of their western rawness, their trail wisdom, their profitable mastery of savage mountain ways.

Others were more visibly marked. Unlike the little girl on the Lander Cutoff, they survived; but they did not prosper. At the desolate crossroads and Main Streets of northeastern California, Audrey saw both kinds of people. She saw some of the barbarians, tanned, strapping, and spitting, dressed (as Timmy was dressed) in T-shirts and bluejeans, with brown arms and faces, and a long loping stride just like his.

But others she saw seemed, a century after the fact, still to be worn out from their four months' journey west. It obviously wasn't cholera, or scurvy, or mountain fever they were sufffering from, though there may have been something of dysentery or dehydration in their systems: they did look, these weaker Californians, as if they needed more juice, and had trouble with their bowels.

On roads that were nothing but nineteenth-century trails, paved and widened, they drove past isolated shacks and tin trailers baking slowly to death: shacks and trailers surrounded, like the Gleasons' house in Wyoming, by mechanical debris. It was as if the owners had set to raising junk instead of cattle or crops. Audrey found these lone dwellings infinitely sad. She couldn't imagine why or how anyone would live in such places. When the inhabitant was not visible, she imagined him as some pariah, some unspeakable leper exiled from civilization to eat out his heart in this weather-paled prison in the desert.

When she did see the inhabitants it was worse. Shambling, fat old men, as decrepit as the wheelless rusting wrecks out front, would open their screen doors and wave as they passed. Timmy waved cheerily back, but Audrey wanted to cry, and get away, and forget she had ever seen them, sad, subhuman, crazy people who had no place in civilization. There were old women, too, and young men with long beards that flopped over thin chests. A batch of cross-eyed children in bib-overalls stared at them from the back of a broken and motionless truck.

Timmy could hunker down to pass the time of day with the bovine geezers in too-big khaki pants and red baseball caps who sat out on the high sidewalks in front of stores; or, just as easily, joke with the tow-headed boys who hung around one-pump gas stations, doing nothing. He had been one of them himself. When they stopped for gas in Chilcoot, California, Audrey watched a girl her own age, wasted about the eyes, dressed in tight, thin clothes of bright colors, hauling laundry out of a big battered car parked in front of a laundromat. The girl sat drinking cans of Coke and reading comic books in the shade of the covered sidewalk, as she waited for her laundry to get done. In the grocery-general store near Honey Lake, or non-lake, an ancient female,

327

bent over double like an inverted letter L, shuffled around the aisles in slippers stealing cans of cat food, followed by a trail of scaggy cats. The locals either ignored her, or smiled at this genuine village idiot.

The Modoc County Medical center is located in a one-story ranch-style building on the south edge of Alturas. Walls of flagstone and rose-colored plaster support a low-sloped, wide overhanging roof. Leaving the center in your rented car, you drive a hundred shady yards to the Main Street of Alturas. On your left, at the intersection, stands the local office of the California Highway Patrol. As you turn right, out of town, Main Street becomes U.S. 395; the speed limit ends. Across the street, Southern Pacific's Engine 2781 rests immobile, fixed to a length of track in the city park.

U.S. 395 runs down the whole eastern edge of California, from the Oregon border to San Bernardino. It ventures briefly into what passes for urban civilization in Nevada (Reno, Carson City), but generally keeps to the California hinterlands—broad, unpopulated desert and farmland a mile or more above sea level—and clings to the eastern side of the Sierra Nevada ridge. South of Alturas, the road surface is reddish colored and divided by yellow dots, bordered by shoulders of high grass. To the left are level miles of sagebrush and sand, indistinguishable from Nevada's. To the right lie green farms and comfortable ranches. High leafy trees mark the homesites. This far north, the Sierra crest is no more than a low ripple of dark highland to the West. More impressive are the Warner Mountains to the east, where George McCue and his boys used to go fishing. Beyond them (as we know) stretch miles of empty desert.

This is not California at its most original and appealing. The tableland cut by U.S. 395 is as wide-open and untraveled as any other piece of the uncrowded far West: high, monotonous, and flat. Shabby general stores at intersections punctuated the gray sage and green fields every ten or twenty miles. Trailer homes, dry-bed lakes; telephone poles and low hills that run on and on. All clouds fled from the sky, leaving it that blank sun-washed powdery blue color that signifies "California."

They crossed into Lassen County, climbed to Sage Hen Summit. Now there were evergreens: the sage-pocked hills were spiked with ten-foot spruce. They realized how long it had been since they had seen so many trees, seen any trees at all, and loved them for being there. Birds played like butterflies, in pairs, across the road. Past the wide, flat Tule Lake Reservoir, they continued to Madeline, a two-gas-station crossroads. The first sheep ranch— signs of a more gentle land. Then 14 miles to Termo, a one-pump Shell, a disused railroad station, "ICE COOL DRINKS" at the local store. Ravendale: a Texaco, tourist cabins, a café.

In order to retain a rural mood he was enjoying, Timmy avoided Susanville, the county seat, and took a cut-off around the north end of Honey Lake, where he bought food and canned drinks at a general store. They stopped for lunch at a roadside picnic place beneath underfed pines, on what should have been the shore of a huge lake; but all of Honey Lake had dried up the year

328

before. They ate slowly, talked sparingly, as they stared into miles of ochre mud, unrippled by the least vegetation beyond the green border marshes.

After lunch, the easiest thing would have been to continue down 395 to Reno, where they could join Interstate 80, cross the mountains easily at Donner Pass, and roll down to Auburn. From Auburn, it was a short haul north to Grass Valley, Deer Creek, and whatever home they were going to find.

But Timmy wanted no more of Nevada. About 50 miles past lunch, he braked at a signpost marked "HALLELUJAH JUNCTION," and turned to the right.

Audrey looked at him, questioning with her eyes.

"It's the way home," he answered, before she could ask. "The nicest way." They had talked very little since Alturas. Like an old married couple, they could share as much now by not talking as by talking.

It was not enough, Audrey now knew, for love to be a kind of glow, a feeling of bliss. Love must be more of an absolute, like the faith of a fanatic, large enough to contain impossibilities, deceptions, flagrant lies, even hatred: to accommodate self-assertion as well as self-dissolution. Forced by circumstances, they were learning this earlier in their marriage than is common. If whole edges and parts had been ground off in the process, if the process hurt, they were already beginning to fit, one to the other.

A young vine clings for its life to a gnarled, in places already rotting tree. The tree, in its turn, is propped up by the vine. In ten or twenty years, the coils of the vine would grow thick, covered with brown bark and bristles of hair. The tree would put out slender green shoots from dry limbs that had long appeared dead, past any hope of regeneration. Then no one would any longer be able to tell which was vine, which was tree.

Audrey had nursed along the faint little local stations from Lakeview to Chico to Susanville, universal country-western with local Summer Special commercials.

The Chilcoot General Store ("YES, WE HAVE WORMS. DO YOU?"). Vinton. State Highway 49, rough and soft-shouldered.

"They picked the number on purpose," Timmy said. "It runs through all the Gold Country towns."

"What are the orange poles for?"

"To guide the snowplows when they clear the road in winter. They keep this pass open all year. See those road signs turned around so you can't read them?"

"Yes?"

"They're warnings about snow and ice. They turn them back to face you after it starts."

"When will that be?"

"October, November at the latest. Not long now. You'll see it."

"I never thought of snow in California."

"Do you mind?"

"No. It makes it seem more like home."

* * *

Timmy was now on the look-out for the first signs of "home," too; his kind of home. They still passed the forlorn rock shops, the black-eyed Susans, the clusters of junk trailers they had followed for a thousand miles. But gradually the world began to change, warmed by the California sun. The first oak tree: black, thick-sculpted trunk, dark masses of leaves. The first tawny-gold hills, hills the color of an old lion's fur. They eased over the Sierra Nevada on its least-demanding pass, where they stopped to read a stone and brass marker about the pioneer the pass was named for.

Almost immediately over the pass, the homeland Timmy had been looking for began. Loyalton was the first of the Old California towns. It had a fine old saloon, a Main Street made of flat store fronts and shed roofs in weathered Sierra redwood. Out of town, they came upon the first of the great California barns, huge unpainted redwood-sided structures of double and treble-sloped shed roofs, with great cut-out openings instead of doors. Every board was of a different color, every barn of a different shape.

They drove through cattle ranch valleys; open-sided hay barns, noble horses, evergreen hills on either side. After Sierraville, the climb became serious, curving up steeply into a forest of tall pines. A fine black road dotted down the center with yellow and lined with bright orange poles rose through a landscape of green trees, brown hills, and blue sky. Black, yellow, orange; green, brown, and blue: the colors were pure and discrete, and his eyes opened wide to drink them all in. The road S-curved, U-curved, Z-curved steeper and steeper up. Forty, thirty-five was the fastest he could go.

The summer heat dissolved present consciousness into fine sand grains of memory. Timmy looked down on Salmon Creek, and felt the smooth round-ness of granite boulders beneath his bare toes, as he hopped from stone to stone, in and out of the running water, a boy of eight again on a free summer's day.

A curtain of pines was pulled aside, and suddenly the faces of the Sierra Buttes rose up before them, 2,000 feet above the trees. Yuba Pass, at last—6,702 feet; then another set of S-curves for the road back down. Leafy trees now, among the evergreens, near the 5,000-foot marker: summer cabins, summer camps along fishing creeks under high, dense forests. Cloudless vistas, scented shade, dry mountain heat. Sierra City, population 225.

"Do you like it?" he asked.

"It's very strange. Are we near?"

"So near I can hardly stand it."

He looked at children fishing in Canyon Creek, and felt the water around his own ankles, the sun on his bare shoulders, the heft of a pole in his hand.

The very cliff the road had been carved from looked like gold. It broke in flaked layers of diagonally tilted rock. Across the creek, thin black spires detached themselves from the opposite cliff.

At Downieville, they crossed the North Fork of the Yuba on a one-lane iron bridge, and drove into green shade so thick it was like moving through the cool bottom of a salad. The river split the town in two. On the left were bright white houses and shops and fishing cabins. Wooden steps and steep side roads

330

led up to the vine-covered verandas of other houses perched on the hills to the right. Highway 49 ran narrow and deep-shaded between the high wooden sidewalks, the galleried bars.

They followed the north fork for a while, then left it to cut down to the south, crossed that, 5,000, down, 4,000, 3,000 feet, crossed a beautiful fishing bridge. The road was running a journey into time, through tunnels of leaf green or deep cuts in red rock.

GRASS VALLEY, 19. DEER CREEK, 5.

Audrey couldn't yet say freely what he wanted her to say: Yes, I *do* like it. It did all seem strange. On the one hand, California was represented by all these brawny, brown, over-healthy cowboys and their women, natural creatures of the dust and dry heat, as much at home in the tall pines and creek water as chipmunks and crickets and mosquitoes and rattlesnakes.

On the other, these dry towns and open spaces had spawned so many sad freaks, people she wanted to dress warmly and feed well, send back east to the security of brick houses and families. How could they survive here? But then, how could she?

The fir trees and river canyons were handsome. The drive over Yuba Pass had been beautiful. But this kind of beauty seemed to depend so much on wildness and inaccessibility. The heat was as nothing to Nevada's, even to the Midwest at its worst. There were breezes now, and shade, and plenty of dark green among the ochres and tans. Winding down the Yuba River foothills, the air was hot, a hundred degrees hot. But the odors it carried were intoxicating, thick as rare spices: bay, pine, the pollen of wild flowers.

They had come so far.

37

The unmapped county road north out of Deer Creek is an extension of one of its lesser streets, out past the last buildings and abandoned cars. It winds its way up, first among sunbaked hillocks, dry grass, gray-green weeds, crickets; then under a thick cover of live oaks and madrone and redolent bay, which gradually start accommodating pine trees and spruce. The pavement thins to a lane and a half, then barely a lane.

The rented Galaxy, successor to a dead Cougar, drove around cracks, into potholes, over fallen rocks. Then the pavement ended abruptly, and they drove on in a cloud of brown dust, thumping and clunking into ruts and over rocks.

Trees bent benevolently overhead. The unpainted wooden fences on either side were a reassuring sign that someone lived at the end of the road. But for the rest of her life, Audrey would feel insecure and unhappy whenever she found herself riding along an unpaved country road.

Of this road, Timmy had no fears. He had walked it, or ridden it so many times. The way to his parents' farm—which had been, through his childhood, the way to Grandma and Grandpa's farm—was as familiar as the stairway to his own bedroom. He knew where each dip would be, and where the pavement ended, remembered exactly what the trees and grass would smell like in this heat. The very narrowness and bumpiness of the road were a comfort, because they were familiar.

If he was afraid, it was for other reasons.

The road ended at a wide farm gate. He got out, unlatched the gate, pushed it wide open, drove the car on through, stopped it, got out, shut and latched the gate behind him, got back in, and drove on.

Audrey gently stroked his sunburned arm, smiled her faint encouragement. Please God, let it be all right.

332

They drove through an orchard of fat apple trees in fruit, on a gravel road that looped around them like a question mark. And there was the house.

Wide and welcoming it looked, all of wood painted white, under a low pitched, sheltering green roof with its asymmetrical dormers and chimneys. A screened porch ran the full length of the front. A spectacular wisteria twisted its way around the white wooden posts of the porch, spread tendrils and leaves all over the old face of the house. Bright red geraniums, huge bushes of them, a hedge of scarlet and green, grew along the front, behind a row of half-buried abalone shells. Two giant oak trees in front rose far higher than the house. From the nearer one hung an old rope swing.

Timmy parked the car under the near oak, next to his father's truck. He got out, slammed the door, went around and opened Audrey's door, helped her out, closed her door. They stood there, arms around each other's waists, saying nothing. Audrey reached over without thinking and held tight to the rope of the swing.

After a few seconds, the screen door opened with a creak, and a stout, sturdy old woman in gray work pants and a work shirt came on out. She stopped, stared, let the door slap shut behind her.

"George! George, come quick! It's Timmy come home, and . . ."

She waved, beaming with joy, and began running heavily towards the couple.

Before she got to them, the door opened again, and a bald, sunburned man even taller than Timmy stood on the step. He was dressed in denim overalls. The old woman heard him, and stopped, halfway to the oak. All three were now looking at the giant old man on the step. The door opened again. A thin little boy with red hair, also in overalls, came out and stood beside his grandpa.

The old man walked down the steps, past the place where his wife stood, and went towards his youngest son, and his son's new wife, his arms open to embrace them.

The little boy stood alone on the step, not sure what he should do.

38

New Canaan, California
October 10, 1849

We are here, at last, and of course I am pleased to be here instead of on the desert, or in the mountains. Hourly I offer prayers of thanksgiving to Almighty God for his protection and guidance these last five terrible months, and for bringing us safely to the end of this journey, as he finally brought the children of Israel out of their desert.

But so far, this does not seem to be the Promised Land. There is indeed gold, gold aplenty. But it takes the daily labors of a Hercules to obtain enough of it to keep body and soul together, and for our first week here James was felled by fever and dysentery—very common in these camps, by reason of the damp and poor food—and unable to lift a hand. I think he suffered more from his inability to work, and hence to succor *me*, the dear creature, than from his own dreadful illness. More than once he would have dragged his feverish body from the mat to join the hundreds of gold-seekers already down in the creeks, had I not clung to him forcibly, and wept, and prayed him to rest.

There are no houses here, only tents. The community, if it may be called that, has been facetiously named "New Canaan." At the moment, there are perhaps two hundred tents and five hundred people here, all but three of them men; but more keep arriving every day. Some of the tents have wooden floors. Because of his illness, James has not yet had the strength or the time to provide one for ours.

A great many folk already talk of leaving, disheartened as they are by poor health and poor prospects. Some have already left. Others are packing up to take ship from San Francisco. Others are only waiting for the spring, or the first good "strike." All talk sadly and bitterly of "home," by which they mean

334

some beloved house or farm in the States, some place with solid walls, and a roof, and food to eat, and a good fire, and one's own dear people about the fire.

Of course, these are not the first to turn back. How many wagons of dejected parties heading east did we meet as we were heading west—almost from the day we left St. Joseph! Waking and sleeping, I can still see clearly the thousands of cadavers of oxen and mules, left to starve to death where they collapsed in the desert. By now, our own animals must be picked clean to the bone. I can still see, like a vision of Satan's sent me for my sins, the abandoned wagons, half-buried in sand, the cast away fortunes in jettisoned goods. I see the wooden crosses that mark the last resting place of those hundreds who never reached California.

In my dreams, I am every night subjected to another forced march, with no water for us and no grass for the animals, across alkali sands; another boiling deep river to ford, another trail too steep for our cattle or too encumbered with rocks for our wagon to pass. I wake in terror, and thank God it is now only a dream, and a memory, and move closer to James. I wonder if ever I shall be freed from these nightmares.

We are not well. We are not happy. We are certainly not rich. In fact, we have never been more destitute. Now that James is fit enough to go each day to the "digs," he works ferociously from dawn to dark in an effort to glean enough "dust" each day—one ounce seems the best we can hope for—to pay for our daily bread. (Mealy flour here is now 60 cents a pound.) I try to make a home in this sad cotton tent, of what few scraps we managed to salvage from the journey, objects that James has bought with the last of our funds, or kind Christian souls have given us.

When he returns, I try to have the fire going high, and something nourishing for him to eat. I pretend I have overeaten at midday, because there is so little decent food to be had, and James needs all his strength if the two of us are to survive. After our meal, he sits on a log seat he has cut and smokes his pipe and looks at the stars. I tidy away our few pans and things, put two heated stones under the bedcovers, and join him on my log seat. Occasionally, we talk of the past in Vermont, or of the future; but usually we say little. So far, since we have arrived, we have said no more than a few words about the journey itself. I think James is not ready to talk about it yet.

Then, as it grows cold here quite early, I go into the tent and let James sit outside alone, smoking and looking at the stars. I undress and get into bed, and lie awake waiting for him. When he comes to bed, we usually talk for a few minutes about the next day's plans. Then I ask him to join me in a prayer of thanksgiving for the day past and of petition for the day to come. We embrace. He is usually fast asleep before I am. How bitter hard are his days!

I would tell him my great secret, but I think the time is not right. Last night, I woke and he was not at my side; he had got dressed and gone back to his log seat outside. I heard a deep, slow, choking sound. He was crying, and it tore my heart to hear it. He will not yet want to think of the burden of feeding another.

335

But tonight, after supper, he put away his pipe and fetched his old mouth organ out of the satchel. It was rusted and full of dirt, but he managed to get it cleaned out enough to play "Clementine," "Oh! Susannah," and such like tunes. Then, at my request, he played a few hymn tunes I had known ever since childhood, back in Vermont.

Soon the whole encampment grew still, and the only sound seemed to be my dear Jamie's music. The two Williams boys came out from their tent alongside ours, and stood at a short distance in the shadows, listening. Then others came up, till there was a regular circle of homesick Californians standing about our fire. Mrs. Royce came up with her baby Mary, and I bade her sit alongside me on my log seat near the warm fire.

When Jamie began the old hymn setting to the 116th Psalm, Mrs. Royce and I began to sing the words softly, and soon the whole clearing in the woods was full of a hum of deep voices, praising God.

I think we shall stay.